Scandals of
the Ruthless

ABBY GREEN

KATE HEWITT

SHARON KENDRICK

MILLS & BOON

Published in Great Britain 2018
by Mills & Boon, an imprint of HarperCollins*Publishers*
1 London Bridge Street, London, SE1 9GF

Scandals of the Ruthless © 2018 Harlequin Books S.A.

A Shadow of Guilt © 2013 Harlequin Books S.A
Special thanks and acknowledgement are given to Abby Green for her contribution to *Sicily's Corretti Dynasty* series

An Inheritance of Shame © 2013 Harlequin Books S.A.
Special thanks and acknowledgement are given to Kate Hewitt for her contribution to *Sicily's Corretti Dynasty* series

A Whisper of Disgrace © 2013 Harlequin Books S.A
Special thanks and acknowledgement are given to Sharon Kendrick for her contribution to *Sicily's Corretti Dynasty* series

ISBN: 978-0-263-26724-2

10-2018

MIX
Paper from
responsible sources

FSC
www.fsc.org
FSC™ C007454

This book is produced from independently certified FSC™ paper to ensure responsible forest management.

For more information visit: www.harpercollins.co.uk/green

Printed and bound in Spain
by CPI, Barcelona

A SHADOW
OF GUILT

ABBY GREEN

This is for my fellow Corretti Continuity Comrades. Thanks for the cyber help and support, it was lovely exploring and inhabiting the Corretti world with you all x

CHAPTER ONE

HE SHOULD BE in that coffin, and not his irrepressible best friend.

Giacomo Corretti stood in the shadow of the tall pine tree and watched as the coffin was lowered into the ground just a few feet away from where he was effectively hidden. The tight ball of ice firmly lodged in his gut was slowly spreading out to every extremity. He welcomed this even as he castigated himself for being a coward.

The small group of people around the coffin started to move, the priest's final words of blessing lingering on the warm spring air along with the pungent scent of incense. It shouldn't be warm, Gio suddenly realised, it shouldn't be spring. The sea shouldn't be twinkling benignly under a cerulean sky. He desperately wanted apocalyptic clouds to roll in off stormy waters, for everything to darken and for thunder and lightning to lash this place. To lash *him* to pieces.

He could hear the heartbreaking sound of Mario's mother sobbing as she leant on her aged husband. The sound cut him in two. Gio would never have merited this outpouring of grief. The realisation was stark but brought with it no sense of self-pity.

In contrast, beside them with a stoically straight back stood their tall and narrow-shouldered daughter, Valen-

tina. Her long chestnut hair was tied back in a plait and
on her head was a black scarf. The ill-fitting black jacket
and skirt she wore hinted at the coltish seventeen-year-old
body underneath.

She didn't have to look around for Gio to know every
line on her face with instant recall. Pale olive skin as soft
as a rose petal. The lush curve of her mouth and lips which
more than hinted at a burgeoning womanly sensuality.
She had the most extraordinarily coloured eyes, golden
brown like amber.

Tiger's eyes.

He could picture them flashing now with mock anger
and a little bit of very real anger and fear whenever she'd
caught her beloved older brother and Gio flirting with the
danger they had loved so much.

As if the intensity of his gaze and thoughts had touched
her, Valentina Ferranti turned around and pinpointed the
exact spot where Gio stood, those almond-shaped eyes
narrowing on him.

It was too late, he couldn't run. She turned fully and
looked at him for a long moment. She was pale and her
beautiful face was puffy from crying. Her eyes were shadowed and grief-stricken in a way that no one should ever
have to deal with before their time. He had done that to
her. He had caused this irreparable damage.

His careless words came back to him from that night:
*'Don't worry, I'll have him back to his books before mid-
night just like Cinderella....'*

Valentina's desolation reached out to touch Gio and
mock him. And then she was stalking towards him with
long slim legs; her hands were curled to fists much like
his, by her sides. Her face was contorted with the mad
anger of grief.

She stopped just inches away. So close that he could

smell her sweet fresh scent. It was incongruous in the midst of such misery.

'You are not welcome here, Corretti.' Her voice was rough and husky from crying and Gio's insides contracted so much he wondered how he stayed conscious when he couldn't breathe. But he was breathing and he marvelled at the human body's instinct to survive, no matter what.

He took a breath. 'I...' He stopped when the familiar tightening of his vocal chords warned of humiliation to come but he ignored it. 'I...know.'

The fact that he hadn't stumbled over those completely ineffectual words came as small comfort. Mario, her brother and his friend, had been the one who had patiently helped Gio to overcome his chronic stutter which had lasted well into his early teens.

At twenty-two now, the sting of years of humiliation was still like a scar branding his skin. And yet in this moment, he longed to feel that humiliation again. So that he could be subjected to Valentina's cruel laugh and ridicule. Except...she wouldn't do that, she had never done that. She'd always been sweet and shy, and when he had stuttered in front of her she'd never used it as a tool to hurt, as almost everyone else had. Especially his family.

Suddenly Valentina lashed out, taking him by surprise. Her small fist connected with Gio's chest with enough force to send him staggering backwards. Her voice throbbed with pain, 'He was everything to us and thanks to you he's gone. He was going to graduate from university next year and be a success, and you...?'

Valentina's voice was sneering now. 'What can you do for us now? *Nothing*. Get out of here, Corretti. You taint this place with your presence.'

Brokenly she added, 'If you hadn't encouraged him to go out that night—' She stopped and bit her lip fiercely.

The blood drained from Gio's face completely. 'I'm sorry...so sorry,' he said faintly.

Valentina gathered herself once more, eyes dead. 'It's your fault. I hate you, Corretti—I'll hate you for ever because you're alive and he's not.'

Her words fell like splinters of glass all over Gio's skin. She was looking at him now as if she would push him all the way off the nearby cliff and happily watch him crash to pieces on the rocks below.

'Come, Valentina, it's time to go.'

They were both startled from the dark taut energy surrounding them when Valentina's father materialised to take her arm. His voice was thin and weary. 'This is not the time or place.'

Valentina seemed to crumple visibly and without looking at Gio again she allowed her father to turn her and lead her away. After a couple of metres though Mario's father stopped. He looked back to Gio with impossibly mournful eyes and just shook his head sadly. The man had aged ten years in the space of just a few days. It was worse than if he'd spat at Gio's feet or even punched him as Valentina had.

The truth was stark—if Gio hadn't had the unlikeliest of friendships with Mario in the first place, if he hadn't cajoled and pleaded with him to come out that night, this never would have happened.

In that moment Gio wanted to die more than anything else in the world. So badly he could taste it. Everything and anyone he'd ever loved was gone now. For ever. Everything good and promising and hopeful was broken and destroyed.

But, he knew with a bitter taste in his mouth that suicide would be too easy. Far easier than living with this pain every day. Living with the pain of knowing he had decimated an entire family and reduced them to this aching loss. This was his inheritance and he would live with it for the rest of his life.

Seven years later...

It was the wedding of the decade. Two of the most powerful families in Sicily uniting in holy matrimony. Valentina's mouth thinned into a cynical line. Except everyone knew it wasn't a love match between Alessandro Corretti and Alessia Battaglia. It was a bid for the ultimate power play, a way for the Corretti family to go on undefeated into the future for generations to come. If merging with their one-time bitter rivals was what it took, then so be it.

Valentina stopped what she was doing for a moment and put a hand to her chest. Even just thinking of the name Corretti made her feel slightly bilious. Not to mention the fact that she was at this very moment working at their behest.

Much as she would have loved to have been able to tell Carmela Corretti—the mother of the groom—where she could shove her job offer, Valentina didn't have that luxury. She was the owner of a tiny struggling catering company and she'd sweated blood and tears to start it up and try to keep it afloat with her minimal staff. It was the only thing supporting her aged and ailing parents.

Carmela had a reputation, despite the vast Corretti wealth, of being very tight with money, and Valentina knew that part of the reason she'd been lucky enough to get the job had been due to her *very* reasonable prices. Read: ridiculously cheap. But it was the kudos of being hired for something as exclusive as this that would count in the long run, *and* the payment, in spite of not charging as much as her competitors.

As Valentina put the finishing touches to some beluga

caviar canapés she couldn't help recalling Carmela's overly made-up and expressionless face when she'd looked down her patrician nose at Valentina a few weeks previously. 'This has to be the most sophisticated event of the decade—the budget for the food itself will of course be limitless. If you mess this up, Ms Ferranti, you do know you won't ever work on this island again, don't you?'

Valentina had struggled not to look as panic-stricken as she'd felt. The very prospect of having to go to the mainland and leave her parents behind was not an option. Carmela was right though; if Valentina failed at this she would be lucky to get work as a part-time waitress in a pizza joint in Naples.

So she'd stifled the panic and said meekly, 'Of course, Mrs Corretti, I know how important this is.'

And now she and her staff were being paid a pittance to create the most expensive caviar hors d'oeuvres in the world. Carmela had presided over a tasting of the sample menu Valentina had devised and that hour had been the most nerve-racking of Valentina's career so far. And then she'd approved the menu with a mere dismissive flick of her impeccably manicured hand. Valentina had stood there in shock for a long moment before the older woman had spat out, 'Well? What are you waiting for? You have work to do.'

On being given the go-ahead, regal salmon caviar had been flown all the way from Scotland, along with smoked salmon. The beef for the main luncheon had come from Ireland. The beluga caviar had naturally come straight from Russia. The champagne reserved for the head table alone was from the year 1907, salvaged from an infamous shipwreck, its price too astronomical for Valentina to get her head around. The rest of the champagne was merely Bollinger.

No, money was no object when making sure people *saw* and *tasted* the Corretti wealth, they just didn't mind scrimping on the labour behind it.

Valentina blew an errant hair out of her hot face and stood back. Her own two personal staff came by her side and Franco said in awestruck tones at the array of trays of hors d'oeuvres, 'They're like works of art. Val, you've outdone yourself this time.'

Valentina smiled ruefully. 'As much as we need to create the effect, we want them to be eaten.'

She had to admit then that the regal salmon caviar with its distinctive orange colour, wrapped in smoked salmon and in a toasted bread cup, did look enticing. Her stomach rumbled and she looked up at the clock and let out a squeak, tearing off her apron as she did. She fired off commands as she looked for her suit bag which contained her uniform for the day. 'Franco, make sure the chefs are on schedule for the main meal, and, Sara, make sure the serving staff are dressed and ready to take these trays up. We should take the rest of the canapés out of the fridges now. And get Tomasso to check that all the champagne bottles are in the ice buckets upstairs—tell him to replace the frozen rose ice if it's melting.'

Valentina left her staff buzzing around following instructions. Thankfully as the reception was being held in the sumptuous flagship Corretti Hotel—which was right across a verdant square from the beautiful medieval basilica where the wedding was being celebrated—she had full access to their facilities, house chefs and staff. The eponymous restaurant here was Michelin-starred, so she couldn't have asked for more. She merely had to oversee everything but was ultimately responsible for the entire menu.

Valentina found the changing area and struggled out

of her jeans and T-shirt and changed into her one smart black suit and white shirt. She surmised grimly that Carmela was far too canny to have things go wrong in the Corretti name. Far better to be able to blame an outside caterer. Valentina told herself that it was still the opportunity of a lifetime and all she had to do was make sure nothing went wrong. Simple!

After a couple of minutes she stood in her stocking feet and looked at herself in the mirror. She made a face at her flushed cheeks and the shadows under her eyes and scrabbled for her make-up bag, hands trembling from the excess adrenalin as she did her best to counteract the ravages of several sleepless nights.

She'd had nightmares of people choking on a canapé, or epidemic levels of food poisoning after the wedding lunch. The thought of felling the entire Corretti and Battaglia clans was enough to make her an insomniac for years to come! Grimacing at her far too vivid imagination, Valentina wound up her hair into a high bun at the back of her head and gave herself a quick cursory once-over. No jewellery, minimal make-up. All designed to fade as much into the background as possible. Then she gathered up her things and slipped on a pair of mid-height black court shoes.

It was only as she walking back out to the preparation area that the rogue thought slipped into her mind like a sly traitor waiting in the wings. *What if he's here?* He won't be, Valentina assured herself with something bordering uncomfortably on panic. Why would he be here when it was common knowledge he'd left home at sixteen and become completely independent of his family? The fact that he'd since carved out a stupendously successful career breeding and training thoroughbred horses had served to further that estrangement from his own family business and legacy.

He won't be here, Valentina assured herself again. Because if he was… Her mind froze as a yawning chasm of grief and pain and anger washed through her, along with something much more disturbing and hard to define.

He wouldn't be. He *couldn't* be. She was far too vulnerable today to deal with seeing Giacomo Corretti.

If there was any mercy in this world, Valentina told herself fervently, he would be kept away by the sheer psychic force of her anger and hatred. And yet, her heart beat a little faster as she went about her business.

Gio put his fingers between his bow-tied shirt and neck, trying in vain to ease the constriction he felt. He gave up with a muffled curse, leaving his white bow tie slightly askew. The problem was that the constriction was in his chest, and had nothing to do with his tie. He cursed again and wished he was on the other side of the island in his habitual uniform of T-shirt, jeans and boots, with his horses.

He could see people milling about outside the hotel and in the lush landscaped square that was between the huge imposing church and the Corretti Hotel. Clearly the wedding had ended but the luncheon hadn't started yet.

Damn. He'd almost hoped he'd be too late entirely. The only reason he'd come at all had been because his mother had pleaded with him. 'Gio, you never see your brothers, or anyone else. You can't go on isolating yourself like this. *Please* come.'

He'd had to bite back the frustration—the urge to lash out and say something like, *Why the hell should I?* But he hadn't, he'd been immediately disgusted by his own pathetic self-pity and his relationship with his mother was tenuous at the best of times.

As a young boy he'd been witness to his parents' volatile relationship and had watched as his mother had become more and more insecure and self-loathing as she'd tried in vain to keep the attention of her straying husband, Gio's deceased father. Unfortunately her growing instability and self-absorption had coincided with a particularly vulnerable time in Gio's life, and so while affection for her was there…Gio couldn't force an intimacy that had been long ago irreparably eroded.

But he was an adult now and took responsibility for his own actions; it was futile to dwell on the past. He forced his mind back to his mother: if she had some fantasy notion of bringing all of her sons under one roof for their cousin's wedding then would it really be so hard to at least put in an appearance?

So now he was here, hovering on the edge of the square. He smiled grimly at the imagery. He'd been hovering on the edges of his family for as long as he could remember. The youngest male in the Corretti dynasty. The youngest in his own family. Dominated by two older brothers who'd vied for supremacy, and a father who had been mercilessly exacting of all of his sons, not least his quietest one. The one who had disappointed him on every possible level with frailties that were unacceptable in a Corretti male.

Gio ruthlessly pushed aside the memories that threatened to rise and choke him. That way lay madness and even worse memories. Drawing on the icy veneer he'd surrounded himself with for years now, Gio pushed an impatient hand through his unruly hair. He was aware that he wasn't perhaps as clean shaven as he could be, but he just cursed softly again and strode forward and towards the towering Corretti edifice.

Valentina looked blankly at the ladder in her tights. She'd come by way of a ladder in her tights when she'd been all but knocked down by Alessandro Corretti, the groom. Instead of greeting a triumphant married couple after their wedding ceremony, it had been just the groom who had burst into the main reception room like an exploding tornado. She, and a tray of delicate hors d'oeuvres had gone flying, and with Alessandro blissfully unaware of the carnage left in his wake, he'd barrelled on.

As she'd scrabbled around on the ground picking up the detritus before anyone else saw it, her assistant Sara had appeared and bent down to help, hissing sotto voce as she did, 'The wedding is off—the bride just jilted the groom, right there in the church.'

Valentina had looked at her—a sick feeling blooming in her belly. And then she'd heard the sudden flurry of approaching hissed whispers. The stunned and shocked guests were obviously making their way to the reception.

Before she'd had time to figure out what this all meant, Carmela Corretti had swept into the reception hot on the heels of her son, with a face like thunder. She'd spotted Valentina and roughly hauled her up with a hand under her arm. 'The wedding might be off, but you will proceed with this reception for whoever turns up, do you hear me?'

She'd let Valentina go then and looked down that elegant nose. 'As you'll be looking after less than a full guest count, I won't be paying you for services not rendered.'

It had taken a second for her meaning to sink in and then Valentina had gasped out loud. 'But…that's…'

Carmela had cut in ruthlessly. 'I will not discuss this further. Now instruct your staff to tend to the guests who do arrive. I won't have anyone say that we turned them away.'

In shock, Valentina had done as instructed, far too mindful of Carmela Corretti's influence should she defy her. And as she'd watched the staff rushing around serving amongst the arriving shell-shocked guests, as if nothing had just happened, Valentina had felt incredibly shaky with reaction.

She couldn't afford to spill champagne on a haute couture gown or drop a tray into someone's lap so she'd retreated to a quiet corner for a moment to try and steady her nerves and process this information. And the fact that Carmela wasn't going to pay her! The ladder in her tights was the least of her worries…who on earth would now touch the caterer associated with the wedding scandal of the year?

Gio took another full glass of champagne from a passing waiter's tray. He'd lost count of how many he'd had but the alcohol was having a nicely numbing effect on his brain. He'd walked straight into the debacle of the century. Expecting to find his cousin's family jubilant and gloating with their new merger of power, he'd instead found small huddles of guests in the sumptuously decorated reception room, all whispering excitedly of the runaway bride.

The unfolding scandal was so unexpected that it defused much of his simmering anger at the thought of having to play nice with his family. He had caught a glimpse of his older half-sister, Lia, but he'd instinctively shied away from talking to her, never quite knowing what to say to the tall serious woman who'd been brought up in his grandparents' house after her mother, their father's first wife, had died.

Thinking that surely he couldn't be expected to stay here now, Gio decided that he'd more than done his duty and slugged back the champagne before putting the empty glass down. He made his way out of the main function room into the corridor and passed by an anteroom where the wedding band were setting up and doing a sound check. Gio shook his head in disbelief—clearly the word hadn't reached this far yet, or perhaps his formidable aunt Carmela wasn't going to let a runaway bride stop her guests from dancing the night away?

Something suddenly caught Gio's peripheral vision. He stopped in his tracks. He was passing another room now, a store room. He could see that it was the figure of a woman sitting on a chair in the empty room, surrounded by boxes and other chairs piled high. Her head was down-bent, glossy chestnut hair caught up in a bun. Shapely legs under a black skirt. A white shirt and jacket. Slim pale hands clasped on her lap.

As if she could feel the weight of his gaze on her, her head started to come up. Déjà vu was so immediate and strong, Gio nearly staggered back from it. *No*, he thought, *it couldn't be her*. Not here, not now. Not ever. She was only in his dreams and nightmares. Cursing him. Along with the ghost of her brother.

But now her head was up fully and those glorious tiger eyes were widening. *It was her*. The knowledge exploded something open, deep inside him. Something that had been frozen in time for seven years. He saw colour leach from her cheeks. So much more angular now that her teenage plumpness had disappeared. *So much more beautiful*. He could see her throat work, swallowing.

She stood up with a slightly jerky move. She was taller than he remembered, slimmer and yet with very womanly curves. The promise of the burgeoning beauty that he re-membered had been truly fulfilled. So many things were impacting Gio at once that he had to shut them all down deep inside him.

He had alternately dreaded and anticipated the possibil-ity of this day for a long time. He couldn't crumble now in front of her. He wouldn't allow himself the luxury.

He walked to the entrance of the room and totally redundantly he said, 'Valentina.' And then after a pause, 'It's good to see you.'

Valentina was in shock. More shock heaped on top of shock. Without even realising she was speaking out loud she said, 'You're not meant to be here.' *The sheer force of my will should have kept you away.* But she didn't say that.

Gio's mouth turned up on one corner in a tiny movement that wasn't quite a smile, 'Well, my cousin is, *was*, the groom so I have some right to be here.' He frowned slightly. 'What are you doing here?'

Valentina's brain wasn't working properly. She answered almost absently, 'I'm the caterer.'

Gio was so much taller and broader than she remembered. Any hint of boyishness was gone. He was all stark angles and sinuous muscle and power. The suit hugged his muscular frame like a second skin. The white shirt and white bow tie made him look even darker.

His hair was still messy though, giving him a familiar devil-may-care look that rang bells somewhere dimly in Valentina's consciousness. His eyes were a light brown and a wicked voice whispered that she knew very well they could look green in certain lights.

She used to watch him and her brother for hours as they'd egged each other on in a series of daredevil stunts, either on horseback or on the mud bikes Gio had had first on his father's property, and then later, on his own property. But by then they'd been proper adult motorbikes and he and her brother had relished their death-defying races. She remembered the way Gio would tip his head back and laugh; he'd looked so vitally masculine, his teeth gleaming whitely in his face.

She remembered turning fifteen and seeing him again for the first time in about four years, because he'd been living abroad in France, building up his equine business. He'd returned home a conquering hero, a self-made millionaire, with a bevy of champion thoroughbred horses. But that had had nothing to do with how she'd instantly had an altogether different awareness of him. Her belly would twist when she saw him, and then there were the butterflies, so violent it was like feeling sick. Her gaze had been shamefully captivated by his tall rangy body.

Much to her everlasting mortification she'd tagged along on her brother's visits to Gio in his new home near Syracuse whenever he'd been home from college, during his long summers off. Gio had bought a palatial *castello* complete with a farm, where he'd installed a state-of-the-art stud and gallops. He'd been in the process of doing up a nearby run-down racetrack which by today had become the famed Corretti racetrack where the eponymous internationally renowned annual Corretti Cup race was held.

Gio had caught her staring once and she'd been so mortified she'd been red for a week. She hadn't been able to get out of her head how he'd held her gaze for a long moment, a slow smile turning up his mouth, as if something illicit and secret had passed between them. Something that scared her as much as it had exhilarated her.

He had a beautiful face, sculpted lips. High cheekbones and a hard slashing line of a nose. A strong chin. But something in his demeanour took away any prettiness. A dark brooding energy surrounded him like a force-field.

Gio lifted a hand to point to her hair and said, 'You have something…just there.' It shattered her memories and brought her back to the present. He was pointing above her right ear and Valentina reached up and felt something wet and sticky and took her hand down to see a lump of viscous orange salmon caviar.

And then it was as if the deep baritone reality of his

voice made the bells ring loud and clear in her head. He looked devil-may-care because that's what he was, and that attitude had led directly to her brother's death. For the past few moments she'd been protecting herself from the reality that he was here, in front of her, and now that protection was ripped away.

She remembered. And with that knowledge came the pain. The memories. That lonely grave in the graveyard. Seven years of an ache that didn't seem to get any better, only fade slightly. Until it caught you unawares and the wound was reopened all over again. Like right now.

How dared he stand there and talk to her as if nothing had happened? As if civility could hide the ugly past. Anger and something much darker bubbled up inside Valentina. A kind of guilt, for having remembered another time for a moment; disgusted with herself she strode out of the room and straight up to Gio. She clenched the hand that held the remnants of the once-perfect canapé and looked up at him, focusing on the blazing incinerating anger of grief, and not something much more dangerous in her belly when she realised how tall he was. 'Get out of my way, Corretti.'

Gio flinched minutely as if she'd slapped him. He could remember in vivid recall how it had felt that day when she'd punched him in the chest. And he welcomed it now. For a few seconds when she'd looked stunned and not angry, he'd thought that perhaps, with time, a mellowing had taken place. But then he mocked himself—the pain of losing Mario still as fresh as it had been on the night he died. And the shock to cushion that blow had long gone. Now there was just the excoriating and ever-present guilt.

Valentina was looking up at him, her eyes glowing gold and spitting. She hated him. It was in every taut and tense line of her body.

She gritted out, 'I said get out of my way, Corretti.'

CHAPTER TWO

GIO STEPPED BACK, his voice was stiff. 'I'm not in your way, Valentina.'

Valentina didn't move though. She was vibrating all over with anger. It was like a tangible thing.

'You need to go. You need to leave this place.'

A small flare of anger which he had no right to feel raced up Gio's spine. His mouth tightened. 'As this is my cousin's wedding I think I have a right to stay.' He didn't bother to mention he'd been about to leave.

'The wedding is off, or hadn't you heard?' Valentina supplied with a measure of satisfaction.

Something Gio didn't understand made him bullishly stand his ground. 'The reception is still on, or hadn't *you* heard?'

He saw her face pale and instinctively put out a hand to touch her but she flinched backwards, disgust etched all over her. 'Don't touch me. And yes, I know the reception is still on—half a reception, that is, which your aunt expects me to cater for without handing over one euro in payment. Your whole family are poison, Corretti, right to the core.'

Gio wanted to say, *Stop calling me that,* but instead he frowned and said, 'What do you mean? She's not paying you?'

'No,' Valentina spat out, hating that she'd blurted that

out, or that she was still even in a conversation with Giacomo Corretti.

'But that's ridiculous, you should to get paid regardless.'

Valentina laughed harshly and forced herself to look at Gio. 'Yes, call me old-fashioned but it is customary to be paid for services rendered. However, your aunt seems to feel that in light of the unfortunate turn of events, she's absolved of the duty of payment.'

'That's crazy…' Gio raked a hand through his hair, fire entering his belly. He was fixing on something, anything, he could do by way of helping Valentina and he knew it. The anger at his aunt's heavy-handed and bullying tactics was a very easy target to focus on.

He started to stride back towards the main function room and then he heard behind him, 'Wait! Where do you think you're going?'

Gio turned around. The sight of Valentina standing just feet away with a stray lock of glossy silky hair caressing one hot cheek sent something molten right into his gut. He was shocked all over again that it was her, *here*, and he was captivated, momentarily forgetting everything.

He felt as if he'd been existing in a fog and had suddenly been plunged into an icy pool. Everything was bright and piercingly clear, the sound check of the band nearby almost painful in its intensity.

And something was happening in his body. After five years of strict sensory denial, it, too, was surging to life. Blood was rushing to every vein and artery. *Becoming hard.*

Valentina was oblivious to this cataclysm going on in Gio's body. She pointed a finger at him. 'I asked you where you think you're going?'

Gio sucked in a breath and felt dizzy—as if someone had just spiked the air around him with a mind-altering drug. He struggled to focus on what she'd asked and not on the lush curve of her mouth, the perfect bow of its shape. He hadn't even been noticing women for so long and now this—it was like an overload on his senses.

'My aunt...' he managed finally, focusing carefully on the words. 'My aunt, I'll tell her she can't do this to you.'

He turned again, as much to put some distance between himself and Valentina as anything else but wasn't prepared for when a hand gripped his arm, pulling him around. She was suddenly too close. Gio all but reeled back and Valentina dropped her hand and looked him up and down scathingly. 'You're drunk.'

He could have laughed. He knew very well that after the shock of seeing this woman again he was no more drunk than she was.

Gio forced control on his wayward body, but he was tingling all over. He still felt the touch of her hand like a brand.

'I'll go to my aunt and tell her she—'

'No, you won't,' Valentina interjected hotly. 'You'll do no such thing. I do not need you to fight my battles for me, Corretti.'

Something snapped inside Gio and he gritted his jaw. 'It's *Gio*, or have you forgotten you once called me that?'

Valentina's face was carved from stone. 'No, I haven't forgotten, but apparently you've forgotten why I'd never call you that again.'

The cruelty of that statement nearly felled Gio but he stayed standing. 'No,' he said faintly, 'I haven't forgotten.'

Their eyes were locked, amber with hazel. For a moment there was nothing but simmering emotion between them, so strong and tangible that when one of the band members started to walk out of the room they'd been rehearsing in, he took one look at the couple locked in silent combat and retreated back inside, closing the door softly.

'I'll pay you—I'll cover whatever my aunt should be paying you.'

Valentina reared back, her hands curled into tiny fists, two spots of hectic colour on her white cheeks. *'You?'*

Gio steeled himself.

'I wouldn't take your filthy money if it was offered to me on a silver platter.'

Of course, he conceded bitterly, she would have nothing to do with him, or his money, no matter how hard he'd worked for it.

Valentina pointed a finger at her chest then and Gio swallowed hard and fought not to let his eyes drop to those provocative swells underneath the plain white shirt. 'I am a professional and I've been hired to do a job and that's what I'm going to do. I will not let your aunt jeopardise my reputation by running out now. And I will not take your guilt money, Corretti.'

Guilt money. The words fell on him hard. This time Gio didn't correct her use of his name. For the first time he saw the bright sheen of tears in her eyes and something inside him broke apart. The memory of her stoic back that day by the graveside was vivid. But he couldn't move or say a thing. She wouldn't welcome it.

Suddenly the doors to the main function room opened and a young girl appeared with a worried face beside them. 'Val, *there* you are. We need you inside, *now*. Mrs Corretti is looking for you.'

Valentina's chin came up but she looked at Gio. 'Thanks, Sara, I'll be in in a second.'

She waited until the girl had left and then she said to Gio with icy emphasis, 'I think the least you can do is leave. And I sincerely hope never to have to see you again.'

And then she walked by him, giving him a wide berth as if afraid to even come close to touching him. Gio heard the doors open and close behind him. Her scent lingered on the air, light and musky. *Her.*

I think the least you can do is leave. Gio hadn't needed much of an excuse before. And he certainly didn't need one now. The past seven years had just fallen away like the flimsiest of sets on a stage to expose all of the ugliness and pain that was still there.

As much as Valentina never wanted to see him again, he echoed that sentiment right at that moment. He didn't think he could survive another encounter with her.

A week later...

'*Who* did you say?' Gio's voice rang with incredulity. Was he hearing things? He shook his head and focused again on his PA, a comfortably middle-aged woman called Agata.

She spoke again slowly, enunciating every word carefully. 'Val-en-tina Ferr-anti. She's outside right now, she wants to see you. And she looks determined.'

Gio turned his back on Agata for a moment and spiked two hands through his already messy hair, his whole body knotting with tension and something much hotter, darker. Already he could feel blood pooling southwards. His mouth tightened. So it hadn't been an aberration. It was her, uniquely her, who was having this effect on him.

Perfetto. His body and libido were being awoken by the only woman in the world he could never have. Or more accurately who would never have *him.*

He turned around again, hiding his tumultuous thoughts behind an impassive expression. Valentina would not affect him today. She'd obviously just come to hurl a few more spiked arrows in his direction and he would withstand it if it killed him. It was his due.

'Send her in.'

Valentina's hands were clammy, and she smoothed them again on her worn jeans. She resolutely pushed down the memory of the words she'd hurled at Gio Corretti just days ago: *I wouldn't take your filthy money if it was offered to me on a silver platter.* Her cheeks got hot with guilt.

What was taking his assistant so long? Perhaps she should have dressed up more? Instead of these old jeans, sneakers and a T-shirt that had definitely seen better days. Too late now. And anyway, it wasn't as if she was trying to impress Giacomo Corretti. She was only here because he was literally the only person on the island of Sicily outside the sphere of his aunt's influence.

Even though Valentina knew that Gio had built up a successful business, she'd been surprised when she'd come to his offices at his racetrack in Syracuse—to find everything so pristine and gleaming. She wasn't sure what she'd expected, some level of obvious debauchery?

For a couple of years after Mario's death, Gio Corretti became the most hedonistic playboy in Europe. Always a lover of extreme sports, he'd seemed to relish doing as many dangerous things as possible. He'd been pictured jumping out of planes, rock climbing with his bare hands, scaling the highest mountains in the world.

He'd also been pictured on yachts in the south of France, in the casinos of Monte Carlo and in the winners' enclosures at Epsom and Longchamp, where he'd regularly won and lost millions of euros in the space of hours. And in each place a stunning woman on his arm, clinging to him with besotted adoration and euro signs in her eyes.

But contrary to that feckless image, his racetrack was a

veritable hive of industry with smartly turned-out grooms wearing black T-shirts emblazoned with the Corretti Race-track logo, leading sleek-looking thoroughbreds through the grounds, and gardeners tending the lushly flowering borders.

The most impressive part of the location was the race-track which overlooked the Mediterranean Sea, giving it a vista unlike any other in the world. This wasn't where Mario had died—Valentina didn't think she could have come here today if it was. Mario had died on the smaller training gallops at Gio's *castello*, because this racetrack hadn't yet been ready.

Valentina heard the low hum of voices in Gio's office where the friendly middle-aged lady had disappeared moments before and her belly knotted. Anger at seeing Gio again had been her impetus through this horrific week and the spectacular implosion of her career—anger is what had impelled her here because one Corretti had ruined her but only another Corretti could save her—but what if he was telling his assistant that he didn't want to see her?

Just then she heard a sound like the door handle jiggling and she flinched and stood up, her heart thumping at the thought of seeing Gio again. What had she been think-ing? She couldn't do this. She was in the act of turning to leave when she heard a calm mellifluous voice announce, 'Sorry to keep you waiting, Ms Ferranti, he'll see you now.'

Gio's body was locked tight as he waited for Valentina to appear in the doorway and when she did, in jeans and a T-shirt, with her hair loose over her shoulders in chestnut waves, a whole new tension came into his body.

Her T-shirt was moulded over the firm globes of her breasts. Gio felt like he couldn't breathe and dragged his gaze back up to those feline amber eyes. The same eyes that had been haunting him all week.

He put out a hand and said stiffly, 'Please, won't you sit down?'

Valentina hovered uncertainly just inside the door, which Agata had closed behind her on her way out. She shook her head. 'No, I'd prefer to stand.'

Gio inclined his head and stayed behind his desk, as if that could offer some protection.

Valentina crossed her arms then, inadvertently pushing her breasts together and up, and Gio nearly groaned out loud. He cursed himself—he was acting like a hormonal teenager.

More tersely than he intended, he rapped out, 'You'll have to forgive me for being a little surprised to see you. After all, it was hardly your intention the last time we met.'

Valentina found herself floundering, badly. Seeing Gio again last week, her response then had been visceral and a reflex to years-old grief and anger. After all, she hadn't seen him since the funeral. But now that raw emotion was stripped away somewhat and left in its place was something much more ambiguous. And a physical awareness of the man which was very disturbing.

A huge window behind him looked out over the racing ground and stands, the sea beyond. But Valentina could only see him in a dark polo shirt which was stretched across a hard muscled chest, and long, long legs clad in lovingly worn jeans. Without even looking properly she could imagine his thighs—like powerful columns of sheer muscle.

When he and Mario had been on horseback they'd been a sight to behold, but Gio even more so. He'd moved with such fluid grace that it had been hard to tell where he ended and the horse began. Her brother hadn't had such an innate ability.… Valentina gulped. She couldn't think of that now.

She struggled to recall his words, something about her not wanting to see him again. Her throat felt scratchy. 'No…it wasn't my intention.'

One of Gio's black brows arched. 'And it is now?'

Valentina cursed herself for ever thinking of this as a plan of action and tried desperately to articulate herself. 'Yes. Well, it's just that…things have happened in the past week.'

Gio came around his desk then and perched on the corner, legs outstretched before him. His scent tantalised Valentina's nostrils and just like that she was flung back in time to when she'd turned seventeen, weeks before Mario's death. She'd taken her moped to Gio's *castello* to look for Mario for their father, who'd needed him to do chores. In those days Valentina hadn't needed any excuse to go to Gio's *castello* or the track.

She'd gone to the stables looking for Mario and had seen no one, aware that she was disappointed not to see Gio either. And then a horse had appeared out of nowhere behind her. A huge beast. Valentina had jumped back, startled, ashamed of how intimidated she was around horses.

Someone had come up behind her and before she knew what was happening she'd been lifted effortlessly onto the horse's bare back, and Gio had been swinging himself up behind her, an arm snug around her waist, thighs hard around hers. She'd been so shocked to find herself that high off the ground and with Gio in such close proximity that she'd struggled for breath as terror and excitement had constricted her lungs.

He'd said in her ear, 'You'll never get comfortable with horses if you don't get used to riding them.'

He'd put the reins in her hands with his hands over hers and for about half an hour they'd walked around his sandy gallops with Gio murmuring words of encouragement and tuition in her ears. Terror had turned to exhilaration as she'd allowed herself to relax into Gio's protective embrace and when her brother had still failed to materialise Gio had told her that he'd left before she'd arrived, borrowing one of Gio's collection of motorbikes to get home.

Valentina had all but slithered off the horse and on very shaky legs had fled home herself. Mortified to think they'd been entirely alone for all that time. She'd been unable to look at Gio for weeks afterwards without blushing, achingly aware of how her whole body had tingled next to his, and how hot she'd felt between her legs.

'What things?'

Valentina looked blankly at Gio now, her mind still dazed from the memory.

'You said things have happened?'

Valentina came crashing back to earth. Why on earth was she remembering such traitorous memories when only one was important? The memory of when she and her parents had rushed into that hospital in Palermo only to be stopped by a doctor and told that their son was dead.

Valentina focused on that now and crossed her arms even tighter across her chest. This man owed her. Owed her parents. Owed her brother. 'Your aunt refused to pay me for the catering at the wedding.'

Gio frowned. 'Did you tell her you wouldn't accept non-payment?'

Valentina flushed. She'd been so angry and emotional after seeing Gio that when she'd come face to face with Carmela Corretti and the woman had still refused to pay her even though people were sitting down to the six-course meal, despite the shambles of the wedding, that she'd threatened legal action.

Even now Valentina could almost laugh at the folly of her naivety! As if a mere mortal like her could take on a Corretti. Carmela had looked at her and her face had gone white and then red with anger at this impudence.

'You dare to threaten me with legal action.'

Hands on hips, gone too far to back down now, Valentina had fumed. 'Yes, I do. You don't scare me, you know.'

Carmela had just smiled and said as if she were remarking on the weather, 'You can consider yourself not only not paid, Ms Ferranti, you can also consider yourself blacklisted from every catering job on this island. I did warn you, did I not?'

Valentina had gasped at the unfairness of this attack. 'But there's nothing wrong with the menu or the catering service.'

'No,' agreed Carmela almost cheerfully. 'But, there is everything wrong with you and your attitude, young lady.'

That had been too much for Valentina, to be spoken to so patronisingly by a Corretti. She'd seen an ice bucket nearby full of water and her hands had itched to pour it over the woman's head. But she'd been saved from that impetuous action when the abandoned groom had reappeared and suddenly Carmela had pushed Valentina out of the way to go to him.

Gio said nothing for a long moment and then, 'I think I would have paid to see my aunt with a full ice bucket over her head.'

Valentina snuck a look at Gio's expression. And then as she watched, his eyes sparkled and his mouth twitched. It was so unexpected to see this, that to her horror, Valentina could feel a lightness bubbling up inside herself too.

No! her brain screamed. *Do not let him close, do not let him charm you.*

Fighting the lightness down with an iron will Valentina suddenly realised that she'd been totally and utterly wrong to come here. Had she come because seeing Gio last week had precipitated a dangerous need to see him again? The very thought of such a susceptibility made her feel nauseous.

Without even thinking about it, she'd whirled around to the door and had her hand on the handle before she felt a much larger hand around her upper arm, tugging her back. That touch sent tremors of sensation and *wanting* into her blood. She had to leave now.

She pulled her arm free and looked up at Gio, who was too close. 'I made a mistake coming here.'

All lightness was gone from Gio now; his eyes were flashing green, his mouth was tight. 'You hardly came all the way here from Palermo for nothing, Valentina.'

She shook her head, feeling sick. Memories were coming up too thick and fast, jumbling everything up, when she had to remember why she hated this man. 'I shouldn't have come. I thought you could help me with something but I forgot—I don't want...*need* your help.'

And then she yanked the door open and ran all the way out of his building and didn't stop till she got to her rusty old car.

Gio slammed the door shut after Valentina left and put his two hands against it and dropped his head. 'Damn, damn, *damn.*'

That evening when Valentina got home from checking on her parents she paced the floor of her tiny spartan apartment. Things were not good. Her father hadn't looked well at all, pasty and slightly sweaty, but he'd brushed aside her concerns. Worry knotted Valentina's insides. She hadn't told them yet of the debacle of her career which had effectively been ruined by Carmela Corretti. Between her parents—with her father's ominous chest pains and her mother's arthritis and only access to the most basic health care—it was a serious worry.

She stopped pacing and put a weary hand to her head. She *had* to work. But thanks to Carmela she'd be lucky to get a job as a chambermaid in a three-star hotel in Messina. And that wasn't all—her two staff were also unemployed thanks to her impetuous actions.

Valentina sat down on a rickety chair and cursed herself soundly. Why did she have to get so emotional and react to Carmela like that?

Gio. Because seeing him had pushed her over the edge. Had made her reckless and had brought up all the simmering anger at the Correttis in general for their lavish and effortlessly powerful ways. The way they didn't have to think of anyone but themselves.

But Valentina's conscience smote her—Gio hadn't always been like the others. He'd been shy and quiet. Withdrawn. Her father had worked doing odd jobs and maintenance for the Corretti palazzo near Palermo all his life and her mother had done their laundry. They'd lived in a tiny humble house nearby.

At first Gio and Mario hadn't been friends—they'd circled each other for a long time like two suspicious animals. Valentina had witnessed how their friendship had bonded after a particularly nasty fight. She'd been just five and had been trailing her beloved father and brother as she usually did, in awe of the palazzo and its extensive grounds. Mario had been goading Gio with fists raised. 'Come on, say something, why don't you? Don't you have a tongue?'

From her hiding place, Valentina had seen how Gio

had launched himself at Mario with a feral grunt. Her father had found them and taken both boys by the scruffs of their necks and ordered them to apologise to each other.

She'd watched as Gio had struggled to get the words out, his face smeared with dirt and dust. It had been excruciating to watch. 'I…I…I'm…s-s-s-s…' He'd stopped and then tried again, eventually saying 'sorry' in a rush.

She could remember the look on his face, as if he'd been waiting for Mario to laugh or make fun of him. He had a stutter. That's why he never spoke. Even though she'd only been five, Valentina had been aware of her ten-year-old brother's sheer maturity and grace when he'd ignored Gio's debilitating stutter and had held out his hand and said, 'I'm sorry too.'

Since that day they'd been inseparable. Valentina fought against this memory, much as she'd fought against the ones earlier—she didn't want to remember Gio like that.

Her hands clenched to fists. If Mario hadn't been so in thrall to Gio, he would never have put aside his studies that night and gone to Gio's *castello* to race horses with him. She could remember the conversation when Gio had turned up on his motorbike to entice Mario away. Mario had protested. 'I really should be studying for my exams.'

Gio had made a face. 'That's the lamest excuse I ever heard, Ferranti.'

Mario had chuckled and then said teasingly, 'Well, at least some of us *want* to get an education!'

Gio had growled at that and had launched himself at Mario and the two had mock fought for a few minutes. Valentina had been watching all of this surreptitiously from behind the door, her eyes glued in fascination to Gio's lean muscular form. Then they'd stopped and Mario had stood back breathing heavily, a dangerous glint in his eye that

Valentina recognised all too well. 'I'll come if you let me ride Black Star.'

Immediately Valentina had tensed and looked at Gio, who was scowling. 'No way, Mario…you know I won't let you near him—he's too dangerous.'

Mario had taunted, 'You're saying you're the *only* one who can handle him?'

Gio had flushed and Valentina had leapt out of her hiding place to stand between the young men, looking at Gio. 'Don't let him near that horse, Gio. I swear to God—'

Her brother had taken her shoulders and gently moved her out of the way, saying, 'This is none of your concern, Val.'

But Valentina had implored Gio with her eyes. She'd seen Black Star in action on his gallops. He was a mythically huge thoroughbred that Gio had bought recently in France. He was very controversial because while he had the potential to be a great champion, he'd already run a few races and in each one had unseated his jockey. In one tragic instance, the jockey had been killed.

The authorities in Europe had wanted to put the horse down but Gio had stepped in to buy him, claiming that he could tame him into acquiescence, putting forward the argument that the horse shouldn't be punished for the failure of the trainers. But when Gio had shown the horse off to Mario and her when he'd returned home, she'd seen a madness in his eyes that had terrified her. So far, the only one who'd been able to get near him was Gio. And now her brother wanted a go?

There'd been a stand-off between the two men. Mario had cajoled, 'Gio…come on.'

Gio had just looked at Mario for a long moment and then shrugged lightly and said, 'We'll see.'

Mario had grinned in triumph and clapped his friend on the shoulder, saying, 'Wait here, I'll just change.'

He'd left and Gio had looked at Valentina, causing that inevitable self-conscious flush to rise up through her whole body. She ignored it. 'Gio…you can't let him near that horse…something will happen to him. You know he's not as good as you.'

Gio had come close and touched his finger to Valentina's chin, tipping it up slightly, making her heart beat fast and her body ache with a peculiar restlessness.

'Don't worry, *piccolina*, I won't let anything happen to him.'

Indignant fire had raced up Valentina's spine and she'd jerked her chin free. 'Don't call me that, I'm not little.'

Gio had said nothing for a long moment, just looked at her so intensely that she'd felt breathless, and then in a slightly rougher tone of voice, 'I know you're not…and don't worry. I'll have him back to his boring books before midnight, just like Cinderella.'

Mario had reappeared and gave Valentina a hug and walked out the door, Gio had followed with a quick glance backwards. *'Ciao, bellissima.'*

And that had been the last time she'd seen Mario. When she'd seen Gio in the hospital later that night she'd run to him, distraught, hysterical. 'You let him go on that horse, didn't you, *didn't you*?'

Gio had just stood there, white-faced, and said, 'I'm so sorry.'

Her mother and father had been so proud of Mario. Everything, all of their hopes and fears, had rested on him. Valentina had resigned herself to the fact that she wouldn't have the same opportunities. She was genuinely happy for her brother to succeed and he'd often told her, 'Val, when I become a lawyer and I'm making lots of money, I'll send you to a cordon bleu school in France….'

Tears pricked her eyes, but just then a knock came on Valentina's apartment door, wrenching her back to the present. Surprised, because she wasn't used to visitors, she dashed away the dampness on her cheeks and stood up. When she opened the door and saw who it was she sucked in a breath. *'You.'*

CHAPTER THREE

GIO LOOKED GRIM in the dim light of the corridor. 'Yes, it's me.'

Still too shocked to make much sense of this she just said, 'How did you get up here?' The front door was at ground level and there were five apartments in the ancient crumbling building which was on one of Palermo's less salubrious streets.

'Someone was coming in just as I arrived.'

'How did you know where I lived?'

Gio's mouth tightened. 'I asked around.'

Valentina could just bet he had—and who wouldn't give a Corretti the information they wanted? Seeing him here like this in the flesh when she'd just been feeling so vulnerable made Valentina prickly.

'What do you want, Gio?' She saw the flash in his eyes and realised she'd just called him *Gio*. Flutters erupted in her belly.

'I'd like to come in for a minute if that's OK?'

'No, it's not OK.'

Valentina started to close the door but was surprised when she felt the resistance of Gio's hand. Suddenly he looked quite intimidating.

'We can conduct this conversation here in the doorway

and give your neighbours something to listen to or you can invite me in.'

Valentina heard the tell-tale creak of her neighbour's door just then and very reluctantly let Gio come in. He went and stood in the middle of the small living area, which had the kitchen area just off it and a tiny bedroom and bathroom on the other side. Palatial it was not, especially when she thought about his *castello*.

She smiled with saccharine sweetness. 'Well, I don't think you're here for tips on how to live in a small space.'

A corner of his mouth turned up and the flutters in Valentina's belly intensified. Damn him.

'No. That's not why I'm here.' He turned to face her then and she noticed that he'd changed out of his polo shirt and jeans, into a white shirt and chinos. His overlong hair curled over his collar, a lock falling near his eyes.

'I'm here because you ran out today after saying you didn't need me to help you. But clearly you were prepared to ask for help up until that point. You wouldn't have driven across the island for nothing.'

Valentina cursed herself again for having gone to him at all. She lifted her chin. 'It was a bad idea. Everything is fine.'

Gio crossed his arms. 'I know my aunt Carmela—I'd imagine that everything is not fine at all.'

Valentina's belly lurched. Things weren't fine. They were awful. But she wouldn't ask Gio for help. She *couldn't*. There was too much history between them. Along with all sorts of dangerous undercurrents she didn't want to look at. *So*, a small voice asked her now, *so why did you go to him today*?

Firmly Valentina opened her door again and stood aside. She looked at Gio but avoided his eyes. 'I shouldn't have gone to you today. I'd like you to leave *now*.'

Gio looked at the woman standing so stiffly by the door and wanted to shake her. She'd come today for *something*. Exasperated now he said, 'Look, Valentina, you know you can talk to me. You can tell me whatever it is, if you need something.'

She looked at him then and for the first time he noticed that she was pale and she looked tired, shadows under her eyes. Worry on her face.

'No, *you* look. Pretend you never saw me today. Now for the second time, I'd like you to leave. You shouldn't have come all the way here.'

'Valentina, for crying out loud—' Gio broke off when a shrill ring pierced the tense atmosphere. He looked down and could see a mobile vibrating on the small coffee table. Automatically he bent to pick it up and saw that it said, *Home*. His gut clenched. Valentina's parents. He handed it to her, saying, 'It's your—'

But she cut him off. 'I know who it is.'

She took the phone and turned her back to him saying, 'Mama?'

Gio's gaze travelled down over the glossy hair in messy waves over shoulders and slender back and then his eyes went to the rounded curve of her bottom. He wanted to walk up to her and pull her hair aside and press a kiss to the side of her neck. He wanted to encircle her waist with his arm, and feel the brush of her breasts on his skin. He wanted to pull her back into his body, moulding her to him. Instantly his body responded with a wave of heat. The sudden need was so intense he shook with it.

It was a few seconds before he noticed that Valentina had turned and was looking at him, her face pale and stricken. Immediately he was alert, eyes narrowed on her. 'What is it?'

'My father has collapsed.'

Gio was moving before she'd even finished speaking and they were outside and in his car a few seconds after that. Valentina rattled off the address. Luckily she didn't live far from her parents, who had moved into Palermo after her father had retired from working at the Corretti palazzo.

They pulled up outside the modest house and Valentina was out of the car and through the front door when Gio got out of the car. He followed her in, an awful hollow feeling in his belly. If anything happened to her father... Just then he saw the man on the floor, his face white. Valentina's mother was sobbing over the body and he could see Valentina starting to shake violently.

Gio came in and gently moved Valentina aside and then in cool authoritative tones instructed her to call an ambulance. While she was on the phone he knelt down beside Emilio Ferranti and listened for a heartbeat and heard nothing.

Expertly Gio opened the man's shirt and started CPR. He felt someone pulling his arm and saw Valentina's face, white with worry and shock. 'What are you doing?'

Gio shrugged her off gently but firmly. 'I'm giving him CPR.' And then he bent to his task and didn't look up until the paramedics arrived and pulled him to one side. He was breathing fast and sweating as he watched them hook Emilio up to various things. Then they put him on a gurney and wheeled him into the ambulance, with Valentina's mother getting into the back. One of the paramedics was talking to Valentina, and then they were gone with the ambulance lights flashing and the siren wailing intermittently.

Gio went up to Valentina. She looked at him, dazed. His heart turned over in his chest. 'Come on, I'll take you to the hospital.'

He led her to the car and put her in, fastening the safety belt around her when she made no move to do so.

When they were on the road with the lights of the ambulance just visible in the far distance he felt her turn to him. 'The paramedic told me you probably saved his life. I…I didn't know what you were doing.'

Gio shrugged minutely. 'Don't worry about it, it can look scary.'

'Where did you learn to do that?'

A bleakness entered Gio and he didn't say, *I learnt how to do it after Mario died, when I couldn't save him, or help him.* Instead he just said lightly, 'I run a business—I insist that all my staff have basic first aid training, including myself.' Gio's experience was a bit more than just in first aid, he'd actually done a paramedic training course. The way he'd felt so helpless next to Mario's inert body had forged within him a strong desire never to feel that helpless again. The awful thing was that Mario had been alive for a while, but Gio hadn't known how to keep him alive. And he'd died in Gio's arms before the medics had arrived.

'I…thank you.'

Gio winced. 'You don't have to say anything.'

The rest of the journey was made in silence and when they got to the hospital Gio pushed down the awful sense of déjà vu. The night of Mario's accident, he'd hoped against hope that somehow miraculously they'd brought Mario back to life but when he'd got there he'd seen the small huddle of Valentina with her parents, crying. Valentina had rushed at him with her fists flying. 'I knew something would happen. You shouldn't have taken him out. He wouldn't have gone if you'd not asked him.…'

The memory faded, to be replaced now by the frantic chaos of the emergency room. Valentina went and asked at the desk and then, with a quick glance at Gio, who just nodded at her, she disappeared with a nurse.

Gio made a phone call like an automaton to one of his staff to come and switch his impractical sports car for something more practical. It was shortly after that had been delivered when he saw the bowed figure of Valentina's mother, with Valentina all but holding her up. *Please God*, he prayed silently.

But when they got close Valentina looked at him and smiled tiredly. 'He's stable. It was a massive heart attack and the doctor said if he hadn't been given CPR he wouldn't have made it.'

Gio felt uncomfortable and just said, 'I have a car outside, let me take you home.'

Valentina's mother acknowledged Gio but to his relief she didn't seem too upset to see him there, or surprised. He solicitously helped them into the jeep that had been delivered and then Valentina said, 'You can take us to my mother's. I'll stay with her tonight.'

When Gio pulled up outside the house again he jumped out to help Valentina's mother. At the door she stopped and looked up at him. 'Thank you, Gio.'

He looked into her lined and careworn face and couldn't see anything but tired gratitude. She patted his hand and then went inside the house. When Valentina was about to pass him he stopped her with a hand on her arm. She looked at him and he had to curb his response to her.

'If you need anything…*anything* at all, you know where to find me. I mean it, Valentina.'

She started to say, 'I…' and then she stopped and said, 'OK.' And then she went inside and closed the door.

A week after he'd left Valentina at her mother's house, Gio was trying not to think of her and was looking at a picture in the local newspaper. A huge headline was proclaiming: Scandals in the Corretti Family! There was a salacious rumour that the runaway bride had actually run away with his older brother Matteo after the non-wedding. And it had been revealed that his cousin, Rosa, was not actually his cousin but another half-sister, thanks to an affair between his aunt Carmela and his father.

Gio's mouth twisted in disgust. He wanted nothing to do with the sordid details of these stories. He did feel a twinge of sympathy for Rosa, who had always been quite sweet to him on the rare occasions they'd met. He could imagine that this must be devastating news to deal with.…

Gio's phone rang at that moment and it was a number he didn't recognise. Unconsciously his insides tensed. He threw down the paper and picked the phone up. *'Pronto?'*

There was nothing for a few seconds and then *her* voice came down the line. 'It's me.'

Gio's belly tightened. Carefully he said, 'How is your father?'

Valentina sounded weary. 'He's doing OK, still in hospital, but it looks like he needs a major bypass operation.'

There was another long silence and then, 'Gio…I…'

Gio clutched the phone, suddenly feeling panicky. *If she hangs up…* 'Go on, Valentina, what is it?'

He heard her sigh audibly and then she said, 'I need you to give me a job.'

'I don't have any formal training—I'll work in the kitchen…I'll work wherever you want.'

Gio schooled his expression, but his chest tightened at the pride in Valentina's voice. She'd come to him today, the day after she'd phoned, dressed in black slacks and a white shirt. Hair tied back in a low ponytail. Face pale. Avoiding his eyes. She must hate this.

Something piqued his curiosity. 'Where *did* you train?'

Valentina looked at him then and he had to keep an even more rigid control on his control.

'You remember my nonna?'

Gio nodded. He had a vague memory of their grandmother, a small woman with sparkling brown eyes. She'd been at the grave that day too, a wizened matriarch who should never have had to see her grandson buried before her. Gio fought down the predictable tightness in his chest, and Valentina continued. 'She was a cook for a local trattoria, and she was my first teacher. From when I was tiny she taught me all the basics and her secrets. When I left school I went to work with her, and then when she passed away, I worked for Marcel Picheron as a commis-chef.'

Her mouth twisted minutely. 'My parents had pooled all their resources into—' She stopped abruptly and the name hung silently in the air like an accusation—*Mario*. Then she looked away for a moment before continuing through the thick tension in the air. 'They had no more money to send me to college, but I heard about Marcel's open days when he would audition unknowns so I auditioned and got in.'

Gio remembered well how Mario's parents had put every cent into his education. And yet Valentina had never shown any signs of being bitter about her own education being neglected. She'd been as proud as they had.

He could only imagine how good Valentina must have been to impress the cantankerous old French chef who had more Michelin stars than any other chef in Italy and who ran the most exclusive restaurant on the island. It had a waiting list of six months.

Valentina glanced at Gio again. 'I worked my way up to sous-chef but I found that my forte was in devising menus and creating hors d'oeuvres.'

Dryly he remarked now, 'You probably have had a better training than most people out of a cordon bleu school in Paris.'

Valentina shrugged, her cheeks going pink. 'I set up my own catering company with two friends a year ago. We come up with menus for events, and then we hire outside chefs to come in and cook. I make all the canapés. In general I supervise everything, and step in to chef if I need to.'

Gio recalled the small part of the reception he'd seen a few weeks ago. He could remember the intricately delicate canapés, how appetising and original they'd looked even though he'd had no appetite for them, his gut too churned up to be there in the first place.

He got up from behind his desk and stood at the huge window with hands in his pockets, observing but not really seeing the hive of activity out on the racecourse. He turned back to face Valentina, who was sitting in a chair. She looked as delicate and brittle as spun glass.

'The annual Corretti Cup race meeting is coming up in three weeks. It runs for three days with the Corretti Cup race on the last day. We provide a full entertainment package here, including a set menu for lunch every day. I'd like you to come up with the menu for that main luncheon each day, and also look after catering for the evening champagne receptions.'

His words took a minute to sink in. Valentina stood up, feeling a little shaky and disbelieving. She'd imagined Gio telling her she could work on the lowest rung of the ladder in his kitchen. Not that she could be handed the entire catering job for the Corretti Cup! Suspicious now she said testily, 'I'm not a charity case.'

His eyes flashed and his jaw tightened. 'I don't hire people out of the goodness of my heart. I hire them because they're good. I've got a new chef that I'm not sure about so I want you to devise a menu for him to work to. I saw what you did at the wedding reception—your work is good, very good. Quite apart from the recommendation that my aunt hired you in the first place when she's a notorious stickler for perfection.'

A warm flush of pleasure took Valentina by surprise and she realised what an opportunity she was being presented with. The annual Corretti Cup was a very prestigious international fixture. Whatever the kudos of doing a Corretti wedding, this was on another level. Suddenly she felt giddy at the thought.

She bit her lip. 'I had two full-time staff working for me. I trust them.'

Gio waved a hand. 'Hire them back. Whatever you need.'

He came back around his desk and sat down and looked up at her, completely business-like. 'Let's discuss your fees.'

An hour later Valentina's head was whirling. She'd been despatched with one of Gio's assistants and given a thorough tour of the kitchens and dining areas. It was all state of the art and luxurious without being ostentatious. There were VIP corporate boxes that overlooked the stadium, with their own balconies. There was even a couple of royal suite boxes.

When they emerged back out onto the main track area her guide pointed behind the huge stand and said, 'That's where the stables and practice gallops are situated, and the staff living quarters. Signor Corretti keeps the rest of his horses at his *castello* nearby where his stud is based.'

Valentina pushed down the lancing pain when she thought of the *castello* grounds where Mario had died and asked, 'What's it like to work here?'

The assistant answered enthusiastically, 'Signor Corretti is a tough boss but fair. He always knows exactly what's going on, and we get better paid than at any of the other racetracks in Italy.'

Valentina told him she was fine to wander on her own after that. The truth was, Gio had been more than fair with her pay. He'd been positively generous. When she'd balked at the amount, he'd said, 'I pay all my staff well, Valentina. I'm not interested in having people working for me who are grumbling about pay or overtime. I can do this, and so I do.'

Valentina surmised now that the vast wealth he'd built up from his horses came in handy when you wanted to keep your employees loyal. But for some reason that churlish thought didn't sit entirely right. Gio hadn't struck her as the type of person to buy his staff's favour. They all seemed to genuinely like him.

She saw his tall form now in the distance and it made her heart kick in a very betraying manner. He'd spotted her and was striding towards her. Valentina had the abrupt urge to turn and run away fast but she didn't. When he stopped before her he asked her how she'd got on and she told him. Dark glasses hid his eyes and Valentina had the perverse urge to take them off so she could read those changeable green depths.

She curled her hands to fists at her sides.

'So you'll start tomorrow then? There's a lot to do in three weeks.'

Valentina nodded and looked away. 'Yes, I'll start tomorrow.' She looked back to Gio and said haltingly, 'I… just wanted to say thank you. You didn't have to do this.'

Mario. Of course he had to do this.

The name hung in the air between them again, even though neither of them had said it. Gio shrugged lightly.

'I'm always on the lookout for good staff and I think you'll add an edge to this year's Corretti Cup.'

He was perfectly solicitous and polite, much as Valentina would imagine him being with anyone else, and she suddenly hated that. She didn't want to be just another employee. So what did she want to be then? The dangerous revelation of that thought made her step back hurriedly. 'OK, well, I'd better get going.'

'You know you can move into the staff quarters here if you like?'

Valentina shook her head. 'No, with my father in hospital I'd like to see him every day. And my mother needs me.'

'That's going to be a killer of a commute. I don't need you falling asleep in your canapés.'

Valentina glanced quickly at him and away again when she saw his rigid jaw. 'It'll be fine. I won't let you down.'

She moved to leave and Gio put his hand on her arm. She stopped in her tracks, breathless.

'I didn't mean that you would let me down. I'm concerned it'll be too much.'

Valentina forced down the tender feeling rising up and looked directly at Gio's dark glasses where she was reflected as a tiny figure. She pulled her arm free and said coolly, 'I'm not your concern.'

Gio's jaw clenched tighter. 'You are if you're my employee.'

Valentina faced him directly, something dark goading her to say, 'Since when have you cared so much for others or their safety?'

Gio seemed to blanch before her eyes and Valentina wished the words unsaid but it was too late. She stepped back before she said anything else. 'You don't need to worry.'

Gio watched Valentina hurry away in her black slacks

and white shirt with her hair pulled back and he wanted to throttle her. Well, he wanted to kiss her, and then throttle her. He was glad of his glasses because he'd been staring at her mouth for the past few minutes, until she'd let that little barb slide out: *Since when have you cared so much for others...*

Gio swung away abruptly from following Valentina's progress to the car park and paced angrily towards his own jeep which was nearby. He gunned the engine and made the fifteen-minute journey to his *castello* with his hands clenched tight around the wheel.

When he saw the familiar lines and ramparts of his home he breathed out and turned into the impressive driveway lined by tall cypress trees. As the *castello* came into view he had to concede as he often did that it was entirely too huge for just him, but he'd bought it more for the surrounding land which contained his small farm and more importantly his stud and stables.

It had used to also contain a small training ground and gallops but after Mario's death he'd got rid of them, unable to look out his window and not see the prone figure of his best friend lying on the ground.

It was one of the reasons he'd taken off for Europe after Mario's death and had spent the best part of two years in a blurry haze. Anything to avoid coming home and dealing with his demons. But he had eventually found his way back out of that black hole to come home. Now, he still trained horses but he was fanatical about safety and hadn't been on a horse's back in seven years.

Cursing this uncharacteristic introspection Gio swung out of his jeep and instead of going into the house, took a detour around it and made directly for the stables where he found Misfit, who whinnied in acknowledgement as soon as Gio drew near. Just being near his prize stallion made a level of peace flow through Gio, even though having met Valentina again he realised peace was bound to be elusive.

He caressed the sleek thoroughbred's neck and face and chuckled softly before taking an apple out of his pocket, which the horse gratefully received. 'You're a rogue,' Gio chastised easily. 'You only love me for my apples.' Familiar emotion welled up when he thought of how far he'd come with this thoroughbred.

His father, who had fancied himself as a bit of a horseman on the side, had installed state-of-the-art stables and training grounds at the family palazzo. It had quickly become a sanctuary for Gio, who'd had an innate affinity for the horses from the first moment he'd seen one.

Benito Corretti had bought Misfit as a yearling, unbroken, from a stud in Ireland. The colt had had a good pedigree but after several failed attempts to break him in by the head trainer, his father had declared curtly, 'Send him to the meat factory. He was a waste of money.'

Gio had gone to his father. He'd been sixteen years old and hadn't stuttered in a couple of years but in front of his father he could feel his vocal chords closing up the way they always had, but he'd swallowed hard and concentrated. 'Father, give me a week—if I can't break him by then you can do what you want.'

His father had been drunk and had taunted Gio cruelly, 'Are you s-s-s-s-sure, G-G-G-Gio?'

His father couldn't resist the chance to goad him. Gio wanted to punch him in the face but held his fists by his side. How many times had Mario counselled him that it wasn't worth it to show emotion to his old man? As soon as he could he'd be gone from his family palazzo to set up his own business. Somewhere far, far away.

His opportunity to do just that had come much sooner than he'd thought. Gio had confounded everyone by tam-

ing the horse within a week and his father had said grudgingly, 'You can have him then, seeing as how you put so
much work into him—perhaps you're not a complete loss
to the Corretti name after all.'

Gio had seized his opportunity. He'd never excelled at
school anyway, so he'd left his house that night and with
the help of Mario had taken his horse to a stables nearby. In
the following weeks Gio had searched for and found work
at another stables near Syracuse, and had made a deal with
the owner so that he could work for food and board while
stabling his horse there for free. He'd trained his horse in
his free time, honing him into a champion.

His boss had seen something in Gio and the horse—
when he'd been transporting his own horses to race in
England, Ireland and France, he'd offered to include Gio's
horse, Misfit. Gio had never looked back after that. Misfit had become a champion racer almost overnight and
Gio had paid back his mentor and boss many times over.

He'd been winning millions at the biggest racetracks in
Europe by the time he was nineteen, making a name for
himself as a prodigiously natural trainer and then breeder.

Misfit had been retired for a long time now, but with
his stellar track record, horse breeders from as far away
as the Middle East and Ireland sent their mares to Sicily
to be covered by the renowned stallion for astronomical
fees. He'd already sired at least another dozen champions.

Gio ran a cursory but expert eye over his horse now and,
satisfied that he was in good condition and comfortable,
gave him a last affectionate pat on the neck. As he was
walking back out of the stables all he could think about
though was how the hell he was going to get through the
foreseeable future with Valentina Ferranti around every
corner....

* * *

By the end of the first week Valentina could hardly see straight she was so tired. She was driving almost two hours each way every day in her clapped-out car and after calling in to see her father in hospital it was usually after midnight before she got to bed, before getting up again at 5:00 a.m.

Her father's condition was not good. He was on a waiting list for a major heart operation but it could take months for him to be next in line. The very real fear that he could have another heart attack, and this time a worse one before the operation, was constantly on Valentina's mind. Not to mention her mother, who was beside herself with worry.

She was in the act of turning with a plate of pastries in her hands when the door to the kitchen opened, startling her. When Valentina saw who it was, the plate slipped out of her fingers, smashing all over the floor.

Even the sound couldn't really jar her out of her exhaustion as she bent to start picking up the pieces.

'Wait, let me do that.'

Valentina stood reluctantly and watched as Gio bent down at her feet and started picking up the biggest pieces. One of the evening cleaners came in then and Gio instructed him to clean up the mess. He took Valentina by the arm and led her out, protesting, 'I should clean it up—it's my mess.'

'Leave it,' growled Gio before letting her arm go and turning to face her outside the kitchen door. Nearly everyone else had already left for the evening.

Gio looked at his watch and asked, 'What on earth are you doing here at 8:30 p.m.?'

Valentina flushed, far too aware of Gio's earthy smell—musky and masculine. He must have been working with the horses. He seemed very tall and imposing right then, his broad shoulders blocking everything out behind him, making a curious ache form in Valentina's belly. She hadn't seen him much during the week and she only realised now as some tension ebbed away that she'd been unconsciously *waiting* for him. It made her angry and she glared up at him, hands on hips. 'I'm working late because it's the only quiet time in the kitchen when I can experiment with new recipes.'

'Working late isn't a problem, as long as you start work late, but you've been in every morning this week at 7:00 a.m., well before most other people.'

'How do you know?' Valentina asked suspiciously.

'Because it's my business to know these things.'

Valentina bit her lip when she could feel a retort springing up. She remembered the last time and how her cruel words had rang in her head for days afterwards.

'Fine,' she said grudgingly, 'I won't work so late from now on.'

Gio sounded grim. 'You look exhausted, and I don't believe you.'

Valentina looked up at him and was actually too tired at that moment to argue. All she could do was wearily pull her apron over her head and say, 'Well, then you won't stop me going home.'

Gio took her arm and all but frog-marched her out to where his jeep was waiting. 'I'm driving you—you're a liability.'

Valentina started to protest but he all but lifted her into the passenger seat and secured the seat belt around her. Her mouth was open to say something but when the hard muscles of his arm brushed her breast she shut it abruptly, heat flashing up through her body.

As grim-faced as Gio, Valentina crossed her arms and once they were on the main road to Palermo she managed to get out a strangled, 'How am I supposed to get to work in the morning or are you providing a personal chauffeur service to your staff now?'

Gio sent her a quelling look. 'It's Saturday tomorrow so you shouldn't be working anyway, but I'll have someone drop your car home for you.'

When they were reaching the outskirts of Palermo, in about half the time it would have taken Valentina, she said, 'I need to stop at the hospital first.'

Gio obliged and took the road to the hospital and when he got out of the jeep and met her at the front she stopped and said, 'What are you doing? I can get a taxi home from here.'

'I'd like to pay my respects to your mother if I may, and your father if he doesn't mind.'

Valentina couldn't speak. Guilt flooded her and she avoided Gio's eyes. Under his questioning look she blurted out, 'The truth is that my parents don't know about…my job. That I lost it, or that I'm working for you.'

Gio folded his arms; his belly felt leaden. 'And you think they'd be upset if they knew?'

She looked up at him. 'Well, what do you think?'

A bleak feeling rushed through Gio. How could he have forgotten for a moment the intense and awful grief of that day by the graveside. He ran a hand through his hair and stepped back. 'You're probably right…it's not a good idea.'

'What's not a good idea? Gio, I'm glad you came— Emilio has been asking for you.'

They both turned at the same time to see Valentina's mother on the steps of the hospital where she'd clearly been getting air and had heard their last exchange. With no choice now, Gio followed a stony-faced Valentina and her mother into the hospital, his stomach churning at the thought of what lay ahead.

CHAPTER FOUR

'WHAT DID YOU say to my father?' Valentina hissed at Gio as they walked back out of the hospital an hour later.

Gio was still in shock himself at how Emilio had reacted to seeing him. Alone in the hospital room with the old man, Gio had steeled himself for whatever Mario's father was going to say, expecting a diatribe or a level of hostility matched by his daughter. But the man had completely taken the wind out of his sails by saying a little stiffly, 'First of all, thank you. I believe the reason I'm still alive is because of you.'

Gio had muttered something unintelligible, embarrassed.

And then Signor Ferranti had held out his hand. 'Come here, boy...let me look at you.'

Gio had walked over and given his hand to Emilio, who had taken it in a surprisingly strong grip. His voice was rougher, emotional. 'When we lost Mario...we lost you too.'

Gio's mouth had opened and closed. His own emotion rising thick and fast. Eventually he'd got out, 'But...don't you blame me? Hate me for what happened?'

Emilio had let his hand go and pointed to a chair for Gio to sit down and he'd done so, heavily. Stunned.

'I did,' the old man admitted, 'for a long time. It was

easier to blame you than to believe that it could have just been a tragic accident. But ultimately, that's what it was. I know well how reckless Mario was, you were as bad as each other.'

'If I hadn't had that cursed horse though—'

Signor Ferranti put up a hand, stopping Gio. He arched a brow. 'Do you really think you could have stopped Mario when he wanted to do something?'

Gio's chest was so tight he could hardly breathe. He half shrugged.

Mario's father said gently now, 'Mario followed you around like a puppy, wanted to do everything you did....'

A granite weight settled in Gio's belly, the all-too-familiar guilt rearing up when he thought of the countless reckless activities he'd encouraged Mario to join him in over the years. Anything to alleviate his own sense of yawning loneliness. 'I know,' he'd just answered quietly.

As if sensing his self-flagellation though, Valentina's father had said gently, 'Gio, he worshipped the ground you walked on...just as I know you did him.'

Gio looked at Signor Ferranti in surprise. There was no condemnation in his voice, only weary acceptance.

'For Valentina though...it was very hard for her to come to terms with. She was so angry...is still angry, I think.'

'Gio!'

Gio looked down at Valentina blankly for a second. He was still in the room with her father. They were outside the hospital doors now and her arms were folded and she was glaring up at him. There were smudges of weariness under her eyes and that made Gio's resolve firm even more.

Now she'd got his attention she continued. 'So are you going to tell me how on earth you had the nerve to propose moving my father to a private specialist clinic in Syracuse, let alone taking him to a hospital on the mainland for a major heart operation?'

Gio reigned in his temper which seemed to be growing a shorter and shorter fuse around this woman. He took a deep breath. 'I offered to help your father and I'm glad to say he accepted. By moving him to Syracuse while he waits for the operation, you will be able to move into the staff accommodation at the racetrack. It'll wipe out your commute and give you an easy mind with your parents so close. It'll also ease their minds to know you're not over-exhausting yourself.'

'So you're doing this to make things better for yourself?' Valentina sneered. 'Because you don't want a fainting staff member serving your VIP guests?'

Valentina wasn't sure why she was so angry, just that she was. Blistering. It was something to do with the way her father had shown no enmity towards Gio. And it was more than just gratitude for having saved his life. After a long private conversation, she and her mother had been allowed back into the room and the first thing her father had said to her was, 'You should have told us about your job, *piccolina*....'

So not only had Gio told them about her disaster, they also now knew that she was working for him. And didn't seem fazed by that knowledge at all. She'd looked at Gio accusingly but his face had been completely impassive.

If anything, her parents had been looking at Gio almost adoringly. And then her father's consultant had come into the room and Gio had cleared his throat and announced what he would like to do to help.

Her parents had been taken aback by his audacious offer and Valentina had looked on in shock as her mother had gripped her husband's hand and begged him with tears in her eyes to do as Gio suggested.

'What's the problem, Valentina? I would have thought you'd be happy to know that your father will be receiving the best treatment.'

Valentina uncrossed her arms and her hands curled to fists by her sides. 'You put them, *all of us*, in an awkward position—how could they say no? But you know we can't afford this treatment. How do you think we can ever pay you back?'

Gio's face tightened. He waved a hand. 'You don't need to worry about that. I'll take care of it.'

He started to walk towards his jeep and Valentina called impetuously from behind him, 'Do you really think money will make up for it?'

Gio stopped in his tracks and after long silent tense seconds he turned around from the bottom of the steps. His face was stark. 'What's that supposed to mean?'

Valentina had gone too far now. Something very personal and dark was pushing her over this edge. 'You know what I'm talking about. You're trying to atone—'

Gio bounded up the steps again so fast and with such ruthless intent that Valentina took a step back.

'So what if I am?' he asked rawly. 'Is that so bad if it saves your father?'

Valentina felt like something was breaking apart inside her. 'Yes. Because it won't bring *him* back.'

Gio took her arms in a tight grip with his hands. 'Do you think I don't know that?'

For a second Valentina glimpsed a depth and level of stark pain in Gio's eyes that made her want to cry out. It echoed within her like a keening cry. And another echo sounded deep within her, telling her she was a fraud of the worst kind, because she was deliberately pushing Gio away to avoid facing up to a dark truth inside her.

It was the same reason she'd hurled those cruel words

at him last week at the track: *Since when have you cared so much for others...*

She'd been able to push it down for seven years, but standing in front of him now—it was rising inexorably within her, demanding that she acknowledge it. And she couldn't. Gio was unwittingly forcing her look at herself and she didn't like what she saw. Breaking the intense eye contact Valentina ripped herself free of his grip and stepped around him to hurry down the steps. She went straight to a nearby hospital taxi rank.

Before Gio could stop her she'd got into the first taxi and was pulling out of the hospital forecourt. He looked at the taxi's break lights winking just before it disappeared completely. A wave of bleakness washed over him. Was Valentina right? Was he interfering where he shouldn't? Acting out of a crippling sense of guilt? Trying to buy his soul back by saving Mario's father?

The fact that Mario's parents had apparently forgiven Gio was small comfort now. Gio knew that the only hope he had for his soul to find some peace was through Valentina's forgiveness, and her father's words came back to Gio then: *It was very hard for her to come to terms with... she was so angry...she still is.*

The anger Valentina felt was palpable, not in question. She'd only come to him for help because he was literally the only person on the island who would defy his aunt to employ her. His mouth firmed and he made his way to his jeep. He would not apologise for wanting to help her father and he was *not* doing it to buy forgiveness. He was doing it because Mario wasn't here to take care of his family, but Gio was. And Valentina could rant and rail all she liked.

Valentina stared blindly out of the taxi window, the lights of a busy Friday Palermo night flashing past. But the lights blurred as weak ineffectual tears filled her eyes. She'd just run away like the abject coward that she was. Angry with herself for feeling so emotional, Valentina dashed them away, avoiding the driver's curious glances in the rearview mirror.

She hated the ease with which Gio had been so comprehensively all but welcomed back into the bosom of her family. She hated the ease with which he was able to guarantee her father's well-being. And she hated *herself* for being like this.

Gio was highlighting the big flaw that was Valentina in her own family. Mario had been the one on whom all hopes and dreams had rested. So Valentina had been more or less forgotten about. Not the most academic of students anyway, she'd left school at sixteen to work with her grandmother in the small trattoria.

Mario had known of her ambitions to succeed and make something of herself. But when he'd died, that link had gone and her parents had been despondent, left with their only other child who had no glittering prospects.

That's why Valentina had worked so hard to build up a business. But even when it had taken off, her parents had been wary more than proud. They were of the old school and thought that what really counted was academic qualification and a solid career. And also that Valentina should find a nice man and settle down, find someone who would provide for her…and them. Provide them with grandchildren.

But instead, her nemesis Giacomo Corretti had been the one to step into the breach. In more ways than one. Little by little she was becoming more and more beholden to him. She resented him for it but then she'd been the one to invite him back into their lives so she had no one to blame but herself.

She remembered what it had been like to look into his eyes just now, to see the abject pain in those green and brown depths. The way her heart had clenched, the way her conscience had mocked her. And worse, the way her pulse had pounded with a deeply unsettling rhythm just to be near him. As it always did, as it always *had*. Why did he still have to have this effect on her?

The taxi was pulling up outside her apartment building now and Valentina paid the driver and refused to let Gio dominate her thoughts any more. It was only when she fell into a fitful sleep sometime later that he came to haunt her in her dreams.

'What's this?'

Valentina stood in front of Gio the following Monday morning in his office. Her head was still reeling at how fast things had moved in just thirty-six hours. Her father was already settled in the private clinic in Syracuse and she'd moved into the staff accommodation the previous evening.

Gio was sitting behind his desk looking absurdly out of place in his grey T-shirt. He looked far too vital and virile and *sexy* to be sitting at a desk.

Valentina dragged her attention back to his question. 'It's the advance on my pay that you gave me. I need to pay you back for what you're doing for my father. I realise that it'll take a lot—'

Gio stood up abruptly, making Valentina stop talking. His face had darkened visibly and he held the cheque back out to her. 'Don't insult me, Valentina. Please.'

Valentina refused to take the cheque, her own face darkening as blood rushed into it. She felt embarrassed. 'When I came to you looking for work it was to make enough money to support and care for my parents. What I earn should go into their care and as you're paying for that at the moment…' She trailed off, a little scared at the way Gio's eyes had darkened almost to black by now.

'I offered to pay for your father's treatment with no strings attached.'

Valentina observed scathingly, 'There's always strings attached.'

Gio shook his head and looked at her pityingly, making a hot rush of humiliation rush through Valentina. He came around his desk to face her and she wished he hadn't. In flat runners he towered over her own not inconsiderable five feet seven inches.

'What happened to you? What made you become so cynical?' He frowned. 'Was it a love affair gone wrong?'

Valentina nearly choked. A love affair gone wrong? Gio had no idea. She'd had plenty of men chasing after her but she'd kept them all at arm's length. Terrified on some level of getting close to anyone. Terrified of the way one minute someone you loved could be there, and the next minute they could be *gone*. For ever. That realisation seemed to explode into her consciousness like a bomb going off. She'd never even really articulated it to herself like that before. She'd just always instinctively avoided relationships. Losing Mario had made her cynical. It had twisted something inside her soul.

Made weak by this insight, Valentina was barely aware when Gio took her hand and folded the cheque back into it, closing her fingers over it. His hand was big and warm around hers and she looked up at him. They were standing much closer than she'd realised and his scent, musky and warm, unleashed an avalanche of vivid memories in her imagination.

Jerkily she pulled her hand back from his, with the cheque in it, and stepped back. The only coherent thing in her head was that she needed to get out of there *now*.

Before Gio saw something she herself couldn't really understand.

She got to the door and then looked back and blurted out, 'It was you. You made me like this.'

All Valentina saw before she fled was Gio's face darkening even more. She made her way back to the kitchen and busied herself, silently begging everyone around her to leave her alone.

Where did she get the nerve to say these things to him? It was as if every time he came within feet of her she had to lash out. Say the worst thing possible, terrified that if he got too close he might see her cruel words for what they were—a very flimsy attempt to keep him at a distance at all costs.

Valentina knew on some rational level that Mario's death had been a tragic accident; Gio hadn't forced her brother onto that demonic horse. She'd even heard him discouraging it, *initially*. The knowledge that her parents appeared able to forgive him had been a huge blow to her own justification to stay angry at him. But the fact was, for so long now she'd held Gio responsible.

Her anger had been compounded by the way he'd disappeared after Mario's death only to turn up playing the part of a playboy bent on nothing but slaking his basest needs. Disgusted with herself for having been so invested in what he was doing, Valentina had nevertheless stored up every tiny example of Gio carousing and generally acting as if he didn't have a care in the world, while they'd mourned Mario.

Her anger at him had always comforted her on some level. It was familiar and…necessary. For her sanity. In all honesty Valentina knew that she was very afraid of looking at what might be left behind if she couldn't hold Gio responsible. If she couldn't be angry with him. That thought was so terrifying that something must have shown on her face.

'Val? Are you OK?'

Valentina sucked in a big breath and forced a smile at Franco, who was looking at her intently across the island they were working at. She nodded abruptly. 'Fine…I, ah, just remembered something I need to do.'

Thankfully he left her alone and that evening Valentina escaped to the clinic to see how her parents were settling in, rather than unpack in her new accommodation, telling herself it was more than just a ruse to avoid bumping into Gio again.

That evening Gio cursed volubly outside Valentina's suite of rooms. There was no answer. She wasn't there. Even though he knew logically she was most likely visiting her parents, he had to battle a spiking of something very proprietorial. And he didn't like it.

Women had never been anything more than a diversion to him. His long childhood years of feeling less than, and inadequate, had left him with too many scars to trust anyone, apart from Mario. His subsequent successes had done much to chase away that sense of inadequacy, but since Mario's death, the joy had been taken out of it to a large extent.

Gio's mouth twisted wryly just remembering how Mario had been the one who'd fallen in and out of love like some besotted Romeo. Something within Gio had always remained aloof with a woman. They hadn't ever touched some deep secret part of him. In the two years after Mario's death there had been an endless parade of beautiful women but none he'd connected with, and more often than not Gio had found himself waking alone.

Valentina. She'd always been different. She'd snuck into

a place that was locked away deep inside him. But he'd been acutely aware that his feelings and desires for her were strictly forbidden.

When he'd left Sicily first she'd been only ten or eleven. A gap-toothed child only on his radar as his best friend's kid sister who had trailed them with almost religious devotion.

But when he'd returned years later—a millionaire, the new owner of the racetrack in Syracuse with plans to re-build—she'd been fifteen. And Gio had found himself aware of her in a way that had made him ashamed. So he'd flung himself into socialising with Mario, pursuing the local beauties, anything to push dangerous thoughts and desires from his mind.

Over the next two years she'd only grown more and more beautiful and mature. She'd started to flirt with him, but with such sweet innocence that it had twisted his heart. One day he'd been weak. She'd arrived to look for Mario, who'd already left. A miscommunication. Gio had seen her get startled by Misfit and had acted on an impulse, lifting her onto the horse.

He'd swung up behind her, wrapping his arm around her taut young body. The weight of her firm breasts had been heavy on his arm. Those stolen indulgent minutes had been the most erotic in his life.…

Gio grimaced now and turned away from Valentina's door. What was he doing hanging around like some besotted fool? Yes, he still wanted her. More than ever. But that was all. The capacity to feel anything more had long ago withered to dust inside him, poisoned by grief and guilt.

And Valentina…? She hated him with every cell in her body and if she *had* ever felt anything for him, physical or otherwise, it had been destroyed that night in the hospital in Palermo when she'd seen her dead brother laid out on a slab in the morgue.

* * *

The Corretti Cup was fast approaching. Valentina and her staff were flat-out making sure they had everything ordered and organised. That evening as she hung up her apron, she had to concede reluctantly that Gio had done her a favour by insisting she stay on-site. She wasn't half as exhausted as she had been. And the lines of worry and stress had disappeared from her parents' faces.

She'd avoided him since their last cataclysmic meeting the day before and she didn't like the way guilt pricked her conscience *again*. Driving down that disturbing feeling, Valentina walked around the front of the stadium to get back to her accommodation.

She had a suite of rooms to herself, complete with a kitchenette, living area and en suite bedroom. The understated opulence of the accommodation had blown her away. It was in an old reconverted stone stables. She had a private balcony which looked out over the back of the stadium where the gallops, stables and training ground was based.

But she loved this view over the racetrack. The sun was setting over the sea in the distance, turning everything golden and orange. She stood at the railing and sighed deeply, and then heard from not far away, 'It's beautiful when it's like this, with no one around. That'll all change in a few days though.'

Valentina had tensed at the first word. She turned her head and saw Gio sitting on one of the stand seats behind her—that's how she'd missed him. The thought of him watching her for those few seconds made her feel warm. Instantly she doused it. 'Yes,' she said stiffly, 'it's lovely.'

She made to walk on but Gio lifted something out of an ice bucket beside him and she realised he was holding out a beer, and that he had his own one in his other hand.

Ice cold water droplets ran down the side of the cold bottle and suddenly she was parched.

She looked at Gio and all she could see were those broad shoulders and his messy hair, flopping over one eye. She felt weak. He said easily, 'I bring out some beers for the racetrack workers most evenings. It's a tough few weeks getting ready for the cup.'

Torn between wanting to run and wanting to stay, which was very disturbing, Valentina remembered what she'd said the previous day and then stepped forward and took the bottle. Her fingers brushed off Gio's, sending a spark of awareness jumping between them. 'Thanks.'

She stepped over the bottom seat and sat down near him, and then looked at the view again as if it was the most absorbing thing she'd ever seen. She took a gulp of cold beer, not really tasting it. Silence grew and lengthened between them and she fiddled with the label on her bottle. Unable to stand it any more she turned to face him. Awkwardly she started, 'I…I've said things to you…'

She stopped, cursing her inability to be articulate and tried again. 'I owe you an apology. What I said yesterday…' She shrugged one shoulder minutely. 'You seem to bring out the worst in me.'

Gio shook his head, his eyes unreadable in the growing gloom. 'Valentina, what happened in the past—'

She cut him off with an urgent appeal, suddenly terrified he'd mention Mario. 'Let's not talk about it, OK?'

Gio closed his mouth. She could see his jaw clench, but then he just said, 'OK, fine.'

Valentina turned back to the view, an altogether edgier tension in the air now. Desperate to find something, anything innocuous, to talk about she seized on something she'd overheard earlier. 'Some of the staff were talking about the regeneration project for the docklands. It sounds interesting.'

Gio looked at Valentina's profile. The straight nose, determined chin. Long dark lashes. The graceful curve of her cheekbone. She was trying to make small talk. The moment felt very fragile, a tentative cessation of hostilities. Gio's mouth tightened. 'It's a project put in place primarily by my grandfather, Salvatore, in some kind of effort to bring everyone together. Hence the grand wedding that never happened.'

Valentina looked at Gio. 'Isn't that a good thing—I mean, not the wedding failing but bringing everyone together?'

He smiled tightly. 'It would be if everyone's interests were altruistic.'

Valentina frowned. 'Are your interests different to the others?'

Gio shifted; they were straying into an area he wasn't entirely comfortable with now. Reluctantly he said, 'I've been interested in the docklands area for some time. I think it could be a very useful space for youth projects.'

'What kind of youth projects?'

Gio shrugged, tense. 'The kind of projects that brings kids together, teaches them things, lets them explore their limits in a safe environment. Gets them off the streets basically.'

Brings them together so they don't feel so isolated, like I always did even with Mario...

Gio clamped his jaw shut as if those rogue words might spill out. He wasn't sure why he felt so vulnerable telling her about something that was so close to his heart. Was he afraid she'd laugh at him? Accuse him again of trying to atone?

Valentina seemed to absorb this information in silence

and then she asked, 'Your brothers were mentioned too. Do you see them much?'

Gio's mouth tightened. Little did she realise that any question about his family was akin to walking blindfolded into a minefield. He dragged his gaze away from the provocative curves of her body beside him in simple jeans and T-shirt and looked out to the falling night. 'No…is the simple answer.'

'They weren't at the wedding?'

Gio shrugged. 'Not that I saw. They should have been.' He took a gulp of beer, suddenly wondering if he'd been wise to alert Valentina to his presence here.

He felt her turn to look at him. 'You didn't spend much time with them growing up, did you?'

He glanced at her then and took another gulp of beer and swallowed. 'You know I didn't.' Because he spent all his time with Mario. He didn't have to say it.

'Were they mean to you?'

Gio looked away again. *What was this? Twenty questions?* But he unclenched his jaw. 'No, they were never mean to me. They had their own battles to fight. They both took more after my father than I did. I never had that drive or ambition, that sense of competition to be the dominant Corretti. They just…they were preoccupied with their own stuff.'

Gio glanced at Valentina again and she was looking down into her beer bottle, swirling the liquid. Her hands were small and graceful. Capable. He had a sudden memory of being much smaller, when Valentina had been sitting on the sidelines of some game he and Mario had been playing.

At one point he'd gone up to her and asked if she wanted to join in, stuttering over the words. Instinctively he'd been tensed for her reaction, to laugh at him or mimic him, but she'd just stood up and put her hand in his.

Sounding as if it was almost half to herself Valentina said now, 'You've been very successful.'

Gio smiled minutely, brought back to the present, and the reality of a very adult Valentina. 'The horse-racing business is very lucrative and I had a good horse.'

Valentina smiled wryly. That was an understatement. Everyone knew about Giacomo Corretti's meteoric rise to fame and the horse that had won races for almost a decade, turning him from champion into legend. She looked at him. 'Is Misfit still alive?'

Gio nodded and something about the intensity of his focus on her made her nervous, tingly.

'Yes…but he's retired now. He stands at my stud at the *castello*. Mares are sent from all over the world to be covered by him. He's sired two of my current champions—Mischief and Misdemeanour. They're both running in the Corretti Cup this year.'

Valentina fell silent. Misfit had been the horse that he'd taken her riding on that day around the gallops. The sheer provocation of that memory again, and the way this conversation had veered wildly off a comfortable track, made her put her beer bottle down and she stood up.

She sounded breathless. 'I should be going.'

Gio stood up too, and it was only then that Valentina realised how dark it had become. His face was shadowed. He looked even bigger in the dim light. It was as if thinking of that moment on the horse had ripped away some vital part of her defence around this man. She felt naked, vulnerable. Exposed.

She turned around and then felt a large warm hand on her arm, under her T-shirt. Her belly plummeted to some dark hot place.

Gio compelled her to face him, turning her around. He was frowning. 'What did I say?'

'No—nothing,' Valentina stuttered, which made her think of Gio's stutter. How fierce and yet vulnerable he'd looked whenever he had stuttered. She closed her eyes. *Dio*. Would her imagination not cease?

'I've upset you.'

Valentina opened her eyes but avoided his, focusing on the bronzed column of his throat above his dark T-shirt. She shook her head. 'No…I'm just tired. It's been a long day…few days.'

'Valentina, look at me.'

Somehow Gio was right in front of her, his hand hot on her arm. She imagined that she could feel her pulse beating against her skin, as if trying to touch his skin. His blood.

She looked up and was caught by his dark brown gaze. Green flecks like dark jewels. How many times had she dreamt of these eyes? How many times had she coveted his gaze on her, only to feel it and flee like a little coward? His gaze was on her now and it was scorching her alive.

Gio frowned even more, in a question. 'Valentina?'

Her eyes dropped to Gio's mouth. That gorgeous sensual mouth. Made for dark things. When she'd been seventeen she'd kissed her pillow and imagined she was kissing him.

Gio's voice sounded slightly rough. 'Why are you looking at me like that?'

Her eyes rose to meet his. She seemed to have been invaded by some kind of lethargy. She knew she should be cool, step back, push his arm off her, but all those things seemed so difficult to do.

She shook her head faintly. 'Looking at you…like what?'

A long moment burned between them. Valentina had forgotten everything. She could feel herself swaying ever so slightly towards Gio. And then his other hand came onto her other arm and he was pushing her back, pushing her *away* from him.

It was as if someone had just doused her in cold water. Valentina suddenly saw exactly what she must have looked like. Staring at Gio's mouth like a love-struck teenager, swaying like a drunk person, silently begging him— She stepped back sharply, forcing his hands to drop. She felt hot inside, her skin prickly all over, and worse, her breasts felt fuller, her nipples stinging against the lace of her bra.

'Go to bed, Valentina, you're tired.' Gio's voice was curt and flayed Valentina alive.

She couldn't even answer. She stepped down from the seats and had to force herself not to run all the way to her rooms. Mortification was a tidal wave eating her up all over. Gio had pushed her back; he'd had to stop her from making a complete fool of herself. She'd just exposed herself to him spectacularly. No matter what she said or did from now on, she hadn't hidden her attraction to him.

Surrounded by the inky blackness of the night, Gio downed the rest of his beer in a disgusted gulp. When he'd stood in front of Valentina…and she'd looked at him. *Cristo.* He'd been so hot and hungry for her that he'd imagined her looking at him as if…as if she wanted to kiss him, or for him to kiss her.

He'd been so close to pulling her into him, tipping up that chin, running a thumb across the silky skin of her jaw and cheek…. He's almost done it, and then he'd seen her sway slightly…*with fatigue, not lust.*

Thank God he hadn't completely lost it and misread her signals. The last thing he needed was to add one more thing to Valentina's hate list for him.

CHAPTER FIVE

THE FOLLOWING EVENING Valentina was in foul form. It had been a tough day; everyone's nerves were on edge as they put together all the elements for the Corretti Cup. There were many more staff now, all labouring in their various departments. Event micro-managers were making sure all the areas were kitted out. There was one central dining area where a set menu buffet lunch would be served every day for the main crowd.

Then there was the unbelievably opulent cordoned-off vast VIP marquee area, set in its own landscaped gardens, which had the sit-down à la carte menu, and where each evening a champagne reception would be held as the last races were run.

On the last night there would be a gala ball which would include a charity auction. All the staff had been kitted out with security passes for various areas. Valentina had received one for all areas. She was supervising both the main and VIP areas and Gio was adamant that the buffet diners shouldn't feel like they were getting a second-rate service.

It had surprised her; she'd expected him to be more concerned with the VIP section but he'd been almost disdainful of that as he'd led the group of his chief organisers around that morning, making last-minute notes. Some people were paying into the thousands for tickets into the

VIP marquee, or for a corporate box at the stadium stand. Valentina had also been surprised to learn via one of the other staff that all of the proceeds of the Corretti Cup VIP ticket sales were going to various charities Gio supported locally.

On top of all of that she knew he was dealing with the arrival of hundreds of horses for the races. Some of the most expensive and valuable bloodstock in the world was now at the Corretti stables along with an accompanying heavy security presence. The place was buzzing with grooms and cleaners and decorators and assistants.

Gio had been nothing but utterly professional to her all day, and distant—he'd barely looked at her that morning during the walkabout meeting. He'd treated her exactly the same as the others, who'd all been feverishly taking notes. She should be happy; she should be delighted that the previous evening appeared not to have had any effect on his behaviour towards her. She should be ecstatic he was practically ignoring her!

So why was she so out of sorts? She was two days away from the most important opportunity of her career and she couldn't afford to mess up or get distracted.

Thoroughly disgruntled, Valentina went to see her parents after work and brought them some food she'd prepared. They wanted to hear all about the lavish preparations at the racetrack as it was all anyone could talk about in Syracuse. It was the biggest annual event attracting thousands of tourists. It shamed her a little to realise just how much Gio was doing for the local economy.

When she was walking out about thirty minutes later, her mother stopped Valentina in the corridor. 'Gio came to see us yesterday. He's been very good, making sure everything is on track for the operation.'

Valentina's voice was instantly tight. 'Did he? That's

nice.' Another surprise—in the midst of his busiest time of the year he was taking time to visit her parents?

Her mother shook her head, her dark eyes compassionate. 'Valentina…he has suffered too—don't think that he hasn't. You're not the only one who lost Mario that night.'

Valentina's own sense of building guilt mixed with her mother's gentle admonition made her unbearably prickly. She turned to face her. 'Did he, Mama? Did he really suffer? What about when he was cavorting on yachts in the south of France? Or making millions off the rich and idle gamblers in Europe? Or perhaps he suffered when he was staggering out of casinos at dawn in Monte Carlo with a bimbo model on each arm?'

It took Valentina a second to notice that her face had gone pale. 'Mama?'

Her mother was looking over her head and the hairs went up on the back of Valentina's neck. Slowly she turned to see a grim-faced Gio standing behind her. He had a bunch of flowers in his hand. Valentina gulped. He stepped up beside her, a face like thunder, and handed the flowers to Valentina's mother. And then he looked at Valentina, eyes so dark they looked black.

He took her arm and bit out, 'You and I need to talk.' And then he was pulling her unceremoniously from the clinic. Fear and trepidation was uppermost in Valentina's belly now, not even anger, although she'd never let Gio know that. She'd never seen him so angry. When they were outside he all but flung her arm away from him and faced her. Six foot two of bristling angry male, muscles rippling. He was a sight to behold.

Valentina backed away. 'I'm not going to talk to you when you're like this.'

'When I'm like what?' he almost roared. 'You barely talk to me any which way. I can't do anything right.'

Suddenly a wave of emotion came over her and terrified he'd see it in her eyes Valentina walked quickly to her car which was nearby. She heard a muffled curse but got in quickly and locked her doors. She was trembling all over when she pulled out of her car space and it got worse when she hit the open road and saw a familiar dark silver sports car behind her with a broad-shouldered figure at the wheel.

Gio was following her. It had an immediate effect on her body. A wave of heat made tiny beads of sweat break out over her top lip and between her breasts underneath her shirt. Her hands were sweaty on the wheel and her little car wheezed and panted as she pushed it over the speed limit. She ignored Gio flashing his lights behind her. All she knew was that she had to get away from him. Her emotions were far too volatile to deal with him right now. She felt as if she was on the edge of a precipice.

When she pulled into a space at the racetrack with a screech of brakes a few minutes later, Gio was right behind her. He slammed on his breaks too, sending up a shower of gravel and dust. He sprang out of his car, ripping off dark glasses. 'What the hell do you think you're playing at? You could have caused an accident!'

Valentina was shaking with all the strong emotions running through her. 'You know all about accidents, Corretti, don't you? Just stay away from me.'

He sneered. 'Oh, it's like that, is it? We've gone about two steps forward and three hundred back?'

Valentina clenched her hands to fists, her blood thumping in her head, making it spin. 'I quit, Corretti, OK? This isn't working. I should never have come to you in the first place.'

She started to stride away towards her accommodation fully intending to pack and leave and then felt a much larger presence beside her. He took her arm in his hand.

Again. It was too much; she yanked free and glared up into his face. 'Don't touch me.'

Suddenly Valentina became belatedly aware of people stopped in their tracks around them, watching avidly. Gio noticed too. Grimly he took her hand instead, in a grip so tight it bordered on being painful, and said, 'Not another word, Ferranti. We're taking this somewhere private. We are not done.'

Valentina was tight-lipped and white-faced by the time Gio was opening a door on the same floor as his offices. Her hand was still clamped in his and the way his much larger hand engulfed hers was far too disturbing. He finally let her go when he opened the door and all but pushed her through. She snatched back her hand and held it to her chest; it was tingling.

Pacing away from him, she was so pumped up that she barely noticed what was a very starkly designed yet luxurious small apartment. Minimal furnishings in soft greys and muted colours in the living area led into a bedroom and what she presumed to be a bathroom en suite.

Gio closed the door behind him and she heard him turn a key in the lock. Valentina backed away, eyes huge on him, instantly her sense of threat spiked. 'What do you think you're doing?'

Gio was grim. 'We're not leaving here until we've come to some agreement as to how to proceed without you wanting to rip my head off at every opportunity. It doesn't make for a good professional relationship.'

He crossed his arms. 'And first things first, you are *not* quitting.'

Valentina crossed her arms too. She was valiantly ignoring the fact that she was now alone in a locked room with

Gio Corretti and there was enough electricity crackling between them to light up the whole stadium.

'I can quit if I want to.'

Gio arched a brow. 'Really? Have you already forgotten that you came to me as a last resort?'

Valentina flushed. She had forgotten for a moment. She thought she had freedom. But she didn't. If she left now she couldn't allow Gio to pay for her parents' care and she'd be right back to square one. And it would be so much worse because she'd be decimating her father's chances of getting well again. It was inconceivable that she could do that to them.

'Fine.' She felt like a fool. 'I won't quit.'

Gio's brow got higher. 'That's big of you—after that little public display of animosity I would have grounds to fire you if I so wished.'

Fear lanced Valentina. She looked at Gio properly. 'But you just said that I couldn't quit.'

Gio looked at Valentina and suddenly the bravado was gone and she looked achingly young and vulnerable. Her hair had been tied up in a ponytail but long tendrils had come loose and drifted about her shoulders. She was wearing tight black skinny jeans, flat shoes and a white button-down shirt. It was slightly too short and he could see a sliver of pale flat belly underneath.

She wore no make-up and she was the most beautiful woman Gio had ever seen. A shaft of desire hit him right in the solar plexus, spreading outwards to every cell in his body, even as the realisation that he could never have her failed to douse that desire. It only served to rouse it.

Anger made Gio spit out, 'Let's get to the real issue here, the elephant in the room—*Mario*.'

He saw how Valentina blanched and her eyes got bigger. He pushed down the urge to apologise. Saying his name out loud was like exploding a soft yet lethal bomb between them. 'Come on,' he sneered. 'Aren't you just waiting for another opportunity to hurl some more insults and accusations my way?'

Perhaps it was the easy forgiveness of Valentina's parents working on him subconsciously, but for the first time in a long time, Gio actually felt a subtle shift in his ever-present sense of guilt. It wasn't so black or all-encompassing.

Valentina was struggling to hold on to something real, tangible. Her hatred for this man, for what he had done. She clung to it now like a drowning person clinging to a buoy. Her voice shook with tension. 'Don't you dare mention his name.'

Gio looked fearsome, his face tight with anger, eyes blazing. Muscles popping in his jaw. 'I have as much of a right to mention his name as you do.'

Valentina shook her head. 'No, no, you don't, you—'

'I what?' Gio cut in. 'I *killed him*? Is that what you're going to say?'

Emotion, thick and acrid and cloying, was rising up within Valentina, but it wasn't the easily understood grief for her brother. *That* she recognised and knew well; this was something much more ambiguous and disturbing. It was something to do with this man and how he made her feel, how he'd always made her feel.

Not understanding this visceral feeling he effortlessly evoked within her and hating him for it, Valentina suddenly flew at him with her hands balled to fists. She took him by surprise and he fell back against the door with a thump. His arms came around her to protect them both just as she registered that his chest was like steel under her hands. And, in the same instance, that she wanted to unfurl her hands and run them up over his muscles and not beat him.

Valentina sprang back, breaking his hold, aghast at her bubbling emotions. She was breathing hard and she looked up at Gio, who straightened up carefully from the door, hands behind him. His polo shirt strained over his hard chest. He was breathing hard too, his chest rising and falling. Tension was even thicker now between them along that ever-present crackle of electricity.

She was suddenly desperate to cling on to something, *anything* that could keep a distance between them, because for a moment it had fallen away. Dissolved in a rush of heat. Dissolved by the shocking extent of her awareness of him.

Valentina turned away for a moment to try and collect herself when she felt as if she was coming apart and then turned back, her control flimsy. 'You might not have killed him but you're responsible.'

A stillness seemed to surround Gio now, making Valentina even more nervous. When he spoke he sounded weary. 'And how long are you going to keep punishing me for that? Don't you think I've been punishing myself for it?'

Valentina tried to ignore the way something in his voice caused an ache inside her. She emitted a hoarse laugh and put out a hand to encompass their general surroundings. 'You call this punishment? Living in luxury? Making millions? Cavorting on yachts with celebrities?'

Gio's face got even starker and inwardly Valentina quivered. She had to concede uncomfortably that it had been some time since he'd been pictured on the hedonistic social scene. It had all ended abruptly after those couple of years, when he'd returned to Sicily and immersed himself in his racetrack. He hadn't even been pictured with a woman since then.

He came closer to her and she fought not to move back, every muscle screaming with tension. She felt as if she'd woken a slumbering lion.

'For two years I lived like that and it was no fun.'

'That's not the impression you gave to the world.' Valentina ignored the little voice of conscience that reminded her that Gio hadn't looked *happy* in any of the photos she'd seen of him in the press. He'd looked intense, as if driven by something.

Now Gio emitted a curt laugh that made Valentina flinch. He put a hand through his hair and stalked away from her to stand looking out the window with his back to her. Finally Valentina could breathe again. Every line of his body was taut. Shoulders broad, leading down to slim hips in low-riding worn jeans. Even now, in the midst of this high emotion, her attention was wandering, gaze captivated by his perfect backside, those powerful thighs and long legs.

Disgusted with herself, she swallowed back a curse and crossed her arms and lifted her gaze to the back of that dark head. And something inexplicably tender lanced her. She didn't have time to question it before Gio started talking in a cool voice.

'I ran away from here, something I'm not proud of.'

He turned around then and Valentina sucked in a breath at the bleakness on his face, in his eyes. 'If I could have been the one to die, do you not think I wished it a million times? Every time I woke up in the morning? I knew what I had done…I *know*. If we hadn't been friends, if I hadn't badgered him into coming out that night, if I hadn't had that damaged horse at my stables…' He broke off and then continued huskily. 'Do you not think I know that Mario's death was my fault? If I hadn't been arrogant enough to assume I could tame the most untameable of horses…Mario wouldn't have wanted to try himself, to prove me wrong.'

Bitterness laced Gio's voice now. 'I came from a life of excess I hadn't even earned, from a family connected only by their disconnectedness. Mario came from everything that was good and real.'

His eyes seemed to be skewering Valentina to the spot. She couldn't move. His voice roughened. 'The night Mario died…I went back to the palazzo and put Black Star down, even though he was physically uninjured. He *was* untameable, there *was* something wrong in his head, or genes, but I'd let him live. *Me.* He should have been put down months before, when that jockey had died.'

Gio's mouth was impossibly flat. 'It took another death before I saw through my sheer arrogance. When I left here I wanted to die too. I wanted to kill myself but that would have been too easy, too self-serving. So I did everything imaginable to court death, without it actually being by my hand.

'I jumped out of planes, I climbed impossible mountains, I went to war-torn regions in Africa—ostensibly for charity purposes but secretly hoping I'd find myself a target of some drug-crazed faction.'

Something cold went down Valentina's spine when she thought of the cavalier way in which Gio had played with his life.

But he wasn't finished. His mouth twisted in evident self-disgust. 'Instead I found myself being lauded as a champion of philanthropists, and became a pin-up for extreme-sport enthusiasts. So then I immersed myself in the debauched and shallow world of the truly idle and rich. Because that's what I deserved.'

He laughed curtly. 'After all, isn't that what I was? I'd never done a decent day's work in school and yet Mario, with infinitely less resources, had succeeded against all the odds. Do you not think that I *know* how much Mario's life was worth over mine?'

Valentina felt as if she'd just been punched in the gut with his words. She even put a hand there as if she could stop pain from blooming outwards. She couldn't say anything though, too stunned, too shocked....

Gio continued in a flat voice. 'The days were meaningless and morphed into one another, interspersed with whatever my next desperate flirtation with death would be. I lost and won back my entire fortune in the space of twenty-four hours many times over. One night in a casino I was so drunk I could barely see straight, but I was about to use Misfit as collateral in a bet with a renowned and very ruthless gambler. He'd been waiting for his moment to get my horse.

'And right then, I truly didn't care about Misfit, I didn't care about anything. I'd slept with a woman the night before and couldn't have even told you her name. She was just one of many.'

Valentina was silent. In shock. Not disgusted. Everything about him spoke of his own self-recrimination. She found herself inexplicably understanding his need to lose himself in something, anything.

Gio's mouth tightened, even as one corner turned up imperceptibly. 'It was in that moment, as I was about to let everything I'd ever cared about go, that I heard Mario's voice as clearly as if he were standing here now, in this room. He just said, *Enough*. And somehow...I got up and walked away.'

He looked directly at her. 'So no, those two years were not fun. I was living the empty life of an even emptier hedonist. I was half alive but not as dead as I wanted to be.'

Gio's words sank in and choked Valentina's vocal

chords. She believed his wish to die; she'd seen it on his face that day at the graveside and she'd welcomed it at the time because she had wanted to hurt him as she hurt. Yet only now she was realising how etched into her memory it had always been.

Helpless tears pricked her eyes at the thought of Mario's presence coming to Gio like that. She believed that too, because she'd felt him around her at certain times. It's exactly what he would have said to Gio.

Overcome and floundering badly at Gio's emotionally stark confession that gave her no room to attack him, Valentina put her hands to her face to hide her blurring vision as if that could hide the emotion that was rising like a dam breaking deep inside her. She faintly heard a sound and felt Gio's presence come closer and suddenly Valentina could do nothing but obey a deep need and instinctively she reached for Gio, wrapping her arms blindly around his waist. Within seconds she was sobbing into his chest.

For a long moment he did nothing and Valentina knew she was clinging to him like a limpet but she couldn't stop it. And then slowly, his arms came around her and he was holding her so tight she thought her bones might crush. She cried for a long time, until little hiccups were coming out of her mouth. She'd cried for Mario so many times she'd lost count, but this was infinitely different. There was something cathartic about this.

When the hiccups had stopped and Valentina's breaths evened out again, she felt wrung out but also very aware of being held so tightly in Gio's arms. Her breasts were crushed to his belly and her nipples were tight and hard against the lace of her bra. Sensitised and tingling.

The material of Gio's shirt was damp under her wet cheek and she could feel the delineation of hard muscle, the rise and fall of his chest. His heartbeat was slightly fast under her cheek, his scent musky and earthy. And down lower, where her hips were all but welded to his hard thighs, Valentina could feel his arousal pressing into her soft belly.

This realisation didn't shame her or disgust her. It excited her, and thrilled her. She didn't want to move, or breathe. Didn't want to break the spell that seemed to hover over them. It was as if the intense flood of emotion had washed something acrid away.

Finally, reluctantly, Valentina pulled back within Gio's arms. She couldn't stay welded to him forever.

His hold slackened fractionally and she looked up. His face was stark, intent. She could still feel him, rigid against her, and she wanted to move her hips. Her sex tingled in response and her heart thumped because she knew she wanted this man. No other man had ever managed to touch or arouse this very secret part of her.

Gio lifted his arms and brought his hands to Valentina's face, cupping her jaw, his thumbs wiping away the moisture from her cheeks. She knew she must look a sight, and Gio's shirt had to be sodden from her tears and runny nose. But she didn't care. A fierce burgeoning desire was rising within her, something which had been there before but had been put on ice for seven years.

For a long time it had been illicit and forbidden, *guilty*. But from the moment she'd seen him again it had flamed to life. Yet the contradiction had duelled within her: how could she hate him and want him at the same time? But now those questions faded in her head. *Hate* felt like a much more indefinable thing and the desire was there, stronger than hate, rushing through her blood and making her feel alive.

She lifted a hand and touched Gio's hard jaw. He clenched it against her hand. Desire thickened the air around them, unmistakable. As if questioning it, Gio looked down at her, a small frown between his eyes. 'Valentina?'

It was the same look he'd given her the other night when she'd exposed herself and she understood it now. He'd been asking the question then, unsure of what she'd been telling him with her body language. The knowledge was heady. He *wanted* her.

One of Valentina's fingers touched Gio's bottom lip, tracing its full sensuous outline. Words were rising up within her, she couldn't keep them back. 'Gio…kiss me.' She'd wanted this, *ached* for this, for so long.

It was only after an interminable moment of nothing happening that she looked up into Gio's eyes and saw something like torture in their dark green depths. He shook his head. 'This is not a good idea. You don't want this, not really.'

Gio heard himself say the words and felt his erection straining against his jeans, against her soft curves. He'd never felt harder in his life and it had nothing to do with being celibate for five years. He wanted to kiss and plunder this woman before she changed her mind but he knew he couldn't. She hated him already; she would despise him for ever for this.

Valentina's gaze narrowed on his. A light was dawning in her eyes. He braced himself for the moment when she would pull herself free and demand to know what the hell he was doing.

And then she said, 'Damn you, Gio Corretti, *kiss me.*'

Had she really said those words? Valentina looked up at Gio, the question screaming in her head, *Why won't he just kiss me?* She could feel his erection, even harder now, and imagined it straining against his jeans, against her.

She felt damp heat moisten between her legs. Desperation wasn't far away and suddenly it hit her: she was a warm female body who had all but thrown herself at him. Few men *wouldn't* respond to that.

Horrified to think that she'd so badly misread the situation, very belatedly she tried to move, to get free of Gio's embrace, but suddenly his hands tightened on her jaw, fingers reaching around to her neck.

Gio had had a moment of doubt when she'd uttered those words. *Damn you, Gio Corretti, kiss me.* He thought he'd been hallucinating. But then she hadn't moved away; she'd looked up at him with a distinctive light of determination in her eyes. And more than that, he'd seen the stark need in those amber depths. Unmistakable. The same need he felt right now.

But then he'd seen the flicker of doubt and uncertainty cross her face. Clearly she thought he didn't want her when such a thought was laughable. Couldn't she *feel* his need straining against her? Gio knew a stronger man would take the opportunity to push her back. A more moral man would tell her to go and not take advantage of this heightened moment. But he was not that man. He'd been damned a long time ago and he wanted Valentina.

All he could think of now was of the lovers she must have already had and jealousy burnt up his spine. A woman as beautiful as her, the kind of woman who had just demanded he kiss her—she wasn't innocent. And he couldn't bear to think of her with anyone else. He wanted her to want only him. Think of only him.

And she did want him. A fierce exultant force rushed through him and it was so strong that Gio had to control it with effort. She was moving in earnest now, trying to get away and a fierce primitive force surged through him, making his hands tighten. He growled softly, 'Where do you think you're going?'

Valentina's breath hitched and she looked into his eyes. Gio was responding now; his eyes were slumberous and blazing. His need was laid bare for her to see, as if she hadn't already felt it in his body, and while one part of her exulted, another part contracted. Suddenly she felt out of her depth.

'I...I changed my mind,' she said almost hopefully, even as her treacherous body was responding to the heat in Gio's eyes, the way his body felt next to hers.

He shook his head slowly and Valentina felt herself being mesmerised. 'It's too late for that. You asked to be kissed and so I'm going to kiss you.'

His hands were tight around her jaw, fingers caressing the back of her head. Valentina felt completely exposed and vulnerable as Gio's head started to descend. Intense flutters of excitement and anticipation shot through her abdomen and she had the stark realisation of how much she'd always longed for this moment. She wasn't strong enough to pull away and she wasn't sure Gio would even let her go.

There was a feral intensity in his eyes as his head dipped closer and closer and, like a coward, Valentina let her eyes drift shut. When his mouth finally touched hers, the sensation of those hard sensual contours was so exquisite against her sensitive lips that she had to grab on to his T-shirt to hold on.

His touch was hard, but gentle. Exploratory. Valentina was aware of his hands moving, thumbs trailing across her jaw as his hands went to the back of her head, where he found and pulled out her hairband. She could feel her hair falling around her shoulders, and one of Gio's big hands cradled the back of her head, angling her so that he could move his mouth on hers with lazy expert sensuality.

Valentina only realised she wasn't breathing when Gio coaxed her mouth to open to his, his tongue touching the seam of her lips. When she drew in a breath the full reality of kissing Gio Corretti hit her like a steam train. His scent hit her nostrils, even muskier now, laden with the promise of something so carnal that her toes curled.

His hand tightened on her head, and his other hand found its way to her back, pulling her into him, arching her spine. And it wasn't enough. As their tongues touched, Valentina pressed even closer.

The sensation of tongues touching and tasting, exploring, was so exquisite that Valentina never wanted it to stop. Everything was heightened. Valentina was aware of how hard his arousal felt, pressing into her. Restlessly, her hips moved, and as if in answer Gio's hand went to her hip, where he flattened it across the small of her back, pressing her in even tighter.

When she felt the faintly calloused skin of the palm of his hand against the bare skin just above the waist of her jeans she only knew that she wanted *more*.

His hand drifted up to her bra strap and Valentina's breasts seemed to swell and tighten in response, she broke away from the kiss. She opened her eyes to look up into those dark green depths. Her mouth felt swollen, bruised. Her heart was thundering and she felt dizzy. She realised that she was on her tippy-toes; her arms were tight around Gio's neck and she was so close to his mouth that their breaths intermingled. If she could have climbed into his skin right then she would have done it without hesitation.

Gio's hand was spread flat across Valentina's smooth back; her skin was like silk. Her bra strap was a provocative inducement to just flip it open, slide his hands around and cup those firm swells. His whole body *ached* with want.

Somehow he managed to get out, 'Do you want this?'

Valentina was aware of what Gio was asking. This wouldn't end with just this kiss. If she said yes, it would be everything. All of her. There were voices in her head urging her to stop, think. But they were dim. Stronger was the urgent primal desire she felt. This man and this moment was all she could focus on. She wanted him with a hunger that was completely alien and new to her, and she couldn't walk away from it. Right then she seriously doubted the ability of her legs to hold her up anyway. Gio was all but holding her up.

Slowly Valentina nodded her head. 'Yes, I want this.'

Looking slightly tortured Gio just asked, 'Are you sure?'

He was giving her a chance to go, to think about this. Her heart lurched. She nodded again and said firmly, 'Yes.'

Valentina was lifted into Gio's arms against his chest so fast that her head swam. He shouldered his way into the bedroom off the main living area and Valentina could see a huge bed dressed in dark grey linen. The sun was setting outside, bathing the room in a dusky glow.

'What is this place?' she asked far too belatedly, a little stunned at how fast everything was moving.

'It's mine, sometimes I stay overnight.'

Gio carefully lowered her to stand by the bed. For the first time in what felt like aeons there was space between them and already Valentina felt bereft. It scared her. But not enough to put more space between them.

Gio's face was flushed and the first indication of stubble darkened his jaw. He opened his mouth and Valentina quickly put her hand up to cover it, afraid he was going to ask her again if she knew what she was doing. She didn't want to think or rationalise what was happening. She just wanted to feel.

Gio took her hand down and a small smile touched his

mouth as if he understood. He held her hand against his chest where she could feel his heartbeat fast but strong, and with his other hand he wrapped it around her neck and pulled her towards him.

This time the kiss was hungry and devouring. It became heated in seconds, and Valentina curled her hand into his shirt, bunching it up. Her other hand went to his hip and found the hot skin underneath his shirt. Emboldened, she slid it around to his back and explored under his jeans, feeling the cleft of his smooth buttocks. Gio broke the kiss and said thickly, 'I need to see you.'

His hands were on her shirt, undoing her buttons. Valentina shivered with anticipation and looked down. Gio's hands looked huge and very dark, long fingers grappling with tiny buttons. She heard him curse softly when the buttons eluded his grasp and brought her own hands up to do the job. To be standing here, undressing in front of Gio…it was too huge to think about.

When her shirt fell open to reveal her lacy bra, Valentina blushed hotly. Gio pushed her hands aside and pulled open the shirt even more, until it came off her shoulders and down her arms and fell to the floor.

She couldn't look up at him. A hand snaked around to her back and undid her bra. He pulled the two straps down her arms and her bra joined her shirt on the floor. Instinctively Valentina went to cover her breasts but Gio stopped her arms. 'Don't…'

He tipped up her chin so that she had to look at him and his eyes were molten with heat and need, dissolving Valentina's inhibitions. 'You're beautiful.'

She saw his eyes drop to take in the swells of her breasts and their tips tingled painfully. With two hands he cupped them, and moved his thumbs across the sensitised peaks.

Valentina moaned softly, closing her eyes. It was too much to see his hands on her flesh like that.

Somehow Gio manoeuvred them so that he was sitting on the bed and he brought Valentina between his hard thighs, trapping her between them. With one hand on her waist holding her steady, he cupped a breast with his other and brought his mouth forward, and fed that hungry aching tip into the hot cavern of his mouth. Valentina sucked in a tortured breath and her hands went to his shoulders, holding on for dear life as shards of intense pleasure went from her nipple to between her legs.

Gio was remorseless, sucking and teasing the peak into throbbing stiffness. Flicking it with this tongue before sucking fiercely again. Valentina wasn't even aware of her hand going to the back of his head to hold him there. She cried out when he moved to the other breast and administered the same exquisite torture. Valentina had never known a pleasure like it. It was awakening an even more intense need in her body, down low, where her legs were pressed together by Gio's thighs.

Suddenly Valentina pulled back from his wicked mouth and looked down. Her eyelids felt heavy. Thickly she muttered, 'I want to see you too.' And she bent down to pull Gio's polo shirt up and over his head. When his magnificent torso was revealed she could only look at it as reverently as he'd looked at her.

He was beautifully muscled, not an ounce of fat. Dark olive skin and a very masculine dusting of hair. Gio's eyes glittered fiercely and he said, 'Come here.'

Valentina obeyed without question but this time she straddled Gio's thighs so that she was sitting on his lap. He brought both arms around her and the sensation of her bare breasts and wet nipples against his chest made her gasp. He pulled her head down to his and covered her mouth, swallowing her gasp. Her arousal levels rose to fever pitch. She'd never known there could be so many kinds of kisses. This was dark and wicked and she could feel the bulge of his erection underneath the apex of her legs. She wriggled, heightening the sensation. Gio's hand went to the front of her jeans and Valentina broke off the kiss with a gasp when she felt his fingers come between her jeans and skin.

Her hair was falling down her back, making every nerve end stand on edge. Gio's fingers were hot against her lower belly and as she looked into his eyes he flicked his thumb and opened the top button. With the top button gaping open and the zip pulled down, Gio spread his hand around the back of her waist and delved underneath, cupping one firm buttock.

Valentina arched upwards against him, and Gio took advantage, his mouth and tongue unerringly finding a turgid nipple and sucking fiercely as his hand went deeper and his fingers found the damp cleft of her body.

Valentina cried out, her legs pressing tight against his thighs as if that might assuage the delicious torture, but then suddenly the earth was moving and she was on her back on the bed with Gio looming over her, his shoulders impossibly broad, a lock of dark hair falling messily onto his forehead.

Valentina wanted to reach up to touch that lock, invaded by a dangerous tenderness, and had to clench her hand to a fist to stop it. Thankfully Gio was far too busy distracting her to see anything of this turmoil within her.

With a fast economy of movement he had opened her jeans fully and was pulling them down and off so now she was in nothing but her knickers. This was more naked than she'd ever been in front of anyone apart from her mother and Valentina bit her lip when trepidation and insecurity lanced her.

Something pierced through the heat haze in Gio's brain when he saw the flicker of trepidation on Valentina's face, and the full plumpness of her bottom lip caught between small white teeth. Like a cold bucket of water being thrown in his face, something occurred to him. His hands stilled on the button of his jeans and he frowned. 'Valentina... are you a virgin?'

CHAPTER SIX

GIO SAW VALENTINA'S face flush and a heavy weight settled in his gut. She brought up an arm to cover her breasts and just like that the temperature in the room zoomed down from about a million degrees to minus forty.

Stifling an almost overwhelming urge to smash his fist into the nearest solid object, Gio stepped back from the sinful provocation of Valentina's practically naked supine body. A body he would have been sinking into right now and discovering for himself just how innocent she was, with scant thought of being gentle.

On stiff legs he went straight to the bathroom and lifted the robe from the back of the door and came back, holding it out to Valentina, who he avoided looking at on the bed. Discovering she was innocent was not something he'd expected in a million years and this changed everything. She could not really want him to be the one to take her innocence, and when the heat of passion died away, she'd realise that and hate him even more.

'What are you doing?' Her voice, soft and husky, grated over his exposed and sensitive nerves. The muscles in his arm bunched and he said more curtly than he intended, 'Take the robe, Valentina, I don't sleep with virgins.'

Valentina was sitting up on the bed holding the robe to her naked chest, in shock, for a long minute afterwards. Gio had left the room, pulling on his shirt as he did with just a curt, 'I'll wait outside.'

She felt cold all over and yet still hot and tingly inside. The sense of something momentous being ripped out of her grasp was huge. There was an awful sting to his rejection of her because she was a virgin, a sting that cut much deeper than she liked to acknowledge. To avoid looking at that far too controversial subject, Valentina allowed anger to rise into her overheated brain. How dared Gio react like that?

The anger gave her the impetus to move and with stiff arms she pulled on the robe and belted it tightly around her and stalked out to the living area. When she emerged it was to see the rigid lines of Gio's body as he looked out the window with his back to her. He clearly knew she was there as she saw him tense even more.

Valentina resisted the urge to pick something up and fling it at his head. Instead she said with saccharine sweetness, 'I'll just go and divest myself of my virginity and be back so we can continue where we left off, shall I?'

Gio whirled around, arms crossed and muscles bunched. Tension stamped all over his features. He looked wild and uncivilised and it made Valentina feel even hotter.

'You should have been honest with me.'

Valentina crossed her arms and laughed out loud. 'You are such a hypocrite! You just told me that you've slept with women and not even remembered their names—how do you know that they weren't virgins?'

Gio winced. Why on earth had he spilled his guts like that? He'd never articulated to anyone how empty and meaningless those two years were. How low he'd sunk.

He tried to ignore how achingly sexy Valentina looked in nothing but the robe with her dark hair spread out across her shoulders. Frustration coursed through his veins, making his body hurt. He bit out, 'They weren't. Believe me.'

Valentina taunted, 'So I should preface every kiss I have with a man with "By the way I'm a virgin"?'

Something dark went into Gio's gut at the thought of her kissing any other man. 'Yes, especially if every kiss ends up with you lying half naked on a bed.'

Valentina sucked in a gasp at the injustice of that comment and felt the prickle of humiliating tears. All she could think of right then was how ardently she'd thrown herself at Gio, how she'd begged him to kiss her. Make love to her. She'd been gyrating on his lap like some kind of an exotic dancer. He'd tried to stop her, had asked her twice if she wanted this, and each time she'd said a resounding *yes*.

As if sensing her turmoil Gio uncrossed his arms and put out a hand. Valentina backed away and fire raced up her spine, obliterating any lingering desire. 'I hate you, Giacomo Corretti. And I wouldn't sleep with you now if you were the last man on this earth.'

Valentina whirled around and hated that tears were blurring her vision. She dashed them away and went back into the bedroom where she ripped off the robe and dragged on her clothes, every move she'd made and kiss she'd just given this man running through her head like a bad B-movie.

When she re-emerged she stalked straight to the main door, turned the key and had her hand on the handle before she felt a hand on her other arm. Instantly sensations ran all the way down to her groin and her still-sensitive breasts peaked.

'Look, Valentina, wait—'

She ripped her arm free and looked up into Gio's face. The contrition she saw there sent her over the edge. She could handle anything but not this…*pity*. She lifted a hand and before she was even aware of the impulse, it had connected so hard with his face that his head snapped around. Trembling all over from an overdose of adrenalin and emotion she said, 'Don't touch me again. *Ever.*'

The first day of the Corretti Cup race meeting was dawning and Gio stood in his study office looking out the window at the hive of activity in every corner of the racetrack. It was usually his favourite time of the year but this year he was impossibly distracted. Distracted by a five-foot-seven chestnut-haired, amber-eyed temptress and a level of sexual frustration he'd never known could exist. Not to mention the ever-simmering cauldron of emotions in his gut—ever since he'd seen her again. Gone was the numb shell that had been encasing him since he'd returned to Sicily.

Valentina.

Her name was on his mind, his lips, every waking moment. He could still feel the sting of her hand across his face. It had been no less than he'd deserved.

When he'd realised she was a virgin he'd reacted viscerally. He could never be the one to take that prize from her. It would be a travesty. Yet she had been ready to give it—in the heat of the moment. Gio knew damn well that in the aftermath Valentina would have realised the magnitude of what she'd just done and with *who*, and she would have felt nothing but disgust for giving in to such base desires.

Grief for Mario—talking about him had defused something between them, but no way was it strong enough to withstand the bitter and deep anger she undoubtedly still felt towards Gio. The chemistry that sizzled between them had obscured that momentarily.

She might hate him for rejecting her now, but he'd saved him and her from that simmering enmity deepening even more.

Gio knew all this and repeated it over and over again

to himself but the truth was that he was lying to himself.
Because for all of his lofty assertions to Valentina that he
didn't sleep with virgins, all he wanted to do was close
the gates to his racetrack, turn everyone away, find her
and put her over his shoulder like a caveman. And then he
wanted to take her to a quiet place and make love to her
until they were both weak and sated.

Until she was no longer a virgin. Until she was *his* and
no one else's.

Valentina should have been focusing on the task at hand—
the first day of the Corretti Cup—but her mind kept veer-
ing off track back to the other evening and the excruciating
humiliation of having Gio reject her because she was a
virgin.

Even now, hot tears pricked her eyes and to counteract
the weak emotion she stabbed a fork with unnecessary
zeal into a piece of pork. She felt so conflicted…the hate
she'd always felt for Gio was disturbingly elusive now. She
wanted to think of his rejection, hold that to her like a cold
justification, but she kept thinking about what he'd told her.

He'd ripped apart a huge part of her defence around him
by revealing what he'd gone through after Mario's death.

And then he'd taken her in his arms…and Valentina had
turned into a complete stranger. She'd *begged* him to kiss
her, to make love to her. Self-disgust filled her now. Few
men would turn that down…and Gio had merely proved
himself as susceptible to a warm willing body as the next
man. What he hadn't counted on was her unwelcome innocence.

The hurt that seized her in the pit of her belly reminded
Valentina that his rejection had cut far deeper than she
wanted to acknowledge.

Stabbing the pork viciously again, Valentina told herself

that he'd done her a favour by not sleeping with her. Her conscience pricked her to think of the emotional fall-out if she *had* slept with him and for the first time she considered the rogue idea that perhaps he'd done it out of some moral sense of integrity.

One thing was certain: there was no way that Valentina was ever going to allow him to make her feel so vulnerable or exposed again.

'Val?'

Valentina looked up feeling a little dazed to see her assistant Sara, who was eyeing the very overpierced piece of pork warily.

'Yes?'

Sara looked up. 'I, ah, just checked the main buffet tent and it's all moving like clockwork. No one is waiting for their food.'

Valentina forced a smile and her mind back to the task at hand with effort. 'Thanks, Sara, I'll go and check the VIP tent. You can start to organise the canapés for the drinks reception later.'

As Valentina hurried off she forced all thoughts of Gio out of her head but then she suddenly caught a glimpse of him in the distance and instantly all efforts to put him out of her head were reduced to naught. She cursed loudly.

'You look stunning tonight.'

The tiny hairs rose all over Valentina's body and her breath automatically quickened and her heart missed a beat. She looked up from where she was running a pen down the list of VIP names to see Gio standing in front of her, ludicrously handsome in his black tuxedo. He'd changed since she'd caught that sighting of him earlier. His normally unruly hair was tamed into some kind of order, making him look even more debonair.

She'd been burningly aware of him since he'd walked into the huge and lavishly decorated marquee about an hour before but to her relief he'd been on the other side of the room, talking to people. Mainly a steady stream of women which had aroused very dark and disturbing feelings inside her. But now he was here. And she couldn't breathe.

Somehow she found the wherewithal to breathe in and said coolly, 'It's the only formal dress I have—I didn't have time to go shopping.'

Gio's dark eyes ran over her from where she'd put her hair up in a simple high knot, down over the black structured dress with its flared skirt and a pair of peep-toe black shoes. She was markedly dressed down compared to all the other women in the room who were dripping in jewels and dressed in the latest slinky silky fashions. Which was only appropriate, she'd told herself, hating that she felt somehow *less*.

Despite the vivid recall of the other night and her lingering sense of humiliation and anger, Valentina felt hot colour seeping up her chest when face to face with Gio again and the memory of how she'd slapped him. She'd never hit another human being in her life. The compulsion to apologise was suddenly acute. Her emotions had betrayed her and she didn't want him to think she still felt so volatile. Avoiding his eyes, she said stiffly, 'I'm sorry… about hitting you.'

'I deserved it.'

Gio's quick answer had her looking up to see him put a hand to his jaw as if to test it. Her belly clenched when she noticed a tiny scar high on his cheekbone. Had she done that? Treacherously her intent to be cool dissolved. 'Did I really hurt you?'

Gio's mouth curled up on one side, making Valentina's insides feel curiously liquid.

'Let's just say I wouldn't want to be on the other end of your right hook.'

'I'm sorry,' she said again, her voice sounding frigid as she tried to disguise her emotions.

Just then a petite and very groomed dark-haired woman came up to Gio's side and he dipped his head to listen to what she had to say. The woman blushed prettily and something dark pierced Valentina's composure to see this evidence of another woman finding him attractive. *Attractive?* a snide voice in her head mocked—he stood head and shoulders above every other man in the room and she knew it.

The woman had moved away and Gio was looking at her. Valentina realised her hands were curled to fists and she consciously relaxed them.

Gio was saying smoothly, 'If you'll excuse me—my mother's father is looking for a recommendation for tomorrow's race.'

Valentina nodded her head vigorously, and Gio mocked softly but with an undefinable light in his eyes, 'You don't have to look so pleased to see me go.'

He walked away and Valentina couldn't help recalling the bleakness she'd seen the other evening, the way Gio had called himself *worthless*. He seemed to her to strike a poignantly lone figure amongst the teeming crowd.

To Valentina's relief she was kept too busy after that to think about Gio or where he was. And much later when she came up for air, he seemed to be firmly ensconced on the other side of the tent with the last of the guests. She was supervising the start of the clear-up. The jazz band that had been playing were putting their instruments away. Franco, her other assistant, came up to her and said, 'Why don't you take off? I'll make sure this is all done. You've got an early start tomorrow.'

Valentina smiled at her assistant ruefully and pointed out, 'So do you.'

But just then she saw Gio look over to where she was, and he stood up, before threading his way through the small tables with his easy leonine grace. Flutters of sensation erupted in her belly and she felt very vulnerable when she remembered the volatile mix of emotions this man had aroused earlier. He was getting closer. Her smile faded and she blurted out to Franco, 'Actually, I'd really appreciate that if you don't mind.'

Franco was assuring her it was fine but Valentina was already halfway out of the marquee and didn't look back to see how Gio's expression darkened to one of thunder as he took in her escape.

Gio stopped dead in the middle of the tent and watched as Valentina's slim back disappeared through the doorway. He cursed softly at his impulse to snatch her back. What was he going to do? Demand she wait until every last person had left? She'd been working more tirelessly than almost anyone else involved in the Cup and had made the first day a resounding success. More than one person had come to him to ask him who was doing the catering. The champagne reception had gone without a hitch. Her staff were more than capable of dealing with the clean-up.

He ran a hand through his hair and cursed again. The truth was, he had no interest in talking to her about the day, or business. He only wanted *her*. He'd thought earlier that something had softened between them when she'd apologised for hitting him. She'd looked genuinely contrite. But her words from that night came back to him now, ringing in his ears: *Don't touch me again. Ever.*

She'd just been polite and professional. That was all.

It didn't help that all evening he'd been acutely aware of her as she'd greeted guests at the door, a wide smile on her face. She'd stood out from the other women who looked like ridiculous birds of paradise—overdone and over-made-up—with the simplest of black dresses which had highlighted her slender figure. The V-neck design had allowed tantalising glimpses of her smooth pale cleavage and Gio had had to battle against the images of her bared breasts, nipples wet from his tongue, racing through his head at the least opportune moments.

An acquaintance, a renowned French playboy, had asked him earlier, 'Who is the stunning woman greeting us this evening?'

Gio had all but snarled at him, 'She's not available.' The intensity of emotion he'd felt as it had coursed through his blood had blindsided him. He'd wanted to grab the man by the neck and throw him out. As it was he'd watched him with an eagle eye all night.

His mouth tightened. Valentina might desire him but she would never allow him close again. And if he had a shred of conscience, he wouldn't touch her again. The problem was, Gio didn't think his conscience was strong enough to overcome the physical craving racing through his blood, or the possessiveness he felt.

The following afternoon Valentina went back to her rooms to change for the second evening's champagne reception. The second day had passed off as successfully as the first, so far, and she was finally allowing herself to relax a little. She'd even managed to stop for a moment earlier, while checking one of the corporate boxes, and had got swept up in the spine-tingling finish of the main race of the day.

The sheer scale of the event and amounts of money being bet and won made her eyes boggle. She'd never seen such luxe wealth in her life. And amongst all the excess had been Gio—surveying everything and everyone around him. More than once she'd seen him dip his head discreetly to one of his staff who would rush off and avert a potential crisis or situation. But what had struck her again more than anything was how *alone* he'd looked, and how that had made her feel.

One of her very first memories was of playing outside her father's workshop at the palazzo while Mario helped him inside, and watching the lone figure of a young Gio as he'd watched his father's stable hands exercise the horses on their gallops.

Just a couple of hours ago as she'd stood in the background with a tray of empty glasses, Valentina had had to suppress the almost overwhelming urge to put down her tray and go up to him and slip her hand into his. She'd found herself imagining him looking down at her and smiling back…and squeezing her hand.

The tray of glasses had been shaking in her hands before she'd come to her senses and rushed off again. And now as she let herself into her rooms she shook her head. What was wrong with her? Why was her mind taking such flights of fancy? She had to admit that her virulent anger had become something else, but it was not tender. No matter how many times that soft emotion seemed to be taking her unawares.

When Valentina had put down her bag and was in the centre of her room she noticed the clothes through the open bedroom door. She went in to see that there were two floor-length evening dresses and one shorter cocktail-length dress in clear protective covers hanging off the doors of her wardrobe. Lined up below were three pairs of shoes all colour coded to go with the dresses. Laid out on her bed she could see more bags and on her dresser she could see jewellery boxes.

Stunned, she walked closer. The dresses were gorgeous, the stuff of fantasy. One was dark red, another royal blue and the cocktail dress was strapless and black with a beaded lace overlay that made it sparkle.

She backed away and saw the boxes on the bed. Feeling a sense of dread she opened one and lifted back gold tissue paper to see the wispiest, most delicate underwear she'd ever seen in her life. Hurriedly she closed it back up again.

It was only then that she noticed the white square of paper with a typewritten message near the biggest box..

Valentina, I hope you don't mind that I took the liberty of ordering you some dresses. You'd mentioned that you hadn't had time to shop....

At the bottom of the note there was just a simple *G*.

First of all Valentina felt the predictable rise of hot rage—how dared Gio presume to buy her clothes? But then the note was so impersonal—he hadn't even written it by hand. He must have got his secretary to type it out.

Then her cheeks got hot with embarrassment. Had he thought she looked completely out of place last night in her chain-store dress? He'd told her she looked stunning but the truth was that he'd probably offered up that platitude to every woman there. She'd never catered for such a prestigious event before; she'd never had to dress up.

She saw her dress now, hanging where she'd left it last night on the back of the bedroom door, and it looked unbearably shabby and worn next to these designer concoctions of perfection. Her embarrassment levels went up a notch. Gio evidently didn't want her showing him up with his important guests and friends.

For a second intense vulnerability hit Valentina when she entertained the notion of putting one of these dresses on, and seeing Gio's reaction to her. Would he want her then? In spite of her unwelcome virginity? Did she want to seduce him?

Humiliation, never far, made hot colour seep up into her face and rebellion fired her blood as she ignored the beautiful creations and resolutely pulled on her own dress and shoes. Valentina pushed down the voice telling her she was being ridiculously childish and when she was ready she left her room to go back to work.

It was some hours later before Valentina felt the familiar tingle of awareness. Much to her chagrin, she'd just dropped a pen from nerveless fingers for about the tenth time that evening and was bending down to pick it up.

His impeccably polished shoes came into her line of vision and she sucked in a deep fortifying breath before straightening up.

Her mouth dried. Tonight Gio was wearing a white shirt and that white bow tie. It was slightly askew as if he'd been pulling at it impatiently, giving him a rakish air. Faint stubble lined his jaw. Valentina struggled to find her equilibrium, hating that he'd caught her before she had a chance to compose herself. And then she thought of the typed note and the dresses, and forced ice into her veins.

She hitched up her chin and said in her coolest voice, 'You didn't have to go to the trouble of sending someone out to buy me dresses. If you'd told me what was required I could have taken an hour to go out and buy something myself.'

Gio's eyes flashed with displeasure. 'The idea was that you choose one to wear tonight.'

Valentina welcomed the surge of anger and glanced

around to make sure no one was near before hissing at him, 'I'm not one of your mistresses, Gio.'

Gio opened his mouth to respond but suddenly they were interrupted by one of his aides, who Valentina dimly recognised as working on the equestrian side of things.

He was saying sotto voce, 'Excuse me Signor Corretti, but Sheikh Nadim of Merkazad has just arrived with his wife. I thought you'd want to know. We've settled his horses into the stables already.'

Valentina knew that Sheikh Nadim was one of the most important guests Gio had been expecting. She saw a muscle clench in Gio's jaw and felt quivery inside. He just looked at her for an intense moment and then bit out a curt, 'We'll continue this later.' And he strode off with his PA.

Valentina had little time to think about his thinly veiled threat because she was quickly swamped by more guests and making sure that everyone was being catered to, and that the champagne was kept flowing.

Much later, Gio was ripping open his bow tie and opening the top button of his shirt as he made his way to Valentina's rooms. It was long after everyone had finished up for the night.

Sheikh Nadim of Merkazad, an old friend of Gio's, had invited him back to his hotel for a nightcap and he hadn't been able to refuse. Gio usually loved any chance he got to talk about horses and racing with Nadim, but not this time. Eventually his friend had chuckled ruefully and said, 'I'll release you from your misery. Go and find her, my friend. I know that tortured look well. I saw it in my own mirror often enough.'

Gio shook his head now—he couldn't ever imagine when Nadim and his Irish wife, Iseult, hadn't been completely and soppily in love. In truth he found it hard to be around them—to witness that level of utter devotion and absorption. It made him feel all at once claustrophobic and yet curiously restless, yearning for something he couldn't articulate.

Ruthlessly pushing aside such incendiary lines of thought, Gio took the stairs now two at a time, his blood humming at the thought of seeing Valentina.

Valentina was still pacing in her room an hour after she'd returned from the empty marquee. Gio had disappeared at some stage and she hated the way she'd felt disappointed that he hadn't returned to explain whatever he'd meant by 'We'll continue this later.'

He'd obviously gone back to the luxurious hotel in Syracuse where most of the guests were staying, and where she knew there was an exclusive nightclub. Her hands curled to fists without her even realising it as she had a vision of Gio standing at the side of the dance floor with throbbing music and lights highlighting any number of beautiful women he could have within a mere flick of his fingers. *Experienced women.*

A peremptory knock sounded on her door and Valentina stopped dead, breath caught in her throat. Superstitiously she didn't move and it came again, along with a familiar voice that sounded positively angry. 'Valentina!'

Livid with herself for the relief she was feeling but also because she'd let him get to her so much she stalked to the door and said through it, 'It's late, Gio, what do you want?'

On the other side of the door Gio bit back the succinct answer he wanted to give: *you.* Instead he said, 'I told you I'd talk to you later.'

Valentina's voice, husky enough to set his nerve endings alight and yet cool enough to try, and fail, to douse them floated through. 'I'm tired and going to bed. We can talk tomorrow.'

Valentina had a sudden morbid fear of Gio coming through the door. The sting of rejection came back vividly. She knew if she was in close proximity to him she might not be able to disguise her far too disturbing emotions. Or the fact that she wanted him with a hunger that was shameful.

Gio's voice came back hard and implacable as the wood of the door. 'Either you let me in, Valentina, or I use the master key to let myself in.'

Valentina crossed her arms and hissed out, 'That's a blatant infringement of my employee rights. If you do any such thing I'll quit right now and sue you for harassment!'

The eloquent answer to that was the unmistakable sound of a key going into her lock and turning. The door opened to reveal a dark and dishevelled-looking Gio with bow tie hanging completely askew now, his jacket hanging off one finger. And Valentina felt the inevitable surge of electricity between them like a doom-laden klaxon going off.

He was in and the door was shut firmly behind him again before she'd recovered from the shock. Gio's dark eyes were running over her and he said throatily, 'We hadn't finished our discussion about your wardrobe.'

Those words returned Valentina to reality with a bump. She moved away, tightening her arms across her chest. 'I am not discussing this with you now. So if you don't mind…?'

Gio casually threw his jacket onto a nearby chair and leant back easily against the door, and looked at her. 'I don't mind at all—you can do what you like once we've finished our conversation.'

CHAPTER SEVEN

VALENTINA LOOKED FROM the strewn jacket to him and then
turned and paced away, glad she'd at least taken off her
shoes because her legs felt wobbly enough at the moment.
She turned back, feeling seriously jittery now and threatened to have her private space invaded like this, especially
when she thought of the frothy lace excuses for underwear
in the boxes in the other room. 'I told you, Gio—I'm not
one of your mistresses so please don't feel like you have
to kit me out in a similar manner.'

Gio flushed and Valentina took a step back.

His voice rang with indignation. 'I've never had a mistress in my life—lots of one-night stands that I'm not proud
of, but no mistress. I've never wanted to spend that much
time with a woman.'

It was Valentina's turn to flush. She felt confused and
didn't like the warm glow his words left in her gut. 'So…
why did you…?' She trailed off and then tacked on, 'Look,
if you felt that I was letting you down with my own clothes
you could have just said something and I'd have gone shopping myself.'

Gio straightened up from the door and ran a hand
through his hair, messing it up. '*Dio*. I didn't feel as if you
were letting me down. Damn it, Valentina, you could have

been dressed in a sack and still outshone every woman there. You'd mentioned that you hadn't had time to shop....'

The glow of warmth in Valentina's gut spread and she panicked when she recalled her earlier vulnerability, the temptation to put on one of the dresses, wanting to look beautiful for Gio. That suddenly galvanised her into movement and Valentina stalked into the bedroom and gathered all the dresses up, along with the shoes, underwear and jewellery, in her arms.

Uncaring of the fact that she was leaving a trail behind her, she was only intent on getting rid of Gio and this reminder of how fragile she was around him. She came back and dumped it on a chair near him, the red dress slithering to a silken mound on the floor.

Valentina was breathing far more heavily than that little trip had warranted. She crossed her arms again and looked at Gio, who caught her gaze with a suspiciously impassive expression.

'Look, I appreciate it, really. But I can buy my own clothes and I'll go shopping tomorrow.'

A little scared by Gio's lack of reaction Valentina blurted out, 'It's not as if you went to the trouble of getting them yourself....' She flushed when she thought of the exquisite underwear and had a sudden fantasy that Gio *had* looked at it and imagined her in it. That spurred her back into the bedroom and she returned holding out the typewritten note. She held it up like evidence at a trial. 'Look! Your assistant wrote this—you probably weren't even aware of what you were signing.'

Gio's arms were crossed now and he growled softly, 'Yes, I was, because *I* wrote that note. No one else. Just like I had the boutique send over a selection of dresses and I chose the ones I thought would suit you best.'

Valentina's hand dropped and the note fell from numb

fingers to the floor. *Dio*. He had picked it all out. He had looked at it. Had he imagined—? Her mind seized at the thought.

Heat suffused Valentina to have it confirmed that he had chosen it. Himself. Increasingly panicked now she crossed her arms and said, 'It doesn't matter. I just want you to go.'

'But it does matter,' he insisted softly, coming closer. 'You see, I don't like you thinking that I could be insensitive enough to order you something as intimate as underwear via my secretary. After all, how would she even know your size?'

Gio continued. 'I have severe dyslexia. It's a condition I've had to learn to live with all my life and thankfully there is now a plethora of software out there to help people with my condition. That note was dictated by me, into a very handy machine which then printed it off, whereupon I signed it with my customary signature of *G* because it's simply easier. And distinctive to anyone who knows me.'

Valentina's arms were crossed so tightly across her chest now she feared she might cut off the blood supply to her brain. Gio's mention of his dyslexia was throwing up memories of Mario sitting patiently beside him, laboriously working through homework assignments from Gio's expensive prep school. She'd forgotten. And didn't like the reminder, or the tender urges that came with it.

On jelly legs Valentina went to the door and opened it wide and stood back. 'Thank you for that explanation. I appreciate it. I'll return the dresses tomorrow and buy something suitable. I'd just like it if you left now. Please.'

But Gio didn't appear to be listening. He was pacing back and forth and then he stopped suddenly and turned to face her, something so carnal and stark on his face that her whole body went slowly on fire.

'The fact is that I did buy those dresses for a reason... and it wasn't because you weren't dressed appropriately. It was because I wanted to see you in them. I bought the underwear too, and I imagined how it would fit....'

Valentina felt faint; her sweaty hand nearly slipped off the door handle. All she could feel was searing heat and all she could see was Gio.

He came towards her before she had time to react and pushed the door closed again behind her and locked it. Valentina was trapped against the door but had a curious inability or wish to move. She could only look up at him and ask redundantly, 'Why?'

Gio's arms were braced either side of her head. His whole body was caging her in. His scent, his proximity... Valentina couldn't move, couldn't think straight.

'Because of *this*.' And then Gio bent towards her and, without touching another part of her body, pressed his mouth to hers, and the world went on fire.

It felt like aeons later when Valentina surfaced from the kiss to look up into Gio's dark green-flecked eyes. Her lips felt swollen. His hand was on her waist and she was clinging to his shirt; it was bunched in her hands. She hadn't even been aware of doing that. She could see herself reflected in his pupils, a tiny figure, and suddenly she remembered the excoriating rejection of the other night, how she'd vowed to him and herself that she wouldn't let him touch her again. She'd just broken that promise with little or no persuasion.

Disgusted with herself she let go of Gio's shirt and pushed away from him, and tried to ignore the way the beat of her blood was calling her back to him like a magnet. When she felt able, she turned around and wrapped her arms around her body in an unconsciously protective gesture.

She looked at Gio with huge eyes. 'I can't do this with you. I won't do this with you. With anyone else but you.

'After all,' she reminded him bitterly, 'I'm still a virgin, Gio. I haven't managed to offload that burden yet.'

Fire and rage rushed through Gio with frightening force, at the *very thought*.… He ground out with an almost savage intensity, 'And you won't…with anyone else, except me.'

He came towards her and Valentina stepped back holding out an arm, as if that could stop him. Fires were racing all over her skin at the way he'd just sounded and the look of intent on his face. The magnitude of what could happen here if she let it. *And how much she wanted it*. Valentina had to fight it. She called up how it had felt when he'd handed her that robe and avoided her eyes. *I don't sleep with virgins*.

'Wait.' Her voice shook. 'How dare you suddenly decide that you've got any kind of right to make such a statement. You were very clear in your rejection the other evening.'

'I didn't want to reject you.' Gio's voice was rough and husky, weakening Valentina's resolve. 'Walking away was the hardest thing I've ever done but I did it because I knew if I'd taken you, you would have woken afterwards and despised me even more than you already do.'

Those words lanced her deep inside. She thought he'd rejected her because he just didn't want to sleep with her *enough*. She felt like an abject fraud because, if anything, she might have despised herself for being so weak, not him, but this was her only defence against Gio now. She tipped up her chin. 'And what makes now any different?'

'What makes it different is that I'm willing to risk your hatred because I want you too much. I'm not strong enough to stand back and watch some other man become your first lover.'

Valentina saw Gio's hands curled to fists and felt his very tangible passion. The thought of some other man touching her, kissing her, almost made bile rise from her gullet.

Without Valentina realising it, Gio had come closer. He reached out a hand now and cupped her jaw, his fingers trailing against her neck where she could feel her pulse beating almost out of control.

He just said, 'You want me…you can't deny it, not here and now.'

'I…' she croaked and stopped, feeling seriously out of her depth. She couldn't deny it. To deny it would be to utter the worst of falsehoods. Gio knew it. She knew it.

And in that moment she also knew that she was tacitly acquiescing because she had no choice. This had been building and building between them from the moment she'd seen him at the wedding just weeks before. *And a long time before that*, a small rogue voice insisted.

Gio smiled and it was unbearably bleak. 'I'm giving you full permission to despise me all you want in the aftermath, Valentina, because I know you will. At least this way there can be total honesty between us. It's physical, that's *all*.'

His acceptance of her antipathy made something ache inside Valentina, but the promise of no emotions also freed something. She knew she could never love someone and risk losing them again, the way she'd lost Mario. Something pure and innocent inside her had been lost for ever that night. The grief was too deep, too raw. Gio was too inextricably bound up with pain for her, and guilt. The guilt of the shameful secret she was still too cowardly to acknowledge.

The shadow of Mario's death was too long. But she wanted him. She'd never connected with another man on such a visceral, physical level. This would burn out, it had to. Intensity like this couldn't last.…

As if reading her thoughts, Gio said, 'This will burn out, and when it does…we'll move on.'

We'll move on. Valentina wondered if they really could move on, find some kind of closure. For a long moment nothing was said. Valentina looked into Gio's eyes until she felt as if she were drowning. And then she felt some great resistance she'd been clinging on to dissolve within her. She couldn't fight this.

She put her hand over his on her jaw and turned her face so that she could press a kiss to his palm. She closed her eyes but she could feel the tremor that went through his body, or was it hers? She couldn't tell.

Gio moved closer to her, putting a hand to the small of her back, and tugged her closer. Valentina sent up a fervent prayer that they could move on from this, because she didn't have the strength to stop now. And as his mouth met hers and she melted into him and his kiss, it felt so *right*.

Gio was trying to curb the rush of desire sending his brain into a fiery orbit. Valentina felt so unutterably good in his arms. Soft and pliant and curvy. Her breasts were pressed against his chest and he could feel the thrust of hard nipples. Letting his hand drop he found the sweet curve of her bottom and cupped it, softly at first and then harder when he felt the instinctive sway of her hips towards him.

Victory was heady and he was rapidly getting lost in the nectar of the sweetest kiss. As sweet as it was though, he wanted more; he wanted harder, darker. He wanted to be inside her, and he had to be careful. She was innocent. Exerting extreme self-control Gio managed to somehow break the connection and pull back, almost groaning when he saw how long it took for Valentina to open heavy-lidded eyes, their dark depths even darker, pupils huge. Her lips dark red and swollen.

'Let's take this slow...OK?'

Valentina sucked in a breath, trying to force oxygen to her short-circuiting brain. That had just been a kiss and a relatively chaste one and already she felt as if she were burning up from the inside out.

Before she could articulate anything that might sound vaguely coherent Gio was taking her by the hand and leading her into the bedroom. He pushed her back gently towards the bed and she collapsed onto the edge to find him at her feet, those big capable hands moving up her legs and under the dress.

He looked up at her for a second. *Lord*. Valentina could feel her lower belly muscles clench hard. She couldn't speak, could only watch as Gio's eyes went back to her legs and watch how they cupped behind her knees before inching ever higher, pushing her dress up inexorably until her legs were bared.

Gio's cheeks were flushed and Valentina felt the warmth of his calloused palms move up until they cupped her buttocks intimately. She gasped. He was right between her legs now, pushing them apart. She half collapsed back onto the bed, her elbows the only thing holding her up.

Gio looked up at her and said throatily, 'Trust me?'

Valentina bit her lip and after a heated moment nodded her head. Without taking his eyes off hers Valentina could feel him lift her gently so that he could push her dress all the way up; now her entire lower body was exposed to him. For a fleeting second she wished ardently that she *was* wearing one of the impossibly delicate lace panties and not her very plain black ones.

But she soon forgot about that when she felt Gio's hands

find her panties and slowly start to move them down and Valentina felt herself lifting her hips ever so slightly to help. Somewhere she was aware of a shocked part of herself wondering how on earth she was letting this happen. With this man? When only minutes ago she'd been trying to throw him out of this room. But like a coward she blocked it out; this growing, pulling desire in her body was too strong.

Gio pulled Valentina's panties off and threw them somewhere on the ground; now she was exposed to him completely, her dress bunched up over her waist. They seemed to have passed go and gone straight to level one hundred but all Valentina could see was the way Gio was looking at her with such awe and reverence, his big hands now on her thighs, spreading her for him.

He bent and pressed kisses along her sensitive inner thighs and she could feel the bristle of his stubble. It enflamed her nerve endings and she squirmed against his mouth, only to have his hands tighten on her, silently ordering her to be still.

His mouth was getting higher and higher, rising inexorably to the apex of her legs where she felt so hot and yet indecently damp. When his breath feathered there Valentina's elbows gave out and she collapsed onto the bed, just as Gio's mouth found her and she felt his tongue touch her moist cleft.

She had to put a fist to her mouth and bite down hard against the pleasure he was now wreaking on her body with such shocking intimacy. He was licking her, tasting her and ruthlessly pushing those legs apart when they wanted to close against this exquisite invasion.

And then she felt his tongue opening her up to him, exploring and stabbing deep inside, tasting her very essence. Valentina felt faint. A finger joined his tongue, pushing and stretching. She could feel her hips moving against his mouth, seeking more, a deeper penetration. She felt so stretched and yet unfulfilled and wanted more. A tight feeling was coiling deep inside her, getting tighter and tighter, making her move even more restlessly.

Then she felt two fingers, pushing deeper, and his tongue found and circled her clitoris with ruthless sucking intensity until Valentina broke free of the building tension to soar high to a place she'd ever seen before. Waves of pleasure more intense than she could have ever imagined broke through her and over her. It was so stupendous she couldn't even cry out, absorbing it in shocked silence, biting into her fist even harder in a bid to contain what she felt.

As she floated back down into some sense of reality Valentina became aware that she was still throbbing in spasms, deep inside her. Her fist fell from her mouth, too heavy to hold up any more. Gio's hands were gone and she looked up languorously to see him rise up like some kind of avenging God to rip open his shirt to reveal that magnificent chest. His eyes burnt into hers, and his hands went to his trousers, making quick work of his belt, buttons and zip.

Valentina couldn't even lift her head, it felt so heavy. She was aware of being displayed wantonly towards him but couldn't drum up a sense of shame. Not after what she'd just experienced. She'd never known it could be like that....

'I want to see you,' Gio muttered thickly, finding her hands and pulling her gently upwards. Valentina sat up and felt light-headed. Gio was pulling her to her feet and found her zip, yanking it down, and taking her dress with it so that it dropped at her feet with a soft swishing sound. Now she stood before him in nothing but her own plain bra and Gio's dark eyes were molten as they looked her up and down.

To her surprise, Valentina could feel some of the delicious lethargy move and shift, dissipate, so that she was being infected by a rising sense of tension again. It coiled deep inside her. Gio was naked and she looked down to see his erection thrusting towards her. Instinctively she reached for him, wanting to touch him, and wrapped a hand around his thick impressive length.

He breathed deep and his hands tightened on her arms where they'd gone to steady her a moment ago. Valentina was fascinated by the feel of him under her hand; he was like steel encased in velvet, infinitely strong and hard and yet so vulnerable. She looked up and her hand stopped when she saw the stark and almost feral need imprinted on his face. She gulped.

Gently he took her hand off him and said, 'I don't know how long I can last if you touch me like that. And I need to last—this is your first time....'

Valentina's heart seemed to miss a beat. Her first time, here with this man. The reality suddenly hit her, along with the very fervent assertion that she didn't want to be anywhere else. That threw up all sorts of emotional contradictions within her and to drive them down where she didn't have to analyse them Valentina stepped up to Gio and put her hands on his face.

'Gio...' Her voice was husky and rough. 'Make love to me.'

Her words hung in the desire-saturated air for a long moment and then Gio wrapped his arms around her and pulled her into him, driving his mouth down onto hers and kissing her so thoroughly she felt dizzy with need.

Valentina was barely aware of Gio undoing her bra so that it dropped to the floor between them. She only came back to her senses when she felt herself being lowered back onto the bed and looked up to see Gio hover over her on two hands, huge and dark and devastating. Shoulders broad, chest wide, hips narrow and lean. And lower, where the trail of very masculine hair ended, jutted his arousal. Valentina's eyes widened. She could see a pearlescent bead of moisture at the tip of his erection and her lower body clenched in instinctive response to such a display of male virility.

Gio started to press his mouth in a series of hot kisses all the way up from her belly to her ribs. Valentina held her breath. After an achingly long moment she felt him stretch out beside her on the bed and he cupped one breast, before his breath feathered over the distended tingling tip and he drew it into his mouth. The sheer sensation of that torturous delicious tugging sucking heat made Valentina's hips buck off the bed, her feet desperately searching for anything to dig into.

When Gio's mouth went to her other breast Valentina was nearly sobbing aloud from the sheer pleasure. She could feel heat gather between her legs, and as if guided there by her mind, Gio's free hand gently pushed her thighs apart, as he sought access.

Valentina was too incoherent to stop him. With skilful precision, Gio parted her thighs wider and his fingers found the aching core of her body, fingers stroking and spreading her moist arousal. Valentina's hands clutched at Gio's shoulders, fingers digging deep into satin skin, dewed with sweat. Their combined scent, musky and tart with desire, only served to make her feel even hotter.

Gio took his mouth off Valentina's breast and moved up to her mouth. She met him blindly, tongues lashing together as need mounted. She could feel a tremor run through Gio's body beside her and had a fleeting sense of just how much he was holding back. As his tongue delved deep into her mouth, his fingers thrust inside her, deeply intimate. It was so sudden and yet shockingly arousing that Valentina gasped against his mouth. Tiny waves and tremors of another incipient orgasm started up and she drew back to look up at Gio in wonder. His eyes were black, molten. No more green flecks.

His fingers slowly started to move in and out. Valentina could feel herself being stretched and on the periphery of the mounting excitement and pleasure was the slight tinge of pain.

'I want to prepare you…make sure you're ready for me.'

At that moment Valentina felt Gio's arousal, heavy against her hip. Long and thick and hard. She sucked in a breath as his words sank in. 'Oh…'

'Yes…' He smiled wryly. 'Oh…'

As Gio's fingers picked up pace though, Valentina quickly stopped being able to rationalise anything. Her hands clutched at his shoulders again and her head went back, hips raising of their own accord. She moved them restlessly, seeking something…more.

'Gio…' she whispered brokenly. She felt something give inside her. It was a fleeting moment of sharp pain and Gio pulled his hand away. Valentina looked at him, blinking. Her body was still crying out for his touch, despite the pain.

'Gio?'

Gio moved his body so that he hovered over her now, pushing her legs apart with his hips. She could feel the heavy length of him brushing against her sex. He took himself in his hand and Valentina looked down to see that he'd sheathed himself with protection with no idea of when or where he'd had the wherewithal to do it.

He was running the thick head of his penis along where

she felt drenched with desire. So much that it embarrassed her. With that realisation she turned her head to the side, suddenly overwhelmed.

She felt him still and a hand come to her chin, turning her back. His face was etched with desire but also something else that made her quiver: *concern*.

'Valentina?'

She took refuge from the tender feeling his concern aroused by focusing on the needs of her physical body. 'I want you…'

The concern faded from Gio's face and a stark primality took over. She could feel him position himself, feel his fingers on himself and on her as he slowly fed himself into her, inch by thick inch. The initial sensation was overpowering. Valentina sucked in a breath at the intrusion. This was so much more devastating than his fingers. But even as she thought that, her body seemed to recognise something she didn't, or trust something she didn't, and she could feel her muscles opening, admitting entrance.

With a guttural groan Gio took his hand away and rested on both hands over her body. With a hoarse calling out of her name, he thrust deep and hard and sheathed himself in her completely.

Valentina's eyes opened wide and her chest expanded with the breath she'd drawn in. Her hands were on his biceps where she could feel them quiver under her fingers. He was shaking, or she was shaking; she wasn't sure which.

She felt impossibly full and impaled, invaded. Gio was looking down at her, that concern edging back. 'OK?'

Valentina jerkily nodded her head. 'Please…Gio…'

Slowly he started to move, out…and then back in. His movements within her were so exquisite, bordering between pain and pleasure, that Valentina could only breathe in short gasps, struggling to hang on to whatever control she still had. She felt as if she was in danger of exploding into a million fragments with each long slide of Gio's body back into hers. And with each stroke, the pain faded to be replaced and eclipsed by pleasure.

Without even realising what she was doing, her feet were digging into the bed beside Gio's hips; her own were moving restlessly. As if sensing her inner turmoil over all this newness, Gio bent and pressed a kiss to her mouth, tongue stroking along hers for a long moment, soothing but also inciting.

'Wrap your legs around me,' he whispered in her ear, 'and I'll help you to fly.'

She could feel him find her leg and lift it up over one hip and blindly she lifted her other leg, wrapping both legs around those lean hips, ankles crossed just above his buttocks. He sank even deeper within her and their moans mingled. Valentina could feel his chest hairs scrape her sensitised breasts, making her arch upwards, seeking that contact again.

Gio's movements became more urgent. He was thrusting so hard and so deep now that Valentina saw stars. And then without any warning at all, her entire body clenched tight before exploding into a million pieces. Valentina gasped, head back, bucking uncontrollably against Gio as he pounded into her, his own release finally stilling that huge body just as he touched the very core of her.

In the aftermath Valentina's brain couldn't wrap itself around the magnitude of what had just happened. The pain mixed with a pleasure more intense than she'd ever experienced. She was vaguely aware of Gio pulling free of her body and disappearing for a moment before returning. She was vaguely aware of him lifting her body so that her head touched a pillow. He drew a thin cover over her body. When he tucked himself around her, she found that she was instinctively twining her legs around his, holding him to her tightly.

He lifted an arm and she felt his fingers smoothing damp strands of hair from her face. She opened sleepy eyes and caught a glimpse of a mark on the inside of his upper left arm. In the dim light she hadn't noticed it before. Without thinking Valentina reached up to trace what looked like black marks etched into his skin. A tattoo of some sort. She frowned. 'What's this?'

Gio's fingers in her hair stilled and she felt him tense. After a long moment he drew his arm back from her questing fingers and just said, 'It's nothing…rest now.'

He shifted his body so that Valentina was curled into his side, and with her cheek resting on his chest over where his heart beat steadily, she found herself slipping down into a dark dreamless place. She would think about those marks…later. She would think about it all.

As the dawn light filtered into Valentina's room, bathing everything in a pinky gold, Gio sat in a chair in the corner of her room. He'd pulled on his trousers, leaving them open, and just watched the woman who lay sleeping in the bed.

She was on her front, the sheet provocatively resting just over her buttocks, revealing the long smooth curve of her back. One arm was curled up to her chest where he could just make out the swell of her breast. His body tightened predictably and Gio grimaced at the response.

Her other arm was flung out by her head and her cheek rested on the pillow, long black lashes casting a shadow on flushed cheeks. Still flushed. He remembered how it had felt to sink into her velvet hot embrace, how tight she'd been at first.… His own body tightened even more and Gio gave up castigating himself for such a helpless response.

It had been the hardest thing in the world to extricate himself from Valentina's embrace but a part of him hadn't relished the prospect of her expression when she woke to find herself curled around him so comprehensively. And another part of him had needed to get some space…to try and rationalise the sheer scale of what had just happened.

Gio had never experienced sex like that…so intense and primal. His face grew stark—admittedly, many of his previous experiences were a blur from those two hellish years. But even before that…it had never been like this. He'd never lost control, lost himself so completely. Mario had used to tease him mercilessly: *You won't be able to cut yourself off forever, Gio. One day you'll meet someone who won't let you stay so aloof.…*

The truth was, Gio had envied the ease with which Mario had fallen in and out of love. Gio just hadn't had that capacity. Emotions for him were a dark and dangerous place to explore. Once, when he'd been tiny, he'd gone to his father with something he'd made, desperate to try and get his attention, acutely aware of how his older brothers seemed to effortlessly get and hold their father's attention in a way he couldn't.

Gio had stood in front of his father holding out the model airplane he'd spent hours working on. He could remember that all he'd wanted to say was, *I made this for you.* But under his father's arctic judgemental glare the words just wouldn't come out.

His father had snapped at him, irritated at this hesitance, and Gio could remember how his hands had trembled. The less he'd been able to speak, the more angry his father had become until he'd ripped the airplane out of Gio's hands, thrown it to the ground and stamped on it.

A lot of his father's vile words from that day were forgotten, but not the acrid sense of betrayal and hurt. Or the way his mother had shrank into the shadows, unable to stand up for her youngest son, too scared of directing that wrath towards her when she was so desperately trying to get back into her husband's favour.

He'd learnt to draw inwards that day, to protect himself.

A movement from the bed made Gio focus on Valentina again. He welcomed the distraction. She was uncurling her arm from her side and Gio could see the swell of her plump breast. With fire igniting in his veins again he stood up and went over, sitting beside her on the edge of the bed.

Slowly she opened her eyes. He saw her try to focus, to assimilate the information her body was undoubtedly giving her. And then she saw him. Those amber feline eyes widened, the flush on her cheeks deepened. Gio's chest constricted when he could see the myriad questions about to come out of her mouth.

Without thinking he put a finger to her lips, their softness making him ache. 'Shh…don't think…don't say anything…just let it be….'

Gio watched her wary response, and then as if some inner turmoil had been resolved she nodded imperceptibly. He took his finger away and said throatily, 'How do you feel? Are you sore?'

Even as he watched he could see the glowing embers of desire in her eyes, and his arousal soared. Looking endearingly shy now, she just shook her head against the pillow.

'Good,' Gio said and bent down to press a kiss to her mouth. She turned onto her back, opening up her body to him again and Gio fell back into the glorious blaze once more.

CHAPTER EIGHT

VALENTINA WAS IN deeply unchartered waters. She was standing in her shower with her eyes closed and Gio was massaging shampoo into her hair. She felt like purring. She also felt like turning around and pushing him up against the wall and kissing him all over. She could feel his erection brush against her buttocks and had to put her hands out to touch the tiles, afraid she'd fall down in a heap at his feet under the teeming hot spray.

She felt him turn her around and kept her eyes closed, too scared to look and see that gorgeous physique up close. That physique that had taken her to heaven and back more times than she could remember during the previous night and then again that morning. She'd never known the human body was capable of such pleasure, of such base carnal desires. Or that those desires could be felt, and *met*.

But more than all of that, she was too scared to open her eyes and look into Gio's. To see the same expression she'd seen in them this morning when she'd woken to find him looking at her so intently, as if he could see all the way into her soul, where she hid her deepest secrets.

But she couldn't avoid it. Not when Gio pronounced her clean and tipped her chin up with a finger. With the utmost reluctance she opened her eyes and looked up. Gio had stopped the water but they were still surrounded by steamy warm air, like a sensual cocoon. Lazily he put his arm out, hand touching the wall behind her. It was then that Valentina noticed the marks again, on his arm. The tattoo.

He saw where her gaze had gone and in an instant the atmosphere went from hot and sultry to cool as ice. He quickly took down his arm again, reaching out for towels. So fast that her head span, Gio had manoeuvred her out of the shower and was wrapping her in a huge soft towel and hitching one around his own hips.

Curiosity well and truly stoked now, Valentina followed Gio into the bedroom. He'd lifted the towel off his hips and was roughly rubbing his hair before running it over the rest of his body in a very perfunctory manner, clearly doing his utmost to get out of her room quickly. Valentina tried desperately not to let his naked back and those firmly sculpted buttocks distract her. Just looking at his powerfully muscled thighs made her think of how potently masculine he'd felt between her legs.

She hitched her own towel under her arms sarong-style and ignored the fact that she was dripping water all over the floor. She went over and stood in front of a very naked and damp Gio. She crossed her arms against the betraying rush of heat to her groin.

'What are those marks?'

Gio scowled and for a second looked endearingly young. Oozing reluctance he wrapped his towel around his hips and crossed his own arms, effectively hiding the tattoo in question.

Growing exasperated now Valentina reached out and pulled at his arms, making him loosen them, and then she held his left arm up, so that she could see the tattoo clearly. 'Why on earth don't you want to talk about this? It's just a tattoo....'

Saying something finally, Gio bit out, 'Exactly, it's nothing.'

He tried to pull his arm back but Valentina held on tenaciously, inspecting the uniform black ink marks. Out loud she said, 'They look like roman numerals...some kind of a date? Four...five...'

She could read the first part, but the last piece eluded her—her knowledge of roman numerals only went up to about ten but this was clearly a much larger number, and as she realised this, she also realised the significance of *four* and *five*. Mario had died on the fourth of May....

Valentina dropped Gio's arm and looked up at him. She could feel the blood draining southwards. Gio cursed under his breath and guided her to the bed to sit down on the edge. He stood in front of her and admitted with stark reluctance, 'It's the date Mario died.'

Valentina's belly clenched hard. Every line of Gio's body was screaming at her to *stay out of this.*

'But...' She tried to formulate words, to understand. 'Why?'

Gio cursed again and turned away, pacing impatiently to the window, presenting her with his rigid back. Without turning around he said bleakly, 'I needed to mark the date...when Mario's life ended, and mine.'

Before, Valentina knew she would have jumped down his throat and reminded him that his life hadn't ended. But after what he'd told her of his experiences she had to concede that it *had* ended on some level.

After the intimacies of the previous night it was very hard to call up the rage she'd clung to for so long. *This is what she'd been afraid of.*

The thought of him asking some stranger to carve an indelible mark into his skin made her feel unaccountably emotional. Before she knew what she was doing she'd stood up and went over to Gio. She inserted herself between him and the window, his jaw was as rigid as the rest of him and he looked at her warily.

Dropping her gaze to his arms, she once again undid them from where they were crossed so tightly. She took his marked arm and held it out again, turned up so she could see the tattoo. With her finger she traced the lines, feeling the indentation in his skin, marked for ever with this brand of the date her brother had died.

His guilt reached out to envelop her in that moment and it was so suffocating that she stepped back, letting his arm drop heavily. Panic prickled in her belly. For one awful second she'd wanted to place her mouth over that tattoo, to kiss Gio there, to assuage his pain…and that was a revelation she wasn't ready for.

Feeling rigid all over, the previous night all but forgotten in her bid to put some space between herself and his man, Valentina stepped back and said, 'I should get ready for work.'

She went into the bathroom and turned the lock in the door. And then she rested her back against the door. She half expected to hear Gio demand autocratically that she open up and remembered his own reluctance to admit what the tattoo was. But nothing happened.

It was only when she heard her main apartment door open and close and she knew that Gio had left that she allowed herself to sink to the floor and silent tears leaked from her eyes.

She wasn't even sure what she was crying for…but for once it wasn't grief for Mario; it was for something much deeper and more ambiguous. Allowing herself that glimpse of Gio's pain and guilt had shaken her to her very core. And deep down, in that dark and secret place within her, the shameful truth she'd harboured for seven years was rising back to the surface.

Valentina was aware that if she were to acknowledge it now, it would blast apart everything that had been holding her together since Mario had died...and if she didn't have that, who was she?

As Gio walked away from Valentina's accommodation his gut churned. *The tattoo.* Of course she'd noticed the tattoo. He'd been drunk when he'd got it, full of bile and self-recrimination. Guilt. A perverse part of him had liked the thought of being marked for ever, so he could never forget. As if that were possible.

For a crazy second back there, he'd almost fancied that Valentina had been moved enough by the tattoo that she'd... She'd *what*? a voice mocked him bitterly. That she'd understood something of his experience? That she possibly didn't hate him as much as he thought she did?

His mouth firmed. She would never forgive him. And she certainly wasn't interested in absolving him.

Gio resolutely pushed tender emotional roots back down into the murky darkness of his damaged soul and vowed that if the physical was all he was going to get with Valentina, then he would take it. And let her walk away when she'd had enough. Even though the thought of that made him want to smash his fist through the nearest solid object.

'Mini doughnuts to go with mini coffees for dessert...and the sweet fig starter...truly inspired...'

Valentina smiled weakly and cursed herself inwardly. This was what she'd been waiting for, an opportunity to showcase her skills in front of the very people who could take her forward with her career and yet she couldn't concentrate. She was too keyed up, her whole body quivering because she knew Gio was just feet away in the crowded throng. Guests were finishing lunch in the VIP marquee and moving back outside for the biggest race of the three days.

Valentina gave up trying to focus on what the guests were saying to her and murmured her thanks and excuses, cursing herself again that she was so distracted. She turned to head back out to the main tent to make sure that everything was set up for the inevitable celebrations after the race and ran straight into a wall of steel.

Gio.

She looked up. His hands were on her arms and her legs felt like jelly. His gaze raked her up and down and dimly she realised that he'd shaved since the morning. He looked…edible. Her insides melted. She thought of the tattoo and her heart clenched.

'OK?'

It took a second for his question to register. She was too caught up in her reaction to him. Jerkily she nodded her head and then she realised that he was standing with another couple. The man was tall, as tall as Gio. There was a startling resemblance even though Valentina knew it wasn't one of his brothers. A woman stood beside the man, his hand in a proprietorial hold on her arm, much the same way Gio now held Valentina's arm. It was only then that she became aware of the crackling tension between the men.

In that instance some flicker of affinity passed between the women, even though Valentina had never seen her before. She was beautiful, with long straight brown hair and stunning blue eyes.

'Angelo, I'd like you to meet Valentina Ferranti, the woman who has been in charge of catering for this year's Corretti Cup.'

The man smiled and Valentina felt Gio's hand tighten on her fractionally. He was stupendously handsome, even though he did nothing for Valentina. He put out a hand and said urbanely, 'Nice to meet you. I'm Gio's illegitimate cousin. I'm also betting against his horse today and I expect to win.'

Before Valentina could respond Gio was biting out, 'She's got nothing to do with our pathetic family dramas.'

Valentina took Angelo's hand and felt something inexplicably primal rise up within her. She smiled sweetly. 'We'll be serving Prosecco and elderflower cocktails after the race to help you drown your sorrows when you lose to Gio's horse.'

Angelo kept ahold of her hand and after a long moment he looked from Valentina to Gio and said with steel in his voice, 'We'll see.'

Shocked at that protective surge she'd felt to defend Gio, Valentina took her hand back and jerked her arm out of Gio's hold. Focusing on no one in particular she muttered something about needing to check something and left the tent.

Thankfully things were gearing up for the big race so Valentina knew that Gio would be busy and unlikely to come after her and she needed some space. She couldn't keep avoiding her own conscience after last night and that morning.

She found a secluded spot hidden away from everything and leant against the railing of a nearby paddock, resting her forehead on her hands. Her insides felt as if they were cramping. Her breath was choppy. She shouldn't have slept with Gio…and yet, Valentina had enough honesty to admit that if she went back in time, was confronted with Gio all over again…no force on earth could have induced her to resist.

But the tattoo...what he'd been through after Mario's death—it all whirled sickeningly in her head now.

'What is it? What's wrong?'

Valentina was being pulled up from the railing, her heart slamming to a halt before she even realised that Gio had followed her. Sudden anger at this invasion of privacy when she felt so vulnerable made her lash out. 'Nothing is wrong, Gio, apart from the fact that I despise myself for being so weak!'

Every line in Gio's face stood out in stark relief. 'I told you last night, Valentina. I give you full permission to despise *me*. And believe me, I have every intention of making you despise me over and over again.'

He reached out with two hands and pulled her into him before she could take a breath and then his mouth was fusing to hers. The kiss was desperate and brutal but electrifying. Anger and pain and remorse all clawed up within Valentina seeking release. Desperately she clutched at his head, holding him to her, allowing no escape. Teeth bit and drew blood before Gio stopped, breathing harshly, his forehead resting on Valentina's. She was dizzy with the sudden overwhelming surge of need mixed with adrenalin.

'Hate *me*, Valentina...not yourself. This thing...it's out of our control.'

Gio stood up straight and pulled back even though it was the hardest thing in the world. Valentina's smooth top knot was coming undone. Her mouth was red and swollen, her chest rising up and down as she tried to regain her breath. A few buttons had opened on her white shirt, giving him a tantalising glimpse of her lacy bra and cleavage. And Gio knew he had to get out of there now or he'd take her on the ground like an animal.

He turned and walked away before he did anything else

and realised that, by the time this insanity was over between them, he'd be torn apart completely.

Valentina looked after Gio, struck dumb by his curt, *Hate me, Valentina.* Tears pricked her eyes. She wanted to call out; she wanted to make him stop. She wanted to say *sorry*. But like a coward, she didn't. The truth sat heavily in her belly. She didn't despise herself for being weak…she despised herself for feeling so many disturbing emotions for this man and for not having the courage to own up to them, or analyse them.

Distaste flickered across Gio's face. The gala auction had been under way for some time now and the huge sums of money were becoming more outrageous as people helped themselves to increasing quantities of alcohol.

Not so long ago he had been one of those people, flinging huge sums of money into the ether in some desperate bid to seek solace.

His cousin Angelo had come to him before leaving with his date and had shook Gio's hand in recognition of the fact that he had indeed lost to Gio's far superior horse in the race. But to Gio's surprise, while their conversation was sharp and cool, he'd felt a burgeoning respect for the man and they'd parted on more than civil note. He found himself slightly amazed when his usual reaction to anyone in his family was to walk quickly in the other direction.

A flash of dark red caught Gio's eye then and he looked, his gaze stopping and fixing on Valentina where she'd just arrived into the VIP tent. *She was wearing one of the dresses.* The knowledge sent something very primal into his blood.

She'd somehow managed to avoid him all evening—always flitting to and fro on the opposite side of wherever he was, and too surrounded by people eager to share in his Corretti Cup race success Gio had been trapped. Until now. His whole body tingled and arousal was fierce and immediate. He'd had a vision of her in this dress as soon as he'd seen it but the reality was far more stupendous.

Her hair was up, in a slightly messy chignon, exposing her long delicate neck. Her shoulders were bare and pale. Her breasts swelled against the heart-shaped neckline of the dress and tight bodice before it fell to the floor in a swathe of silk and chiffon.

She wore no jewellery, and a minimum of make-up. And she was more beautiful than any other woman there. A fact which seemed to have impacted on not only him. Gio saw a lurching movement towards her and recognised the French playboy.

Gio was moving before he'd even realised his intention and he pushed down the memory of her words earlier, how deeply they'd cut into him. He'd followed her outside after their exchange with Angelo because he'd been stunned at how she'd defended him. He should have realised that it had meant nothing.

The hurt from earlier solidified in his belly and he blocked it out, welcoming the heat in his blood. This was all he wanted, this oblivion she could give him. And hate herself for, a small voice reminded him. He was too weak to turn back now and his vision went red when he saw his erstwhile friend reach Valentina and clamp a hand around her arm.

Valentina had just arrived back into the VIP tent. Instinctively she found herself searching out a familiar tall and broad figure when her eyes adjusted to the artfully lit space. When she didn't see him immediately she blocked out the way her belly hollowed out. She felt very exposed, as if she was sending Gio some silent message because after a long intense internal struggle earlier, she'd finally put on one of the dresses Gio had bought for her.

It, and the matching underwear, felt exactly as decadent as she'd feared it would, along with the very scary sense of being on tenterhooks all evening, waiting to see Gio and his reaction. Before she could look further though, her arm was taken in a harsh grip.

She looked up, surprised, into the arrogant features of the French playboy who had been trying to chat her up the other night. She could see in an instant that he was inebriated. His already harsh grip tightened and immediately Valentina recoiled back, and tried to free herself but he hung on.

'Please let me go, Monsieur Lagarde.' She tried to keep her voice calm and reasonable over the sound of the crowd and the auctioneer.

'Oh, please…' he slurred. 'Surely we can be on first name terms, *non*? Call me Pierre….'

Valentina struggled again to free her arm, feeling a sliver of trepidation snake down her spine when she realised that he'd somehow manoeuvred them so that they were hidden from view behind a tall plant.

'You are so beautiful….'

He had both her arms in his hands now and Valentina felt panic claw upwards. He was huge, looming over her with his huge bulk. And then just as suddenly as the panic had risen, he was being lifted away from her as if by some magical force, his hands gone from her arms, making her stumble forward slightly.

He was replaced by a grim-looking Gio and all Valentina could see of Pierre was two of the discreet security men escorting him outside.

Gio cursed and came closer. 'He's bruised your arms.'

Valentina looked down stupidly and saw the red marks of his fingers. It was only then that she realised how scared she'd been for a few seconds. She looked up at Gio, aghast at the helpless emotion rising up within her, and knew shamefully that it had more to do with the man in front of her than what had just happened. She blinked rapidly to keep it back, but failed miserably.

Gio cursed again and she was being enveloped in his arms. Valentina felt faint with relief and how good it felt to have him hold her. Guilt compounded her as she soaked in his strength when she thought of what she'd said earlier.

She pulled back within his arms and looked up, words trembling on her lips. But once again Gio just put a finger to her mouth, silencing her. He shook his head. 'Don't say it.'

Valentina swallowed and spoke against his finger. 'But you don't know what I'm going to say.'

'I don't need to hear it, all I need is you.'

Valentina knew that if she was to pull free of Gio now, step back and say she didn't want him, he would let her go. He might not want to, but he would. It was etched into every tightly held muscle in his body.

Valentina knew there were a million and one reasons why she should take this opportunity to walk away. There was too much between them, too much that was tangled and dark and unspoken. But all she could feel was *him*. That dark seductive energy winding around her, binding her to him in some silent pact.

His assurance that she could do this and hate him for it made her feel riven with guilt...but she couldn't walk away. Just as she couldn't stop breathing.

But if she did this she also had to stop lashing out and blaming him. She had to take responsibility for her actions and hope that, soon, this temporary madness would cease and she could get on with her life. Even though right at that moment the thought of a life without Gio in it was inconceivable.

Valentina knew that if she tried to articulate any of this to Gio he'd just stop her. So she said, 'Can we just leave? Now?'

Valentina felt the faint tremor that ran through Gio's body and knew that he'd been as aware as her of how significant this moment was.

'Of course.'

His arms dropped and he stepped back, taking her hand. Valentina bit her lip and stopped him, suddenly aware of their surroundings. 'But…don't you have to stay? For the end of the auction?'

Gio just looked at her and flashed a sudden smile, making her breath stop momentarily. When he smiled like that he reminded her so much of *before*.

'I can delegate. Anyway, I don't think too many people here will be in any fit state to recall if I'm here or not at the end…and your work is done?'

Valentina nodded. Her staff were only concerned now with topping up glasses and the clear-up. It was over. She'd weathered her first bona fide exclusive event. As if reading her mind and sensing her relief Gio came close again and cupped her jaw before settling a sweet kiss on her mouth. He drew back. 'I meant to say thank you, you did a formidable job. I thought you'd appreciate knowing that my aunt Carmela nearly choked on her starter when she saw you directing proceedings earlier.'

Valentina melted inside at his words and couldn't help smiling too. She'd studiously ignored the frosty glares from the older woman but had been human enough to relish the second chance Gio had given her. Not only that, she'd been inundated with enquiries as to her availability for future events.

Gio was pulling her out from their secluded spot and Valentina tugged his hand again. 'Gio...'

He looked at her and she saw the fleeting trepidation on his face.

'I just wanted to say thank you...for the opportunity.'

'My pleasure...' He touched her jaw with a finger, leaving a trail of tingling fire in its wake, and said throatily, 'And it will be...'

Blazing heat seemed to consume Valentina like a flash fire. Both her hands were around Gio's where he held hers in a bid to stay upright as he all but pulled her from the tent. He stopped only momentarily to have words with one of his assistants and then he was striding out into the warm night air.

When she could see that Gio was heading in the direction of her rooms she found that she wanted to get away from here completely. She stopped in her tracks so Gio had to stop too. He looked back at her and the stark impatience on his face nearly made her change her mind. But she said, 'Not here...somewhere else.'

Gio frowned down at her. A wary light dawned in his eye. 'My *castello* is close...'

Where Mario died... Valentina waited for the inevitable pain to lance her but it didn't come. It felt right to want to go there and she couldn't explain it, but bizarrely it felt like a link to the past, a positive link.

'Your *castello*...yes.'

'Are you sure?'

Valentina nodded, impatience firing her own blood now. Abruptly Gio turned in his tracks and Valentina followed him to the private staff car park. He was unlocking his sports car but Valentina saw the huge monster of a motorbike beside it. She asked impetuously, 'Is that yours?'

Gio followed her look from where he was undoing his bow tie with long fingers. 'Yes, it's mine.'

His hand stilled. 'Why? Do you want to go on that instead?'

Valentina had a vivid memory of seeing Gio pull up outside her parents' humble home shortly after he'd come back from Europe. In jeans and a white T-shirt. No helmet.

She looked at him. 'Can we?'

Gio shrugged lightly. 'Sure...' He closed the car door and went to the bike, dislodging it from its parked position. With lithe grace he swung his leg over the pillion and settled into the main seat, his thighs straining against his trousers.

Looking back at Valentina he held out a hand. 'Hold on to me and step up onto the side and swing your leg over.'

Valentina bent down and slipped off her high-heeled sandals and hitched up her dress between her legs. Infectious excitement flared in her belly. Holding her shoes and dress in one hand, she balanced on Gio's shoulder with the other and felt his hand steady her, on her waist.

And then she was on the bike, nestled so snugly behind him that she could feel the indentation of his hard buttocks between her legs. A warm heat flooded through her. Gio was facing away from her again and then twisted back, holding out a helmet.

Valentina looked at it and then at him. 'Do I have to?'

'Yes,' he said firmly. 'If you want to go on this bike with me.'

Looking mildly amused at her mutinous expression Gio carefully put the helmet on her head and secured the strap before attending to himself.

Then he said over his shoulder, 'Put your hands around my waist and hold on.'

Valentina leant into him and did that, her shoe straps dangling from one hand. Gio's belly was hard and flat and she felt his muscles clench as he pushed forward and then back to get them moving. Her arms and hands tightened instinctively around him as the engine roared to life and suddenly they were moving out and into the darkness beyond the racetrack.

The ride was exhilarating through the inky night with the wind whipping past their heads. Valentina gave up worrying about her dress. Her thighs were completely bare by now, clenched tight around Gio's hips.

Her hands were low against his belly and she could feel the tell-tale bulge of his arousal brushing her knuckles. Suddenly emboldened by the decision she'd made, Valentina's fingers opened, exploring, finding Gio's belt, opening it and sneaking her hand underneath to his hot skin.

His hand came over hers and Valentina held her breath thinking he would move it, but he held it there, over his erection, which grew under the palm of her hand, separated only by thin briefs.

It was unbearably sensual, this dark ride into the night, feeling Gio's body respond to her. When at last they turned into his driveway lined with tall trees, Valentina could have wept with relief.

When the bike came to a stop with a throaty roar outside Gio's house, he sat there for a moment, holding her hand on him, before gently taking it off. He turned the engine off and the night was suddenly very still around them. Valentina felt him take a breath and finally unwelded herself from his back, taking her other arm away too.

Gio removed his helmet and then turned around and removed hers. She could feel her hair tumble down around her shoulders. He threw the helmet to the ground and cupped her face in his hands. She could feel the faint calluses against her cheeks.

'What do you do to me, Valentina?'

'The same as you do to me, I think,' she whispered, before Gio slanted his mouth down over hers and kissed her.

When Valentina's hips were rolling impatiently against Gio's buttocks he finally pulled back. They were both breathing hard.

'I think we can do better than kissing on a bike....' His voice was dry.

Gio got off the bike in one lithe move. He bent down and scooped Valentina up into his arms before she knew what was happening. Her sandals were still dangling from her fingers and they trailed down Gio's back now when her arms went around his neck and she clung on.

Gio shouldered the front door open and Valentina asked dryly, 'No key?'

Gio muttered, 'The security guards knew I was on my way.'

'Oh...' Valentina was stunned again at the sheer evidence of Gio's wealth and reminded herself that he had extremely valuable bloodstock here, some of the most valuable in the world.

He walked them through the dark house. Valentina couldn't make out much in the gloom, just that they seemed to pass through some cavernous empty rooms with big windows before Gio climbed an ornate staircase to the first floor.

He walked them into a room with the door wide open and Valentina could see a huge bed revealed in a shaft of moonlight. Instinctively her arms tightened around Gio's neck. The thought of Gio sleeping in this bed, possibly naked, made her inner muscles clench hard.

Gio stopped by the bed and let Valentina drop to the floor. Her sandals dropped too, from nerveless fingers. His hands were on her bare shoulders and gruffly he said, 'I didn't tell you how beautiful you look.'

Valentina blushed in the gloom and she looked down. Gio tipped her chin back up. 'I'm glad you didn't send them back.'

Her throat felt very constricted but Valentina finally admitted, 'Me too.'

Gio seemed to study her for an infinitesimal moment before he instructed, 'Turn around.'

Silently, tingling all over, Valentina turned around. His hands kept contact with her skin. And then she felt him brush her hair over one shoulder before his fingers trailed from the back of her neck down her spine until they reached the top of the zip.

He pulled the zip down all the way, until she felt his knuckles graze just above her bare buttocks and she shivered. The dress fell open under its own weight and when Gio tugged it gently from her hips it fell to the floor. Gio then undid the clasp of her bra and that, too, was dispensed with.

Turning her back gently to face him, Valentina was glad of the dim light so she couldn't fully make out the expression on his face, in his eyes. She could feel his gaze on her though, making her breasts feel heavy and her nipples spring hard and tight.

When he cupped her breasts in his hands and rubbed his thumbs back and forth over the puckered tips she had to hold on to his biceps to stay standing.

'I want you so much....'

Valentina took a breath and reached her hands up to his jacket, pushing it off his shoulders and down his arms, dislodging his hands from their torturous touch for a moment. Then she made quick work of removing his shirt.

The languor of a few seconds ago was gone. Valentina heard the soft slick of leather as Gio removed his belt and then opened his trousers, pulling them down and off, taking his briefs with them. Desperation mounted. Inexperienced and shaky with the extreme desire rising within her, Valentina all but fell back onto the bed at the merest nudging from Gio. He came down beside her and stretched out so that they touched from thigh to thigh, hip to hip, chest to chest.

Valentina shifted so that she could put her head down on the soft mattress. She reached out a tentative hand to touch Gio's jaw, suddenly suffused with shyness and said, 'Take me…'

CHAPTER NINE

WHEN VALENTINA WOKE she could feel the sunlight caressing her bare skin and a warm breeze, the scent of grass and earth. Superstitiously she didn't open her eyes yet. She was lying face down, on one cheek, and could feel the sheet just covering her bottom. Her legs were splayed with wanton abandon and she had the distinct impression of strong arms that had been around her not so long ago.

She remembered how Gio had tucked her into his body, arms wrapped tight around her, powerful legs cupping her back and bottom as she'd slid into a dreamless sleep with her body humming from the overload of recent pleasure.

She knew Gio wasn't in the room any more. Her skin wasn't tingling with that preternatural awareness. Reluctantly Valentina moved onto her back and winced when aching muscles protested. She blushed when she thought of how tightly she'd gripped Gio's hips with her legs, the way she'd dug her heels into his buttocks, urging him to go harder, *deeper*. She blushed even more when she thought of how she'd dug her nails into his back…he might be marked. And then that thought caused a curiously satisfied glow within her.

Slowly she opened her eyes and took in the room which had been shrouded in darkness last night. It took a few seconds to adjust to the bright light and to realise that there were no curtains on the huge window nearby. Valentina came up on her elbows and looked around.

The room was starkly bare with only a minimum of furniture that looked old and used. A low table with a lamp nearby, a chest of drawers and a wardrobe. The walls were stripped back as if in readiness to be painted. A chandelier light hung over the bed on an exposed wire. Old and unadorned floorboards were unvarnished and uncarpeted.

The feel was very much faded grandeur but not in the artful way that people paid through the nose for; this was the genuine thing. It was as if Gio hadn't cared enough to do it up and something inside Valentina twisted.

Moving slowly, she got out of bed. Huge and equally faded French doors were half open and led out to a private terraced balcony. The view over the surrounding countryside was stunning. In the far distance Valentina could make out what she thought must be Syracuse with the sea behind it, a faint stain of blue.

Conscious of her nakedness, she looked around and saw her dress neatly folded on a chair near the chest of drawers along with her underwear and shoes. She blushed again to think of Gio handling them and then she spotted a T-shirt and a pair of sweatpants laid out over the footboard at the bottom of the bed.

She quickly put them on; they were voluminous but Valentina rolled up the sweats and tied the string tightly around her waist. The T-shirt came to her mid-thighs. After exploring the en suite bathroom which was as undecorated as the bedroom and yet had beautiful antique pieces like a stunning chandelier and a gilt mirror, she went in search of Gio with a distinct prickle of apprehension.

She didn't like to remind herself that they'd avoided this morning-after scenario the other day when she'd confronted him about the tattoo and had a minor meltdown.

Outside the bedroom was a long corridor but Valentina could see stairs in the distance, the stairs that Gio had carried her up last night.

When she went down to the ground floor she could see the huge front door wide open, revealing the courtyard and Gio's motorbike where he'd left it. Flowers trailed haphazardly from pots around the door. Rooms led off the main entrance and Valentina peeked into them. They were slightly more done up than the bedroom but they were still quite bare, with the minimum of furniture.

She came to what had to be the main living room. The walls were white and there was one long low white couch near the middle of the room. A coffee table and a TV seemed incongruous in the huge ascetic room and again Valentina's chest twisted with an emotion she didn't want to look at.

'There you are...'

Valentina whirled around to see Gio leaning against another doorway she hadn't yet noticed, arms crossed. He was wearing a dark T-shirt and faded jeans which hung precariously off those lean hips, the top button open. His jaw was dark with stubble and Valentina recalled how the new growth had felt against her inner thighs only short hours before.

She blurted out, 'I was just looking for you.' She gestured to the clothes awkwardly. 'Thank you...for these.'

He shrugged minutely. 'They look far better on you than they ever did on me.'

Valentina blushed, the enormity hitting her of being here in Gio's house...the morning after the night before.

'Do you want some coffee?'

Seizing any opportunity to block out the revelations coming thick and fast in her head Valentina said quickly,

'Yes, please…and then I really should be getting back to the track.'

Gio lifted a brow as she walked towards him and she stalled.

'It's Sunday, the only thing happening at the track will be the massive clean-up and move-out as people start to transport their horses home. And anyway, it's lunchtime, half the day is already gone.'

Valentina blanched. Lunchtime. Sunday. No escape. Almost desperately now she said, 'My parents…I should see my parents.'

Gio had turned and was walking away, down another long corridor towards the back of the house. He said over his shoulder, 'I rang the clinic earlier and your father is doing fine. They're advising the minimum of fuss before he is taken to Naples tomorrow afternoon.'

Valentina scowled at Gio's back and then immediately felt guilty. He was doing so much for them. Past a constriction in her throat she said, 'Thank you…for checking up on them.'

They were in a huge kitchen now and Gio turned to face Valentina, a small smile playing around his lips as if he knew very well what she'd just been thinking. 'You're welcome.'

Valentina sucked in an involuntary gasp; unlike the rest of the house, the kitchen was pristine. A glorious mix of old and new. Slate floors and rustic wooden worktops blended seamlessly with steel and chrome. Her inner chef sighed with sheer joy. 'This is…stunning,' she breathed out finally, walking towards the central island and running her hand reverently over the surface.

She heard the dry tone in Gio's voice. 'My housekeeper, Eloisa, insisted on the kitchen being finished. It's all to her spec, not mine. She's away this week, visiting family in Messina.'

Valentina thought of the huge cavernous and undecorated rooms. Thankfully Gio's back was to her as he busied himself with the coffee pot. Unable to stop herself, Valentina asked, 'You've lived here for nearly ten years—but it's as if you haven't settled in yet.'

Gio turned around, his face curiously blank, and handed Valentina a tiny cup of espresso. The fact that he knew how she liked her morning coffee made her belly swoop.

Gio took a sip himself and then said, 'In a way I haven't…when I got back from Europe and bought this place it needed a mountain of work.'

Valentina recalled the ongoing construction work whenever she'd been to the *castello* in the past. That's why she'd never been inside before now.

Gio was continuing. 'That took almost two years…and then…'

Valentina's hands clenched so tight around the tiny piece of porcelain that she had to relax for fear of breaking it in two. The significance of what he'd said sank in. Quietly she finished, 'Mario died…'

Gio looked pale and he threw the rest of his coffee back in one gulp before turning to place the cup in the sink.

Valentina put down her own cup and addressed Gio's obviously tense back. 'Where did Mario die?'

He stilled and then he turned around and looked so haunted and bleak for a moment that Valentina quivered inwardly. 'Valentina…' His voice was a hoarse plea.

'Please…I need to know.' To her surprise, she didn't feel angry or resentful. She just desperately needed to know.

As if sensing her intractability Gio moved towards a back door and opened it. Valentina followed to see that it led out to a small herb garden. Obviously the housekeeper's. Gio was holding out a scuffed pair of runners and saying tightly, 'These might fit, they're Eloisa's.'

Valentina took them, avoiding Gio's eyes, and slipped them on. They were a size too big, but fine for now. Valentina had to trot to keep up with Gio as he strode down a path with bushes on either side. Somewhere in the distance she could hear the whinny of a horse.

When they emerged at the bottom of the path the estate was laid out before them. Valentina came to stand beside Gio and saw the vast stables down to their left, surrounded by cypress trees. To the right of that were huge rolling green paddocks, incongruous against the more rocky and bare Sicilian landscape and no doubt carefully maintained by Gio's gardeners.

From what she remembered the gallops where Mario had died were behind the stables but she couldn't see them from here. Gio turned to face her, his jaw tight. 'The gallops are gone, Valentina. I got rid of them…after…' His voice trailed off.

She looked up at him. 'What's there now?'

Gio ran a hand through his hair, reluctance oozing from every taut muscle in his body. 'A garden…I got them to cover it over with a garden.'

Determined now, Valentina crossed her arms. 'I want to see it.'

'Why? Valentina—it won't serve any purpose.…'

She touched his arm then and felt him tense to her touch which sent a cold shiver down her spine. 'Please, Gio…I need to see this.'

After a long tense moment he took his arm from under her hand and turned and stalked onwards. For the first time since they'd met again Valentina had a glimpse of another side of Gio. Cold, inscrutable. She shivered slightly when she imagined the dynamic between them being very different.

They went down past the stables where lots of curious horses' heads peeped out. Valentina thought she recognised Misfit, who whinnied softly, but she wasn't sure. A couple of stable hands passed them by but they were obviously put off by Gio's expression and scurried on. Valentina only realised then that she was still dressed in Gio's oversize clothes and felt her face flame as she hurried to keep up with him.

He'd stopped before she realised it and she crashed into his back. He put out a hand to steady her but she noticed how quickly he took it away again and felt a dart of hurt. They'd come through an arbour of some sort and were standing in a huge walled garden. Valentina was taking it all in and noticed that Gio was standing on the edge of an elaborate green structure, about a foot high. Valentina came to stand beside him and frowned. 'It's a maze.'

Gio's voice was tight. 'It's a labyrinth. The one path which leads in also leads back out.' She heard him take a breath. 'Mario told me about them once…he'd always been fascinated by them.'

Valentina had a vague memory of Mario mentioning something about them now too.

Gio said from beside her, 'I'll leave you.'

And then he was gone. She could hear him striding away again. It was almost too huge to take in—the fact that there now existed a walled garden where the gallops had been, and then this…labyrinth. Valentina was standing at the entrance and slowly started to walk the path.

It was a curiously meditative experience. Every time she thought she was coming close to the centre of the labyrinth, the path would diverge far away again. She felt exasperated at first until she realised that this was undoubtedly part of the process. She was surprised when she finally found herself stumbling into the centre at last. It was so unexpectedly peaceful that she stood there for long minutes.

She knew her parents would be incredibly emotional to see what Gio had done in Mario's name. And she? Like a coward, Valentina didn't want to explore deeper than the peace she felt right then. Her emotions were far too close to the surface as it was, ambiguous and volatile.

Eventually she wound her way back from the centre to the entrance of the labyrinth and reluctantly left the garden behind. She couldn't shake the feeling that some bruised part of her heart had been healed.

When she got back up to the kitchen door of the *castello* a grim-faced Gio met her. He'd shaved and changed and was holding car keys, and a bag which she suspected contained her dress. 'I can take you now if you're ready to leave?'

Valentina knew that she should be jumping at this opportunity to run as far away as she could, as fast as possible. But in light of Gio's clear desire to have her gone something inexplicably rebellious rose up within her.

She lifted her chin. 'What makes you think I'm ready to leave?'

She saw the quickly hidden flare of confusion in his eyes before they narrowed again. Almost as if wanting to goad her now he said, 'I assumed that seeing where Mario had died would be a passion killer.'

Valentina sucked in a breath at his crude words. But amazingly, hurt didn't grip her. She couldn't articulate it to Gio but it felt *right* to be here with him. Her blood was already flowing thicker in her veins just standing in front of him, his freshly clean scent on the air between them.

'I was the one who wanted to come here, remember?'

Again that flare of confusion. Valentina focused on Gio

and not on the confusing tumult of emotions within her. She walked up to him and took the keys out of his hands and dropped them to the nearby countertop. Then she took the bag out of his other hand and dropped it to the floor.

Gio's eyes were dark, burning. Almost censorious. 'Do you know what you're doing, Valentina?'

Her voice sounded thick to her ears. 'I want you, Gio, that's all.'

Gio smiled and it was grim and hard. 'As long as that's all. I'd hate for there to be any confusion.'

Valentina's heart lurched but she forced herself to say, 'No, there's no confusion.'

Gio reached out and pulled her into his body and Valentina had to fight not to close her eyes at the way her body sang.

'You're right,' he said harshly. 'There's nothing but this.' And then his mouth was on hers and the confusion in Valentina's heart faded away to be replaced by heat.

Just over twenty-four hours later Valentina was standing in a private room in a state-of-the-art clinic in Naples listening to a consultant tell them about the operation which her father would undergo the next day. Her father was in bed, pale, and her mother was sitting by his side, looking worried but stoic, holding his hand tightly.

Gio stood in a corner of the room, arms crossed and face stern as he, too, listened. Dressed in chinos and a white shirt, he looked cool and crisp. And gorgeous, and *remote*.

Valentina's body ached minutely in very secret places. She trembled with awareness just to be this close to Gio. Her brain was still reeling from an overload of sensation and lack of sleep.

She darted Gio a quick glance now but he wasn't looking at her. His jaw was tight, impossibly stern. She felt conflicted, confused. From the moment she'd challenged him in his kitchen yesterday, something unspoken but profound had shifted between them.

She hadn't had time to dwell on it though—Gio had used his considerable skill and experience to render Valentina all but mute with pleasure.

When Valentina had woken late that morning, disorientated and more physically replete than she could have imagined possible, it had been to a cool and fully dressed Gio telling her, 'It's time to go. The plane is ready to take your parents to Naples.'

Valentina's attention came back into the room, guilt washing through her to think that Gio was distracting her even now, when her father's life was being discussed. She did her utmost to ignore him and her roiling emotions and concentrated on her parents.

When the consultant left the room and Valentina had made sure her mother was comfortable in the private room that had been set up for her beside her husband's, all courtesy of Gio, she left, feeling incredibly weary all of a sudden.

She was surprised to see Gio outside the clinic, not sure what she'd been expecting, but half expecting him to have left. Gio faced her now and held out what looked like a plastic hotel room key. 'It's to a suite in the Grand Plaza Hotel. It's not far from here.'

Valentina blanched. It was also one of the most expensive hotels in Italy. She started to protest but Gio took her hand and curled it almost painfully over the card and said curtly, 'I don't want to hear it, Valentina. Take the key and use it. You need to stay somewhere while you're here.'

Valentina reeled at the further evidence of this cool stranger. As if his silence on the journey over here hadn't confirmed that something was very wrong. Suddenly she didn't know where she stood any more; she was on shifting sands. This wasn't the same man who had been clutching her hair, thrusting so deep inside her just hours ago that she'd wept openly.

'I have to go back to Syracuse this evening. But I'll be back to see how the operation went tomorrow.'

Valentina crossed her arms tight against how badly she wanted to touch Gio, have him touch her. To have him explain this abrupt emotional withdrawal. But a deep and endless chasm seemed to exist between them now.

She fought to match his cool distance in a very belated bid to protect herself. 'You don't have to come back tomorrow, you're busy.'

In the same curt tone he replied, 'I'll be here.'

He gestured with a hand to where a driver stood by a car at the bottom of the clinic's steps. 'Dario will take you to the hotel and wherever you need to go. He's at your disposal while you're in Naples.'

'Gio…' Valentina began helplessly before stopping at the look on his face. She threw her hands up. 'Fine, all right.'

Gio stepped back. 'Till tomorrow.'

And then he was gone, down the steps and sliding into the back of his own car before it left the clinic car park and disappeared into the noisy fume-filled Naples traffic, and in that moment Valentina felt as if something very precious had just slipped through her fingers.

Less than an hour later Gio was watching the bright lights of Naples recede from beneath his small private Cessna plane. His gut ached. His whole body ached with a mixture of pleasure and pain. His hands were clenched to fists on his thighs and he had to consciously relax them. He smiled bleakly in recognition of the fact that he could relax them now because Valentina wasn't near enough to him to tempt him to touch her.

Standing on the steps of the clinic he'd had to battle not to pull her into him, bury his face in her hair, feel how those soft curves would fit into his body like missing pieces of a jigsaw.

He'd gorged himself on her for the past twenty-four hours. And it wasn't enough, it would never be enough. But it would have to be enough.

When she'd insisted on seeing where Mario had died, it had spelt the end of the affair to Gio as clearly as if it had been written on a board with indelible ink. When he'd left her standing in that garden, he'd been fully prepared for her return, and for her demand to leave straightaway.

But...she hadn't asked to leave. She'd asked to stay.

And yet it hadn't filled him with a sense of triumph. She'd said, *I want you, Gio, that's all.* And that had reminded him more succinctly than anything else of what was between them. And what *wasn't.* There wasn't even the anger any more.

Valentina had cut herself off from what had happened in the past between them, and she had no problem continuing the physical relationship with him because there was no emotional investment. That's why she hadn't reacted the way he'd anticipated to seeing where Mario had died. That's why she'd had no problem going to the *castello* in the first place.

Gio accepted a tumbler glass of brandy from the attentive air steward. He threw it back in one gulp and winced as the liquid turned to fire down his throat. He cursed himself for having thought for one weak moment that perhaps emotions were involved.

If anything, Valentina's emotions where Gio was concerned had become the worst possible of things: benign.

Soon, Valentina's desire would wane and she would look at Gio with nothing but pity. He'd already seen a flash of it when she'd asked about his house and why it wasn't furnished.

That would be the worst thing of all…to endure Valentina's pity for him. After everything, that was the one thing he wouldn't stand for.

The knowledge sat heavy in his gut. He'd always believed that he was empty inside, after years of contracting inwards to protect himself from his father's cruelty and his mother's ineffectualness. Mario had been the only one he'd trusted and allowed himself to love like a brother. *And Valentina*, a small voice mocked gently.

However, that capacity had died and withered with his friend. He'd believed he'd never love again. But he'd been wrong. The knowledge didn't precipitate joy within him—to discover that he hadn't lost that ability at all. Valentina Ferranti had the power now to tear him apart, there would be no recovery.

'I'm not gone yet.…'

'No, Papa, you're not.' Valentina smiled but it felt very precarious as tears burnt the backs of her eyelids. She could feel her mother's steadying hand on her shoulder. The operation had been a big success.

Much to her shame, she couldn't deny that her see-sawing emotions had just as much to do with the huge and silent presence of Gio standing a few feet away in the recovery room, as it had to do with the success of her father's operation.

He hadn't wanted to intrude but her father and mother had insisted on him coming in. Valentina could see her father flagging and immediately a nurse stepped in, saying briskly, 'That's enough for now. You'll have plenty of time to visit again tomorrow. He's going to be here for a while.'

Valentina allowed herself to be hustled out, sharing a quick kiss with her relieved mother, who was staying behind.

Once out in the corridor after Gio had made his goodbyes too, Valentina felt shy and awkward, not knowing how to navigate this new tension between them. It felt like aeons since she'd lain in bed with this man, arms clasped tight around him, her breasts crushed to his chest and her head nestled between his shoulder and neck while his fingers had trailed little fires up and down her spine.

The sense of peace she'd felt in that moment mocked her now.

'I—'

'You—'

They both spoke at the same moment and then stopped. Gio said tightly, 'You first.'

Valentina swallowed. 'I need to get back to Sicily. My mother needs some things from home, now that they're going to be here while my father recuperates.'

'I'm going back now. You can come with me on the plane. I'll arrange for your return when you need to come back.'

So sterile. Valentina shoved down the hurt and forced a smile. 'OK, thanks.' She indicated to the small holdall she held. 'I packed my things and checked out of the hotel just in case....'

Gio was already striding out of the clinic, issuing terse instructions into his phone, and Valentina struggled to catch up to him, a dart of anger piercing her insecurity. What had she been hoping for? She welcomed the anger because it had been a long time since she'd felt it for this man and it gave her the illusion that she still had a shred of control around him.

On the plane Gio made no effort to converse and stared out of his window in silence. The tension grew as the short flight wore on. Eventually Valentina couldn't take it any more and undid her seat belt, turning to face Gio's remote profile.

'Gio…' Her voice sounded unbearably husky.

She could see how his whole body tensed before he turned his head, a brow arched in polite enquiry. Valentina wanted to thump him.

Instead she drew up all her courage. 'Is there something…' She stopped and cursed. He was so damn intimidating like this.

'Is there something wrong? You've…barely said two words to me since…' She gulped and forged on. 'Since we left the *castello* the other morning.'

For a split second Valentina thought she saw something unbearably bleak flash in Gio's eyes but it was gone. She had to have imagined it.

Gio sighed audibly and Valentina felt a shiver of trepidation.

'I don't think we should see each other again.'

'You don't.' Valentina's entire body seemed to go hot and then cold all over. Icy cold.

'Do *you*?' That brow was raised again, like a polite enquiry. As if he wasn't experiencing the same nuclear fallout that seemed to be happening in her body. Valentina had to concentrate on what he'd asked and when she registered how he was looking at her so dispassionately, just waiting for an answer, she blurted out, *'No!'*

She flushed, 'I mean, yes…I think that's a good idea. After all…there's nothing…'

Valentina stopped; she was feeling very light-headed,

breathless. Pain was blooming in her chest and Gio was saying from somewhere distant, 'There is nothing. I think it's for the best. You have your job to get on with. After the Corretti Cup getting work should be the least of your worries. My aunt won't stand in your way again.'

Somehow Valentina thought she managed to get out something that sounded like, 'Yes…thank you…'

The previous couple of weeks flashed through her head, the way Gio had stepped into her life and so comprehensively turned it around. He'd felt obligated; he'd felt the yoke of history heavy around his neck. And he'd desired her. But it was all over now. Finished. Duty and obligation had been seen to and delivered. *There was nothing left.* A small voice mocked her—since when had she wanted anything else? Anything more?

Then the air steward was interrupting them and telling them they'd be landing in a few minutes. Blindly Valentina found her belt buckle and fastened it. The click seemed to reverberate around her head and she looked out the window as the familiar Sicilian landscape rushed up to meet them and kept telling herself, *Breathe, just keep breathing.*

Once the plane had landed and they were on the tarmac Gio turned to Valentina. A muscle ticked in his jaw. 'One of my assistants will take you to get your car at the racetrack. You can let him know when you wish to return to Naples and he'll arrange for your flight.'

Pride stiffened Valentina's spine and to her everlasting relief she felt strong enough to say, 'I can take a scheduled flight, Gio, you don't have to—'

He slashed a hand through the air, making her flinch minutely. And then he cursed softly. 'Just…don't argue, Valentina, please. Take my plane.'

Valentina felt like childishly stamping her foot and demanding why the hell he cared if she went by his plane or not when he clearly never wanted to lay eyes on her again. But just then his phone rang and he lifted it to his ear, not taking his eyes off Valentina, as if daring her to defy him. *'Pronto?'*

As Valentina watched she saw Gio's face turn ashen. He said faintly, 'I'll be right there.'

Impulsively she reached out a hand, scared. 'Gio, what is it?'

He was distracted, looking for his assistant, who came running before turning back to Valentina. 'It's Misfit, he's been taken ill.'

'Oh, Gio...' Her throat constricted and all anger drained away. 'Is there anything I can do?'

Gio stopped for a moment and looked at her, his assistant hovering nearby, and then he just said with chilling finality, 'No, there's nothing you can do. Goodbye, Valentina.'

And then he'd turned and was walking to his low sports car nearby. He swung into the vehicle and with a muted roar was gone. The assistant approached Valentina and took her small case out of numb fingers. 'Ms Ferranti? If you'd like to follow me?'

Two days later Valentina was returning on Gio's private plane to Sicily in the early evening. She'd delivered her mother's clothes and supplies from home. Her father was gaining strength every day and, in all honesty, Valentina knew she hadn't seen him look better in years. What Gio had done, with such effortless ease, had ensured a renewed lease of life to her parents that they could never have attained on their own.

Gio. Valentina felt numb when she thought of him. She still had to clear her things out of the accommodation at the racetrack but felt too weary to think about it straightaway. Her heart clenched when she remembered how ashen Gio had gone on hearing that Misfit was ill. For the first time Valentina realised fully how no one had been there for Gio after Mario died; Mario had been his only, closest friend. A friendship and trust that had been hard won, and which had encompassed her too, once.

When the plane landed Valentina went to her car which was parked in the car park. She sat in it for a long time before making a decision.

When she approached the closed and unfriendly looking gates of Gio's *castello* about thirty minutes later she cursed her impetuosity. A guard approached from an artfully hidden small Portakabin she hadn't noticed before.

'Can I help you?'

She took a deep breath. 'I'd like to see Signor Corretti, please.'

'Is he expecting you?'

Valentina stuttered, her bravado failing her, 'N-no, but if you tell him it's Valentina Ferranti…' *Then he'll tell them that he absolutely doesn't want to see you*, a voice mocked in her head.

Valentina shivered when the security guard disappeared again. She now had an inkling of what it would be like to be on the other side of Gio's affections, and just how much she'd taken his attention for granted.

A long minute later the guard returned and opened the gate saying, 'He's at the stables.'

'Thank you.' Valentina shifted her gears awkwardly as nerves suddenly gripped her. What was she doing here with some misguided notion that she could somehow comfort Gio when he might need it? *You didn't worry about his well-being seven years ago*, her inner conscience mocked her.

Valentina pushed down all the nerves and voices. She

owed Gio at least the courtesy of seeing how Misfit was doing. She knew how much the horse meant to him. She pulled up behind some other cars parked near the stable courtyard and got out.

Dusk was falling but she could see light spilling from the main stables and went towards it. When she entered it took a minute for her to see that Gio had his back to her. He was on his haunches at the entrance to one of the stalls. His back looked impossibly broad as it tapered down to those narrow hips. Hesitantly she went forward and wasn't prepared for when Gio's voice, sounding harsh and husky, said, 'What are you doing here, Valentina?'

CHAPTER TEN

'I…' THE WORDS FROZE in Valentina's throat as Gio stood up and turned around. He looked wild. Unshaven, bleary eyed. His hair was mussed up. He looked as if he hadn't been to bed since she'd last seen her.

She swallowed. 'I was concerned. I wanted to know how Misfit was doing.'

Gio wiped his hands with a towel and threw it down on the ground, then he stepped back and gestured with a hand. 'See for yourself, he's dying. The vet is coming back in an hour to administer the final shot to put him out of his misery.'

Valentina could feel the blood draining from her face. She moved closer to see the huge majestic horse lying on his side with his eyes closed. His whole body was sheened with sweat and his breaths were impossibly shallow.

Eyes huge, she looked at Gio and whispered, 'What happened?'

Gio's voice was sterile, clipped. 'A virus, a very rare virus. It gets into a horse's brain and induces paralysis among other things. The horse sinks into a coma and dies within a couple of days. There's no cure.'

'Gio…I'm so sorry.'

'Why? It's not your fault.'

Valentina winced when she was hurtled back in time

to the graveyard when she'd told Gio it was his fault that Mario had died. Never more than at this moment did she have a full understanding of the pain she'd caused with her grief and anger. Guilt, bitter and acrid, rose upwards.

'Gio…' Her throat ached. 'I'm so sorry…about everything.'

Gio looked at her, his eyes burning in his face. With that uncanny prescience that he seemed to have around her, he knew exactly what she meant. His grim smile did little to raise Valentina's spirits.

'Once…I wanted nothing more than to hear you say that. To know that you possibly didn't despise the very air I breathed.'

The ache in her throat got worse. Valentina shook her head. 'I don't despise…you, the air you breathe.'

'It's too late, Valentina.' He gestured towards his horse. 'Don't you see? It's all too late. Everything turns to dust in the end—it's all completely futile.'

Tears pricked Valentina's eyes now to see the bleak despair on Gio's face. 'No, Gio, it's not all futile, it's *not*. It's terrible that Misfit is dying and I wish he wasn't but he's had a wonderful life with you.'

Gio laughed curtly. 'Just like Mario had a wonderful life until it was snatched out of his hands.'

Valentina reached out a hand but Gio backed away, rigid with tension. He put his hands up as if to ward her off.

Slowly he lowered his hands back down. 'Do you know that I've slowly begun to believe that what happened that night wasn't all my fault? That it *was* just a tragic accident.'

He shook his head. 'We'd finished with the horses and were calling it a night. I still had plenty of time to get Mario home…but then he saw Black Star, loose in the paddock. Mario started to plead again, just for one attempt to ride him, to see if he could possibly have the magic touch....'

Valentina's heart was breaking in two in her chest. 'Gio...'

But he wasn't listening to her, or was ignoring her. 'I wasn't going to let him. I said no and walked to the stables with Misfit. When I got back outside, Mario was putting a saddle on Black Star...I could see the stallion was already edgy. I told Mario to leave it alone...but he wouldn't listen. He'd swung up onto his back before I could stop him, and Black Star went berserk. He jumped the paddock fence but his back leg got caught. Mario went down and Black Star landed on him, crushing him before I could get to him. The damned horse just got up and walked away, dragging Mario behind him until I could get to him and free him... but it was too late.'

Tears were streaming down Valentina's face now, silent sobs making her chest heave. She struggled for control. When she could speak she said thickly, 'You're right, it wasn't your fault...and I should never have—'

Gio put up a hand to stop her speaking. 'No. You had every right to be angry with me. I won't let you take that back now. Nothing can change the fact that it was my fault I had that horse here in the first place when it should have been put down months before....'

Valentina felt exposed and raw. More than anything she wanted to touch Gio...to comfort him. It was like an ache in her whole body. She remembered how cold he'd been when he'd told her it was over. No wonder he never wanted to see her again.

'You won't...' She took in a shuddering breath. 'You won't see me again if you don't want to. I'll stay out of your way.'

Gio just looked at her and Valentina wiped at a tear

on her cheek. And then quietly he said, 'You don't get it, do you?'

'Get what?' She frowned slightly.

Gio took a step closer and something about his intensity made Valentina take a step back. 'See, even now, you show how you really feel.'

'What are you talking about?'

Gio laughed curtly and looked up at the ceiling before looking back down again at Valentina. 'I'm in love with you. I love you so much and it's tearing me to pieces. What was purely physical for you was…*is* soul deep for me. I think I've loved you forever. When you were seventeen I had to pretend to like other girls to stop Mario suspecting that I was only interested in one girl—his sister.'

Gio ran a hand through his hair impatiently. '*Dio*, he would have killed me. *I* would have killed me if I'd been Mario.

'And you?' Gio posed a rhetorical question. 'I know you had a crush on me. I always felt your gaze on me. I noticed the way you'd blush whenever I looked at you.'

Shock was rendering Valentina mute. Her head was spinning. She felt weak and light-headed, like she wanted to sit down on something solid. She couldn't possibly believe Gio had just said he loved her. It was too fantastical, unbelievable.

Gio's mouth firmed; unmistakable pride lit his eyes, turning them green in the soft light. 'I know you don't feel anything for me—I never expected it. Anger and grief fuelled this madness between us.'

Valentina just looked at him, barely hearing his words. She could feel her heart expanding in her chest, as if it had already realised what he'd said and believed it. *Welcomed it.* For a second she saw something like hope in his eyes and her own heart beat faster in response.

She opened her mouth, not even sure what she was going to say, feeling the edges of incredible joy reach out to grab her. The moment hung suspended between them, but then just like that, the spectre of deeply ingrained fear and guilt rose up like a huge shadow to choke her. Memories: the shock of being told Mario was dead, the huge gaping hole left in the family. The excoriating grief and insecurity that had followed. The erosion of belief in anything good, solid, dependable. The awful chasm of loss.

That night in the hospital when for a moment— Valentina shut it down. She couldn't bear for him to see that in her eyes now. The guilt she still felt.

She was standing on the edge of that chasm of loss and pain all over again and she knew she wasn't brave enough to take the leap, to lay herself bare. Her heart spasmed once, painfully. She could feel it contracting in her chest, withering.

She closed her mouth and shook her head minutely in answer to some question that Gio hadn't even asked out loud. The flare of hope died in his eyes, and something died inside her.

Gio turned away from her and picked up the towel from the ground and walked back to the stall. Without turning around he just said, 'The vet is due here soon. Just go, Valentina. We're done.'

Valentina couldn't move though. She was rooted to the spot. She saw Gio's hands come up to the stall posts and grip them so tight that his knuckles shone white. 'Valentina, for the love of God, just…*go*.'

Finally, she could move and Valentina whirled around on the spot before rushing from the stables. Her throat was burning and her eyes were swimming. She almost knocked down the vet, who was just walking away from his car.

When she got into her car it took her an age to start it

up because her hands were shaking so much and when she drove out of Gio's *castello* she had to pull over into a layby where she doubled over with the grief and pain. As she wept and hugged her belly she told herself that this was better, this had to be better than loving and losing all over again, because if she loved and lost Gio…she'd never recover.

Three weeks later…

Valentina looked at herself in the cracked mirror of her tiny bathroom in Palermo. She was pale and wan, dark shadows under her eyes. And her eyes…they looked dead. Valiantly she pinched her cheeks as if that could restore some colour but it faded again just as quickly.

She felt empty and her body was one big ache of loss. She sighed deeply. This wasn't meant to be so painful. The choice she'd made when she'd stood in front of Gio three weeks before… Her mouth twisted at herself. It hadn't been a choice. It had been a deeply ingrained reflex action to protect herself. She was a coward. The worst kind of coward.

Gio. Valentina's hands tightened on the sink—just his name was causing a physical pain in her belly. She'd been terrified she'd see him yesterday when her parents had been brought to a private clinic in Palermo, so that her father could continue his convalescence closer to home.

But it hadn't been Gio who'd come to make sure everything was OK; it had been an assistant, the same assistant who had taken over informing Valentina what was happening. When Gio hadn't shown up, the mixture of relief and pain had been almost crippling.

Her mother had taken one look at her and pulled her aside. 'Valentina—'

And Valentina had cut her off, afraid that the maternal concern would undo her completely. 'Mama, please... don't.'

But her mother had ignored her and said gently, 'Valentina, talk to him. He deserves that much at least.'

Valentina stood up straight. Did Gio deserve that? Did he deserve to hear what she had to say? To hear the awful shameful secret she'd kept secret for so long? The secret her mother knew because she'd witnessed the moment when— Valentina bit her lip so hard that she tasted blood.

For the first time in weeks, Valentina felt a sense of purpose. She would tell Gio...everything. And then if he still wanted her to leave, she would go and perhaps one day this awful yawning ache in her heart would ease.

A couple of hours later Valentina pulled up in the staff car park of the Corretti racetrack. When she got out she asked someone if they knew where Gio was and they directed her to the training ground.

When she got there she could see Gio in the training enclosure. One or two people were gathered around, watching him at work.

The horse pranced skittishly but Gio held the reins firm and murmured low soothing words. Valentina felt weak, her eyes automatically devouring his tall broad form. He looked thinner, leaner. His hair looked messier, as if he hadn't cut it. The lines of his face were unbearably stark and she recalled his bleakness when Misfit had been dying. She recalled the flare of hope dying in his eyes.

She stopped a few feet away from the railing and as if sensing her presence he looked right at her and the air flew out of Valentina's lungs. It was like a punch to the gut and the thought reverberated in her head: *How on earth did I think I could live without this?*

Gio's eyes widened and his mouth opened. And then

everything seemed to happen in slow motion.… As he mouthed her name—*Valentina*—she heard the intense yapping of a dog and saw a flurry of movement to her right as someone burst into the enclosure, clearly chasing the small terrier dog who had no business being in this area.

People started shouting as the dog ran between the horse's feet, barking energetically. Gio's eyes were still on *her* though, with a kind of sick fascination, as the horse reared high and his front hoofs caught Gio on the chest, knocking him backwards. There was a sickening crunch as Gio's head hit off the railing behind him and then he was inert on the ground.

Valentina was unaware of moving; she was only aware of kneeling beside Gio's supine form and holding his head in her lap, his face deathly pale. She took one hand away from the back of his head and it was covered in blood.

She wondered who was screaming hysterically for an ambulance and only realised it was her when someone put a hand on her shoulder and said, 'It's here.'

CHAPTER ELEVEN

'He's as stable as can be. He was lucky that his skull wasn't fractured and that his ribs are just badly bruised. He'll be in a lot of pain for a couple of weeks.'

'OK, thank you.'

The doctor looked kindly at Valentina. 'You should go home and get cleaned up. The sedative will have knocked him out for a while.'

Valentina smiled but it felt brittle. 'I'm fine, I'd like to stay.' The doctor eventually shrugged and left the private Palermo hospital room. Valentina had asked them to call Gio's mother but they'd been told that she was away on a short trip. Yet another stark reminder of Gio's isolation which had made her heart bleed.

Valentina turned back to the man lying on the bed. He was covered by a sheet from the waist down, but he was naked from the waist up, with strapping around his chest where his ribs had been injured.

A white bandage was around his head and his face was still almost as white as the bandage. Valentina felt tears burn her eyes again and she went back to the chair beside the bed.

He looked so young and defenceless like this. Sniffling and wiping at the tears that just wouldn't stop, Valentina took Gio's nearest hand in hers. It was completely lifeless.

She bit back the surge of panic and reassured herself that the doctor had said he'd be fine.

A lock of hair had fallen down over the bandage on his forehead and Valentina reached up to push it back. The feel of the silky strands under her fingers made them tremble and she quickly clasped his hand again in both of hers.

Somehow with Gio here like this, not looking at her with that distant expression, it was easier to start talking....

'Gio,' she whispered, 'I know you can't hear me but I need to tell you something—a few things actually. And I know I'm being a coward when you can't hear me....

'The thing is, I don't know if I'm strong enough to tell you when you can look at me and see me for what I really am...and then watch you turn your back on me. I don't think...I could survive that.'

Valentina took in a deep shuddering breath and focused on his mouth. 'The thing is that I love you too. I've loved you for so long, Gio—far longer than I ever admitted it to myself.' Her voice dropped even lower. 'I remember being seventeen and wanting you so much, craving your attention and yet being scared witless of how you made me feel.'

Valentina smiled a watery smile. 'You and Mario together...you were so dynamic, full of life. He never could quite keep up with you but yet he never resented you for it. I think he felt accomplished enough in his own way, separate to you.

'There's something though that I have to tell you—to explain why I've been so angry with you. The evening Mario died...' Valentina stopped for a moment and then went on painfully. 'We got the phone call to say someone was injured, but not *who*. All we knew was that one of you was in trouble and that you were being transported to the hospital in Palermo....'

Valentina felt as if she were standing apart from herself, listening to the story too.

'When we got there, frantic, a doctor came to us and said, "We couldn't save him."' Valentina's hands tightened unconsciously on Gio's.

'The fact was that we still didn't know *who* had died. And I thought…' Valentina's voice broke slightly. 'I assumed that it had been you. The pain was indescribable. But then…I saw you. You were standing there, in the corridor, and the relief was so overwhelming…and then I suddenly realised what that meant. That Mario was dead, not you. And that my worst fear had been losing you, not my own brother.'

Valentina smiled wanly. 'You see, it was only when we saw you that we realised who was dead. My mother had seen my reaction. She *knew* and that merely compounded my own guilt and confusion, along with the pain of realising that it was Mario who was dead.'

She looked down at Gio's hand in hers. 'I've been so ashamed for so long…when I saw you at the funeral I lashed out, unable to bear the fact that you were making me remember that I'd have preferred my own brother to be dead, and he *was.*…

'When I saw you again at the wedding…it all came back. I thought I'd buried it. I thought I'd forgotten you… but I hadn't. And I still wanted you which made things even harder.

'When you told me you loved me, I couldn't believe it. The thought of saying those words back to you…of loving you and possibly losing you the way I'd lost Mario… It was too terrifying…it *is* terrifying. But not as terrifying as it was to see you lying on that ground today.'

Sobs rose upwards again and Valentina choked out, 'The past three weeks have been hell…but I thought that's what

I could live with for the rest of my life. I thought I could protect myself by leaving you…but I can't. I love you, Gio.'

Suddenly overwhelmed with all she'd said, Valentina went to take her hand out of Gio's but to her shock her hand was taken in a tight grip and a soft growl came from the man on the bed, 'Where do you think you're going?'

'Gio…' Valentina breathed out, her heart pumping.

His eyes flickered open slowly and he winced at the bright light for a few seconds before they came to rest on Valentina. Her breath caught in her throat. She was suddenly ridiculously aware of how deranged she must look after hours of crying and the panic-filled helicopter ride to the hospital.

'You have blood on your cheek.…' Gio let her hand go and lifted his to touch her cheek with a finger.

Valentina closed her eyes and prayed for control. 'I… must have got some of your blood on me.…' When his hand dropped again she tried to wipe at it ineffectually with the sleeve of her top.

Nervousness made her babble, and also not wanting to see Gio's reaction as to why she might be there. 'The doctor says you'll make a full recovery. Your ribs are bruised and you've got a nasty crack to the head but it's not fractured.'

Just saying the words though was bringing it all back and Valentina struggled to hold back the tears of emotion.

'I don't give a damn about that.' Gio's eyes were very dark all of a sudden, and alert and intent, on Valentina.

'You don't?'

'No.' He shook his head and then winced minutely when it obviously caused him pain. He opened his eyes again and found and took Valentina's hand in a tight grip. 'What I want to know is did I really just hear you say you love me, and all that other stuff, or was I dreaming?'

Blood was rushing to her head and Valentina whispered, 'How much other stuff did you…think you heard?'

'Everything…I think…' Gio said grimly.

Hesitant, Valentina said, 'About Mario and the hospital?'

'Yes, dammit… Valentina…'

Valentina gripped Gio's hand back and closed her eyes as if that could help. Not to see Gio's face when she said this. 'It wasn't a dream. You heard it, and I meant every word.'

There was silence and after long seconds Valentina opened her eyes again to see Gio with his head back on his pillow and a smile playing around his mouth. 'You love me….'

Feeling slightly disgruntled at his easy insouciance when Valentina felt as if she'd just been pulled from a train wreck she said curtly, 'Yes, I do.'

Gio's smile faded then to be replaced by something more serious. His hand moved up her arm and he said, 'Come here, I need to touch you.'

'But your ribs—your head…I'll hurt you.'

Gio shook his head, this time more gingerly. 'You could never hurt me as much as you did when you walked away after I told you I loved you.'

Fresh tears pricked Valentina's eyes and Gio's hand tightened on her arm. 'But I'll forgive you everything if you just come here right now.'

Carefully Valentina stood up and perched on the side of the bed. Gio's voice was husky. 'Closer.'

Giving in, Valentina kicked off her sneakers and came down full length beside him and tried to ignore his painful intake of breath when he lifted his arm to move it around her so that she was cocooned against him, her head in his shoulder, her hand resting on his abdomen, below the strapping. She felt herself relaxing into his hard form, her curves melting into his body.

She felt him draw a breath into his chest and he said in a carefully neutral voice, 'Why did you decide you wanted to stay at the *castello* after seeing the garden, where Mario died?'

Valentina lifted her head to look at Gio. She remembered the excruciating way he'd shut her out—how ready he'd been for her to flee, because he'd obviously expected her to be upset. She could see now how he might have misread her reaction.

She willed him to believe her, to understand. 'When I saw the garden...and walked the labyrinth, I didn't feel as if Mario was there, or I did...but in a very peaceful way. He always loved visiting you at the *castello* so much. He was so proud of your achievement. I just...I felt happy there, secure. That's why I wanted to stay.'

Gio's arm tightened around her and his eyes looked suspiciously bright for a moment. He sounded gruff. 'I thought...I thought it meant that you'd divorced yourself so much from your emotions around me and what had happened that you just didn't care enough to leave.'

Valentina shook her head. 'Never...my emotions are very much intact.'

Gio touched her chin and jaw with his other hand as reverently as if she were made of china and Valentina felt a profound peace steal over her.

Gio smiled. 'You know what this means, of course?'

'What?'

Gio's eyes glowed dark green with emotion. 'Kiss me first,' he said throatily. Carefully Valentina reached up and pressed her lips to his. Despite the delicacy of Gio's injuries, she could feel his arm tighten around her as the inevitable spark lit between them.

Groaning softly Gio pulled back. Colour was in his cheeks now, replacing that deathly pallor, and Valentina touched his jaw with her hand, her fingers tracing his mouth. Gio kissed her fingers. 'What it means is that you're going to marry me and we're going to live happily ever after....'

Valentina's hand stilled and her eyes widened on his. Giddiness rushed through her entire body but along with it came a tendril of trepidation and she bit her lip. She whispered, 'I'm scared, Gio...I think I'm scared to feel this happy....'

Gio pulled her closer. 'We have love—as long as we have love, there's no need to fear anything.'

'Love..' Valentina smiled tremulously. 'We definitely have love.'

Two years later...

Valentina felt the baby kicking in her belly and automatically put her hand there. She smiled when she sensed a presence and a much larger hand came over hers and an arm snaked around her distended midriff to cup her close to his body. *Gio.* Even now, tremors of awareness went through her especially when she could feel him hardening against her bottom.

One of his hands came up to cup one very full and sensitive breast and her blood got even hotter. Valentina blushed and whirled around within Gio's arms, dislodging his questing hand, and looked up with mock outrage. 'Do you really think your guests have paid to see you mauling your heavily pregnant wife?'

Unnoticed in the background the crowd were going wild as the annual Corretti Cup race was drawing to an exciting finish. Neither Gio or Valentina gave two hoots right then if a unicorn suddenly appeared and won the race instead of the hotly tipped favourite, who was, of course, one of Gio's horses.

Gio smiled lazily, his hand coming back up to cup her breast again, this time kneading it gently so that Valentina couldn't help but moan softly.

'You seemed to enjoy being *mauled* in bed this morning very much if I recall.'

'You're insatiable, Signor Corretti. I'm merely doing my wifely duty to keep you happy.' She smiled prettily and he threw back his head and laughed out loud, infusing Valentina with a bone-deep sense of contentment to hear him sound so happy.

Just then she spotted something out of the corner of her eye and said with happy resignation, 'I think it's time to rescue my parents. Maria's looking suspiciously overexcited and tired which spells trouble.'

Gio turned to follow his wife's gaze and smiled indulgently when he saw his fifteen-month-old daughter squirming to be free of her doting grandparents' embrace. She was trouble, all right, more than taking after her late uncle Mario with her mop of dark brown curls and mischievous eyes.

Gio turned back to Valentina and looked down, his heart swelling with love. Her pregnant belly pressed against him and he felt full up…with love and contentment and peace— for the first time in his life, *peace*.

'We'll rescue them in a minute, but first…'

He didn't even need to say it. Valentina lifted her mouth to his, wound her arms around his neck and they kissed as if for the first time all over again while the crowd went wild behind them, the favourite horse striding easily home to victory.

* * * * *

AN INHERITANCE
OF SHAME

KATE HEWITT

To Gabri – thanks for all your help with Italian phrases. I don't know what I'd do without you! Love, K.

CHAPTER ONE

It was his. All his. *Almost* his, for tomorrow he had an appointment to sign the papers transferring the ownership of the Corretti Hotel Palermo from Corretti Enterprises to Corretti International. Angelo Corretti's mouth twisted at the irony. From one Corretti to another. Or not.

Slowly he strolled through the hotel lobby, watching the bellhops catch sight of him, their eyes widening before they straightened to attention. A middle-aged woman at the concierge desk eyed him apprehensively, clearly waiting to spring into action if summoned. He hadn't been formally introduced to any of the hotel staff, but he had no doubt they knew who he was. He'd been in and out of the Corretti offices for nearly a week, arranging meetings with the major shareholders who had no choice but to hand over the reins of the flagship hotel in view of their CEO's absence and Angelo's controlling shares.

It had, in the end, all been so gloriously simple. Leave the Correttis alone for a little while and they'd tear themselves apart. They just couldn't help it.

'Sir? Signor...Corretti?' The concierge finally approached him, her heels clicking across the marble floor of the soaring foyer. Angelo heard how she stumbled over his name, because of course everyone knew the

Correttis here, and in all of Sicily. They were the most powerful and scandalous family in southern Italy. And he wasn't one of them.

Except he was.

He felt his mouth twist downwards as that all too familiar and futile rage coursed through him. He was one of them, but he had never—and never would be— acknowledged as one, even if everyone knew the truth of his birth. Even if everyone in the village he'd grown up in, from the time he was a little boy and barely understood it himself, had known he was Carlo Corretti's bastard and made his life hell because of it.

He turned to the concierge, forcing his mouth upwards into a smile. 'Yes?'

'Is there anything I can do for you?' she asked, and he saw the uncertainty in her eyes, the fear that he'd come in here and sweep it all clean. And part of him was tempted to do just that. Every single person who worked here had been loyal to the family he despised and was determined to ruin. Why shouldn't he fire them all, bring in his own people?

'No, thank you, Natalia.' He'd glanced at her discreet, silver-plated name tag before meeting her worried gaze with a faint smile. 'I'll just go to my room.' He'd booked the penthouse suite for tonight, intending to savour staying in the best room of his enemy's best hotel. The room he knew for a fact was reserved almost exclusively for Matteo Corretti's use, except since the debacle of the called-off Corretti/Battaglia wedding, Matteo was nowhere to be seen. He wouldn't be using the suite even if he could, which from tomorrow he couldn't.

No Corretti, save for himself, would ever stay in this hotel again.

'Certainly, Signor Corretti.' She spoke his name more

surely now, but it felt like a hollow victory. He'd always been a Corretti, had claimed the name for his own even though the man who had fathered him had never admitted to it or him. Even though using that name had earned him more black eyes and bloody noses than he cared to remember. It was his, damn it, and he'd earned it.

He'd earned all of this.

With one last cool smile for the concierge, he turned towards the bank of gleaming lifts and pressed the button for the penthouse. It was nearly midnight, and the foyer was deserted except for a skeleton staff. The streets outside one of Palermo's busiest squares had emptied out, and Angelo hadn't seen anyone on his walk here from his temporary offices a few blocks away.

Yet as he soared upwards towards the hotel's top floor and its glittering, panoramic view of the city and harbour, Angelo knew he was too wired and restless to sleep. Sleep, at the best times, had always been difficult; he often only caught two or three hours in a night, and that not always consecutively. The rest of the time he worked or exercised, anything to keep his body and brain moving, doing.

The doors opened directly into the suite that covered the entire top floor. Angelo stepped inside, his narrowed gaze taking in all the luxurious details: the marble floor, the crystal chandelier, the expensive antiques and art. The lights had been turned down and he glimpsed a wide king-size bed in the suite's master bedroom, the navy silk duvet turned down to reveal the six hundred thread count sheets underneath.

He dropped his key card onto a side table and loosened his tie, shed his jacket. He felt the beginnings of a headache, the throbbing at his temples telling him he'd be facing a migraine in a couple of hours. Migraines and

insomnia were just two of the prices he'd had to pay for
how hard he'd worked, how much he'd achieved, and he
paid them willingly. He'd pay just about anything to be
where he was, who he was. Successful, powerful, with
the ability to pull the sumptuous rug out from under the
Correttis' feet.

He strolled through the suite, the lights of the city visible and glittering from the floor-to-ceiling windows. The
living area was elegant if a bit too stuffy for his taste,
with some fussy little chairs and tables, a few ridiculous-
looking urns. He'd have a refit of the whole hotel first
thing, he decided as he plucked a grape from the bowl
of fresh fruit on the coffee table, another fussy piece of
furniture, with fluted, gold-leaf edges. He'd bring this
place up to date, modern and cutting edge. It had been
relying on the distinctly tattered Corretti name and a
faded elegance for far too long.

Restless, his head starting to really pound, he continued to prowl through the suite, knowing he wouldn't
be able to sleep yet unwilling to sit down and work.
This was the eve of his victory after all. He should be
celebrating.

Unfortunately he had no one to celebrate with in this
town. He hadn't made any friends here in the eighteen
years he'd called Sicily home, only enemies.

You made one friend.

The thought slid into his mind, surprising and sweet,
and he stilled his restless pacing of the suite's living area.

Lucia. He tried not to think of her, because thinking
of her was remembering and remembering made him
wonder. Wish. *Regret.*

And he never regretted anything. He wouldn't regret
the one night he'd spent in her arms, burying himself

so deep inside her he'd almost forgotten who he was—and who he wasn't.

For a few blissful hours Lucia Anturri, the neighbour's daughter he'd ignored and appreciated in turns, with the startling blue eyes that mirrored her heart, had made him forget all the anger and pain and emptiness he'd ever felt.

And then he'd slipped away from her while she was sleeping and gone back to his life in New York, to the man of purpose and determination and anger that he'd always be, because damn it, he didn't *want* to forget.

Not even for one night.

Even more restless now, that old anger surging through him, Angelo jerked open the buttons of his shirt. He'd take a long, hot shower. Sometimes that helped with the headaches, and at least it was something to do.

He was in the process of shedding his shirt as he came into the bedroom and to an abrupt halt. A bucket of ice with a bottle of champagne chilling inside was by the bed—and so was a woman.

Lucia froze at the sight of the half-dressed man in front of her, three freshly laundered towels pressed to her hard-beating heart.

Angelo.

She knew, had always known, that she would see him again, and occasionally she'd embroidered ridiculous, romantic fantasies about how it would happen. Stupid, schoolgirl dreams. She hadn't done that for years though, and she'd never imagined this.

Running into him without a second's notice, totally unprepared—

She'd heard whispers that he was back in Sicily but

she had assumed they were, as they'd always been, mere rumours, and she'd never expected to see him here.

From just one shocked glimpse of him standing there, his hair rumpled and his shirt half undone, she knew he didn't recognise her. Meanwhile in the space of a few seconds she was reliving every glorious and agonising moment she'd spent with him that one night seven years ago, the feel of his satiny skin, the desperate press of his lips against hers.

Such thoughts were clearly the furthest from his mind. His eyes had narrowed, his lips thinned, and he looked angry. She recognised that look, for God knew she'd seen it enough over the fraught years of their childhood. Yet even angry he was beautiful, the most beautiful man she'd ever known.

Known and loved.

Swallowing, she pushed that most unhelpful thought away. She hadn't seen Angelo in seven years. She didn't love him any more, and she absolutely knew he'd never loved her.

Which, of course, shouldn't hurt all this time later, yet in that unguarded moment as she stared at him, his shirt hanging open to reveal the taut, golden expanse of his chest, she knew it did.

Angelo arched an eyebrow, obviously annoyed, clearly waiting. For what? An apology? Did he expect her to do the little chambermaid stammering act and scurry away?

Two desires, both deep-seated, warred within her. On one hand she felt like telling Angelo Corretti exactly what she thought of him for sneaking out of her bed seven years ago. Except she didn't even know what that was, because she thought of Angelo in so many ways. Desire and despair. Hope and hatred. Love and loss.

In any case, the far more sensible impulse she had was

to leave this room before he recognised her, before any awful, awkward reunion scenarios could play out. They may have been childhood friends, he may have been her first and only lover, but she was next to nothing to him, and always had been—a shaming fact she did not need reminding of tonight.

'I'm sorry,' she said, lowering her head just a little so her hair fell in front of her face. 'I was just getting your room ready for the night. I'll be out of your way.'

She started to move past him, her head still lowered, hating the ache this simple, terrible exchange opened up inside her. It was an ache she'd had for so long that she'd become numb to it, learned to live with it the way you might a missing limb or a permanent scar. Yet now, in Angelo's uncaring presence, she felt it throb painfully to life and for a second, furious with herself, she had to blink back tears.

She was just about to slip past him when his hand curled around her arm, jolting her so hard and deep she almost stumbled.

'Wait.'

She stilled, her heart hammering, her breath caught in her chest. Angelo let go of her arm and walked towards the bed.

'I'm celebrating, you know,' he said, but he didn't sound like he was. He sounded as sardonic and cynical as he'd ever been. Lucia tensed, her back to him, her face angled away. He still didn't recognise her, and that realisation gave her equal parts relief and deep disappointment.

'Why don't you celebrate with me,' he continued, clearly a command, and she stiffened. Was this what he'd become? The kind of man who solicited the housekeeping? 'Just a drink,' he clarified, and now he sounded coolly amused as he popped the cork on the complimentary bottle of champagne that always came with the penthouse suite. 'Since nobody else is here.'

Lucia turned around slowly, her whole body rigid. She had no idea how to act. What to say. This had gone on way too long for her to keep pretending she was a stranger, and yet—

Maybe that's what she was to him now. A stranger.

He was pouring the champagne into two crystal flutes, his mouth twisted downwards, and something in the shuttered bleakness of his expression called to that ache deep inside her, the ache she'd been trying so hard and for so long to ignore. When he looked like that it reminded her of when he'd shown up on her doorstep seven years ago, when he'd stared at her so bleakly, so blankly, and his voice had broken as he'd confessed, *'He's dead, Lucia. And I don't feel anything.'*

She hadn't thought then; she'd just drawn him inside by the hand, led him to the shabby little living room of the house she'd grown up in and where she then lived alone.

And started something—a single night—that had changed her life for ever.

She swallowed now, forced herself to lift her chin and look him in the eye. She saw him tense, *felt* it, one hand still outstretched, a flute of fizzing champagne clasped between his long, lean fingers.

'All right, Angelo,' she said, and thankfully her voice remained steady. 'I'll have a drink with you.'

Angelo stood completely motionless, his hand still outstretched. The only sound in the room was the gentle fizz of the champagne's bubbles popping against the sides of the crystal flute and his own suddenly ragged breathing.

Lucia.

How could he not have recognised her? How could he have not known her from the moment he'd seen her in his suite? The first thought that seared his brain now was the completely irrelevant realisation of how *blue* her eyes were, so startling against her dark hair and olive skin. How wide and clear and open they'd always been, open to him.

Then chasing the heels of that poignant memory was a far more bitter realisation—and with it a dawning fury.

'You work for them? Those *sciacalli*?'

Her chin tilted up a notch and those blue, blue eyes flashed even bluer. 'If you mean am I employed at this hotel, then the answer is yes.'

Another thing he'd forgotten: the low, husky timbre of her voice, sounding sensual and smoky and still so tender and sweet. He had a sudden, painfully clear recollection of her asking him in that same low voice what he'd expected to feel that night, the night of his father's funeral, what he'd wanted to feel. He'd answered in a ragged gulp that just stopped short of a sob, *'Satisfaction. Happiness. Something. I just feel empty.'*

She hadn't replied, just put her arms around him, and he'd turned into her embrace, burying his head in the sweet curve of her neck before his lips had found hers, seeking and needing the total acceptance and understanding she'd always so freely given.

And now she worked for the Correttis? The family who had made his childhood a living hell? He shook his head slowly, his head throbbing so hard his vision blurred. 'So what, you're on your knees for them? Scrubbing their filth, bobbing a curtsey when they come by? What happened to your promise, Lucia?'

'My promise,' she repeated, her voice completely expressionless.

He pressed one fist against his temple, closed his eyes briefly against the pain that thundered in his head—and in his heart. 'Do you not even remember? You promised me you'd never even talk to them—'

'As a matter of fact, Angelo, I don't talk to them. I'm a chambermaid, one of dozens. They don't even know my name.'

'So that excuses—'

'Do you really want to talk about excuses?' she asked levelly, and he opened his eyes, pressed his fist harder against his temple. Damn it, his head hurt. And even in the midst of his shock and pain he recognised how ridiculous he was being. She'd made those silly promises when she was a child, a girl of no more than eleven or twelve. He remembered the moment, stupidly. He'd been jumped on his way back to school, beaten bloody but he'd come up swinging as always. She'd been waiting on her doorstep, her heart in her eyes. She'd tried to comfort him, and in his hurt pride and anger he'd shrugged her off.

But she kept trying—she'd always kept *trying*—and he'd let her press an ice pack to his eye and wipe the blood away. He'd caught her looking at him, her eyes so wide and serious, and he'd grabbed her wrist and demanded roughly, *'Promise. Promise you'll never speak to them, or like them, or even work for them—'*

She'd blinked once, twice, and then answered in a voice that was low and husky even then. *'I promise.'*

No, he didn't want to talk about excuses now. He knew he didn't have any. Seven years since he'd left her in bed and he still felt that needling pinprick of guilt when he allowed himself to feel it—or anything.

Not that he'd allowed himself to think of her often.

By eight o'clock the morning after they'd slept together he'd already been on a plane back to New York, having resolutely shoved her out of his mind.

And now she was back, and the memories cascaded over him, a tidal wave of unexpected emotion he had no desire to feel.

He shut his eyes again, his fist still pressed to his temple.

'You're getting a migraine, aren't you,' she said quietly, and he opened his eyes, dropped his hand. He'd used to get headaches even as a child, and she'd given him aspirin, rubbed his temples when he'd let her.

'It doesn't matter.'

'What doesn't matter? That you have a headache, or that I work for the Correttis?'

'You don't work for them any more.'

Her eyes widened for one fraught second and he knew she thought he was firing her. 'I own the hotel now,' he explained flatly, and he heard her slight indrawn breath.

'Congratulations,' she said after a tiny pause, and he couldn't tell a thing from her tone. She seemed so different now, so calm and controlled, so *cold*. So unlike the warm, generous person she'd been, giving him her body and maybe even her heart in the course of a single night—

No, not her heart. Long ago he'd wondered briefly if she had romanticised their one encounter, thought she might have because of their shared history. He'd worried that she might have expected more from him, things he knew he wasn't capable of, couldn't give.

Looking at her impassive face now he knew any uneasy concerns he had once had were completely unfounded, and he wasn't even surprised. Of course Lucia had moved on.

'Do you have any tablets?' she asked calmly, and the pain was bad enough that he answered her.

'In my wash kit, in my bag.'

She slipped past him, and he inhaled her scent as she went by. He sank onto the edge of the bed, the flute of champagne still dangling from his fingers. Distantly over the pounding in his brain he heard her moving about, unzipping his suitcase.

A few minutes later she came back in and knelt by his side. 'Let me take this,' she said, and plucked the champagne from his fingers. 'And give you this.' She handed him a glass of water and two tablets. 'I checked the dosage. It said two?'

He nodded, and he felt her hand wrap around his as she guided the glass to his lips. Even through the pain pounding in his head he felt a spark of awareness blaze from his fingers all the way to his groin. He remembered how sweet and yielding she'd been in his arms, without even so much as a word spoken between them. But then Lucia had always been sweet and yielding, always been willing to take care of him, even when he'd pushed her away again and again.

Clearly she'd changed, for she pulled her hand away from his, and he stamped down on that spark.

'Thank you,' he said gruffly. They may have shared one desperate, passionate night, but he knew there was nothing between them now. There couldn't be.

Lucia sat back on her heels and watched Angelo struggle with himself, as he so often did. Feeling weak and hating to show it. And her, wanting to help him and hating how he always pushed her away. The story of both of their lives.

A story she was done with, she told herself now. Seeing Angelo again might have opened up that ache inside her, but she wasn't going to do anything about it. She wasn't going to be stupid about it, even though part of her, just as before, as always, yearned towards him and whatever little he could give.

No. He'd wrecked her before, and broken not just her heart but her whole self. Shattered her into pieces, and she wouldn't allow even a hairline crack to appear now. It had taken years to put herself together again, to feel strong if not actually ever complete.

She rose, picking up the towels she'd dropped when she'd gone for his pills. 'Will you be all right?' she said, making it not so much a question as a statement.

'I'm fine,' he said, the words a growl, and she knew he was already regretting that little display of vulnerability.

'Then I'll leave you to it,' she said, and Angelo didn't answer. She took a few steps and then stopped, her back to him, one hand on the doorframe, suddenly unwilling to go so simply. So easily. Words bubbled up, bottled in her throat. Words that threatened to spill out of the hurt and pain she felt even now, so many years later. The pain and hurt she didn't want him to see, because if he saw it he'd know how much she'd cared. How weak she'd been—and still was.

She swallowed it all down, those words and worse ones, broken, wounded words about a grief so very deep and raw that he knew nothing about. She couldn't tell him tonight.

Maybe she wouldn't ever tell him. Did he really need to know? Wouldn't it be better to simply move on, or at least to let him think she had moved on?

'Lucia?' Angelo said, and it was a question although

what he was asking she didn't know. *What do you want? Why are you still here?*

'I'm going,' she said, and then she forced herself to walk out of the suite without looking back.

CHAPTER TWO

ANGELO FINGERED THE typewritten list of the hotel's employees that lay on his desk. Matteo's desk, because there
had been no time to change anything since signing the
papers on the hotel this morning. He'd gone directly from
the meeting of unhappy shareholders to here, sweeping
into his rival's office and claiming it as his own.

His mouth twisted as he glanced at the tabloid headline he'd left up on his laptop. Not that he actually read
those rags, but this one blazed bad news about the Correttis. Alessandro Corretti was meant to have wed Alessia Battaglia, but she'd run off with his cousin Matteo at
the very last second. Angelo smiled grimly. The chaos
that had ensued was devastating for his half-brothers
and cousins, but good news for him.

With Matteo out of the way and the other Correttis
scrambling to make sense of the chaos, he could saun-
ter in and take another slice of the Corretti pie, starting
with the docklands regeneration. Antonio Battaglia, the
Minister of Trade and Housing as well as Alessia's father, would be all too willing to consider his bid, since
he was already funding a housing project in the area.
Angelo had made initial overtures, and planned to ce-
ment the deal this week.

He glanced back at the list of employees. *Anturri,*

Lucia was the first name under the housekeeping section. As soon as he'd arrived back at the hotel he'd pulled up the employee files and seen that Lucia had been working here for seven years, the entire length of time since he'd last seen her.

Why did that hurt?

No, it didn't hurt. Annoyed him, perhaps. From his bed to making the Correttis'. Had she had a moment's pause, a second's worth of regret, before she took a job working for the family he hated, the family who had rejected him even as his association with them had defined and nearly destroyed his life?

Or had she just not cared?

Yet Lucia had *always* cared. She'd always been there when they were children, waiting for him to come home, ready to bathe his cuts or just make him smile with a stupid story or joke. More often than not he'd pushed her away, too angry to accept her offers of friendship. *Mi cucciola*, he'd called her. My puppy. An endearment but also a barb because she *had* been like a puppy, dogging his heels, pleading for a pat on the head. Sometimes he'd given it, sometimes he'd ignored her and sometimes he'd sent her away.

Yet still she'd come back, her heart in her eyes just like it had been the night he'd shown up at her door, too numb to feel anything except the sudden, desperate passion she'd awoken in him when she'd taken him in her arms.

Guilt needled him again as he thought of that night, how he'd slipped from her bed before dawn without a single word of farewell. He should have said goodbye, at least. Considering their history, their shared childhood, she'd deserved that much. Even if it didn't seem like it mattered to her any more. It mattered, annoyingly, to him.

He stood up, pacing the spacious confines of the office with his usual restlessness. He should be feeling victorious now, savagely satisfied, but he only felt uneasy, restless, the remnants of his migraine mocking him.

He'd spent another sleepless night battling memories as well as his migraine. For seven years he'd schooled himself not to think of that night, to act as if it hadn't happened. Yet last night in the throes of pain he'd been weak, and he'd remembered.

Remembered the sweet slide of her lips against his, the way she'd drawn him to herself, curling around him, *accepting* him in a way he'd never been before or since. How he'd felt tears spring to his eyes when he'd joined his body with hers, how absolutely right and whole that moment had felt.

Idiotic. He was *not* a romantic, and a single encounter—poignant as it may have been—didn't mean anything. It obviously hadn't meant anything to Lucia, who had seemed completely unmoved by his appearance last night. And if *Lucia*, who had hero-worshipped him as a child, could be indifferent and even cold towards him now, than surely he could act the same. Feel the same.

In any case he had too many other things to accomplish to waste even a second on Lucia Anturri or what had happened between them. Nothing would happen between them now. He'd come back to Sicily for one purpose only: to ruin the Correttis. To finally have his revenge.

Determinedly Angelo pulled the phone towards him. It was time to call Antonio Battaglia, and start carving up that Corretti pie.

* * *

Lucia felt the throb in her temples and wondered if headaches could be contagious. She'd had one since she'd left Angelo in the penthouse suite last night, and spent a sleepless night trying *not* to remember their one night together.

Yet far worse than the pain in her head was the ache seeing Angelo had opened up in her heart. No tablet or pill would help that. Swallowing hard, she pushed the trolley of fresh linens and cleaning supplies down the corridor. She had to finish all the third-floor rooms by lunchtime. She had to forget about Angelo.

How can you forget him when you haven't told him?

Last night, she knew, hadn't been the right time. She'd even half convinced herself that he need never know the consequence of their one night together. What point was there, really, in raking up the past? It wouldn't change things. It wouldn't change him.

And yet Lucia knew if the positions had been somehow reversed she would want to know. Yet could she really assume that Angelo would feel the same? And if she did tell him, and he shrugged it off as irrelevant, wouldn't that break her heart all over again? Just one brief conversation with him last night and already she felt it starting to splinter.

She was almost finished the third floor, her head and heart both aching, when she heard the muffled sobs coming from the supply room at the end of the hall. Frowning, Lucia pushed open the door and her heart twisted at the sight inside the little room stacked with towels and industrial-size bottles of cleaner.

'Maria.'

Maria Dibona, another chambermaid, looked up at her with tear-streaked eyes. *'Scusi, scusi,'* she said, wiping at her eyes. Lucia reached for a box of tissues used to supply the hotel bathrooms and handed her one. 'Is it Stefano?'

Maria nodded. Lucia knew her son had left Sicily for a life in Naples, and his sudden defection had broken his mother's heart.

'I'm sorry, Maria.' She put her arm around the older woman. 'Have you been in touch?'

'He hasn't even called.' Maria pressed the tissue to her eyes. 'How is a mother to live, not knowing if her son is healthy or not? Alive or not?'

'He will call,' Lucia murmured. 'He loves you, you know. Even if he doesn't always show it.' She meant the words for Maria, yet she felt their mocking echo in herself. Hadn't she told herself the same thing after Angelo had left? Hadn't she tried to convince herself that he would call or write, *reach* her, even as the heaviness in her heart told her otherwise?

When she'd rolled over and seen the smooth expanse of empty sheet next to her she'd known Angelo wasn't coming back. Wasn't writing, calling or keeping in touch in any way…no matter how desperately she tried to believe otherwise.

Maria blew her nose. 'He was such a good boy. Why did he have to leave?'

Lucia just shook her head and squeezed the woman's shoulders. She had no answers, no real comfort to give besides her own understanding and sympathy. She'd lived too long and experienced too much heartache to offer anyone pat answers. There were none.

She heard the sound of someone striding down the hall, someone walking with purpose and determination. Instinctively she stiffened, and then shock iced through as an all too familiar face appeared around the door of the little supply cupboard.

'Lucia.'

She straightened and Maria lurched upright, dabbing her face frantically. '*Scusi, scusi*, Signor Corretti…'

Angelo waved a hand in quick dismissal of the other woman. His grey-green eyes blazed into Lucia's. 'I need to speak with you.'

'Very well.' Lucia hid her trembling hands in her apron. She hadn't expected to see him again so soon, or even at all. She had no idea what he intended to say, but she knew she wasn't ready for the conversation.

'In my office.' Angelo turned away, and Lucia glanced back at Maria, whose eyes had rounded in surprise. Maria was no gossip, but Lucia knew the news would still spread. Angelo Corretti had summoned her to his office for a private conversation. All the old memories and rumours would be raked up.

Closing her eyes briefly, she followed Angelo out into the corridor. They didn't speak as they stepped into a lift that took them to the second-to-top floor that housed the hotel's corporate offices, yet Lucia was all too achingly aware of the man next to her, the suppressed tension in every taut line of his lean body, the anger apparent in the tightness of his square jaw. She tried not to look at him, because if she looked at him she'd drink him in and she knew her need and want would be visible in her eyes, all too obvious to him.

Still. Still she felt that welling up of longing for him, a hopeless yearning that had her almost swaying towards him. It infuriated her, that her body and even her heart could want a man who had so little regard for her. At least her mind was strong. She straightened, lifted her chin. Angelo would never know how much he'd hurt her.

The lift doors pinged open and Lucia felt her cheeks warm as Angelo strode past a receptionist whose jaw dropped when she saw Lucia in her standard grey maid's uniform, complete with frilly apron and ridiculous cap, follow him into his office like a scolded schoolgirl…or a summoned mistress.

No, she wouldn't think like that. Couldn't, even if everyone else would. Again.

Angelo strode towards the floor-to-ceiling windows with a view of Palermo's harbour, one hand braced against the glass, his back to her. Lucia waited, her heart pounding even as her hungry gaze swept over him, the long, muscular stretch of back, the narrow hips, the powerful legs. The elegant, expensive suit that reminded her just how out of her league he was now.

Angelo swung around suddenly to face her, his eyes narrowed. 'Why did you start working at this hotel?'

Lucia blinked. 'Because I needed a job.'

'Surely you could have found a suitable position somewhere else.'

She drew herself up even though she felt like curling into a protective ball, hiding her hurts. How could he be angry about her *job*? 'Are you still angry that I broke my promise, Angelo?' she asked, an edge to her voice. 'That seems rather hypocritical.'

'I didn't make any promises,' he said flatly, and she drew in one short, sharp breath. Felt the truth of his words cut her as if he were wielding a sword.

'I know that.'

'So why did you?'

She gritted her teeth, forced herself to sound calm. Strong. 'I told you, I needed a job. Did you really call me up here to ask me that—'

'Did you even think of that promise you made, Lucia?'

he cut her off harshly. His hands clenched into fists at his sides. 'Did you think of me?'

Every day. She drew a painful breath into her lungs. 'Did you think of me, Angelo?' she asked quietly, knowingly, and he swung away again, his silence answer enough.

Lucia waited, her hands clenched in the folds of her apron. A minute ticked by in taut silence, and then another, and Angelo still didn't speak.

'Who was that woman you were with?' he asked suddenly, and she blinked in surprise.

'Her name is Maria Dibona. She works here, with me.'

'I gathered that.' Angelo turned towards her, but she couldn't tell anything from his face besides the fact that he still seemed angry. But then Angelo had always seemed angry, except perhaps for when he'd been sad. And the few times he'd made her laugh, when they were children…precious memories she kept locked away, deep inside. Memories she couldn't let herself think about now. 'Why was she crying?' he asked, and she shrugged.

'Her son has left suddenly for Naples. She misses him.'

Angelo said nothing for a moment, but his eyes blazed into hers and his mouth twisted downwards. 'And you were comforting her?'

Where was this going? 'Trying to. Sometimes there's very little comfort to be had.'

He didn't answer, but she saw a flash of recognition in his eyes and she knew he thought she'd been talking about them. What little *them* there was. And had she? Perhaps. Perhaps she wasn't above such a sly implication.

'You still live in Caltarione,' he said suddenly, a statement, and she raised her eyebrows.

'Obviously you must know that, since you've looked

at my employee file. What is this about, Angelo? Why have you brought me up here?'

She saw, to her surprise, a faint flush touch his cheek-bones. He glanced down at some papers on his desk. 'We were friends once, weren't we?'

Once, not now. His meaning was clear. 'As children, yes,' she said flatly.

'I want to know what has happened to you in these past years.'

'Oh, really? Funny, then, that you never called or wrote. Not a postcard or email or anything. If you wanted to catch up on old times, Angelo, I'm sure you could have found a way other than summoning me to your office like some scolded schoolgirl.'

His blush deepened, and his eyes glittered. 'I didn't—'

'Didn't think of me once in the past seven years while you were away becoming a billionaire? How surprising. And yet you're angry because I took a job working for the Correttis.' She shook her head. 'You may not have made any promises, but you're still a hypocrite.'

'You're angry with me,' he said, and she forced herself to laugh, the sound hard and humourless.

'Angry? That takes too much effort. I *was* angry, yes, and I'm annoyed you think you can order me around now. But if you think I'm hurt because you stole from my bed—' She stopped suddenly, her breath catching in her chest, and swallowed hard. She knew she couldn't continue, couldn't maintain the charade that what had happened seven years ago hadn't utterly broken her.

So she simply stared, her chin tilted at a determinedly haughty angle, everything in her willing Angelo to believe that she didn't care about him. That he hadn't hurt her. Let him believe she was only angry; at least it hid the agony of grief she couldn't bear to have exposed.

'I'm sorry, Lucia,' Angelo said abruptly, and Lucia could only stare. He didn't *sound* sorry.

'For what?' she asked after a taut moment when neither of them spoke.

'For...' He paused, a muscle flickering in his jaw, his eyes shadowed with some dark emotion. 'For leaving you like that.' Lucia let out a shuddering breath. She'd never expected an apology, even one so grudgingly given. She didn't speak. Angelo stared.

'Aren't you going to say anything?' he finally demanded.

'What do you want me to say?'

'You could accept my apology, to start.'

'Why should I?'

Angelo's jaw dropped, which would have made her laugh save for the leaden weight of her heart. *'What?'*

'Just because you've finally deigned to say sorry doesn't make me ready to accept it.' Or act like all that was needed was a carelessly given, barely meant apology. She wanted more than that. She deserved more than that.

Except, of course, Angelo had nothing more to give. And whether or not he said sorry for the past made no real difference to either of their futures. *Why* had he brought her up here? Looking at him now, his face taut with annoyance or maybe even anger, Lucia thought she could hazard a guess.

She was no more than an item to be ticked off on his to-do list. Come back to Sicily, buy a hotel, deal with Lucia. Get any messy emotional business out of the way so he could move on to more important things. She supposed she should be grateful she'd warranted any consideration at all.

She took a deep breath. 'So you've said it, Angelo, you've ticked me off your list, and you can go on happily now with your big business deals and fancy living. And I can get back to work.'

And stop acting out this charade that she didn't care, that she'd only been angry or even annoyed. She couldn't understand how Angelo could believe it, yet he obviously did, for he was annoyed too, by her stubbornness. He still had no idea how much he'd hurt her.

'It's been seven years, Lucia,' he said, an edge to his voice, and she met his gaze as evenly as she could.

'Exactly.'

'I haven't even been in Sicily since that night.'

'Like I said before, there's the phone. Email. We live in the twenty-first century, Angelo. If you'd wanted to be in touch, I think you just might have found a way.' He bunched his jaw and she shook her head. 'Don't make excuses. I don't need them. I know that one night was exactly that to you—one night. I'm not delusional.' *Not any more.*

'So you didn't even expect me to call? Or write?'

'No, I didn't.' Even though part of her had stubbornly, stupidly hoped. 'But expecting and wanting are two different things.'

He stared at her for a long, hard moment. 'What did you want?' he asked quietly, and Lucia didn't answer. She would not articulate all the things she had wanted, had hoped for despite the odds, the *obviousness* of Angelo's abandonment. She would not give Angelo the satisfaction of knowing, and so she lifted one shoulder in something like a shrug. 'A goodbye would have been something.'

'That's all? A farewell?'

'I said it would have been *something*.' She tore her gaze from his, forced all that emotion down so it caught in her chest, a pressure so intense it felt like all her breath was being sucked from her body. 'It's irrelevant anyway,' she continued, each word so very painful to say. 'If you brought me up here to say sorry, then you've said it. Thank you for that much, at least.'

'But you don't accept my apology,' Angelo observed. His gaze swept her from head to foot like a laser, searching her, revealing her.

She closed her eyes briefly, tried to summon strength. 'Does it really matter?'

His gaze narrowed, his lips compressed. 'Why do you ask that?'

'Because you've managed to go seven years without saying sorry or speaking to me at all, Angelo. How can I help but think my opinions—my feelings—matter very little to you?' He frowned and she shook her head. 'I'm not accusing you. I'm not angry about it any more.'

'You still seem angry.'

Seem, Lucia thought, being the operative word. If only it was as simple as that; if only she felt angry that he'd been so thoughtless as to leave her bed without a word. If only she felt clean, strong anger instead of this endless ache of grief. 'I suppose seeing you again has brought it back, a bit, that's all,' she finally said. She couldn't meet his gaze. 'Why do you care anyway?'

'I suppose…the same.' Angelo sounded guarded. 'Seeing you again has made me…want to make amends.'

Make amends? As if a two-word reluctant redress made up for years of emptiness, heartache, *agony*? Did he really think that was an equal exchange?

But he didn't know. He couldn't know how much she'd endured, the gossip and shame, the loss and heartbreak. He had no idea of the hell she'd been through, and she wouldn't weaken and shame herself by telling him now.

'Well, then,' she said, and her voice sounded flat, lifeless. 'I suppose that's all there is to say.'

Angelo nodded, the movement no more than a terse jerk of his head. 'I suppose so.'

She made herself look at him then, for surely this was goodbye. The goodbye they'd never had. They lived in different worlds now; she was a maid, he was a billionaire. And while she cherished the memory of who he'd once been, she knew she didn't even recognise this haughty man with his hostile gaze and designer suit. He was so different from the tousle-haired boy with the sad eyes and the sudden smile, the boy who had hated her to see him vulnerable and yet had sought her out in the sweetest, most unexpected moments. What had happened to that boy?

Staring at Angelo's hard countenance, Lucia knew he was long gone. And the unyielding man in front of her was no more than a wealthy stranger. She felt a sudden sweep of sorrow at the thought, too overwhelming to ignore, and she closed her eyes. *She missed that boy.* She missed the girl she'd been with him, full of irrepressible hope and happiness. The girl and boy they'd been were gone now, changed forever by circumstance and suffering.

She opened her eyes to see Angelo staring at her, a crease between his brows, a frown compressing his mouth. He had a beautiful mouth, full, sculpted lips that had felt so amazingly soft against hers. Ridiculous that she would recall the feel of them now.

'So may I go?' she asked when the silence between them had stretched on for several minutes. 'Or is there anything else you'd like to say? You might as well say it now, because if you summon me to your office twice the gossip will really start flying.'

Angelo's frown deepened into a near scowl. 'Gossip?'

Lucia just shook her head. She shouldn't have said

that. Angelo didn't know how difficult those months after he'd left had been for her, how in their stifling village community she'd been labelled another Corretti whore…just like his mother had. She didn't want him to know. 'It looks a little suspicious, that's all. Most maids never see the CEO's office.'

'I see.' He paused, glanced down at some papers that lay scattered across his desk. 'I'm sorry. I didn't mean to make things difficult for you.'

'Never mind. May I go now?'

Angelo stared at her for a long moment, and she saw that glimpse of bleakness in his eyes again, and that ache inside her opened right up, consumed her with sudden, desperate need. She wanted to take him in her arms and smooth away the crease that furrowed his forehead. She wanted to kiss him and tell him none of it mattered, because she loved him. She'd always loved him.

Pathetic. Stupid. What kind of woman loved a man who had treated her the way Angelo had treated her?

Her mother, for one. And look how *she* had ended up.

'Yes,' Angelo finally said, and he sounded distant, distracted. He was probably already thinking of his next business deal. He turned away, to face the window. 'Yes, of course you can go.'

And so she did, slipping silently through the heavy oak doors even as that ache inside her opened up so she felt as if she had nothing left, *was* nothing but need and emptiness. She walked quickly past the receptionist and felt tears sting her eyes.

Alone in the lift she pressed her fists against her eyes and willed it all back, all down. She would not cry. She would not cry for Angelo Corretti, who had broken her heart too many times already so she'd had to keep fitting it back together, jagged pieces that no longer made a healthy whole. Still she'd done it; she'd thought she'd succeeded.

Alone in the lift with the tears starting in her eyes and threatening to slip down her cheeks, she knew she hadn't.

Angelo stared blindly out the window, his mind spinning with what Lucia had said. And what she hadn't said.

His first reaction had been, predictably, affront. Anger, even. What kind of person didn't accept an apology? He'd had no need to call her up here. He could have ignored her completely.

Yet even as he felt anger flare he'd known it was unreasonable. Unjust. He'd treated her badly, *very* badly considering their childhood friendship, their history. He'd always known that even if he tried not to think of it. Tried not to remember that one tender night.

Seeing her last night had raked up all those old memories and feelings, and he knew he couldn't be distracted from his purpose here. So she'd been right; his apology had been, in a sense, an item on his to-do list.

Deal with Lucia and then move on.

Except as he stood there and silently fumed, staring out the window without taking in the view, he knew he wasn't moving on at all. Seeing Lucia had mired him right back in the past, remembering how he'd been with her. Who he'd been. She'd seen him at his most vulnerable and needy, at his most shaming and pathetic. The thought made his fists clench.

He'd hoped apologising to Lucia would give them both a sense of closure, but he didn't think it had. At least for him it had only stirred things up even more.

Gazing blindly out the window, he saw the bright blue of her eyes, the determined tilt of her chin. When had she become so strong, so *hard*? He'd thought, he realised now, that she'd be glad of his apology, grateful for his attention. He'd expected her to trip over herself accepting his grudging *sorry*.

Instead she'd seemed…indifferent. Uncaring. *Hard*.

He spun away from the window.

He hated this feeling of restless dissatisfaction that gnawed at him, ate away any sense of achievement he'd had over his recent business successes. He hated the raw emotion he felt about Lucia, an uncomfortable mix of guilt and vulnerability and need. Why couldn't he just forget about her? Regardless of whether she had accepted his apology or not, at least he'd given it. The matter was done. It should have been, at any rate.

He sat down at the desk, pulled a sheaf of papers towards him, determined not to think of her again. He'd managed not to think of her for seven years; surely an hour or two wouldn't be difficult.

Yet the minutes ticked by and Angelo just sat there, staring at the papers in front of him without taking in a single word.

CHAPTER THREE

'FRESH TOWELS ARE needed in the penthouse suite.'

Lucia glanced up from where she'd been stacking laundered linens in one of the supply cupboards.

'The penthouse suite?' she repeated, and felt dread—as well as a betraying anticipation—sweep through her. 'Can't someone else go?' She'd been avoiding the penthouse suite or any of the hotel's public places since her confrontation with Angelo.

She'd seen the speculative, sideways glances when she'd walked out of his office, had heard the whispers fall to a hush when she'd entered the break room. She knew people were wondering, some of them remembering, and she couldn't stand the thought of any more speculation or shame. She also couldn't stand the thought of seeing Angelo again, knowing he would look at her as if she were no more than an irritating problem he had to solve. She didn't have the strength to act indifferent, uncaring. He'd see through her thin facade at some point, and she could bear that least of all.

'Signor Corretti asked for you in particular,' Emilia, one of the other chambermaids, returned with a smirk. 'I wonder what he wants besides the towels?'

Lucia stilled. She knew Emilia from her childhood, knew the other woman had never liked her—had in fact seemed jealous of her, which was ridiculous considering how lonely her life had been since Angelo's sudden departure. Emilia would certainly relish any gossip Angelo's personal requests stirred up now. Swallowing, she nodded.

'Fine.' And she'd tell Angelo to leave her alone while she was at it. She took a deep breath and reached for several of the velvety soft towels. If Angelo owned the hotel, she'd have to see him again at some point. The more she got used to it, the less it would hurt. She hoped.

Still Lucia couldn't keep the dread from pooling like acid in her stomach as she headed up the service lift to the top floor, the towels clutched to her chest. Maybe he wouldn't be there. Maybe he'd put in the request for towels and then gone out…*somewhere*…

Except of course that was ridiculous, if he'd made the request himself. He obviously wanted to see her, was summoning her like a—

No. She wouldn't think that way.

The lift doors opened directly into the suite, and Lucia took a step into the silent foyer. She couldn't see or hear Angelo anywhere.

She glanced cautiously towards the living area before she decided to just head for the bathroom, deposit the towels and get out of there as quickly as possible. Taking a deep breath, she hurried down the hall and had her hand on the doorknob of the bathroom when the door swung open and Angelo stood there, dressed only in a pair of dress slacks, his chest bare, droplets of water clinging to his golden skin.

Lucia stood as if rooted to the spot, the towels clutched to her chest, every thought evaporating from her brain. Finally she moistened her lips and managed, 'You wanted towels—'

'Towels?' He frowned, glancing at the towels still clutched against her chest. 'I didn't ask for any towels.'

Lucia felt colour rush to her face. 'You—you didn't?' Which meant Emilia had been mistaken—or lying. Had the other maid set her up for more gossip? Now she could whisper to everyone how Lucia had sneaked up to the penthouse suite late at night? Lucia knew what it would look like. And from Angelo's narrowed gaze, she had a feeling he knew what it looked like too.

Angelo gazed at Lucia, her cheeks touched with colour but her eyes still frustratingly blank. Once he'd been able to see so much clear emotion in those blue, blue eyes of hers. He'd read her so easily because she'd never tried to hide what she felt. How much she felt. He'd taken for granted, he saw now, the hero-worship she'd had for him when they were children. He'd always known it wasn't real, couldn't be, and yet he missed it. He missed, if not the childish adoration she'd once had for him, then at least the affection. The regard.

She looked now as if she didn't care for him at all. As if he were a stranger of no importance. Anger or even hatred would have been easier to accept. It would have been understandable.

But this cold indifference in her eyes—it chilled him. Reminded him of Carlo Corretti's uncaring stare when he'd confronted the man who had fathered him with the hard truth of his identity.

All you were meant to be was a stain on the sheets.

He couldn't stand for Lucia to look at him that way, as if he didn't matter. Didn't exist.

'I didn't order any towels,' he said again, wondering if she had possibly used it as an excuse to see him.

But no—she looked like she'd rather be anywhere else. With anyone else.

'It must have been a mistake,' Lucia said stiffly. 'I'll go.'

She turned and started down the hall, and some insane impulse had Angelo springing forward, reaching for her wrist. 'No—'

She stilled, his fingers still wrapped around her wrist. 'Angelo,' she said in a low voice. 'Don't.'

He could feel the pulse in her wrist hammering hard, and it gratified him. Underneath that cold indifference she felt something. Just as he did. 'Don't what?' he asked softly.

'Don't do this,' she said helplessly. 'What happened between us is over. I know that. It's fine.'

'It is not fine.'

She turned back to him, genuine confusion clouding her eyes to a stormy grey. '*Why?* Why do you ever care what I think or feel?'

'Because—' He heard his voice rise in frustration. *Because I can't stop thinking about you. Because when I finally fall asleep at night I dream of your eyes, your mouth, your softness.* What would it take to stop thinking about this woman? To get her out of his head completely?

Lucia's gaze swept over him and then she angled her head away, hiding her face. Her eyes. 'I must go.' She turned towards the lift, extended one hand towards the button.

Without thinking about what he was doing Angelo lunged forward, trapped her hand with his against the panel of buttons. 'Don't.'

She stilled, and he realised how close he was to her, his body pressing hers against the wall next to the lift. He could feel the heat coming off her lithe, athletic frame, and also the awareness. It coiled and snapped between them like a live wire, an attraction he'd felt—and surrendered to—all those years before. An attraction he still felt now—and with a thrill of satisfaction he knew she felt it too. It *wasn't* over.

He lowered his head so his lips brushed the dark softness of her hair, inhaled the clean, warm scent of her.

'Lucia,' he murmured, and he felt her tense even more.

'Let me go, Angelo.' Her voice trembled and broke on the note of his name and he felt a savage surge of triumph at knowing how affected she was. How attracted.

His lips brushed her hair again and with one hand he drew her own away from the lift button. A shudder wracked her body at his touch, and Angelo felt another thrill surge through him at her blatant response.

He laced his fingers with her own and put his other hand on her shoulder, gently turning her around so her back was against the lift, her body towards him.

He pressed against her and although she remained tense he could still feel her response, her body arching helplessly towards his. This was what he'd wanted all along, he acknowledged with a sudden, primal certainty. This was what he couldn't forget. What he wouldn't forget.

And this was how he would finally exorcise himself of her.

She'd lowered her head, her hair sliding in front of her face. He tucked a tendril behind her ear.

'Don't—' she whispered, but the single word ended on a shudder of longing.

'Don't what?' Angelo asked huskily. 'Don't touch you, or don't stop?' He trailed his fingers down her cheek, let his thumb caress the intoxicating fullness of her lips. Another shudder, and he felt the answering ache inside him. She was so soft. Lips, hair, the curve of her cheek. 'Don't kiss you?' he murmured, and then he did.

Her lips were as sweet and warm as he remembered, and after only a second's pause they parted beneath his own. He swept his tongue into her mouth's softness, his hands sliding from her shoulders to her waist and then to her hips, pulling her closer to him, fitting her against his arousal.

Her hands came up to his shoulders, her fingers curling around as she responded to his kiss, her tongue meeting his, her mouth and body accepting him as they had before.

Triumph and something far deeper and needier surged through him. How had he ever lived without this? Without *her*?

He moved his hand upwards to cup the warm swell of her breast, felt her shuddering response. Then he felt a tear splash onto his cheek and he jerked away as if that single drop had scorched him.

'*Maledizione*, you're crying?'

Lucia dashed the tear from her face. 'You think I want this?' she snapped, her voice choked and yet still filled with furious pride. 'You think I want a repeat of what happened before? Another one-night stand?'

'I...' At a loss, Angelo just shook his head. He'd thought her so hard, so indifferent, yet in that moment it seemed no more than a charade. She couldn't hide the honest emotion in her eyes, and it was despair. *Grief.* 'Lucia...'

'Don't.' Her voice came out clogged and she shook her head. 'Please don't, Angelo.' She turned from him, her whole body trembling, and pressed the button for the lift.

She didn't say anything else and neither did he as they waited for the lift doors to open. He was still reeling from shock at the naked sorrow that had swamped her eyes when the doors opened and she stepped inside. She didn't turn around to face him and Angelo felt that familiar pressure build in his chest, throb in his temples. He didn't want her to go. Not like this—

The doors closed on both of their silence.

He stood there for a moment, his head aching, his heart aching. Damn his heart. Damn *hers*. Why had she looked so sad? So lost? He'd thought she was strong, hard. Indifferent…yet she hadn't been indifferent to him in his arms. He'd thought then she felt the same consuming desire and need he felt, not sadness. Grief.

When he'd gazed down at her she'd looked…*broken*.

He didn't want to think about why.

He turned from the lift and stalked over to his laptop, pulling it resolutely towards him, determined to forget about Lucia once and for all.

He couldn't be distracted from his purpose here. He had work to do, more deals to make, more plans to put into motion. Battaglia wanted to meet him and discuss the docklands regeneration project. Luca's fashion business could be ripe for a hostile takeover. Even Gio and his horses on the other side of the island might show a weakness. The Corretti empire was surely starting to crumble, and he'd be the one to sweep up the pieces.

He was on the cusp, Angelo reminded himself, of having everything he'd ever wanted.

So why now, as ever, did he feel so empty?

CHAPTER FOUR

LUCIA'S LEGS TREMBLED and she sagged against the side of the lift as it plunged downwards, away from Angelo. She could still feel the taste of him on her lips, the strong press of his hard body against hers. Even now desire flowed through her in a molten river, making her sag even more against the wall. Making her even weaker.

For she was weak, so pathetically weak, to still respond to him. To still want him, even though she knew he would never think of her as anything more than—*what?*

Why had he kissed her? The answer, the only possible answer, was glaringly apparent. Because he knew he could have her—and then walk away. Because he knew that just as before she would take him in her arms, into her body, and then he could leave without so much as an explanation. She was the easy option, just as her mother had been, accepting a man who treated her like dirt. Wanting him, even begging him, back.

She had never wanted to be like that. She still didn't. She *wouldn't*.

Lucia closed her eyes, forced back the sting of tears. Forced back all the emotion, all the useless regret and anger and hurt. At least she'd shown him she was different now...if only just. At least this time she'd been the one to walk away. If only just.

Two hours later, her heart and body aching, she climbed the steps to the tiny apartment she rented over a bar in Caltarione, the small village near the Correttis' palazzo. She's grown up in a tiny, terraced house farther down the main street, next to Angelo and his grandparents. She'd thought of leaving the village after Angelo had gone, after she'd endured the bold stares and muttered curses that had accompanied her wherever she went for months after his departure, but she hadn't.

Perhaps it was stubbornness or maybe just sentimentality, but she wasn't willing to leave the only place she'd considered home. She wouldn't be driven out, even if the busy streets of Palermo might offer more anonymity and acceptance.

In any case, the whispers and rumours and sneers had died down in the years since Angelo had left. They'd returned, a little, with him; she recognised the speculative looks Emilia and some of the other housekeeping staff who knew her history had given her in the past week. But she ignored it all, with a determination that had sapped all of her strength.

She certainly didn't feel like she had any left now. Resisting Angelo had taken everything.

Kicking open the door to her apartment Lucia discarded her sensible shoes and stripped the soiled maid's uniform from her body. She headed towards the tiny bathroom in the back of the flat and turned the taps on the small, rather dingy tub. She sank onto the edge of the bath and dropped her head in her hands. She felt so unbearably, achingly tired, tired of pretending all the time that she was strong, that she barely cared or remembered about what happened seven years ago. Why had she insisted on this ridiculous charade of indifference? Was it simply out of pride?

But no, she knew it was not as simple a matter as that. She knew this charade was as much for her own benefit as Angelo's. Some absurd part of her believed, or at least hoped, that if she acted like she didn't care, she wouldn't. If she told him it didn't matter, it wouldn't.

And yet it did matter. So very much. It had mattered then, and it mattered now. And while she'd convinced herself that he didn't need to know the truth, maybe she needed him to.

The thought was both novel and frightening. She didn't want to tell Angelo the truth of their night together, and yet as long as she kept it a secret it festered unhealed inside her soul. What if she lanced that wound, drained it of its poison and power? What if she told Angelo, not for his sake, but for her own?

Would she finally be able to put the whole episode behind her, put Angelo behind her?

If only.

She stayed in the tub until the water had grown cold and then she slipped on a pair of worn trackie bottoms and a T-shirt. After a second's pause she took an old cardboard box from the dusty top shelf of her wardrobe, brought it out to the sofa in the living room. She didn't take this box out very often; it felt like picking off the scab of her barely healed soul. She knew it was dangerous weakness to take it out now, when she already felt so raw, yet still she did it, unable to resist remembering.

Carefully she eased the lid off the box and looked at the few treasures inside: a scrapbook of old travel postcards she'd been given from the people whose houses she and her mother had cleaned. She and Angelo had used to make up stories about all the different places they'd travel to one day, the amazing things they would do. A single letter Angelo had written her from New York, when he'd left at eighteen years old. She'd practically memorised its few lines. A lock of hair.

She took the last out now, fingering its silky softness, a tiny curl tied with a bit of thread. She closed her eyes and a single tear tracked down her cheek. It hurt so much to remember, to access that hidden grief she knew she would always carry with her, a leaden weight inside her that never lightened; she had simply learned to limp along under its heaviness.

A sudden, hard rapping on the front door made her still, tense. The only person who ever knocked on her door was the owner of the bar downstairs, an oily man with a sagging paunch who was always making veiled— and not-so-veiled—references to what he thought he knew of her past. She really didn't feel like dealing with him now.

Another knock sounded, this one even more sharp and insistent.

Drawing a deep breath, Lucia put the box and its contents aside. She wiped the tear from her face and looked through the fogged eyehole in the door, shock slicing straight through her when she saw who it was. No oily landlord, and definitely no paunch.

Angelo raised his hand to knock again and, her own hands shaking, she unlocked the door and opened it.

'What are you doing here, Angelo?'

His hair was rumpled like he'd driven his fingers carelessly through it, his expression as grim as ever. 'May I come in?'

She shrugged and moved aside. Angelo stepped across the threshold, his narrowed gaze quickly taking in the small, shabby apartment with her mother's old three-piece suite and a few framed posters for decoration. It wasn't much, Lucia certainly knew that, but it was hers and she'd earned it. She didn't like the way Angelo seemed to sum it up and dismiss it in one judgemental second.

'What do you want?' she asked, and heard how ragged her voice sounded. 'Or do you not even know? Because you keep trying to find me, but God only knows why.'

He turned slowly to face her. 'God only knows,' he agreed quietly. 'Because I don't.'

'Then maybe you should just stop.'

'I can't.'

She shook her head helplessly, every emotion far too close to the surface, to his scrutiny. 'Why not?'

'I…' He stared at her, his eyes glittering, wild. His lips parted, but no sound came out. Lucia folded her arms, conscious now that she was wearing a thin T-shirt and no bra.

'Well?' she managed.

'Back in my hotel suite,' Angelo said slowly. 'At the lift.' His gaze roved over her, searching. 'Why did you look at me like that?'

'Like what?'

'As if…as if you were sad.'

Lucia swallowed. 'Don't, Angelo,' she said, her voice no more than a rasp. 'Please, just leave it.'

'I can't.'

'You *can*. You're like a dog with a bone.' She shook her head, anger warring with the agony as well as the deep-seated desire she had to hide it. 'Just leave me alone.'

'You think I don't want to?' Angelo asked quietly, and she let out a sudden, wild laugh, the unfettered sound surprising them both.

'Oh, I know you want to. You've always wanted to. Everything you've taken from me has been against your better judgement, even your will. You think I don't know that?'

Angelo was silent for a long moment. 'Why do you offer it, then?' he finally asked. 'All the kindnesses when we were children—and before…that night—'

That night. She did not want to remember the hope, the *joy*, that had coursed through her when Angelo had kissed her. When she thought he'd felt just as she did, had built a castle in the air of her dreams, as insubstantial as the mist on the sea, gone by morning, as she'd surely known he would be.

'Because we were friends, Angelo,' she forced out. 'Because, when we were children, I saw the sadness in your eyes and I wanted to wipe it away. I wanted to help you—' *I wanted to love you.* She swallowed down the words.

'I've never wanted *help*.'

'I know that. How could I not know that, when you constantly pushed me away? And yet I kept trying.' She shook her head, forced herself to laugh, as if it was all in the distant, unimportant past. 'I was foolish, as a kid.' And as a woman.

'And that night?' Angelo asked in a low voice. 'Why did you sleep with me?'

'Isn't it obvious?' She turned around with a shrug, every atom of her being focused on appearing hard, strong. 'I wanted you. I've always been attracted to you.'

'And that was it? A one-night stand, pleasurable for both of us?'

She jerked her head in the semblance of a nod. She couldn't manage anything more.

Angelo shook his head. 'There's more.' He took a step towards her, his mouth a hard line, his gaze seeming to bore right into her. 'If that's the truth, Lucia, you wouldn't have looked like you did back there, by the lift. You wouldn't have looked like I'd broken your heart—'

'You *did* break my heart.' The words exploded from her like a gunshot, a crack in the taut silence of the room. She saw shock flash in Angelo's eyes and she turned away quickly.

'Then—'

'It's not what you think.' She drew in a ragged breath. Now was the time for truth, or at least part of it. She still couldn't tell him how much she'd loved him, admit all that weakness, but she could tell him about the consequences of their one night. Perhaps he'd already guessed it; perhaps that was why he kept at her, asking questions, demanding answers. He knew she was hiding something.

'What do I think, Lucia?' Angelo asked quietly.

She shook her head, her back still to him. 'It doesn't matter what you think.'

'No?'

'You don't *know*, Angelo.' She dragged in a breath, the very air hard to breathe, heavy inside her. 'You don't understand—'

'Then tell me.' He came to stand behind her, one hand hard on her shoulder. 'Tell me what I don't know.'

Lucia closed her eyes, tried to find the words. She hadn't been able to find them in all the letters she'd written and never sent, and she searched uselessly for them now. She licked her lips. 'That night...'

'Yes?' Angelo prompted, impatient now, his fingers digging into her shoulder.

'There were...consequences....'

'Consequences?' Angelo's voice sharpened and she couldn't answer. 'Look at me, damn it.' With his hand on her shoulder he turned her around, forced her to face him. 'What have you been keeping from me?' he demanded, and she saw the anger in his eyes, but worse, far worse, she saw the fear. She felt it.

He knew. Maybe he didn't realise he knew, but he knew.

'I was pregnant, Angelo,' she whispered. 'I had a baby.'

CHAPTER FIVE

ANGELO DROPPED HIS hands from her shoulders and stared at her utterly without expression, his body completely still. Lucia had no idea what he was thinking or feeling. Maybe it was nothing. Maybe he didn't even care. He certainly wouldn't grieve their daughter the way she had. He might not even believe her.

His gaze moved over her slowly, as if searching for answers, for weaknesses. 'Are you saying,' he asked in a voice devoid of expression, 'that you became pregnant, after that night? That one time?' She nodded. 'You had a baby? A child?' She nodded again, the words to explain stuck in her throat, jagged shards of memory and loss that cut open everything inside her. He continued to stare at her, hard, first in assessment, and then in acceptance.

She saw the emotions move over his face: first the shock, followed by a flash of anger, and then an understanding. And finally, the most unexpected emotion of all, an eager hope softening his features as his mouth half quirked into an incredulous, tremulous smile. 'A boy,' he asked hoarsely, 'or a girl?'

Lucia closed her eyes against the agonising emotion so apparent on his face. She'd steeled herself for anger, accusations, maybe even disbelief. But hope? *Happiness?* They hurt so much more. 'A girl,' she whispered.

'But where—where is she?' She opened her eyes and saw Angelo looking around as if he expected a bright-eyed, curly-haired six-year-old to come bounding up to him with a smile. 'What is her name?'

'Angelica,' Lucia whispered, the word tearing her throat, hurting her.

'Angelica...' She saw a smile dawn across Angelo's face then disappear. His eyes narrowed, the hope fading from them. 'Where is she, Lucia?'

She just shook her head, unable to speak, to tell him. 'Where is she?' he demanded, urgent now, rough. He took her by the shoulders again, stared at her hard, and through the mist of her own tears she saw the bleakness in his eyes, and she knew just as before he already knew.

'She's dead.'

She felt Angelo's fingers clench on her shoulders before he released her and turned away. Neither of them spoke and Lucia drew a ragged breath into her lungs.

'How?' he finally asked tonelessly.

'She—she was stillborn. At seven months. The cord was wrapped around her neck.' She drew another breath, just as ragged. 'She was perfect, Angelo.'

Angelo shook his head and made some small sound, his back to her, and she had the sudden urge to comfort him, just as she had many times before. Take him in her arms, draw his head to her shoulder. This time she didn't move. It was too late for that. Far, far too late.

Slowly he turned back around, his face now wiped of any emotion or expression at all. Lucia remained still, everything in her aching. She wanted him to say something, *do* something, but he didn't move or speak.

After an endless moment his gaze fell on the box of treasures she'd left on the sofa. Lucia made one involuntary move towards it, as if she could hide the evidence of her sentimentality. Angelo's letter, the scrapbook they'd once pored over…

The lock of hair.

His gaze remained steadfastly on that little curl of sadness and then he lifted it to hers. 'May I?' he asked, and wordlessly she nodded.

She watched as Angelo took the silky bit of baby hair in his hand and ran its softness between his fingers. He didn't say anything, and his head was lowered so Lucia couldn't see his face.

'Angelo…' she whispered, although she had no idea what she would say. That she'd never forgotten him? That she'd held their daughter in her arms and grieved not just her precious child but the life she'd thought, for one blissful night, could be hers? That she'd loved him?

And loved him still.

Carefully Angelo returned the lock of the hair to the box. Lucia saw his gaze flick over the other items, but she couldn't tell if he recognised the scrapbook or letter. Then he looked directly at her, and she could see nothing in his grey-green gaze. It was as hard and unyielding as it had ever been.

'I should go.'

Disappointment and even despair flooded her, but somehow she managed to nod again. She didn't trust herself to speak, didn't know what she would say. He nodded back, in farewell, and then she watched as he strode towards the door and out into the night. Once again he'd left her alone and aching, just as he had before.

Angelo didn't remember much about the drive back to the hotel. His mind was a blur of memories and thoughts he could not articulate. He kept his gaze focused on the road, but he didn't even remember driving.

He pulled up to the hotel and tossed the keys to a valet, then strode through the lobby, blind to everyone and everything around him. He rode up the lift up to the penthouse suite and strode through the empty, ornate rooms before ending up in the bathroom, staring at his pale, wild-eyed reflection.

Then he clenched his hand into a fist and punched that reflection as hard as he could. Glass shattered in an explosion of glittering fragments and blood welled up on his knuckles, trickled down his wrist.

Angelo swore and reached for one of the towels—one that Lucia had brought—and pressed it to his bloody fist. What an idiotic, uncontrolled thing to do. Yet even with his hand throbbing he couldn't regret it. He'd needed some outlet for his rage. His agony.

It was sudden, this grief that overwhelmed him, sudden and utterly unexpected. He'd never felt it before, and yet it was also weirdly familiar. He felt as if he'd been feeling it all his life, suppressing it, hiding it— even from himself.

He hadn't grieved his mother when she'd left him at six years old, with a careless kiss and a guilty look. He'd seen her again once, when he was thirteen and she'd come home asking for money.

He hadn't grieved the death of his grandparents, who had taken care of him for his entire childhood and died within a few months of each other when he was eighteen. They hadn't loved him, he knew that. They'd been ashamed of him, the Corretti bastard nobody had wanted.

He hadn't even grieved the father he'd never had, the man who had told him, point blank, he'd have preferred for Angelo not to exist at all. And even when Carlo Corretti had died, Angelo had felt…nothing. He'd always felt nothing.

Until now. Now when that surface nothing cracked like the thinnest ice and revealed the depth and darkness of the emotion churning below. Raw, honest, messy grief rose up inside him, threatened to spill out. His eyes stung and his throat thickened with tears and over what? A baby he'd never expected to have? A life he'd never even thought he wanted?

A daughter. A daughter with silky dark hair and his name. Angelo blinked hard.

With the towel still pressed to his hand he crunched across the broken glass and went back out to the living room, stared unseeingly at the city stretched out before him like a glittering chessboard and he was the king.

That's how he'd seen his life: an arduous journey from pawn to king, strategising and calculating every single move he'd ever made, and all, only to win.

Yet now he felt only loss—unbelievable, unending—flooding through him, filling his emptiness with something far worse. *Grief.*

Slowly he sank onto a sofa, his hand cradled in his lap. He felt as if he were spinning into a void, with no plans, no thoughts. He had no idea what to do now.

Forge ahead, forget what was behind? Forget this daughter he'd never known, and the woman who had been her mother, who might have been his wife?

Could he forget Lucia?

It was a question he'd never asked himself before. He'd never even thought to ask it; forgetting her had been a given. But now…now he wasn't so sure.

Now, Angelo thought bleakly, he wasn't sure of anything.

He closed his eyes, fought against all that emotion surging within him, rising up. Why hadn't she told him about the baby? And if she had, what would he have done? Could he have changed the awful course of events?

He knew, rationally, that he couldn't have, and yet still he wondered. Wished even, for a life he'd never thought to have. And as for the future... He knew there was still something between him and Lucia. Whether it was no more than the remnant of a childhood affection that had long since eroded into antipathy or something more, something good he didn't know. But he intended to find out.

How?

Clearly Lucia wanted him to leave her alone. To forget. And in some ways, it would be easier to forget. To go on as he always had before.

And yet he knew he couldn't. Wouldn't. Grimly Angelo stared straight ahead, his bleeding, throbbing hand momentarily forgotten. He wasn't done here. *They* weren't done...no matter what Lucia wanted or thought.

Lucia woke with her eyes feeling gritty and her mouth dry as dust. She'd barely slept, having spent most of the night trying to blank out the memories that kept looping in a relentless reel through her mind. The doctor's flat voice telling her Angelica was dead. The softness of her daughter's still-warm skin when she'd held her. The blank look on Angelo's face last night.

She'd thought—for a single moment, she'd *believed*—that he cared about Angelica, if not about her. She'd thought, when his back had been turned, he'd been grappling with grief but when he'd turned around again he had looked only blank, as if he'd accepted and absorbed the news in the space of a few minutes, and was now moving on.

Always moving on.

She needed to move on too, Lucia knew, in so many ways. She showered and dressed, plaited her hair and drank a cup of strong coffee. She'd thought she had moved on years ago, had told herself she had. She'd stopped thinking about Angelo, had tried to remember only the good things about their time together as children. She'd thought she'd accepted Angelica's death, had even told herself that it could be better this way. She hadn't really had the resources to care for a child, a baby who would be labelled another Corretti bastard from the moment she'd taken her first breath.

A breath she'd never been able to take.

Firmly Lucia pushed all these thoughts out of her mind. She was done with this. Done with grief, with sorrow, with Angelo. She wished he'd never returned to rake up all these feelings inside her, even as she acknowledged with stark honesty that she was still—*still*—glad he had returned.

She took the bus into Palermo, watched the dust billow into brown clouds along the road and resolutely did not think of Angelo. Of Angelica. Of any of it.

She worked all morning, cleaning bedrooms on the second and third floors, happy to be occupied with hard work. During her break she chatted with Maria, who proudly showed her a letter her son had written from Naples.

'Will you… Will you read it to me?' she asked hesitantly, for like many of the housekeeping staff Maria was not a fluent reader.

Lucia nodded and took the thin piece of paper. She'd finished with school at sixteen, but she'd studied hard and she liked to read. The letter was short enough, just a few pithy paragraphs describing his rented accommodation, the job he had in a canning factory. Lucia read it aloud before folding it back into the envelope and handing it to Maria.

'He sounds like he's doing well.'

'Yes. Yes.' Maria dabbed at her eyes with the corner of her apron. 'I'm a foolish woman, I know, to carry on so. But he's a good boy. And he did write. That's something, yes?'

'Of course it is,' Lucia told her, but inside she felt leaden. Angelo had written her one letter, just as short and matter-of-fact as Maria's son's, yet she'd treasured it. She'd read it so many times the paper had worn thin in places, and her mother had clucked her tongue and told her not to be stupid, not like she was.

Yet she had been. She'd been so incredibly, utterly stupid about Angelo.

How could she be so again, to think of him? Want him? She'd exhausted herself all morning trying *not* to think of him, a pointless endeavour since her brain and body insisted on remembering everything she'd loved about him. Still did. The silvery green of his eyes, the colour of dew drops on grass. The sudden quirk of his smile, so rare, so precious. The sure feel of his hands on her, reaching for her, *needing* her.

'Do you think he'll write again?' Maria asked, and Lucia blinked, focused on the older woman instead of her agonising thoughts.

Swallowing hard, she smiled at Maria. 'I'm sure he will write.'

Maria nodded and put the letter into the pocket of her apron. 'I'll wait,' she said, and Lucia just nodded, unable to keep herself from thinking, *That's what I did. And even though I don't want to be, I still am.*

By six o'clock she was bone-tired, and outside the air was hot, still and dusty. Her feet throbbed as she walked to the street corner to wait for the bus that would take her back to Caltarione.

Traffic flowed by her in an indifferent stream, cars honking and mopeds weaving around dusty taxi cabs. Lucia was just about to sink onto a bench when a Porsche glided up to the kerb and the window slid down.

'Lucia.'

'What do you want, Angelo?' she asked tiredly.

She couldn't see him very well in the dark interior of the car, no more than the hard line of his cheek and jaw, the silvery-green glint of his eyes. 'I looked for you at the hotel but you'd already gone. I need to speak with you.'

She shook her head. Surely they had no more to say each other. 'About what?'

'About Angelica.' And just like that her assumptions scattered and her throat went tight. 'Please,' he said quietly. 'I need to know.' Wordlessly she rose from the bench and slid into the sumptuous leather interior of the car.

Angelo pulled smoothly away from the kerb and they drove in silence down the boulevard towards Quattro Canti, the historic centre of Palermo, its Baroque buildings now gilded in fading sunlight. Lucia watched the buildings stream by in a blur until they were out of the city, and speeding down a dusty road towards Capaci, the sea shimmering in the distance.

'Where are we going?' she asked after the silence had stretched on for several minutes.

'My villa.'

'Your villa?' She turned to him in surprise. 'Why do you stay at the hotel if you have your own villa nearby?'

Angelo lifted one powerful shoulder in a shrug, his gaze still on the road. 'It's more convenient to stay at the hotel.'

They didn't speak again until Angelo pulled up on

a long, curving drive and parked in front of his villa. The place was sleek and utterly modern, made of local stone and built into the rocky hillside so it seemed to blend with the landscape. Lucia followed him inside and stood in the centre of the soaring living room; the furniture was all chrome and leather, top-of-the-line and completely sterile.

Angelo tossed his keys on a side table and loosened his tie. 'Would you like a shower? Or to change?'

She shrugged, although she would have liked to freshen up. 'I don't have any other clothes.'

'That is not a problem. I had some delivered. They're upstairs in one of the bedrooms.'

Shock had her simply staring for a few seconds. 'Why would you do that, if we're just going to have a conversation?'

Now he shrugged, the twist of his shoulders seeming impatient. 'Why not?'

It wasn't, Lucia thought, much of an answer, but she didn't have the energy to question him and the truth was she would kill for a shower. 'Thank you,' she said, as graciously as she could manage, and headed upstairs.

She found the clothes in one of the bedrooms overlooking the sea, several shopping bags' worth from Palermo's most exclusive boutiques. Pocket change to Angelo, of course, but those few bags contained more clothing than she possessed, and were worth far more than anything she owned.

With a ripple of apprehension she headed into the massive marble en suite and stripped off her maid's uniform. It felt good to wash away a day's dirt, but she couldn't shake the uneasy sense that Angelo wanted more from her than just a conversation.

Twenty minutes later, dressed in the most casual

clothes she'd been able to find, a silk T-shirt in pale blue and a matching swishy skirt that ended just above her knee, she went downstairs to find Angelo.

He had obviously showered too, for his hair was damp and curling on his neck and he had changed from his steel-grey suit to a pair of faded jeans and a worn T-shirt in hunter green.

Lucia stood in the doorway of the kitchen and watched him, her breath catching in her chest at the sight of him, the powerful shoulders encased in snug cotton, the flat stomach and trim hips and powerful thighs. He was as beautiful as a Roman statue, and in so many ways just as remote.

Did she really know this man any more? He'd left Sicily fifteen years ago, and she'd only seen him once in all that time. One unforgettable time.

He glanced up, and his eyes seemed even greener as he gazed at her for one long, taut moment before he nodded towards her clothes.

'They fit.'

'Yes. I didn't think you knew my size.'

'I guessed.' He gestured to some containers on the counter in front of him. 'Are you hungry? I realise you probably haven't eaten.'

She was starving and so she nodded, coming into the kitchen to watch Angelo lift the lids off several foil containers.

'I'm not much of a cook,' he said with the tiniest quirk of a smile, 'so I just ordered from the hotel's kitchens.'

'A perk of being the boss, I suppose,' she said, and although she'd meant to sound light she heard a faint note of bitterness creep into her voice, and she knew Angelo heard it too. He glanced up at her, the expression in his eyes veiled.

'Does that bother you? Me being the boss?'

She shrugged, a twitching of her shoulders. 'Why should it?'

'I don't know.'

'Well, I don't know either.' What an inane, childish conversation they were having. Lucia turned away from the sleek granite worktops and prowled around the open living space. 'Has anyone ever lived here?' She had not yet found a single personal item in the entire place, not a book or a photo or even a stray sock. Nothing to tell her more of the man Angelo was now.

'I've never been here before tonight.'

She glanced back at him, shocked. 'Never? Not even to make sure you liked it?'

'I had it built to my specifications, and I have an assistant who handles interior decorating. She knows my preferences.'

Lucia ignored that little splinter of jealousy that burrowed into her at the thought of some female assistant who knew what he liked. More than she knew, because she wouldn't have guessed that Angelo liked such modern decor. She really didn't know anything about him any more.

So how could she still want him? Love him?

Angelo glanced at her, eyebrows raised. 'What do you think of it?'

'You have a beautiful view,' she said diplomatically, and he let out a short, dry laugh.

'I see.'

'It just seems so…sterile. Cold. There's nothing personal about any of it.'

'And why should there be? As I told you, I've never stepped inside the place until half an hour ago.'

'And will you live here? Eventually?'

'No. I'll never live in Sicily.' The finality of his words and tone silenced her. He ladled some manicotti and swordfish onto two plates. 'Let's eat outside.'

Lucia followed him through the sliding glass doors that led to a wraparound veranda with a stunning view of the sea, the setting sun turning its surface to shimmering gold. The surf crashed far below, sending up plumes of white spray onto the railing.

'This is amazing,' Lucia said, gesturing at the view but meaning to encompass everything: the view, the house, Angelo's life. It was all amazing, and she felt a bittersweet pride at how hard he'd worked and how much he'd accomplished.

How far he'd travelled, so far away from her.

Angelo pulled out her chair and she sat, tensing as he spread a cloth napkin in her lap. His thumbs brushed her thighs and even though he'd barely touched her she still felt an ache of longing spread upwards and take over her whole body.

She tried to ignore it, to force it back, because she knew how dangerous that ache of wanting could be. That ache had deceived her, destroyed her. Made her believe in foolish fairy tales and ridiculous happily-ever-afters, even when she'd known they were absurd. Impossible.

'You wanted to talk about Angelica,' she said, smoothing the napkin over her lap once more. That was why she was here, why she'd agreed to come; he deserved to know about his daughter. So she would tell him, and then she would leave. And then, finally, please God, it would truly be finished between them.

Which was what she wanted, had to want, even if everything in her screamed otherwise.

'Yes.' Angelo sat across from her, his gaze fathomless in the near twilight. He reached for the bottle of wine he'd brought out along with their plates and with an arch of an eyebrow indicated if she'd like him to pour.

Lucia shook her head. 'No, thank you.'

Angelo set the bottle back down and reached for his fork. 'You live alone,' he remarked as he started to eat. She nodded, wary, and took a forkful of swordfish. It was buttery-soft and tender, almost dissolving in her mouth. 'What happened to your mother?' he asked.

Lucia swallowed. 'She died seven years ago.' Two months before he'd shown up at her door.

Something flickered in his eyes, although Lucia couldn't tell what it was. What he felt. 'I'm sorry. How did it happen?'

'A heart attack. It was quick.'

'Sudden too.'

'Yes.'

'So you've been on your own a long time.'

'Yes.' He knew from their childhood that she'd been raised by her mother; her father, worthless drunk that he'd been, had left without a backwards glance when she was eight years old, and her mother had never stopped missing him, never stopped wanting him back. Angelo wasn't the only one who'd had unfortunate parents.

'You've been working for the Correttis since I left,' he observed, his tone neutral, and Lucia toyed with her pasta.

'They pay well.'

'Did you mother leave you any money?'

'What little she had.' She glanced up at him, felt a flash of frustration, maybe even of anger. 'Why are you asking all this, Angelo? What on earth does it matter to you?'

'You matter,' he said flatly. 'You were the mother of my child, Lucia. I want to know what has happened to you.'

She shook her head. 'It doesn't change anything.'

'I still want to know.'

They ate in silence for a moment, and Lucia felt tension tauten inside her. She might have been the mother of Angelo's child, but she wasn't—and never had been—anything else to him. It stung that the only reason he'd sought her out now, had spoken to her again at all, was because he wanted to know about Angelica. And even though part of her was gratified and even glad he wanted to know about their daughter, another part shrank back in desolation that he didn't care about *her*.

Still she yearned. Still her stubborn, stupid heart insisted on wanting, on hoping, even when she knew there was no point. No chance.

'Did you try and tell me?' he asked after a long silence, his tone still neutral. 'When you found out you were pregnant?'

'I tried to try,' she answered quietly. 'I didn't know how to tell you. I didn't want you to feel guilty or like I'd trapped you into something, but—' She hesitated, and his mouth twisted.

'But you were afraid I wouldn't believe you? Or come back for you?'

She lifted her chin and made herself meet his hooded gaze directly. 'Would you have?'

'For my child? Yes.' He spoke with complete certainty, and Lucia nodded slowly. For his child. Not for her, never for her. She'd never been enough of a reason for him to stay, or even to consider taking her with him. It was that realisation, she knew, that had kept her from writing. She had never wanted to be his burden.

'In any case,' she said, trying to sound matter-of-fact, 'I wrote a dozen different letters and never sent them. I kept telling myself I had time, and then—and then it didn't matter any more.' She swallowed past the lump that had formed in her throat. Even now it hurt. Especially now.

'I wish,' Angelo said quietly, 'I could have been there. I would have liked to have seen her, to have held her.'

Lucia stared down at her plate, her half-eaten meal blurring in front of her. She knew if she blinked the tears would fall, and she didn't want to cry. Not in front of Angelo. Not when every word he said seemed to hurt her in so many different ways.

He wanted to have been there for their baby, not for her. And even though that knowledge hurt, a far worse pain lanced through her at how easily she could imagine him cradling their daughter, loving her. How much of her still yearned for a life that had never been hers—or theirs.

'She looked just like she was asleep,' she said, her eyes still on her plate. She cleared her throat, the sound unnaturally loud in the sudden stillness. 'I held her for a little while.' She blinked, touched the corner of her eye where a telling moisture had appeared, averting her face so Angelo wouldn't see.

Still she didn't think she'd fooled him.

'Let's walk,' he said, almost roughly, and rose from the table. Lucia looked up, blinking rapidly, and then followed him down the twisting staircase that led to the beach.

CHAPTER SIX

THE WIND OFF the sea was a sultry caress of her skin, the sand soft and still warm under her bare feet. Lucia dabbed at her eyes again, took a deep breath as she wrested her emotions under control. Her composure, her sense of control, was the only thing of value that she had, and she clung to it.

He walked a little ahead of her, his hands shoved into the pockets of his jeans, the wind blowing the T-shirt tight to his body so she could see the powerful, sculpted muscles of his chest and abdomen.

'And afterwards?' he asked after they'd walked for several minutes, the waves washing onto the sand by their feet. 'Was there…was there a funeral?'

'Yes.' She spoke with matter-of-fact flatness, her only defence against the undertow of emotion that threatened to suck her down into its destructive spiral. She hadn't talked of this in so long; she hadn't even allowed herself to remember. Her pregnancy had been a source of shame, so that even her daughter's death had felt like a forbidden grief, not to be spoken of, not to be mourned. More than one woman in the narrow streets of Caltarione had told her she should be thankful Angelica hadn't lived. Lucia had never replied to this repellent sentiment, but everything in her had burned and raged—and now, under the onslaught of Angelo's questions, still did.

'At the church in Caltarione,' she told Angelo in that same matter-of-fact tone. 'It was a very small service.' Just her, the priest and a few friends of her mother who had, to Lucia's surprise, attended with a silent, stolid solidarity. 'She's buried there, in a special area for still-born babies.' She'd used the last of the inheritance from her mother to pay for the headstone.

Angelo nodded, his head lowered, his hands still shoved in his pockets. 'I'd like to go there.' He paused, stopping mid-stride, and reluctantly Lucia turned to him. His gaze moved searchingly over her as he asked, 'Will you go with me?' The request stopped her in her tracks, the grief she'd suppressed for so long like a leaden weight in her chest.

'Lucia?' Angelo prompted, and she couldn't speak, couldn't even shake her head. It was taking all of her strength, all of her will, simply to stand under that oppressive weight, a grief she'd carried with her yet never acknowledged or accepted. Never been able to let go of.

Now it threatened to bury her, and she could not stand the thought of kneeling in front of her baby's grave with Angelo, acknowledging with him the death of their daughter, of all her dreams, the life she'd once hoped to have....

'Lucia.' Angelo took her by the shoulders. 'What is it? What's wrong?'

What was *wrong*? Could he really ask that? Could he really not understand how this was killing her?

She made some small sound, the sound of an animal in pain. Angelo frowned and with the last of her strength Lucia wrenched away from him before he could see the agony on her face. She started running down the beach, back to the villa, anywhere away from him.

She heard Angelo give a muttered curse and then he was coming up behind her, his hands clamping down on her shoulders and turning her towards him. Still she resisted, twisting away from him as the tears streaked down her cheeks and the sobs gathered in her chest, an unbearable pressure finally demanding release.

Angelo wouldn't let her go. His arms came around her, drawing her to him so she was pressed against his chest, his lips on her hair, her face hidden in the warm curve of his shoulder. 'Oh, Lucia…*mi cucciola*…I'm sorry…I didn't realise.… Of course it still hurts. It always hurts.'

The gentleness of his embrace and the tenderness of his words made it impossible for her to fight. Resist. In the safety of his arms she broke, and all the anguish she'd been holding back spilled out of her, so her body shook and tears streamed from her eyes. She couldn't have even said what she was crying for. The loss of her daughter? The loss of Angelo? The loss of everything, all her unspoken hopes, the life she'd so desperately wanted yet had known she would never have.

Angelo drew her down to the sand, his hands stroking her hair as he murmured endearments and words of comfort, his voice low and ragged.

Lucia heard herself saying things and fragments of things she'd never meant to share, hadn't even realised she remembered. 'She had blue eyes, but they were dark. I think they would have been green, like yours.… They wrapped her in a blue blanket and it made me so angry, such a silly thing.… The doctor's hands were so cold and the nurse took her away from me without even asking.…'

And then there were no more words, just sobs tearing

from her chest and coming out of her mouth in ragged gulps as Angelo held and rocked her, offering her the kind of comfort she'd so often given him.

Her face was hidden in the curve of his shoulder, her lips brushing the warm skin just above the collar of his T-shirt, all of it just as he'd once been with her, and acting on instinct and out of need Lucia pressed her lips against his skin in a silent kiss, a mute appeal. She felt Angelo tense, his arms stiffening even as they held her, but she was past caring. Past asking.

The appeal became a demand as she kissed him again, her lips pressing harder against his warm skin. She heard his ragged draw of breath, his arms still around her.

'Lucia…'

But she didn't want words. She wanted this, only this—to take and not to give, to be comforted and not to comfort. Was it wrong? Was it selfish? She didn't care. She needed this. Needed his caress, the only kind of comfort she craved now. She lifted her head from his shoulder and looked at him, but in the twilit darkness she couldn't make out his expression.

She leaned forward and kissed him hard, and his mouth opened under hers even as his hands came up to her shoulders to brace her—or to push her away? She wrapped her arms around him and pressed herself against him. She heard him groan and he deepened the kiss, his tongue sweeping inside and claiming her for his own.

Lucia kissed him back, her hands in his hair and then on his shoulders, sliding beneath his shirt to feel the taut, warm skin underneath. She pushed him back onto the beach and his arms came up around her, their legs tangling together in the sand.

She lay on top of him, shuddered as she felt his hands

slide under her T-shirt, his thumbs brushing across her breasts. She arched into the caress, shifting so she could feel his arousal pressing against her belly. Angelo kissed her, his mouth moving from her lips to her throat, and then the V between her breasts, the pleasure of his touch so intense it felt almost painful, and yet she still wanted more. Needed more.

With one trembling hand she reached down to undo the button on his jeans. Angelo wrapped his fingers around her own, stilling her hand.

'Lucia, no. *Per favore*, not like this.'

'Yes, like this,' she shot back fiercely. 'Exactly like this.'

He shook his head. 'You are sad, grieving—'

'And you were sad and grieving the last time we slept together, Angelo. It helped, didn't it? I helped you forget for a moment.' He stilled, his hand still wrapped around hers, but his grip had slackened and she pushed his hand away, undid his zip. She stroked the hard length of his erection through the silk of his boxers. 'Help me forget,' she whispered. 'Help me forget, even if just for a moment.' She stroked him again, saw him close his eyes, his jaw clenched.

'If you want me to make love to you, I will,' he said raggedly. 'But not here, on the hard sand.'

She let out a wild, trembling laugh. 'Have you become so particular, in the past seven years?' Her creaky, sagging bed had been the setting for their last encounter; he hadn't complained. He hadn't said anything at all.

'Come back to the villa,' he said, and he rose from the sand, buttoning up his jeans before reaching for her hand. Reluctantly Lucia took it. Now that the rawness of the moment had eased she was conscious of how much she'd revealed, from the confessions she'd sobbed out to the tears on her cheeks, and the shameless, desperate way she'd reached for him. Yet even so she still wanted him. Needed what he could give, if just for this one night.

They walked in silence back along the beach, up the stairs to the veranda and then inside to the sterile stillness of the villa. Angelo turned around to face her, his expression watchful, guarded, and Lucia knew he'd suggested they return to the villa not because he had a preference for satin sheets but because he wanted to give her time to change her mind.

Well, she wouldn't. He'd turned to her for comfort and pleasure once; she'd do the same to him. Maybe then it would feel finished between them, a final, equal exchange. Maybe then she could move on.

She lifted her chin. 'Where's the bedroom?'

Surprise flared silver in his eyes and his mouth quirked in a small smile. 'You are constantly amazing me.'

She ignored the warmth that flared through her at his praise. 'Don't patronise me, Angelo.'

'Trust me, I am not. Perhaps tragedy has made you stronger, Lucia, for you have far more spirit now than I ever gave you credit for when we were children.'

'Yes, I do.' Tragedy *had* made her stronger. She was glad he saw it. 'The bedroom,' she prompted, and he smiled faintly even as he watched her, still wary.

'Are you sure about this?'

'Why shouldn't I be?'

'A decision like this should not be made in the heat of the moment—'

'And it's not the heat of the moment right now,' she answered. Still he stared at her, his eyes dark and considering.

'I don't,' he finally said in a low voice, 'want to hurt you.'

Lucia swallowed past the ache his words opened up inside her. He'd hurt so many times in the past, but this time it would be different.

'You won't,' she said. This time she wouldn't let him. She knew what she wanted, what to expect. This time she would be the one to walk away.

It should be simple. He wanted this; clearly, so did she. So why, Angelo wondered, was he not sweeping Lucia up the stairs and into his bed?

Because her tears had been too recent, her grief too raw. Yet he'd turned to her in his own anger and pain; would he not allow her to do the same?

Still he hesitated.

'Don't tell me you have *la gola secca*, Angelo,' she mocked softly. Her eyes glittered sapphire and she walked towards him, determination evident in every taut line of her body, her hips swaying, the silky T-shirt and skirt highlighting the lush curves he'd had his hands on only moments ago.

'No, not a dry throat,' he replied, gazing down at her. 'I'm not afraid.' He just wanted to give her the time to acknowledge *la gola secca* of her own. He didn't want this to be rushed, regrettable. He still didn't know all he wanted from Lucia, but he did know it was more than that.

He tucked a stray tendril of hair behind her ear, trailed his fingers down her cheek. She closed her eyes, drew in a shuddering breath and then opened them to stare straight into his own.

'Make love to me, Angelo. Make love to me, *please*.'

Her broken plea felled him. How could he deny her? How could he resist her? Angelo curled his hands around her shoulders and kissed her softly. At least, it was meant to be a soft kiss, a tender thing, but memory and need crashed over him, reminding him of how accepted he'd felt in her arms, as if her embrace were the only home—the only hope—he'd ever had.

He deepened the kiss, turned it into both a demand and entreaty. His tongue swept into her mouth and he slid his hands under her T-shirt, cupping the lush fullness of her breasts as a sob of longing broke from her throat and she hooked one leg around his, drawing him even closer to her own intoxicating softness.

He'd meant to lead her upstairs, to pull back the satin sheets and lay her down gently, like a treasure. He'd meant to take his time, to make love to her properly, for he knew the last time they'd been together it had been desperate, frantic—and incredible.

And it was just as frantic now—and just as incredible.

Her fingers fumbled with the zip on his jeans and then curled around his erection. He let out a ragged moan as he slid his own hand up the silky length of her thigh and then beneath her underwear straight to the centre of her, his fingers sliding inside her slick warmth even as his brain told him to stop rushing, they had all the time in the world—

Except they didn't. Lucia pulled him closer, arched against him. 'Now, *now*,' she pleaded, her voice almost a sob as she pushed down his jeans and boxers with clumsy, hurried movements. He hoisted her onto the back of the leather sofa, her legs spread wide and open to him. She reached for him, guiding him towards her.

'Lucia…' he muttered, a token protest, for already she was wrapping her legs around his waist, arching against him, and then he was inside her and he let out a ragged gasp of desire because she felt so *good*.

They moved in silent, sweet complicity, and pleasure and something far deeper surged through him, over-whelmed every sense he possessed. He'd thought last time the rightness he'd felt with Lucia had been a prod-uct of his own confused grief over his father's death, but he had no such reason this time. No such excuse. The rightness he felt, the completeness, was just as strong, just as powerful—even more so.

This was where he belonged. He, a bastard child re-jected by his father and abandoned by his mother, barely tolerated by the grandparents who had raised him and reviled by the villagers who could have been his com-munity, his strength. This—Lucia—was the only place where he felt at home. Where he belonged.

He felt her arch against him and she sobbed out his name, her face buried in his shoulder, as he reached his own climax and drew her even closer to him, never wanting to let her go.

Lucia sagged against Angelo, replete. Tears streaked down her face but they had been good tears, healing tears in their own way. She didn't regret anything. She wouldn't let herself.

He moved, slipping out of her, and she felt an immedi-ate and innate sense of loss. Incredibly, she still wanted him. Gently he tucked her hair behind her ears, wiped the traces of tears from her face. He smiled, his features softened into something almost like tenderness.

'*Dio*, I didn't mean it to be as fast as that.'

She laughed shakily; already this was so different from before. From what she knew. Seven years ago there had been no pillow talk, no exchange at all. Afterwards he'd drawn her to him and she'd curled around his body, silent, singing with an ill-found happiness, and they'd both fallen asleep.

When she'd woken up with the dawn he had already left. She hadn't even been surprised, not really.

'There's nothing wrong with fast.'

'Next time it will be slow.'

Next time? The words, spoken with so much certainty, shocked her. Surely there would be no next time with Angelo.

He tugged on her fingers. 'Come upstairs.'

'Where?'

But he didn't answer, just led her up the winding staircase and then into what was clearly the master bedroom, and then into the huge marble en suite bathroom.

'You're covered in sand. And tears. Let me wash you.'

Wash her? It seemed like an incredibly intimate, tender thing to do, so different from the frantic urgency of what had happened before. This was new, uncertain territory, thrilling and scary. She didn't know this Angelo.... And yet as he led her to the huge glassed-in shower with a wry, tender smile she felt like she'd always know him.

That boy. That girl.

She stood still as Angelo turned on the taps and then slowly stripped the clothes from her body, sliding her skirt down her legs and the T-shirt over her head. Underwear came next, his movements gentle and unhurried, until she was completely naked before him.

She shivered slightly as she stood there; this felt, weirdly, more revealing than what they'd done just moments ago. Angelo swept his gaze over her body and she reacted underneath his considering stare, a splotchy blush appearing across her chest. He laughed softly.

'*Mi cucciola*, are you embarrassed?'

'Yes,' she said, blushing further. She crossed her arms over her breasts. 'You've never actually seen me naked before. And…and don't call me that.'

He frowned before yanking his T-shirt over his head and tossing it to the floor. 'Call you what?'

Lucia was momentarily distracted by the sight of his chest, all hard, golden muscle with a sprinkling of dark hair veeing down to the unbuttoned waistband of his jeans. She swallowed dryly. '*Mi cucciola*. You called me that when we were children.' *My puppy.* Lucia had never known if he'd meant it or not, but her heart had thrilled every time the endearment had slipped so carelessly from his lips. And no matter how tender he seemed now, she knew he'd changed. She had. This was still only, and ever could be, a one-night stand. Another one.

'I'm not that girl any more, Angelo,' she said quietly. 'And you're not that boy.'

Slowly he reached out and wiped the trace of a tear from her cheek with his thumb. 'Am I not?' he asked softly, and she shook her head.

'You know you aren't.'

'I don't know anything any more.' Smiling although his eyes were dark he wrapped his hand around the back of her neck and drew her to him, kissing her gently on the lips. Lucia closed her eyes, felt her heart twist inside her.

She couldn't let him be that boy again. She'd fallen in love with that boy, and he'd broken her heart. She knew he didn't love her, had never loved her, and if she believed in an Angelo that was different from the ruthless and determined tycoon he'd become she'd be lost. Broken. *Again.*

If he really was that boy inside, underneath, she wouldn't be able to walk away after one night. And she had to, for her own sake. One night, on her terms this time, and then in the morning she'd walk away. For ever.

Angelo broke the kiss to gaze at her, a question in his eyes. 'What are you thinking?' he asked softly.

'Nothing.' She swallowed, tried to smile. 'Nothing important.'

He smiled, the curve of his mouth primal and possessive as he led her into the shower. Lucia had never bathed with a man before. She'd never *been* with a man except Angelo, had never had the opportunity or the desire. She'd only wanted Angelo. She'd only loved Angelo.

She had to stop thinking like that.

She watched as Angelo poured some expensive-smelling shower gel onto his hands, smiling at her, his eyes glinting in the dim light.

'What are you—?' she began, but then stopped as he slid his soapy hands over her body and she leaned against the wall as the water streamed over them and Angelo touched her everywhere.

'Two showers in the space of about an hour,' she murmured as a heavy languor crept over her, caused by the sure movements of Angelo's slippery hands. 'I feel *very* clean.'

He laughed softly and slid one hand between her legs. Lucia clutched his wrist. *'Angelo...'*

'I'm *very* thorough,' he said, and as his fingers found her so did his mouth. He kissed her deeply and Lucia clung to his shoulders, pleasure coursing through her at the feel of Angelo's hands, his mouth, everything. She forgot about what she wanted or didn't want, what was safe and what was incredibly dangerous. All she could think, feel, *know*, was his touch.

She let her head rest against his shoulder as he stroked her, bringing her dizzyingly near that precipice of pleasure once more, her body boneless and yet throbbing with need—and then he stopped.

'What—'

'Now my turn.'

'*Your* turn...'

'Touch me, Lucia.'

She heard the ragged plea in his voice and lifted her head from his shoulder, saw him gazing at her with a fierce light in his eyes, turning them almost to emerald. With a thrill she realised she wanted to touch him, touch him in ways she hadn't yet, hadn't dared.

With a tentative smile she reached for the shower gel, pouring some into her palms before she slid her slippery hands over his shoulders, down his chest, across his hips, revelling in the feel of hot skin and hard muscle. Angelo had closed his eyes and he threw his head back as she slid her hand farther down still and curled her fingers around the heavy, hard length of his arousal.

There was nothing rushed or frantic about this, nothing desperate. Every caress was deliberate, and it filled Lucia with a tremulous wonder. Thirty-two years old and she'd had no idea sex could be like this, slow and exploratory and *wonderful*. This wasn't a stolen moment, snatched out of grief or pain; it stretched on, infinite with possibility, with an incredible new intimacy.

But it would end by morning. She had to remember that.

'*Lucia...*' Angelo's voice was a groan as he curled his hands around her shoulders and she stroked him everywhere, delighting in the glorious feel of him.

'*Dio*, I'm not going to last,' he muttered, and then he hoisted her easily, his hands cradling her bottom so her legs came round his hips as he drove inside her. Lucia buried her head in his shoulder but he pulled back, forced her to meet his own glittering gaze.

'Look at me,' he commanded hoarsely as he moved inside her. 'Look at me as I make love to you.'

Lucia obeyed, her gaze riveted on his as their bodies acting in perfect synchronicity, her hips rising up to meet his as he moved inside her. Every protective layer she'd ever had was stripped away in the intense intimacy of his gaze, his body buried inside hers. She couldn't hide from it; she'd been laid utterly, gloriously bare and in that moment she revelled in the exposure.

She felt the pressure and pleasure building inside her, spiralling up and up, and she knew Angelo could see it on her face. Knew he would know when she finally fell.

And he did, kissing her lips as she cried out and her body spasmed around his. Seconds later he found his own shuddering climax and she buried her head in the curve of his neck as the water streamed over them.

Lucia didn't know how long she remained there, cradled against him, her heart pounding hard against his. It could have been a minute or an hour, but eventually Angelo gently righted her, turned off the shower and wrapped her in a towel. She remained still as he dried her tenderly and then led her to the bed.

They didn't speak, and Lucia was glad. She didn't want to break this moment that had wrapped around her like a spell of warmth and safety and love. She knew it wasn't real, knew in the hard light of morning it would all be broken, vanished. But she wasn't ready to let go of it yet.

One night. One night of feeling safe and treasured and loved. It didn't seem too much to ask.

Angelo laid her in the bed and then slid in next to

her, pulling her towards him so she naturally curved her body into his. She could feel his still-pounding heart against her back, and after a moment Angelo found her hand with his own and laced his fingers with hers, resting their joined hands against her belly as sleep finally claimed her.

CHAPTER SEVEN

LUCIA WOKE TO an empty bed. She rolled over on her back, stared at the ceiling and let the memories wash over her. The pleasure of last night, and more surprisingly and poignantly, the incredible intimacy. She hadn't expected that. She'd gone into the evening expecting a bargain, an exchange of both power and pleasure. This time she'd be the one to want the one-night stand. And the one to walk away.

The trouble was, she didn't want to.

She rolled onto her side, tucked her legs up towards her tummy. She was an idiot, of course. An absolute idiot to think she could walk away from Angelo. To think that she could want it. She'd loved him since she was seven years old.

And yet she knew, with a heavy, painful certainty, that walking away was her only choice. Angelo wouldn't want anything else, and she refused to surrender her dignity yet again. This time she would choose first…if he hadn't already.

Slowly she swung her legs over the side of the bed, felt aches in all sorts of places. A glance at the clock told her it was after eight, and she was due at the hotel in less than an hour. She pushed her hair out of her face and went in search of her maid's uniform.

Ten minutes later she was dressed, her hair and teeth brushed thanks to the basket of toiletries in the guest bedroom, and resolutely she went in search of Angelo. She found him in the kitchen, slicing fruit, the tantalising aroma of fresh coffee scenting the air.

Lucia hung back for a moment, watching as he moved around the kitchen. He wore another worn T-shirt, this one in heather grey, and a pair of boxers. His hair was tousled, almost curly in the heat, and he looked comfortable, natural, *happy*. She'd never seen him look so happy before.

And for a second, no more, she let herself imagine that this was real. Lasting. This was their home, their life, a normal morning in a loving relationship. She even, treacherously, allowed herself to imagine their daughter slept upstairs, six years old, with Angelo's eyes and her dimple.

A longing so intense it felt as if she were being suffocated took hold of her, stole her breath. Shakily Lucia drew another, forced the images back.

This was what was real: work in half an hour and whatever little she and Angelo had shared over. Throwing her shoulders back, she came into the kitchen.

Angelo raised his head as soon as he heard her; Lucia saw the welcoming light wink out of his eyes as he stared at her, his mouth compressing into a hard line.

'Why are you wearing that wretched uniform?'

She stiffened at the disdain in his voice. 'Because I'm due at work in less than an hour.'

'Work?' He sounded utterly incredulous. 'I called already. You're not expected.'

'You…called?' Lucia stared at him blankly. Why would he call? Why would he not want her to go to work?

'Yes, I called. Of course you're not going to work today.'

'I'm not?' She prickled, fought against the treacherous surge of hope his words caused to rise up within her. 'Why not?'

His mouth quirked in a smile. 'I think the better question is, why would you?'

'Because it's my job and I don't want to get fired?'

His smile widened. 'Since I now own the hotel I don't think you'll get fired.'

'Don't, Angelo.' Even though she knew he was speaking the truth his words made her cringe. Sleeping with the boss. It sounded so sordid, as sordid as the last time he'd breezed in and out of her life, and left rumours and heartache in his wake.

'Don't what?' He frowned, seeming genuinely confused, and Lucia just shook her head and took a deep breath.

'I think,' she said, 'it would be better—cleaner—if we ended this now.'

Angelo stared at her for a long moment. The frown had gone from his face, just like the smile. He looked utterly unreadable, completely expressionless. 'Cleaner,' he finally said, his tone neutral.

'Yes.'

'You want to end this now?'

'I think it would be better.'

He glanced back down at the melon he'd been slicing and arranged the slices on a plate, his long fingers working deftly, his head lowered. 'I don't want to end this now,' he said after a moment, and Lucia's breath hitched, her heart lurched.

It was more than he'd ever admitted to before, and yet it was so damn little. 'When, then?' she made herself ask.

'Does it matter?' Angelo glanced up and she saw impatience flicker in his grey-green eyes. Clearly he hadn't expected this conversation to take so long. '*Dio*, Lucia, after last night—you want to go back to your job? Your life?'

She recoiled, stung by the contempt in his tone. 'I think you rate yourself a little too highly,' she managed through stiff lips.

'I'm saying this all wrong.' He shook his head, still impatient. 'Come have breakfast and we'll talk.'

She glanced at the clock. 'I don't really have time—'

'You don't have time? Don't you think this—us— warrants a little more consideration?'

She let out a hollow laugh. 'There's never been an us, Angelo. You made sure about that.'

'It's different now.'

'Because you want it to be?'

'Why are you angry?' He shook his head, angry now himself. 'I'm offering you something I've—'

'Never offered before?' she filled in, her voice hard. 'So I should grab it with both hands and tell you how thankful I am? Sorry I'm not falling in with your plans.'

His expression shuttered, his jaw bunched. 'At least come and eat something,' he said tightly, and brought a tray of fresh fruit and coffee out towards the veranda.

Slowly Lucia followed him outside, wondered why she was so angry. Surely Angelo was doing everything she'd once dreamt about. Incredible sex, making breakfast, wanting to be with her? What was wrong with this picture?

Because she knew instinctively something was.

Outside the day was already hot, the sun beating down, a slight breeze off the sea the only relief. She sank into a chair and mutely accepted the cup of espresso Angelo handed her.

'So tell me what exactly it is you're offering, Angelo,' she said after she'd taken a sip. 'Why should I take a day off work? What are you suggesting?'

'I'm not suggesting you take the day off, although I suppose that would be a start.'

'A start? To what?'

'To—to us!' He looked, quite suddenly, furious—although whether with her or himself she didn't know. She did know, knew with the unshakeable certainty that she'd always possessed when it came to this man, that he still didn't want to want her. Nothing really had changed except, perhaps, the force of Angelo's reluctant need.

'Us,' she repeated. 'What kind of us?'

'Why are you asking all these questions?'

'Because I want to know what you're suggesting, Angelo. You've been barking out orders since I came downstairs but I still don't know what you want. A day in bed? A *relationship*?'

Shamefully her voice trembled on that revealing word, and from the way he quickly averted his gaze she knew it wasn't that. Never that. He still didn't want a relationship, something real, with her.

He didn't say anything for a long moment, just stared out at the sea, his eyes narrowed against the glare of the sun. 'I don't want you working like that any more,' he finally said, and her mouth dropped open before she thought to snap it shut.

'I don't know which part of that sentence to address,' she finally said, her voice thankfully tart. 'It doesn't matter what you want, and as for whatever *like that* means—'

'On your knees, scrubbing—'

'Since I'm no longer working for the Correttis, it

should hardly matter,' she snapped. 'I'm on my knees for you, Angelo.' And ridiculously she felt a blush heat her face at the suggestiveness of her words, the memory of last night.

Angelo leaned forward, his gaze snapping back to hers, his eyes like molten silver. 'Didn't last night mean anything to you, Lucia? Didn't it change anything?'

She swallowed dryly, memories flashing through her mind, making her blush all the more. 'I never got a chance to ask you those questions the last time we spent a night together,' she replied after a moment, 'but I think I could have guessed what the answers would have been.'

Realisation flared in his eyes and he sat back. 'Are you saying last night was—was just a repeat of what happened before?'

'Wasn't it?'

He didn't answer for a long moment, just stared at her, his gaze sweeping searchingly over her. 'Not for me.'

Her fingers tightened on the cup of coffee and she felt the hot liquid slosh over her fingers. Shakily she put it back on the table with a clatter. 'Just what are you saying, Angelo?'

His mouth firmed, his gaze flicking away before returning to rest on her resolutely. 'I told you, I don't want this to end now.'

What a telling phrase, she thought bleakly. Not now, but maybe later. Definitely later. 'When, then?' she asked, striving to keep her voice even.

He shrugged, the movement dismissive. 'I don't know.'

'When you want it to be over?' she surmised flatly.

'*Dio*, Lucia, isn't it enough that I want to be with you? I want to protect you, provide for you. I can give you so much—'

She felt herself go cold. 'Such as?'

'Clothes, jewels, a villa, a car—whatever you want!' He smiled, relief flashing in his eyes, as if he were glad they were finally understanding each other. 'You don't have to work as a maid. You don't have to work at all. You can live here—'

'And await your pleasure?'

He recoiled, his mouth hardening into a thin line. 'You make it sound…sordid.'

'You're the one doing that, Angelo.' Her voice trembled and she fought against the absurd yearning she still felt, the temptation to accept even this little. She sat back in her chair and closed her eyes. She felt near to crying, and yet too weary to shed any tears.

'I want,' Angelo answered, an edge to his voice now, 'to be with you. You could stay here,' he continued, sweeping one arm out to encompass the villa. 'You could have a maid of your own, an entire staff, clothes and jewels. I'll buy you a car, whatever one you like.'

'I don't know how to drive,' she said flatly. 'And I don't like this villa. I told you that last night. It feels cold.'

He stared at her incredulously. 'Then I'll hire a driver. I'll buy a new villa—you can choose it yourself.'

She shook her head. It wasn't just the villa that was cold; it was the man himself. She didn't know this man any more. She might have had the most incredible, intimate sex with him last night, but this morning he was again a stranger.

A stranger who still could only see what he wanted from her and the most expedient way to get it. Forget asking her out. Forget even a normal, caring conversation. Even now, when he was trying to be thoughtful, clearly expecting her to be pleased with these tawdry suggestions. He had no consideration of her feelings at all, and he didn't even realise it.

Everything in her aching, Lucia rose from the table. 'I need to go to work.'

'I told you, they're not expecting you,' Angelo snapped. He rose from the table, braced his hands on it. His body was taut with emotion, with anger, his mouth a compressed line, his eyes narrowed. 'Lucia, I can see I'm saying all the wrong things. I swear to you, I am not trying to make you angry.'

Which somehow made it worse. He didn't even realise how awful, how *offensive*, his suggestions were. 'I know you're not, Angelo,' she said wearily, and turned away.

He smacked the table with the palm of his hand, rattling the dishes, the crack of his palm echoing through the still air. '*Dio*, don't walk away from me! I'm not done talking to you!'

She stiffened at the autocratic bark of his voice. 'I'm done,' she said flatly. 'And unless you intend to order me not to work as my employer, we have nothing more to say here.'

He stared at her, his eyes flashing with fury, his body tight with suppressed rage, and then on leaden legs Lucia turned and walked back into the house and then out the front door.

Angelo watched Lucia walk away from him in a kind of dazed incredulity. He had not expected this. He still couldn't believe it was happening. She was actually *rejecting* him.

He drove his fingers through his hair, swore under his breath. What was wrong with the woman? He was offering her so much more than she'd ever had before, so much more than she'd ever had with him. He'd spent most of last night awake with her in his arms, trying to think through his own feelings. His own desires. After what they had shared, he knew he wasn't ready to walk away. He didn't think she was either. So he came up with a solution—a solution to give her everything she'd ever wanted—and she refused him?

She was mad.

No, he realised suddenly, the insight causing him to tense, she wasn't. She was angry, because he *hadn't* offered her everything she'd ever wanted. If he had, she surely would have accepted it. So what more did she want?

Swearing again, he strode from the veranda. It took him all of two minutes to ascertain that she'd actually left the villa. Considering the house was miles from so much as a petrol station and she must have known it, the choice to leave on foot was beyond absurd.

Angelo threw open the door of the villa and saw Lucia trudging down the dusty drive. 'Lucia!' he shouted, exasperated with her, with himself, with how this whole morning had unravelled. He'd been looking forward to spending the day in bed, or perhaps again in the shower. He'd been anticipating her incredulous, wondering smile when he'd told her he wasn't walking away.

Instead *she* was walking away…was that what she wanted? Was this actually some kind of *revenge*? God only knew he understood about wanting revenge, yet he could hardly believe it of Lucia.

'Lucia!' he shouted again, and she stilled. Her head came up, her shoulders stiffened and slowly she turned around. 'You cannot walk to Palermo from here,' he called, trying to sound reasonable. 'If you insist on going into work, then let me at least drive you.'

She folded her arms, didn't move. 'Fine,' she called back flatly.

Realising she was simply going to stand there and wait, Angelo swore again under his breath and went back into the house. He pulled on a pair of jeans and leather loafers, grabbed his car keys and headed out. Lucia was waiting by the passenger door of his Porsche, her expression completely unreadable.

Was this the same woman who had cried in his arms last night, both with sorrow and joy, who had told him about their daughter, who had brought him more physical pleasure than he'd had in years…or even ever?

She looked like a stranger. And she acted like a stranger as she slid into the passenger seat and kept her face turned to the window as he started the car.

'It is obvious that I've offended you somehow with my suggestion,' Angelo stated tersely as he headed down the drive. She didn't answer, and he smacked the steering wheel with the palm of his hand. 'At least talk to me, Lucia.'

'I don't think I have anything to say that you'd want to hear.'

That didn't sound good. Angelo blew out a breath. 'I want to hear what you're thinking.'

'Do you really, Angelo? Or will that just make you angrier, because I'm not falling into line with your plans? I'm not falling into your bed.'

'You fell into my bed last night,' he snapped, and then could have cursed himself. *Not* a helpful observation to make at this point.

Lucia kept her face to the window. 'I did,' she said quietly, 'and I don't regret it. But that's all I ever intended last night to be. One night, just as before. I'm not going to be your—your long-term booty call.'

'That is offensive.'

'No kidding.'

His fingers clenched the steering wheel so hard his knuckles whitened. 'You told me that a one-night stand was not something you'd be willing to repeat.'

'I changed my mind.'

'And I changed my mind,' he answered back. 'So you see, we both can change.'

'You think you can change?' She turned to him, eyebrows raised, her tone utterly disbelieving. 'You think, with this suggestion, you *have* changed?'

He forced back the instinctive anger at her incredulous, almost sneering tone. 'You obviously don't think I have,' he said levelly.

She shook her head, folded her arms, the stance clearly one of rejection. 'One night, one week, one month. There's not much difference, Angelo.'

He pressed his lips together and stared straight ahead. All right, he saw her point, but hell, this was new territory for him. He didn't *do* relationships. He didn't have girlfriends or even mistresses. His entire life he'd been focused on work, driven by success and revenge. He had no time for the messy sprawl of romance or, God forbid, *love*. Sex had always been a transaction—

And, he realised, he was proposing such a transaction to Lucia now. He'd dressed it up a bit, yes, but essentially it was a business deal. A bargain.

But he didn't *do* anything else. This was all he had to offer, and damn it, he wanted her to accept it. It wasn't, he thought grimly, such a bad deal.

He glanced at her now, saw she'd turned back to the window. All he could see was the smooth, round curve of her cheek, her plaited hair revealing the vulnerable nape of her neck.

He let out a weary breath. 'Why put a time limit on it, Lucia?' he said, and although she didn't turn from the window he saw her mouth curve in the barest of sad smiles.

'You already did.'

'I did not.' He shook his head, denying the judgement he felt from her. What would make her see sense? 'We didn't use protection last night,' he said after a moment. It hadn't even occurred to him, much to his own shame. 'What if you're pregnant?'

He saw her tense, felt it. 'I don't think that's a possibility.'

'You're on birth control?' Absurd to feel jealous if she was, yet he did. Had she had many other lovers?

'No,' Lucia said after a moment. 'But I—I don't think it's likely.'

'And if it is?'

She turned to him, her expression utterly unreadable. 'You think a pregnancy would force my hand? Make me agree to your…suggestion?'

'It's not such a bad suggestion, Lucia.'

'I think it is.'

'What do you want? Marriage?' He injected the word with the contempt he couldn't help but feel, and he saw hurt flash across her face. *Damn it.*

'And if I did?' she asked quietly.

'I'm not capable of that. I thought—I thought you knew that.'

Her mouth twisted in something like a smile. 'You speak as though it's a chronic condition.'

'I can't help who I am, Lucia.'

'Exactly.'

Frustration bubbled inside him, an unholy ferment of emotion. She was twisting everything he said, taking it completely the wrong way. 'So that's it? You're not even going to give us a chance?'

He heard her draw in a short breath, and knew she was more conflicted, more tempted, than she was trying to act. 'No.'

'*Dio*, Lucia, I think after last night I deserve a little more than that.'

'Did I deserve more than that, before?' she answered. She didn't sound angry though, not the way he felt. She sounded only tired. Resigned, and that made him even more furious. He knew she wanted him. Wanted him as much as he wanted her. Why couldn't she see the sense in what he was offering?

'And so I apologised. I told you I knew I shouldn't have left you like that. God help me, I am trying to make it up to you now. I want to be with you, Lucia. That's what this is about. I thought—I thought you wanted to be with me.' He heard a ragged note enter his voice and stared straight at the road, his jaw so tight he felt as if he might break a tooth. He couldn't believe he was saying these things, much less meaning them.

It felt awful, this helpless confession, like peeling back his own skin. He was raw, vulnerable and completely exposed. And yet still he couldn't help himself. He *had* to say these things. He meant them utterly. He wanted more with Lucia. And yet looking at her averted face he knew his more was still less than what Lucia wanted.

I want to be with you. For a man like Angelo, it was a huge confession. She'd never imagined that he would consider last night the start of something. It hadn't even crossed her mind, because he'd never even hinted at such a thing before. Never remotely wanted it.

And even though it was an amazing admission for him to make, it wasn't enough. It wasn't enough because he didn't even realise how little it was.

Yet Lucia still felt a longing open inside her, that old, endless ache, and she was so unbearably tempted to snatch his paltry offer with both hands. She would have accepted it before. She would have taken whatever crumb he tossed her way, and forced it to sustain her. It was this understanding of her own weakness that made her stiffen her shoulders, harden her resolve.

She really had changed, and she wouldn't let herself accept Angelo's offer of being nothing more than a mistress, even if he hadn't used that word. Even if he didn't understand that was what he was suggesting.

'Lucia,' he said again, his voice still revealingly ragged. 'Say something, please.'

She leaned her head back against the seat and closed her eyes. Willed herself not to say yes…yes, she'd do it, she'd take it, just as long as she could be with him. She would not be that pathetic creature again. Surely she'd had enough rejection for one life.

She'd heard how her mother had begged her father to stay, never mind the drinking, the abuse, the other women. Watched her mother spiral down into despair and bitterness in the following years. Did she really want to be like that?

She had no illusions about how little Angelo was capable of. He'd been pushing people away his whole life. Pushing *her* away. Seven years ago it had been one night; this time it might be a week, a month, perhaps a little longer. And then? He'd push. He'd walk away just as he had before, without a backwards glance. Without even a thought.

'I did want to be with you, Angelo,' she said in a low voice, each word formed with painful effort. 'Once.'

'And not now?'

She swallowed, forced the single word past stiff lips. 'No.'

With her eyes still closed, she didn't see him turn the steering wheel. She just heard the squeal of the tyres and felt her body flung sideways as he pulled the car onto the side of the dusty road. Her eyes flew open and she stared at him in shock, saw his chest rise and fall with ragged breaths as he stared straight ahead.

'Damn it, Lucia,' he said, 'that is *not* true.' He turned to her, his eyes blazing grim determination. 'Look me in the eye and tell me you don't want to be with me. Right here, look me in the eye and swear on your mother's grave—no, on our *daughter's* grave that last night meant nothing to you.'

Lucia stared at him, opened her mouth. No words came out. She couldn't say that, couldn't mean it, and he knew it. 'What do you want from me, Angelo?' she whispered.

'The truth.'

'*Why?*' she burst out. 'Does it stroke your ego to know how much I loved you once? How much I still love you?' She saw shock blaze across his face and his jaw dropped. She laughed, the sound high and wild. 'Yes, I love you. I've always loved you. I loved you when we were children, when I waited for you on my doorstep with a damp cloth for your cuts. I loved you when you told me your dreams of leaving Caltarione, all of Sicily, to make your fortune. I dreamt you'd take me with you, and when you left I still dreamt you'd come back for me. And then you did come back for me—' She broke off, drew in a clogged breath. She was saying so much more than she'd ever intended to reveal, and yet even now she couldn't believe he'd never known. It had been so appallingly obvious to her.

'Lucia—' he said hoarsely, and she flung up one hand.

'*No*. I'll say this now, only now, only once. Loving you doesn't matter. It doesn't make a difference, because I know—I've always known—you don't love me back the same way. You don't love me at all.' He opened his mouth to say—what? Was he actually going to deny something that was so blatantly, brutally true? 'You might think you feel something for me,' she cut him off, 'and perhaps you do. Affection, attraction, something so paltry it hardly matters. I mean no more to you than one of your cars or villas or perhaps one of your corporate takeovers. Something to be acquired, enjoyed and then discarded. That's how you've *always* seen me, Angelo.'

Angelo just stared at her, unspeaking. He still looked dazed.

And he obviously had no answer, for after a few silent seconds he put the car into Drive and swung back onto the motorway, all without a word. Lucia leaned her head back against her seat and closed her eyes. Angelo's silence hurt her far more than she knew it should. Had she actually been expecting him to deny the truth? Hoping for him to insist she was wrong, he really had changed, and he knew now that he loved her?

Fantasies.

Neither of them spoke for the rest of the trip back to Palermo.

Angelo still didn't speak as he pulled in front of the hotel and waited for Lucia to get out. He was still spinning from what she'd said. All of it too incredible, too *much*. He felt too much.

And he'd said too much…more than he'd ever admitted before to anyone *ever*, and she'd thrown it all back in his face. Fury churned through him, along with the shock and the disbelief.

Lucia hesitated as she climbed out of the Porsche, her face still averted, her head bowed. For a second he thought she'd say something—but what? She'd said everything on the side of the road, when she'd told him she loved him and it didn't matter.

Because he didn't love her.

He waited until she'd disappeared into the hotel, and then he pulled away from the kerb with an angry screech of tyres.

His mind a haze, he drove through the crowded streets of Palermo and then along the ocean road towards Messina until he found a deserted stretch of beach. He parked the car on a patch of dry grass along the road and tossed his loafers in the car.

He didn't know how long he walked along the beach, his hands shoved in his pockets, his mind numb. He had meetings to attend, pressure to put on the different Corretti factions. Hell, he had a coup to stage and here he was beachcombing.

Yet still he walked.

I love you. I've always loved you.

How could she love him? Nobody loved him. Nobody had ever told him they loved him before. Not his stony-faced grandparents, not his absent mother and certainly not the father who would have preferred he'd never existed at all.

All you were meant to be was a stain on the sheets.

He'd stopped expecting or even hoping for love or anything close to it long ago. He might have suspected Lucia had had some kind of schoolgirl crush on him at one point, but that's all it had been. It hadn't been real; it hadn't been *love*. It simply wasn't possible.

And he didn't love her. He didn't know how to love, didn't have it in him. He'd accepted that too, understood that about himself. He hadn't loved anyone in his life, hadn't let himself, and so his emotions had atrophied into nothing, an atrophy of the heart. Some might view his lack of love as a weakness or deficiency, but he'd turned it into a strength. If you didn't love anyone it was easier to focus on work, to live for it. Easier to not care when no one loved you back, easier to walk away.

Except now he didn't want to walk away. Lucia was the one walking, and the thought filled him with frustration, fury—and fear. Why couldn't she accept what he'd offered? Why couldn't it be enough for her? It was a hell of a lot more than he'd offered seven years ago, and yet she still wanted more? From him?

Didn't she realise he didn't have any more to give?

Angelo sank onto the sand, his head in his hands. Yes, he realised hollowly, she did, and that was why she'd gone.

He didn't know how long he sat there, unmoving, his mind retreating into numbness once more. Eventually he stirred, saw the sun was high overhead and realised he'd missed at least one, probably two, important meetings.

Resolutely he rose from the sand. He'd spent enough time thinking about Lucia. She didn't want to have an affair? Fine, no problem. There were plenty of other women who did, and in any case he'd gone before without women or sex. Work—revenge—had been his companion, his lover, and it would be again.

He didn't need Lucia.

Seeing her again, he acknowledged, learning about Angelica, all of it had weakened his resolve. Made him want things he knew he couldn't have. That kind of life wasn't for him, could never be for him. It was better this way. It would have to be.

An hour later he was in the corporate offices of the Corretti Hotel, dressed in a designer suit of grey pin-striped silk, about to confirm a meeting with the share-holders of Luca Corretti's fashion company, Corretti Designs. He'd been buying up stock in the company for several months now, quietly, unnoticed by the other shareholders and, it seemed, by even Luca himself. He didn't have enough to stage a takeover like he had with the hotel, but with Luca absent he was going to take the opportunity to put a little pressure on the other share-holders. Hell, maybe they'd even agree to unseat Luca and make him CEO. He already had the hotel after all. It would bring him one step closer to his ultimate revenge.

It was time to think about business—and stop think-ing about Lucia, or love. This was why he'd returned to Sicily, what he'd always wanted. His face now set into familiar harsh lines of determination, Angelo reached for the phone.

CHAPTER EIGHT

SHE WAS DOING the right thing. Lucia repeated that to herself as she walked into the hotel on unsteady legs, everything around her a blur. *She was doing the right thing.* Leaving Angelo, refusing his offer, was the right choice. It had to be, because if one night had nearly felled her seven years ago, what would a week do now? A month? However long Angelo decided he wanted to be with her, all on his terms. *I don't want this to end now.*

Not now, but at some point, yes. He would decide to end it at some point in the not-too-distant future, and when that moment came he would walk away just as before. Just as he always did.

She worked steadily through the morning, grateful to scrub and sweep and spray down counters, and not have to think. Wonder. *Regret.*

She was doing the right thing.

She kept repeating that to herself, a desperate mantra, throughout the next few days. She didn't see or hear from Angelo, and from the sinking disappointment she felt at his absence she knew at least a part of her had been hoping to, even as she knew, bone-deep, that she never would.

Three days after she left Angelo, Maria found her

at break time, sitting alone at a table, lost in her own thoughts.

'Lucia?' The older woman smiled uncertainly, a sheet of paper clutched to her chest.

'*Ciao*, Maria.' Lucia did her best to smile and push away the tangled thoughts about Angelo that turned everything inside her into knots of doubt. 'Did Stefano send you another letter?'

'Not yet, but I want to write him.'

'Again?' Just a few days ago she'd helped Maria write a rather gushing response to Stefano.

Maria nodded, determination glinting in her deep brown eyes. 'Yes... He's not so good a writer, yes? So I keep writing, because I love him.'

The simple, heartfelt statement made Lucia still, those tangled knots inside her loosening just a little. *I keep writing, because I love him.* Maria's love didn't change, no matter Stefano's response—or lack of it. Of course, a mother's love for a son was different from a woman's love for a man, but...

Did she—had she—loved Angelo like that? For years she'd told herself she had, yet she'd never sent him a single letter. Not after he'd left at eighteen, and not seven years later when he'd left her bed. She'd tried, of course, when she'd found out she was pregnant. She'd written draft after labourious draft, yet she hadn't sent a single one. She hadn't got so far as putting any of them in an envelope. She'd never, Lucia saw now with a cringing insight, intended on writing him at all.

Why?

'Lucia?'

'Yes...sorry. Of course I'll help you write him.' She gestured to the seat next to her and Maria sat down, putting the single sheet of paper on the table and smoothing it carefully before handing Lucia a pen. 'What would you like to say?'

Maria smiled shyly. 'Just that I love him. I miss him. I pray for him.' Obediently Lucia wrote this all down, with Maria gazing at her neat handwriting in a kind of incredulous admiration. 'And also that my arthritis, it's better. In case he worries.'

Lucia glanced up, smiling, her eyebrows raised. 'Is it better, Maria?'

The older woman shrugged this aside. 'It's not so bad.'

Lucia wondered if Stefano would think about his mother's arthritis at all. She'd never met the man, and yet she wondered. Doubted. She felt her cynicism coat her heart like a hardened shell, layers and layers built up over time and weary experience. She'd been cynical about Angelo for so long, almost right from the beginning.

She still remembered when he'd left Sicily, how he'd kissed her cheek and turned away, heading off into his far-off future. She'd been seventeen, utterly in love, and she'd told herself if he looked back just once it meant he'd come back for her. He hadn't, and remembering now she knew she hadn't really expected him to. Cynicism coupled with a rather desperate hope—an awful combination. Yet that's how she'd always been with Angelo, wanting something she was quite sure he didn't have to give.

That's how she'd been with him now, when she'd rejected his offer. What if she'd reacted differently? Would Angelo have been able to change? Could they have a chance, if she gave them—him—one?

'I hope he writes you back this time,' Lucia said as she finished the letter, and Maria shrugged, lifted her chin.

'He's a good boy. And even if he doesn't write, he'll always know I love him. That's what matters.'

Lucia felt her throat go tight. 'Yes,' she agreed quietly, 'that's what matters.'

From the shock that had blazed across Angelo's face, she knew he hadn't ever realised she loved him. She'd loved him for years, decades, and yet he'd never known. She'd never told him before, and when she finally had, it had been in anger and exasperation, just another means to push him away.

Yet she *had* to push him away—because if she didn't, he'd surely break her heart.

'It's painfully clear that the Corretti empire is falling apart.' Angelo gazed steadily at each shareholder in turn, watched them fidget and squirm, their uneasy gazes sliding away from his. 'The Correttis simply aren't capable any longer, and the world is noticing.'

More squirming. None of the shareholders at this meeting were related to the Correttis, yet they'd always been loyal. Angelo knew he was taking a risk asking them to switch their loyalty to him, a Corretti of a different kind. He'd called this meeting of shareholders of Corretti Designs in Palermo, knowing that Luca was out of the country. He didn't think it would take too much to nudge the rest of the shareholders into a vote removing Luca as CEO and putting him in his place. They were like dominoes, waiting to fall. And another piece of the Corretti pie would be his. 'The price of Corretti Designs' shares have fallen three per cent in the past week alone,' he continued, knowing that hard facts might sway them more than sly innuendo. 'And it will continue to fall while the Correttis scramble, mired as they are in their own scandal.'

One of the shareholders, a banker from Milan, met his gaze. 'What do you propose?'

'You make me CEO on a trial basis,' Angelo answered swiftly. 'If the share prices improve—'

'The shares have gone down because of the cancelled wedding,' a sharp-looking woman objected. 'It's been all the talk. They'll bounce back in time.'

'Scandal usually boosts share prices of glamour industries,' Angelo replied coolly. 'Yet Corretti Designs' shares have fallen.'

He saw the doubt enter the woman's eyes, felt the mood in the room shift. They might be loyal to Luca Corretti, but all that mattered was the bottom line. 'Six weeks,' he said firmly. 'Give me six weeks and I'll turn this company around.' He held each person's gaze, saw doubts turn into certainties, and triumph surged through him. 'Shall we call a vote?'

'Am I interrupting something?'

Angelo stiffened, then turned his head to see Luca Corretti standing in the doorway of the boardroom, his steely gaze arrowing in on him. He smiled and lounged back in his chair. 'So good of you to join us,' he drawled, and saw a flicker of something almost like admiration in Luca's eyes at his sheer audacity.

'So good of you to invite me,' Luca answered dryly, and came into the room. Angelo felt an answering flare of respect for a man he knew he should hate. Luca Corretti was his cousin, the second son of Benito, his own father's brother. He'd lived in a palace, had grown up with every privilege and luxury. Angelo had hated him on principle for most of his life, yet now he couldn't help but respect the man's steely authority.

He might have been able to buy up the flagship hotel in Matteo's absence, but it appeared taking over Luca's fashion enterprise was going to be a little bit more difficult.

Luca set his briefcase on the table, his gaze moving slowly around the room, pinning every uneasy shareholder in his or her place. 'Now,' he said pleasantly, and Angelo heard the unmistakable undercurrent of authority in his voice, 'where were we?'

Twenty minutes later the meeting had ended and Luca was still in charge. Angelo slid his papers back into his attaché, affected an insouciance he didn't really feel.

Luca glanced at him coolly from across the table. 'Foiled this time, Angelo.'

Angelo gave him a hard smile. 'I don't think we've actually ever been introduced.'

'And yet you seem determined on snatching as much of the Corretti empire as you can.'

'Snatching?' Angelo raised his eyebrows. 'It's business, Luca. It always has been.'

Luca closed his briefcase with a decisive snap. 'Business?' he repeated with a shake of his head. 'I don't think so. Not for you.'

Angelo felt everything in him tense as that familiar rage flashed through him. He hated the other man's mocking tone, that superior sneer. 'Trust me,' he answered evenly, 'it's business.' Without another word he stalked from the boardroom, felt the adrenalin course through him as he took the lift down to the street. Once outside he decided to walk off his anger. He headed towards Pretoria Square, his mind racing along with his heart.

He could certainly do without Luca's fashion house. Buying out the Correttis' flagship hotel had been far more a significant coup and he wasn't going to concern himself with a few dresses. And yet he couldn't keep the resentment from lodging inside him like a stone, heavy and hot, burning through him. Snatching indeed.

How he hated the Correttis, with their smug superiority and their complete indifference to a blood relation, simply because he'd been born on the wrong side of the blanket. Not one of them had ever concerned themselves with him or his welfare. Not one of them had ever cared or considered him at all.

As a boy he'd had the most pathetic, useless fantasies about how they'd notice him. His father would find out about his existence and welcome him into the palazzo. His half-brothers and cousins would become his friends. He had, once upon a time, imagined how they'd become his family, his real family. He'd dreamt of how they'd all love him.

But of course no one ever had.

Except Lucia. Lucia loved you.

He stumbled in his stride and righted himself, tried to push that unhelpful thought away. In the past three days, since he'd left Lucia in front of the hotel, she'd never been far from his thoughts. He'd determined to think of it— her—with cold logic; she said she loved him, so either she was lying or she believed she loved him even though she didn't. Couldn't. There were no other possibilities.

Angelo didn't think she had been lying; she had no reason to lie about such a thing. So she must have somehow convinced herself that she loved him, perhaps as some kind of moral justification for their one-night stand.

And if he disabused her of the ridiculous notion? Convinced her that she couldn't actually love him, that such an idea was mere fantasy? Angelo had at first found himself strangely reluctant to consider such an idea. Yet now as he strode towards Pretoria Square and gazed up at the huge marble fountain—the fountain of shame, it had once been called—he thought again.

Why not? Why not convince Lucia she couldn't love him? Once she let go of such ridiculous, romantic notions she might be more willing to embark on what he wanted: a mutually pleasurable affair. He could still get what he wanted. What she wanted... He just had to convince her that she did.

Lucia was just reaching for another stack of linens when she heard a voice behind her.

'There you are.'

She turned and felt her heart stop right in her chest at the sight of Angelo in the doorway of one of the hotel's supply closets.

'What are you doing here?'

'I need to talk to you.'

'Here? People will talk, Angelo.'

'Let them.'

'Easy for you to say.'

'You never used to care what people thought, Lucia. Remember?' His voice was a rough caress and he stepped into the little room, seeming to take up all the space and air. 'You told me not to care what people thought. What they said to me.'

She focused on counting pillowcases, but in her mind's eye she could see Angelo at ten, eleven years old, bloody and defiant, angry and proud. She remembered trying to tease him out of his hurt, coming up with ridiculous taunts for the ignorant schoolchildren who refused to think of him as anything but the Corretti bastard, the son of a woman they'd said was no better than a whore. More often than not Angelo had just shrugged her off, but once in a while she'd succeeded in making him smile, even laugh. He'd meet her gaze and they'd grin at each other, both of them hurting and yet happy in that moment, united in their understanding of how harsh and unfair the world really was.

'That was a long time ago, Angelo.' Her voice sounded clogged and she cleared her throat, kept her gaze firmly on the sheets and not on the man who seemed intent on breaking her. Again.

'Not so long.' Angelo put one hand on her wrist, stilling her, his touch sure and strong and yet also gentle. 'You don't love me, Lucia.'

She turned to him, surprise temporarily wiping away every other emotion. 'You came here to tell me that?'

'You think you do, but you don't.' He gazed at her steadily, his eyes dark and serious, his tone so very certain.

Lucia shook her head slowly. 'How on earth could you know a thing like that, Angelo?'

'Because.' He frowned, as if he hadn't ever considered the question before. 'Because you can't.'

'I can't,' Lucia repeated. She searched the harsh lines of his face, tried to find some clue as to why he felt the need to tell her this now. 'Does it ease your conscience somehow, to think I didn't love you?'

'It's not about my conscience.'

'What, then?'

The sound of someone pushing a cart came from the corridor, squeaky wheels and a heavy tread. Angelo's breath released in an impatient hiss. 'We can't have this conversation here.'

'I'm working…'

He opened his mouth and she knew he wanted to order her to stop; it was certainly within his rights as her employer. 'When do you get off your shift?' he asked instead, the words coming reluctantly.

'At six.'

'Let me pick you up—'

'And take me back to your villa?' Lucia finished. She felt herself flush and she knew from the answering heat in Angelo's gaze that they were both remembering what had happened the last time they'd done that.

'Then we'll go somewhere else,' Angelo said. 'Out to dinner.'

'A date?' she mocked, even though it hurt. 'Why bother, Angelo? We have nothing more to say to each other.'

'I have something to say to you.'

She stared at the steely glint in his grey-green eyes, and suddenly she remembered her conversation with Maria earlier in the day. *He knows I love him. That's what matters.*

She'd spent so much time and effort pushing Angelo away. What if she stopped? Instead of bearing her love for him like a burden, she'd wear it as a badge.

You'll only get more hurt.

She'd already experienced so much heartache, and yet she'd survived. She was strong; just as Angelo had said. Tragedy had made her stronger.

Yet strong enough for this? To risk her heart one more time, and this more than ever?

She swallowed, made herself nod. 'All right, then.' She turned back to the stacks of sheets. 'You can meet me at the Borgo Vecchio.' She wondered if he'd remember the last time they'd gone to one of Palermo's outdoor markets.

'The Borgo Vecchio? It's no more than a street fair.'

She turned back to him, eyebrows raised. 'Are you too good for a street fair?'

'No, of course not.' Annoyance flashed across his features. 'I just don't see why.'

Obviously he didn't remember. It hadn't been important, at least not important to him. 'I don't belong in fancy restaurants,' she told him. 'And I won't be paraded about Palermo as your whore.'

He recoiled. 'Is that how you see it, Lucia?'

'It's how others see it,' she answered flatly. She saw the surprise in his eyes and knew he hadn't known, had never realised. Never thought for one moment how her pregnancy and his abandonment would have affected her standing in a tiny place like Caltarione.

God help her, what was she doing? How could she risk this—her heart, her life—with a man who had so little consideration or concern for her?

'I didn't realise,' he said quietly. He pressed his lips together, his gaze averted. 'I think there are most likely a lot of things I haven't realised.'

Surprise silenced her. Already he was changing, just a little, but for now she would let it be enough. 'The market?' she prompted, and he nodded.

'I'll meet you at the Borgo Vecchio, a little after six.'

Lucia nodded back, her heart pounding with both dread and anticipation. Yet in the midst of those turbulent emotions she felt a fragile seed sprout to tremulous, trembling life: hope. She hadn't felt it in a long time, perhaps ever. And yet with one quiet word from Angelo she began to believe...and finally hope that things might change between them.

Angelo paced the narrow street of the Borgo Vecchio where he'd agreed to meet Lucia. Stalls heaped with lemons and oranges as well as cheap clothing and electronics jostled for space with the many pedestrians thronging the side street. The smell of fried fruit wafted on the hot air, competing with the stink of unwashed humanity and the diesel fumes from the cars and mopeds speeding by.

Why the hell had he agreed to meet Lucia here? He could have had a reservation at one of the city's best restaurants, champagne chilling in a bucket, caviar and pâté and whatever else they desired immediately on hand. Seated amidst such luxury would have been a much better setting for a seduction.

Yet was that what he intended on doing? Seducing Lucia? No. He was just convincing her of the truth. Making her see the benefits of a loveless affair.

Still he felt uneasy. Unsure. And he didn't like it. He'd lived his life on clear certainties, hard truths, yet Lucia made him doubt. Wonder. *Want.*

'Hello, Angelo.'

He turned and saw her standing before him, her dark hair pulled back in a neat plait, her eyes clear and somehow sad. She'd exchanged her grey maid's uniform for a cheap cotton sundress in pale pink, and Angelo found his gaze helplessly drawn to the smooth olive skin of her shoulders, the swell of her breasts underneath the snug cotton. He yanked his gaze upwards.

'Thank you for meeting me.'

She nodded, hitched her canvas bag higher up on her shoulder. 'Shall we eat?'

'Eat?' He couldn't keep from sounding rather revolted. 'Here?'

She laughed softly. 'You used to like the pizza here.'

And then a memory flashed through his mind, slotted into place. They'd once taken the bus into Palermo, wandered through this market. They must have been fourteen or so; all Angelo had remembered about that day was the burning anger he'd felt at seeing his half-brothers, Alessandro and Santo, out with their father. A happy family, father and sons, strolling through the narrow streets of Caltarione. They hadn't looked his way once.

Lucia, he remembered now, had suggested the trip into the city, probably as a way to distract him from the Correttis. They'd eaten pizza and gelato, and she'd made silly jokes all the while, betting him she could eat more pizza than he could, and he, of course, had proved her wrong. But she'd succeeded in making him laugh, which had surely been her object all along.

Dio, he missed that. Laughing with someone, being stupid and silly and *real*. Lucia, he acknowledged with sudden, flashing insight, was the only person in the entire world with whom he'd ever been remotely real.

'I remember,' he said now, quietly, and he saw her mouth curve in the slightest of smiles.

She turned away, and the end of her plait brushed his shoulder. 'So, pizza?' she asked, and he fell in step beside her.

'Pizza, it is.'

They settled for squares of *sfincione*, the doughy Sicilian pizza scattered with bread crumbs, cheese and anchovies. Angelo eyed his sauce-covered square somewhat dubiously. 'We could be eating fresh flounder at one of the city's best restaurants,' he told her, not even half joking, and she shook her head.

'I wouldn't even know what fork to use.'

It wasn't the first time she'd made a remark alluding to the difference in their stations now, and he wondered at it. 'I'm sure you'd figure it out pretty quickly. And in any case, when you're eating in a restaurant, use whatever the hell fork you want.'

She gave a little laugh. 'That would be your attitude.'

'It would.'

She eyed him over her pizza, her eyes wide and so very blue. 'Why do you think I don't love you, Angelo?' she asked quietly.

Angelo felt something in him shift, lurch. He had the strangest, strongest impulse to deny it, to convince her of the opposite, that she did love him. He swallowed a bite of pizza and shifted his gaze a few inches to the right of her face. 'Because you don't.'

'That's not an answer and you know it.' He just shrugged. He hadn't thought through this very well, he realised. He had no arguments to make beyond what to him was the appallingly obvious: she *couldn't* love him. All on its own it wasn't very compelling. 'How can you say what I feel, or if I really feel it?' she pressed.

'How do you know you love me?' Angelo challenged. 'How can you be sure?'

He shifted his gaze back to her face, saw how still she'd gone, trapped by truth. She *wasn't* sure. Damn it if he didn't feel disappointed. She swallowed, licked her lips, causing a shaft of pure desire to streak through him. Even now, amidst a painfully awkward conversation about emotions, he wanted her. Forget talking. Forget love or lack of it. He'd just haul her into his arms and kiss her until they were both senseless.

'I know I love you,' she said slowly, quietly, 'because whenever I'm with you I feel complete and whole. And when you're gone, I don't.'

Angelo felt his jaw go slack, everything inside him seeming to shut down. He had no words; he had no thoughts. 'You've been living without me for fifteen years,' he finally managed, his voice hoarse, and she smiled sadly.

'I know.' He shook his head, his instinct, his *need*, to deny. 'Tell me this, Angelo,' she cut off whatever unformed reply he'd been going to make. 'Why don't you want me to love you? I'm not asking for anything back. I'm not making demands or a scene. I'm not doing or expecting anything.' She smiled, the corners of her soft mouth curving up tremulously. 'So what scares you about my loving you? About love?'

Everything. He didn't answer, just shook his head. Again. 'You can't love me, Lucia,' he said. He sounded like a broken record, but hell, he didn't *have* anything else.

'You didn't answer my question.'

'That *is* the answer.'

'All right,' she said evenly, 'I'll ask a different question. Why do you think I can't love you? And I want something more than "because."' He heard a slight quaver in her voice, and knew, despite her quiet, utter sincerity, this was hard for her. Maybe as hard for her as it was for him. And he knew then if she could be honest enough to admit that she loved him, then he could be honest enough to admit why he didn't think she could.

'Because,' he said, his gaze averted, each word drawn slowly, painfully, from him. 'No one's ever loved me.' He set his jaw, wished the words right back. Could he sound more pathetic, whining about how nobody liked him?

Lucia didn't answer, and he forced himself to meet her gaze, to see the pity that was surely reflected there. He didn't see pity, only sorrow and a surprising determination. 'Then,' she answered, 'I'm lucky to be the first.'

He blinked back the sudden sting of tears. God help him, he was practically *crying*. 'No,' he said, and that was all he could manage. He forced back all that awful emotion and met her gaze once more. 'What is this really, Lucia? When I first saw you in the hotel—when I brought you up to my office—you didn't tell me you loved me then. You wouldn't even admit to being angry at me. You acted like you didn't care about me at all.' And he'd believed her then. Even now, with everything she'd said, he still believed.

'Loving you,' Lucia said, 'isn't the same as wanting to love you.'

'Ah.' Well, maybe that made sense. Of course she wouldn't *want* to love him.

She sighed and shook her head. 'Angelo, I didn't want to love you because I knew—I know—you don't love me back. Who wants that?'

He shrugged, hating this conversation. 'Nobody, I suppose.'

'Exactly.' She hesitated, and he felt the heaviness of the words she wasn't saying. He just didn't know what they were. 'I said, I *didn't* want to love you,' she said quietly. 'But then, in just the past few days, I started thinking...' She trailed off, biting her lip, and Angelo suddenly, desperately, wanted to know what she'd started thinking about. He *needed* to know.

'You started thinking what?' he asked brusquely.

Her teeth sank in deeper to her lip and he saw cloud-coloured shadows in her eyes, hiding the true emotion underneath. 'I started thinking that maybe I never gave you a chance,' she whispered.

'A chance? A chance for what?'

'To love me.'

The words seemed to hang in the air between them, a hope, a challenge. *A chance to love her.*

What the hell was he supposed to do with that?

'Lucia...'

'I'm not asking you to love me,' she said quickly.

'Not just like that. But…but if you do actually want to be with me, then I won't take some affair, some kind of sordid *arrangement*. If you want to be with me, then you *be* with me. You get to know me again, you ask me out on a date.'

'I did ask you on a date,' he objected, nettled. 'I asked you out to dinner at a proper restaurant.'

'In order to convince me that I don't love you! What was behind that, Angelo? Did you think if I decided I didn't love you, I'd think desire was enough and I'd hop into bed with you? Is that how your twisted mind works?' She spoke with an edge but also with humour, and he actually blushed.

Yes, it appeared that was how his twisted mind worked.

'Love complicates things,' he said defensively. 'It's messy.' And scary. And awful. And loving people usually meant they didn't love you back. They didn't love you at all.

'You think I don't know that?' she answered, still with the edge and the humour. 'My life would have been a whole lot simpler, a lot cleaner, if I'd never loved you.'

He bristled instinctively. 'So don't.'

'I've tried.' She met his gaze squarely, her eyes blazing truth. 'But I can't stop, because I love you too much.'

Her words made him breathless, as if he'd been punched in the gut. He was quite literally winded. 'So why are you telling me this now?' he asked after a moment, when he trusted his voice. 'When you've been denying it all along?'

'Because I decided you should know. I *want* you to know. I'm tired of pretending I've never cared about you, when I do. So very much.' She drew a deep breath and he heard how it shuddered through her. She'd laid everything out there for him, and God help him but he had no idea what to do with it. What to say. What he wanted.

Her.

'So now it's your turn,' she said, and gazed at him with a fragile pride, a tremulous determination. 'You have to decide what you want, Angelo. If you just want sex, find someone else. If you want a fling or an affair, don't look at me.' She let out another breath, threw her shoulders back. Angelo felt a surge of admiration for this woman who was so strong, so proud, so brave. She'd endured so much already, and yet she remained unbowed. 'But if you want something more, something real…if you want to give me—us—a chance, then…' She smiled, barely. 'You know where to find me.'

CHAPTER NINE

IT WAS AMAZING how liberating telling the truth could be. After her painful admission to Angelo last night, Lucia had expected to feel raw, exposed. Uncomfortable, at least, from revealing so much. She hadn't denied or dissembled, hadn't thrown the truth in his face as a defensive ploy. No, she'd given it to him. Presented it to him like a gift, and it was now his to do with as he wished.

The realisation made her feel buoyant. She had nothing more to hide, and it gave her a giddy sense of both relief and joy. Of course she wondered just what he intended to do with her gift, but she refused to let herself become mired in fear or doubt. For the first time her love for Angelo didn't feel like a weakness, a burden to bear. It felt like a strength.

Several chambermaids were huddled in the staff locker room when she arrived at the hotel for work the next morning. They broke apart as soon as they saw her, and Lucia felt a ripple of unease at their suddenly hushed whispers, their averted gazes. Emilia was the only one to look at her directly, and the expression on her face was one of savage jealousy, eyes narrowed and glittering, lips thin and pursed.

'Ciao,' Lucia said with an uncertain smile. 'Come va?'

'Look.' Maria took her by the elbow and brought her

over to a table on the side of the room; a huge bouquet of flowers rested on it. 'For you.'

'Me?' Lucia stared at the gorgeous bouquet—lilies and roses, orchids and carnations. It was the most extravagant, over-the-top bouquet she'd ever seen, and just the sight of it made a silly grin spread over her face. She'd never received so much as a wilted daisy before.

Emilia folded her arms, her eyes sparking maliciously. 'Payment for services rendered, maybe?'

Maria hissed under her breath. '*Stai zitto*, you foolish girl,' she snapped.

For once Emilia's words rolled right off her. Lucia reached for the crisp white card tucked among the blooms and read the message scrawled on it in a bold hand.

I want that chance. Have dinner with me tonight at eight?

Her smile widened even as her heart started beating hard. Chances were wonderful, dangerous things. This could be a chance for Angelo to love her—or break her heart all over again. Shatter it, even, into a million tiny pieces, impossible to put together again, because she'd never given him this kind of chance before. She'd never actually *tried*.

During her midmorning break Lucia took the service lift to the floor of corporate offices. She felt a blush spread across her face as Angelo's personal assistant glanced up at her in cool assessment.

'Is Mr Corretti available?' she asked, to which the secretary merely pursed her lips. 'He might be expecting me,' she added quietly.

'He's in a meeting.'

'Then will you please leave him a message?' Lucia felt the tingly warmth that Angelo's short note had given her spread throughout her body. 'Tell him Lucia said yes.'

The assistant arched her eyebrows, curiosity clearing getting the better of her. 'That's all?'

'That's all.'

She could barely concentrate on her work for the rest of the day; her mind moved dizzily from anticipation to worry to hope, and then back again. She had nothing to wear. What if Angelo took her somewhere fancy? What would they talk about? A *date* with Angelo. An actual date—something they'd never gone on before. What if it went all wrong?

By the time she arrived back at her apartment that evening, she was both exhausted and hyped up with adrenalin. She showered and stood in front of her closet with its paltry few dresses, wishing she had something pretty and feminine to wear. She almost wished she hadn't left the gorgeous clothes Angelo had bought her back in his villa.

Sighing, she reached for a sundress in a pretty, pale blue. It was simple and cheap, and it was all she had. It would have to do. This wasn't about impressing Angelo, she reminded herself as she slipped it on. It wasn't about pretending to be something or someone she wasn't. She wanted him to know and accept who she really was, cheap clothes and all. That was the only kind of chance she was interested in.

She'd just finished her makeup—no more than lip-gloss and a little mascara—when she heard a knock on the door. Taking a deep breath, she hurried to open it, and then found she had no words when she caught sight of Angelo standing there, dressed in a white dress shirt open at the throat and a pair of charcoal grey trousers.

He looked effortlessly elegant and deliberately casual, his eyes blazing grey-green in his tanned face.

He smiled as he saw her, and reached for her hand, giving her a little twirl so her dress flared out around her legs. 'You look lovely.'

'It's not much—'

'Just say thank you.'

She laughed softly. 'Thank you.' They stared at each other for a moment, and Lucia tucked her hair—she'd worn it loose—behind her ears. 'I'm nervous,' she confessed, and Angelo dipped his head.

'So am I.'

She gazed at him uncertainly. 'You don't seem nervous.'

'You might be surprised at this,' he answered, a smile in his eyes, 'but I'm rather adept at hiding my emotions.' She laughed again, felt the fizzing tension inside her begin to ease. Angelo tugged on her hand. 'Let's go.'

He led her downstairs to his Porsche parked by the kerb. She slid into the luxurious leather interior, felt that anticipation rise again. 'Where are we going?'

'A little place inland.' He glanced at her with a smile. 'Nothing too fancy.'

She smiled back, reassured yet still nervous. Everything about this felt strange, new and exciting, yes, but *scary*. So scary.

They didn't talk much on the way to the restaurant, the silence between them expectant yet thankfully not too strained. All around them the sky was settling into twilight, and the last blush of sunset lighted the rugged horizon as Angelo pulled into the dirt lot of a small and unassuming building in a tiny hillside village about twenty kilometres from Palermo.

He'd been telling the truth when he said the place was

nothing fancy, just wooden tables and chairs and plain, whitewashed walls, but a single glance at the menu told Lucia that this was still a high-class restaurant, with high-class prices.

'Not too many forks,' Angelo murmured as they were seated to a private table in the back, and she smiled.

'I can just about manage these.'

'I have no doubt about that.'

A waiter appeared and Angelo ordered a bottle of wine while Lucia fidgeted with her napkin, her glass of water. Few forks there might have been, but she still felt outclassed.

'So,' she said when the waiter left, 'fill me in on the past fifteen years.'

Angelo smiled faintly. 'It could be summed up in a few sentences. I worked. I worked some more. I made money.'

'Give me the long version, then. What did you do after you first left Sicily?'

He shrugged, his long, lean fingers toying with his own cutlery, clearly on edge albeit for a different reason. 'I went to Rome. I didn't have any better ideas, to be honest.'

She imagined him in that huge city—a city she'd never seen—with nothing but a rucksack of clothes and his own burning ambition. 'Did you know anybody there?'

He shook his head. 'I got a job running messages for a finance firm. I learned the city and English, saved up for a moped, and then after about a year I started my own business offering the same service, only faster and cheaper.'

'That was quick.' He would have only been nineteen.

'I spent the next couple of years building that business, and I sold it when I was twenty-three. I wanted to move into real estate, and so with the proceeds from that sale I bought a derelict building in an up-and-coming neighbourhood and turned it into a hotel.' He stopped then, and glanced away.

'And then?' Lucia asked after a moment.

Angelo shrugged. 'More of the same. A bigger building, a shopping centre, and so on. Five years ago I moved to New York and started doing the same thing there.'

'And now you're doing it in Sicily.'

He hesitated for a second's pause and then nodded. 'Yes.'

The waiter came with the wine, and Lucia watched as Angelo swirled it in his glass and tasted it. He nodded once, and the waiter began to pour. When had he learned about such luxuries? she wondered. When had he become accustomed to three-thousand-euro suits, fast cars and fancy restaurants? It was all so removed from her own small world, her shabby apartment and her working-class job. How on earth could a relationship between them ever work?

'Taste,' Angelo said, and she picked up her glass. The wine was rich and velvety-smooth, warming her insides.

'Delicious,' she said, although in all honesty she couldn't really tell one wine from another.

'So tell me what you've been doing these past fifteen years, Lucia, besides working.'

She smiled wryly. 'Not much.'

'You must have other pursuits. Hobbies.'

'I like to read.'

'What kind of books?'

'Anything, really. I like…' She felt herself blushing, which was ridiculous, but there it was. 'I like travel books. Memoirs about people going places, seeing things.'

'And would you like to travel yourself, one day?'

'One day, perhaps.' She hadn't yet had the chance.

'Those postcards,' Angelo said slowly, his considering gaze sweeping over her. 'You used to collect postcards from places all over the world.'

'Just the ones nobody wanted any more,' she said quickly, and he chuckled.

'I wasn't accusing you of stealing, Lucia. I'd just forgotten, that's all. You had a scrapbook.'

'Yes.'

'You wanted to go to Paris,' he spoke slowly, as if the memories were surfacing in his mind, popping like bubbles. 'You had a postcard of the Eiffel Tower, didn't you?'

'Yes.'

'We looked at them together.'

'I bored you with them, more like.'

He shook his head. 'No.'

'You don't need to rewrite the past, Angelo,' she said quietly. 'I know well enough how it was.'

He leaned forward, his eyes glittering. 'Then tell me how you think it was, Lucia.'

She glanced down, felt her face warm. '*Mi cucciola*, remember? I was like an annoying little puppy to you, always frisking at your heels. Sometimes you'd pat me on the head and sometimes you'd kick me away.'

He sat back, silent, and she risked a glance upwards. 'I suppose that's true.'

It was absurd to feel hurt by his admission, but she did. She'd always known he hadn't really cared about her, had tolerated her and sometimes enjoyed her company, but that was all. She'd known that absolutely, and yet…it hurt for him to admit it now.

'That was my problem though,' he added quietly, 'not yours.'

'What do you mean?'

He shrugged one powerful shoulder. 'I didn't appreciate you. I didn't realise what I'd had with you until I'd left.'

She swallowed past the ache in her throat. 'You're still rewriting history, Angelo. You can't expect me to believe you even thought of me once while you were buying and selling your businesses.'

He didn't answer, and that ache in her throat spread, strengthened. She swallowed again, trying to ease its pervasive pain. This really shouldn't have hurt. It was no more than she'd always known, even said to him, yet that had been when she'd been trying to convince herself she didn't care. Now that she'd admitted she did, it hurt more.

'You're right,' he finally said. 'I didn't think of you. But that was a choice, and it took more energy and determination than I ever realised to do it.'

'What do you mean?'

'I missed you,' Angelo said simply. 'I may not have realised it at the time, but I missed you, Lucia. I've always missed you.'

And just like that the ache dissolved into a tentative, hopeful warmth. 'I've missed you too,' she said quietly.

'So tell me what else you've been doing these past years,' Angelo said after a moment. He had to clear his throat, and Lucia took a sip of wine. Admitting you missed someone might not seem like much, but she knew to Angelo it was a big deal. He didn't do emotion, and certainly not vulnerability.

'Not much else, really.'

'You were helping that other maid. Maria.'

'Yes—'

'How?'

She shrugged. 'She has trouble with reading and writing, and so I help her with her letters. I know I didn't get much schooling—'

'No less than me.'

She nodded, accepting. They'd both quit school at sixteen; they'd both needed to work. 'I enjoy it, and it helps her.'

'Have you helped others?'

Another shrug. 'A few. A lot of women in my position can barely read or write. I'm fortunate that I can.'

'That's one way of looking at it.'

She frowned. 'What do you mean?'

'Haven't you ever railed against fate, Lucia? Destiny or God, whatever power that left us both poor and struggling, grateful simply for a job that put food on the table?'

She shook her head. 'What would be the point?'

'Perhaps there's no point in railing,' Angelo answered, 'but in wanting. In doing and having—and *being* more.'

She shook her head again. Here was yet another difference between them. Angelo had always been ambitious, determined to rise above their childhood of the struggling working class in a small Sicilian village; she had never even considered such a thing.

Liar. She'd dreamt of Angelo taking her with him when he'd left, or returning for her. Yet she'd always known they were just that: dreams. Nothing more, nothing real. She hadn't really believed in them.

And even now when they were both trying to make those dreams a reality, she wondered if it were possible. Angelo would never fit into her world, and how could she possibly enter his?

He leaned forward. 'What are you thinking about?'

'Just how different we are.'

'That's not a bad thing.'

'No…' she said slowly, because she couldn't classify it that way, good or bad. Difficult, perhaps. Impossible, maybe.

Angelo reached across the table and laced his fingers with hers. 'Deep down, Lucia, we're not as different as you think.'

She met his gaze, felt his fingers squeeze hers. 'Maybe not,' she answered, but she knew she sounded doubtful.

'Just the fact that you kept that scrapbook of postcards tells me you've wanted something more.'

'That doesn't mean I'd shake my fist at the world if I don't get it.'

'I'm not talking about shaking your first.' He glanced down as he slid his fingers along hers, examining each one in turn, and just that simple touch made her heart beat faster and that lovely, languorous warmth spread throughout her whole body. 'I'm talking about doing something about it.'

'You're the only one of us who did something about it, Angelo. You got out, made more of yourself. I never did.'

He glanced up at her, his fingers still twined with hers. 'Do you regret that?'

'I don't see the point of that either.' She swallowed. 'I had obligations here.'

'You mean your mother?'

'Yes—'

'And then,' Angelo said softly, 'our daughter.' She felt herself stiffen, and Angelo's fingers closed gently around hers. 'What had you planned? To raise her in Caltarione?'

She nodded. 'I didn't have anywhere else to go.'

'You could have moved to Palermo. Even that would

have been a bit of a fresh start.' He didn't sound accusing
or judgemental, just curious. Wanting to understand her.

'Yes, and I did think of it. But it felt like running
away. And I didn't want—' She hesitated, not wanting
to admit how bad it had been for her then.

'You didn't want?' Angelo prompted, his fingers still
linked with hers.

'I didn't want people to think I'd been beaten. Or that
I was ashamed.'

His fingers tightened over hers briefly. 'Is that how
people acted? Like you should have been ashamed?'

'An unwed mother in a tiny village? Of course they
did.' She'd meant to sound light and wry, but she knew
she hadn't managed it. Angelo's face darkened, a frown
compressing his mouth.

'And not just an unwed mother. Another Corretti bastard.'

She clenched her fingers into a protective fist. 'How
did you know?'

'I guessed. It took me long enough. But I've noticed a
few looks.… People know, don't they? Even at the hotel.'

'Only some. But gossip spreads.'

'How did they? How did anyone know I was the father?'

'Oh, Angelo.' She shook her head, smiling even though
a lump had lodged in her throat. 'Carlo Corretti's funeral
was at the church in Caltarione. You walked all the way
from the church down the main street with every old
woman—and young too—peeping from behind her curtains. Everyone knew about the funeral, of course. And
everyone knew you were there.'

'And everyone,' he finished, 'saw me knock on your
door.'

'And come in,' she added with a sad smile, 'and not

leave until morning. I'm amazed both our ears weren't singed by all the gossip.'

Angelo didn't speak for a long moment. He glanced down at their entwined hands, her fingers still pulled protectively into a fist. A tiny movement, pointless, yet some part of her still reacted in self-defence. Carefully he straightened each clenched finger, then laid his palm flat against hers, a warm, comforting weight. 'I should have thought of that,' he said quietly, his gaze still on their pressed palms. 'Back then. I should have considered how it might look for you. Even if you hadn't fallen pregnant, the gossip would have flown.'

'It always does.'

'I should have—'

'What could you have done, Angelo? Your life was in Rome. No matter what might develop between us now, it was still a one-night stand back then.'

He looked up at her, his eyes dark and shadowed. 'Only because I couldn't imagine anything else.'

'What do you mean?'

'This is new territory for me, Lucia.' The smile he gave her was crooked, self-deprecating. 'A relationship of any kind—'

'You must have had relationships before.'

'No.'

'No? None at all?' She frowned, finding that hard to believe. Angelo was thirty-three years old, a man of experience, wealth and power. Of course he'd had relationships.

'I've had…transactions,' Angelo said carefully. 'Of the kind I first suggested to you.' A faint flush touched his cheekbones, and Lucia almost laughed even as his admission made a fresh sorrow sweep through her.

'That sounds like a rather empty way to live.'

'It was. Is. I think…' He paused, his gaze on their hands once more. He slid his fingers through hers, entwining their hands again. 'I think I've always felt empty.'

'Oh, Angelo.' She swallowed, sniffed. He glanced up wryly.

'I didn't mean to make you sad.'

'You haven't, not really.'

'And what about you?' He leaned back, sliding his hand from hers. Self-protection, Lucia knew. He was just starting to realise how much he'd revealed. 'You must have had a few relationships over the years.'

She let out a little laugh of disbelief. 'Oh, Angelo, do you really believe that?'

He frowned. 'Why not?'

'Because of everything I've already said. I've spent my entire life in Caltarione, working as a maid. Every single person there knows my history, my shame, even if I never saw it like that. What self-respecting Sicilian man would want me?'

'I want you,' he said, his voice rough, and she smiled even as a thrill shot through her at the blatant emotion and need visible in his eyes.

'That's certainly enough for me.'

'Still…are you really saying there's been no one? I've been your only lover?' His voice had dropped to a whisper and now Lucia knew she was the one blushing.

'It sounds a bit pathetic, I know.'

'No, not pathetic.' He shook his head. 'It just makes me a little…afraid.'

'Afraid?' She hadn't been expecting that. 'Why?'

'Because most people don't get this kind of second chance, Lucia.' His expression had turned serious, even grave. 'I don't want to wreck it. I don't want to hurt you like I did before.'

She opened her mouth to say—what? What could she say? She had no assurances or promises to make, for she had no idea if he would hurt her or not. No idea if any of this could really work.

Angelo watched the emotions chase across Lucia's face, reveal themselves in her eyes. She was afraid, he knew. Afraid of what? How different they were? Afraid that this—whatever this between them was—wouldn't work? Afraid that he would hurt her, just as he'd said. Certainty lodged inside him, as heavy as a stone. Of course she was afraid of that. So was he.

Her heartfelt admission last night had rocked him to the core, because he'd finally believed her. She *did* love him. It seemed incredible, impossible, and yet he'd believed, and that belief gave life to something far more precious: hope. He wanted a chance to love her back. A chance to show her he was worthy of her love.

Yet already he felt doubt begin its insidious attack on that first, fragile breath of hope. He'd never loved anyone before, didn't know what it felt or looked like, and God help him, he didn't know if he was capable of it. Nothing in his life had prepared him for any of this, not for honesty or vulnerability and certainly not for love. Not even, he realised with a pang, for a conversation like the one they were having right now.

Maybe they needed a break from all this wretched vulnerability. Smiling, he reached for his menu. 'We should order.' Maybe if they kept the conversation light, rather than raking through the cold ashes of the past, the fear they both felt would lessen if not leave them entirely.

Lucia nodded her agreement, and after they'd ordered

their food they spent the next couple of hours chatting about inconsequential things, tasting each other's food and simply enjoying each other's company. Angelo felt himself relax, and more importantly, he felt Lucia relax.

It was late by the time they drove back to Caltarione, and in the darkness of the car Lucia lapsed back into silence once more, staring out the window so Angelo couldn't tell what she was thinking.

'A penny for your thoughts,' he said lightly, although he wasn't sure he wanted to know. As they'd left the restaurant, Lucia's expression had turned pensive, even drawn. Was she regretting this, *him*? Now she just shook her head, and he left it at that.

He climbed the rickety stairs with her to her second-floor apartment, hating the shabby smallness of it all. He wanted to take her to his villa, to give her all the things she'd never even dreamt for herself. Clothes and jewels, yes, but something more. Safety, comfort, the kind of life neither of them had had as children. The kind of life he wanted for her, even if she refused to want it for herself. Giving her those things would be a way to show her he cared, yet he knew she didn't want them, would refuse his offers. She wanted something else—something he didn't know if he had in him to give.

She turned to him in front of the door. 'Do you want to—'

'Come in?' he finished. She looked delectable in her pale blue sundress, the colour a shade lighter than the startling sapphire of her eyes. Her teeth caught her lower lip and she gazed up at him, eyes wide before her lashes swept downwards. 'More than you could possibly know,' he told her gruffly, desire coursing through him in lightning streaks. 'But I won't.'

He was gratified to see disappointment turn down the corners of her mouth. 'Why not?'

Gently he tucked a tendril of hair behind her ear. 'Because I want to do this right, Lucia. I don't want to rush things.' It would be easy, he knew, to let it be about sex. Let their attraction for each other wipe out the need for talking or even thinking. Hell, that would be *much* easier. But he knew she wanted more, and, amazingly, so did he. If he could manage it.

She swallowed and nodded and he leaned forward to brush his lips against hers, allowing himself this much. Yet of course he couldn't stop there. He never had been able to before. One taste of Lucia and he was a drowning man.

Her lips parted beneath his and he deepened the kiss, his hands coming around her shoulders as he pressed against her, losing himself in her warmth and softness so everything else fell away. He slid one knee between her legs, his mouth moving more firmly over hers as he pressed against her.

Behind her the wooden railing gave an almighty crack and, alarmed, Angelo pulled her forward into the shelter of his own body. '*Dio*, this place is falling down around your ears.'

Wrong thing to say. Perhaps even to think. She shook her head and stepped out of his embrace. 'It's my home, Angelo.'

He let out an irritated breath. 'I wasn't trying to insult you.'

'I know that.'

They stared at each other in the darkness, the only sound the tinny music from the bar downstairs, the hitch of their own breathing.

'Come with me,' he said suddenly, 'to the Corretti Cup next week.'

'The Corretti Cup?' she repeated blankly. 'You mean, the horse race?'

He nodded. Gio Corretti, his cousin, ran the island's premier racing track. The Corretti Cup was an important annual event, attended by the rich, the famous, the beautiful, as well as the entire Corretti clan. He'd never gone before, but he certainly intended on showing up this year, and letting the Corretti family tree know they now had to contend with his unfortunate offshoot. He wanted Lucia by his side.

She bit her lip, uncertainty swamping her wide-eyed gaze. 'I don't know, Angelo—'

'You can't hide forever, Lucia.'

'I'm not hiding—'

'Avoiding, then. My world is different from yours now, I know that. But I want you in it. Won't you please come with me?'

She swallowed, and he knew she felt conflicted. Afraid, even, of this too. 'I don't have anything to wear,' she finally said, and he almost laughed with relief.

'That's simple. I'll take you shopping, buy you a dress.'

'I don't—'

'Lucia, I want to buy you something. It would please me. Won't you let me do that?' He didn't know what her difficulty in accepting gifts from him was, but he suspected it stemmed from the inequality she felt in their positions. He had more money than she did, but nothing else had changed. He was, and would always be, the Corretti bastard looking in, wanting more.

Didn't she realise that? He really wasn't any different from the boy she'd fallen in love with...even if he wanted to be. Even if he was determined to show the Correttis and everyone else on this godforsaken island just how damned different he was.

Slowly she nodded. 'All right.'

'We'll go tomorrow, after work.'

'Actually, I have the day off tomorrow.'

'You do?'

She laughed softly. 'It does happen.'

'Then we can spend the day together.'

'Don't you have meetings? Deals to make?'

He had several important meetings, but with only a second's pause he brushed them all aside at the prospect of spending a whole day in Lucia's company. 'I can rearrange my schedule. I'll pick you up at ten.'

She nodded, still hesitant, still shy. 'OK.'

He drew her back towards him, pressed his lips to her forehead. 'It will be OK,' he said, as much to himself as to her.

She didn't pretend to misunderstand. 'You don't know that.'

'We'll take it slowly.'

'I don't think it's the pace that matters.'

He didn't either. He tipped her chin up with his finger so he could meet her clouded gaze. 'What are you afraid of?'

She pressed her lips together, didn't answer, but then she didn't have to. He knew what she was afraid of; he was afraid of it as well.

Was he capable of loving her? Was he capable of love at all?

He didn't know the answer, and he knew Lucia didn't know it either. With one last, soft kiss, he let her go and headed back down the stairs.

CHAPTER TEN

'How about this one?'

Lucia glanced at the skintight leopard print mini-dress Angelo had pulled off the rack and shook her head, laughter bubbling up inside her. 'It's not my colour.'

'Zebra print, maybe?' He took out another dress and this time she laughed aloud.

'I doubt there's been a zebra print dress seen at the Corretti Cup ever.'

'Always time for a first.'

She shook her head, still smiling, and moved down the rack at one of the city's most exclusive boutiques, leopard print dresses and all. They'd visited several boutiques this morning, and her nervousness about being in these exclusive shops with their snooty sales clerks and elegant upholstery had dissolved in the glow of Angelo's smile, the ease of his good humour. She'd forgotten how much fun he could be. It had taken a lot of effort when they were children to make him smile and relax, but when he did…

There was no one with whom she'd rather be.

'All right, since you aren't going to go for the animal prints, how about this?' Angelo had moved to another rack of dresses, these one in various jewel tones.

He pulled out a slim sheath dress of sapphire silk, the fabric possessing an icy glow. Lucia drew in a breath.

'It's lovely,' she said hesitantly, because she couldn't actually imagine wearing it. She couldn't imagine wearing any of these dresses, leopard print included. She felt like a little girl playing dress up, and at any moment someone was going to come in and bark at her to stop pretending. Stop trying to be someone else.

'Try it on,' Angelo urged. 'It matches your eyes.'

Still unsure, she took the dress from him and went back to the sumptuous dressing room, complete with a chaise and three-panelled cheval mirror.

'Would you like any help?' the sales clerk, a tall, blonde woman with cold eyes and spike heels, asked. She'd been gushing all over them ever since Angelo had entered, acting as if he owned the place, but Lucia had a feeling the assistant wasn't fooled by her.

'I'm fine, thank you,' she said, and closed the door.

She knew she should be gratified by such attention, thrilled by Angelo's wealth and power. Surely most women would be, and she suspected he wanted her to be. Yet while she was proud of what he accomplished, all of it still gave her a sick feeling inside.

Sometimes she felt as if she didn't know this man of power and prestige who had the world at his feet. She didn't know how she could fit into his world...how he could love her.

Resolutely she pushed such pointless worries away, at least for the moment, and slipped into the dress, the silk sliding over with a luxuriant whisper. Angelo rapped on the door.

'Let me see.'

'Give me a minute.' With some wriggling she managed to zip up the back, and with a nervous flutter inside she opened the door. Angelo's pupils flared as he took in the fitted sheath dress ending just below her knee. It was simple, elegant, clearly expensive.

'*Magnifico*. We'll take it.'

'Don't you want to ask if I like it?'

His eyes widened with surprise. 'Don't you?'

She sighed, chuckled in defeat. 'Yes, I do.'

'Then there is no problem.'

'No,' she agreed. 'No problem.'

And there really wasn't. Why couldn't she just relax and enjoy all of this, allow herself to be swept along on this luxurious ride? Everything in her resisted it, resisted not just accepting Angelo's gifts, but acknowledging who he was, powerful, wealthy, entitled. She didn't want him to change her, but she didn't want him to be changed either. And she was afraid he already was, afraid Angelo would never be able to love her as she was.

It was an impossible conundrum. *They* were impossible.

Angelo must have sensed some of what she was feeling, for as they left the boutique and strolled down the glamorous Via Liberta, he said, 'You're not happy I bought you the dress.'

'I wouldn't say that,' she hedged, and he laughed dryly.

'You'd rather I hadn't, then.'

She grimaced. 'I don't mean to be ungrateful.'

'But you are.' He sounded amused, but underneath the humour she heard hurt.

'I don't need you to buy me things, Angelo,' she said after a moment, and he glanced away.

'What if I need to buy them for you?' he asked quietly. 'I want to buy them, at least. I want to give you things.'

Lucia stopped on the pavement and turned to face him. 'Why?' she asked, and he shrugged impatiently.

'Why not? I think it is a normal thing to want to do.' His voice was sharp in self-defence. 'I want to see you wearing beautiful things. I want to be the one to give them to you.'

It was, Lucia suspected, a way for him to show her he cared. Perhaps the only way he knew how. And if so, she should surely accept it, be glad for it. Yet still she resisted.

'Here's a question,' Angelo said as they continued walking down the street. 'Why don't you want me to give you things? Because I'm not sure I understand that.'

She didn't answer for a long moment. 'I suppose it reminds me of how different we are now,' she finally said slowly. 'How different you are, Angelo.'

He gave her a sideways glance, his rueful smile somehow sad. 'Do you really think I'm that different? Because from the moment I've been back in Sicily I've felt exactly the same.' He drew a shaky breath, his voice low. 'A ragged boy with a bloody nose and broken dreams.' He shook his head as if to dismiss the admission, and Lucia's heart twisted inside her. Didn't he know that was the boy she'd fallen in love with, not the man he seemed determined to be now, wealthy and powerful, striding through life with arrogant determination?

She opened her mouth to tell him as much, but he was already turning into another shop, this one even more exclusive and expensive-looking, with black velvet cases and diamonds winking in the window.

'Angelo—' she said, his name a warning, and he shook his head.

'You need something to go with the dress. If it makes

you feel better, you can return to me anything I buy after.'

After? After the Corretti Cup, or after he was finished with her? She knew she shouldn't be thinking that way, and yet she couldn't keep the thoughts from slipping into her mind, sly and insidious. As much as she wanted to, she didn't yet believe this could last. Perhaps that was why she refused his gifts. She was trying to protect herself, paltry attempt that it was, because she didn't trust him to love her, not to leave her.

'Try this.'

While her thoughts had been tangling themselves into knots Angelo had spoken to another snooty shop assistant who had brought out a gorgeous diamond necklace, a dozen glittering square-cut diamonds, each one encrusted with a dozen smaller ones. The thing was intricate, ornate and clearly the most expensive item in the shop.

Lucia shook her head.

'Just try it on,' Angelo persisted, and silently she allowed him to fasten the piece around her neck. The stones felt cold and sharp against the fragile skin of her throat, heavy on her neck.

Angelo's mouth curved in a smile of primal possession. *'Bellissima,'* he said in satisfaction, and she shook her head again.

'It's too much, Angelo.' Wordlessly she unclasped the necklace and handed it back to him. 'I'd look ridiculous in it.' Angelo frowned. She was still trying to distance herself, she knew, still acting out of fear and self-protection, yet she wanted to try. Trust could be a choice. Sometimes it had to be.

She took a deep breath and scanned the display cases. 'How about that?' She pointed to a whimsical dragonfly hair clip, its wings winking with diamonds and sapphires.

Angelo's frown deepened. 'You'd rather have that?'

She'd rather have nothing, rather have Angelo as the boy she knew and loved rather than this autocratic man who insisted on draping her in diamonds, yet she could hardly articulate that to him now. 'Yes.'

He gestured to the shop assistant, who took it out of the case. Lucia slid it into her hair, and was gratified to see Angelo's hard features soften into a smile. He nodded to the assistant. 'We'll take it.'

After they left the jewellery boutique they wandered along the waterfront and then into a restaurant that had, Angelo told her, the freshest seafood on all of Sicily.

The mood between them had lightened again, and Lucia revelled in the ease and enjoyment they had in each other's company. When Angelo was being himself.

'The neighbourhood could use some improvement,' she joked as they went inside, for while the restaurant was top drawer it was surrounded by unused docks and abandoned warehouses.

'The government is planning to regenerate this area,' he told her as they sipped chilled white wine on a terrace overlooking the harbour. 'Actually, I'm part of the process. I've secured a bid to redevelop a housing estate in the area.'

'You have?'

He smiled, his eyes crinkling at the corners and flashing grey-green. 'Don't sound so surprised.'

'I didn't realise you had so much business in Sicily.' He shrugged, averting his gaze, and Lucia couldn't keep from adding, 'But you never intend to live here.'

'Not permanently, no.'

She nodded, accepting, even as she wondered if he

simply didn't see that as a problem for their fledgling relationship. Admittedly, there wasn't too much to keep her in Sicily any more. Her mother was dead, her father long gone, and what few friends she had weren't particularly close ones. And yet…

Again, she resisted. Resisted giving more to this man, because she was still bracing herself for the moment when he decided he'd had enough. When he walked away…again.

Firmly she pushed that thought away. She needed to try. *Trust was a choice.* 'What made you decide to come back to Sicily after all this time? Just the business opportunity?'

Angelo's gaze rested on her for a moment, narrowed, shuttered. Then he smiled and took a sip of wine. 'Yes,' he answered. 'Just business.'

They walked along the waterfront for a while after lunch, and then back into the old quarter of the city. The sun was hot overhead and it was pleasant to wander hand in hand through the narrow streets with their crumbling buildings and open-air markets. Despite the elegant, expensive clothes and the pervasive aura of wealth, Angelo seemed like the boy she remembered. The boy she loved.

'This almost feels like old times,' she said, only half teasing.

'Doesn't it?' He turned to her with a smile, although she still sensed that guarded sorrow shadowing his eyes, tensing the lines around his mouth. 'I think you're the only person I've ever been myself with.' The admission, so quietly made, rocked her, because it was so achingly honest—and because she felt the same. Hope bloomed within once more, more powerful than ever.

'Me too,' she said quietly, and squeezed his hand. 'Me too.'

* * *

Angelo couldn't remember when he'd enjoyed a day more. For a whole day spent in Lucia's company he'd felt the tightness inside him ease, the emptiness fill. He felt happy. He felt whole.

The realisation terrified him.

He'd told Lucia love was complicated, messy, and it was. He felt it in all of its uncontainable sprawl now, disordering his thoughts, his ambitions, everything. He'd come to Sicily with a simple plan: to ruin the Correttis. Revenge, simple and sweet, served twenty years' cold. He'd convinced himself it was all he wanted, and yet now…?

Now he wanted this. Her. And not just her, but a life with her, a life he'd never, ever imagined having or even wanting. A life he still could bear to think about only in vague images: a house somewhere, a kitchen with sunlight and a bowl of fruit on the table. A child toddling towards him and loving arms slipping around his waist.

Even those images felt impossibly remote, like fuzzy photographs of another planet. A place he'd never been, and wasn't sure he could go.

A place he wasn't sure he *should* go.

'Angelo?' Lucia turned to him with a smile, although he saw the worry clouding her eyes. Always the worry, the fear. He felt it too.

'I should take you back home,' he said. 'I need to get back to work.'

'I see.'

And she probably did see, all too much. He hadn't meant it as a brush-off precisely, but it served as one. It was time to get back to the reason why he'd come back to Sicily at all. It was time to focus on what really mattered. They didn't speak as he drove her back to Caltarione. As soon as they hit the narrow, dusty streets of the village that time itself seemed to have forgotten he felt himself tense. Resist. He hated this place, hated the memories that came up inside him like the clouds of dust on the road, obscuring everything.

Just like he'd told Lucia, he couldn't escape that old feeling. Here he was once again that foolish boy, ragged and angry, whom everybody had ignored or dismissed. He felt the frustration boil up inside him along with the determination to not be that boy again. Lucia didn't seem to want him to be different, but he needed to be. Needed to be someone who would stand up to the Correttis, who would *count*—

'Stop here,' Lucia said softly, and he glanced at her in surprise for they were still at the top end of the village's main street, at least a quarter of a mile from her house. Then he saw they were outside the church, and realisation slammed into his chest, rocked him to the core.

'Are you sure?'

She nodded, and he parked the car on the kerb. The air was dry and still as they climbed out of the car, and although he couldn't see a single person on the narrow, winding street, he could feel the prying eyes, the pursed lips. How many people were peering out at them from behind latticed shutters, recognising him as the Corretti bastard they'd once ignored and reviled?

And how many people recognised Lucia as the woman who had borne his child, people who would never see her as anything else?

Dio, he wanted so much more for her. He wanted to give it to her. Why couldn't she understand that? Accept it?

He turned to her now, saw her face was pale and set. Before last night he'd never considered what life must

have been like for her after he'd left. She would have
been pregnant, unwed, alone. In a tiny place like Caltarione life must have been intolerable. His throat thickened and at first words wouldn't come.

'I'm sorry,' he said, and she turned to stare at him.

'What for?'

He saw the wariness enter her eyes, her body tensing
in expectation. Afraid—of what? That he would let her
down now, already? 'For not being here when you were
pregnant. And, I suppose, for not even thinking about
how hard it must have been for you in a place like this.
Not until you told me.' She shrugged and he asked quietly, 'Was it very hard?'

'It was worth it.'

'Even though—'

'Yes,' she cut him off with a quiet certainty. 'Even
though.'

He felt the thickness in his throat again, the moisture
in his eyes. What was happening to him? How had he become this weak wreck of a man, devastated by emotion?

'Let's go,' Lucia said, and she took his hand, her own
hand cold in his. Silently she led him around the side of
the church and into the cemetery behind, past the older
headstones now weathered and worn, some toppled over,
to a small garden in the back built into the hillside with
just a few small headstones. And there, in the corner,
a small rectangle of white marble commemorated his
child.

Angelo stared at the few, heartbreakingly simple
words. *Angelica. Molto amata.* Much loved.

He reached out and laid one hand on the marble headstone; it was warm from the sun. He felt tears again,
harder this time to ignore. He couldn't speak; he was

slain by weakness. He should have been here. He should have been here for Angelica, for *Lucia*.

Then he felt her arm slide around his waist and she laid her head on his shoulder, her touch like a healing balm. He took a shuddering breath.

'I'm sorry,' he said again.

'I know,' Lucia answered softly. 'But I didn't bring you here to open up the wounds of the past, Angelo. I brought you here to heal them. To look towards the future.' She spoke tremulously; he felt her uncertainty.

The future. The future scared him, and he suspected it scared her too. What could a future with Lucia look like? A future with love in it, a life he was afraid of because he didn't really believe it could ever be his? It never had been before.

The sun had started to sink behind the church and the cemetery was lost in shadows. Angelo turned away from his daughter's grave.

'We should go,' he said, and silently Lucia followed him back to the car.

An hour later, having dropped her off at her apartment, Angelo strode into his office above the Corretti Hotel. He felt restless, edgy, unfulfilled. The afternoon with Lucia had opened up old wounds, new doubts. He craved being with her, even as he hated the weakness of that craving. The need it showed in him, a need that could surely never be filled.

All you were meant to be was a stain on the sheets.

His father's sneering voice.

You were a mistake, Angelo. It would have been better if you'd never lived.

His grandparents, sighing with weary defeat.

I'm sorry. I should never have had you.

His mother, ashamed and defiant.

No one had wanted him. No one had loved him. He'd learned to live without love, had trained himself not to want it. And now Lucia came once more into his life, with her hope and her love and her *fear*.

He knew she was afraid he would let her down, no matter what she said. He knew it because he felt it too. Wouldn't it be easier for everyone if he just stopped now? Admitted it couldn't work, it wasn't in him? Wouldn't it save them both a lot of heartbreak? And God only knew Lucia had had enough, with his own abandonment and the death of their daughter—

'Signor Corretti? There have been messages....'

Yanked from his thoughts, Angelo glanced impatiently at his receptionist, a woman who had worked for the Correttis and whom he hadn't had time to replace, as she half rose from behind her desk.

'Leave them on my desk.'

He stalked into his office, felt the beginnings of another migraine pulse at his temples. He snatched the scrawled messages on his desk and scanned them, the pain at his temples pulsing harder as he realised what this day had cost him.

A message from one of Corretti Designs' shareholders, the banker from Milan who was having second thoughts about Luca remaining as CEO. Another message from Battaglia, wanting to speak to him about the regeneration bid. A message from Alessandro Corretti, his unacknowledged half-brother, who wanted to set up a meeting about that same bid.

Angelo dropped the sheaf of messages. One damned day might have set back all his plans. Who even knew what opportunities he'd missed while he'd been dallying with Lucia, chasing dreams he had no right to harbour, not even for a moment?

Dio, he'd been so stupid. So *weak*.

Resolutely he sat down at his desk and pulled the phone towards him. Any thoughts of Lucia, of love, had deserted him completely, replaced only by cold, hard purpose. This was why he was here. This was what he had come for.

Lucia gazed at her reflection. The dragonfly clip sparkled in her hair, which she'd styled into loose waves. The sapphire blue of the dress glowed against her skin. She wore cheap shoes.

Funny, but Angelo hadn't thought of that. Neither had she. Dress, check. Jewelry, check. Shoes? A pair of scuffed pumps she'd had for nearly a decade. And as for her underwear…if they ever got that far, Angelo would encounter plain white cotton that had definitely seen better days.

Sighing, she turned away from the mirror.

She wasn't even sure if any of it mattered. It had been five days since Angelo had dropped her off after their day together, and she hadn't seen him at all. Hadn't received so much as a phone call or text message or note. This was all starting to seem horribly familiar. The hope, the dread, the silence.

They hadn't even lasted a week.

Stop it, she told herself. He'd been busy, of course he had. He was an important man, with important deals to make. She understood that, even if she didn't like it. Trust was a choice.

Taking a deep breath, she went into the living room to wait for Angelo. His assistant had sent a message earlier that day that he would pick her up at five. Well, here she was. She only hoped he hadn't changed his mind… about anything. *About everything*.

At ten minutes past five Lucia started to worry. At quarter past, she began to doubt. And at half past, she felt horribly resigned—and that was when she heard quick footsteps on the stairs and a sharp rap at the door.

She opened the door, saw Angelo's gaze sweep over her quickly before he looked away. 'I'm sorry I'm late.'

She nodded, accepting his terse apology even as questions clamoured in her throat. 'What happened?' she asked, keeping her voice light, mild, and Angelo just shrugged.

'A business meeting ran late. Shall we?' He held out his arm and after a moment's pause Lucia slipped her hand through it. She could feel the tension vibrating through Angelo's arm, his whole body. Something had happened. Something was wrong.

That old fear lurched inside her, and she almost pulled away. Almost turned around and went straight back into her apartment. She didn't want this, hated the sense of clingy desperation that flooded through her, just as it must have flooded through her mother. Justify. Excuse. Appease. And all to keep a man around.

Trust is a choice.

'Is something wrong, Angelo?' she asked evenly, and he glanced back at her, his expression sharp and almost hostile until, with effort, he smoothed it out.

'No, I'm sorry. I've been a bit…stressed about work. That's all.' He drew her to him, kissed the top of her head. She slid her arms around him, pressed her cheek against his chest so she could feel the thud of his heart. She felt something in him loosen, relax. He sighed softly. 'You look amazing, you know, and utterly beautiful.'

She felt herself relax too, then. She didn't need to be so suspicious and uneasy. She had to stop waiting, expecting Angelo to let her down. She leaned back to smile at him. 'You look pretty amazing too.'

'And beautiful?' Angelo said with a quirk of his eyebrow, a faint smile on his lips.

'Actually, yes.' Because he was a beautiful man. Long lashes, full lips, high cheekbones. A woman would kill for all of those, and yet Angelo possessed them in an utterly masculine way.

'Let's go,' he said, and linking his hand in hers, he led her downstairs to the Porsche.

They didn't talk too much as they drove along the coast to the racetrack that held the Corretti Cup. Angelo made a few attempts at small talk, but Lucia could tell he was preoccupied—the tension stealing through him again, his fingers tapping the steering wheel—and she wondered how he felt about attending such a prestigious event, hosted by his cousin. Did he still hate his Corretti relations, even as he defiantly bore their name? It was yet another one of his integral contradictions: the ragged boy, the regal businessman. The Corretti who both hated and claimed his name.

As Angelo drove up to the front of the racetrack, a valet came around for the car, and another opened her door. Lucia stepped out, saw an array of women dressed head-to-toe in designer outfits, sleek and privileged and looking world-weary, while she had her pretty dress, her dragonfly hair clip and her cheap, old shoes.

She swallowed dryly, grateful for Angelo's steadying presence as he came beside her, slid his arm through hers.

'What's the schedule of events?' she asked as they joined the decked-out throng streaming towards the main entrance of the track. Angelo sidestepped the crowd and headed towards a separate door marked VIP Only. A dark-suited man allowed them to pass without so much as a blink.

You should be thrilled, Lucia told herself. *VIP!* But she only felt outclassed and uneasy.

'The main race is first,' Angelo said, his arm around her shoulders as he guided her down a private corridor to an even more private box of seats. Lucia sat down on a plush chair, watched as a waiter poured them both champagne. 'And then a champagne reception afterwards.'

'More champagne,' Lucia said as she accepted the crystal flute. 'I've never even had champagne before, you know.'

Angelo smiled faintly. 'See if you like it.'

She didn't. The taste was crisp and tart on her tongue, not sweet at all, and the bubbles went up her nose. She put her glass down on the marble-topped table between them and resisted the urge to wipe her damp palms down the sides of her dress.

She didn't like being here. She didn't like being here with Angelo, who was scanning the different boxes with narrowed eyes, his lips thinned, looking both powerful and predatory.

'Are you going to place a bet?' she asked, and he gave her a quick glance and nod.

'Oh, yes.'

There was something about his grimly certain tone that made her feel even more uneasy. 'Which horse?'

Angelo paused, then answered crisply, 'Cry of Thunder to win.'

Lucia didn't know a thing about horse racing, but from hearing the chatter and gossip in the staff room, she did know that Cry of Thunder was an upstart contender from Spain, a horse that no one was backing because of course everyone wanted Gio Corretti's Sicilian-bred horse to win.

Everyone except Angelo.

'Cry of Thunder?' she repeated after a moment. 'He's not likely to win, is he?'

Angelo hesitated for only a second. 'No.'

'So why are you betting on him, then?'

He shifted in his seat. 'There are more important things than money.'

'Of course there are.' Angelo's tone had been repressive, but Lucia couldn't ignore the deepening unease she felt, prickling along her spine and souring her stomach. 'But a horserace…betting, gambling…that's about money, surely? About winning?'

Angelo glanced at her, and his expression was completely unreadable. All the emotion and need, the hope and happiness, she'd once seen in his eyes was veiled, masked. His eyes were flat and dark, the colour of moss on stone. 'It's definitely about winning,' he finally said, which was no answer at all.

A few other guests entered the VIP box then, and Angelo stood as he said hello to several expensive-suited corporate types. Lucia saw one of the women, a sleek brunette, flick a dismissive glance first towards her frivolous hair clip and then at her shoes. She fought not to blush. Damn her shoes anyway. If she'd been trying to fool anybody, she obviously wasn't. Everyone could see how she didn't belong here.

And she *wasn't* trying to fool anybody, Lucia reminded herself fiercely. This was not her world. She didn't want it to be Angelo's world. She wanted to go home.

'All right?' Angelo asked, and reached for the champagne bottle to top up her barely touched flute.

'Yes.' Lucia smiled tightly. Every muscle in her body ached with tension, and the evening had barely started. She glanced at Angelo, who was leaning forward, his body looking as tense as hers felt. He wasn't enjoying himself either, she thought suddenly, and she felt a flicker of something almost like relief. Maybe they weren't so different at all. Neither of them wanted to be here.

They didn't talk much as more people took their seats and then the race started. Lucia watched the horses, elegantly sinuous, eat up the track, clouds of dust billowing behind them and the sea a sunlit shimmer on the horizon. She couldn't tell what was going on, but it was over soon enough—and Cry of Thunder had come in fifth. Gio Corretti's horse had won.

'How much did you lose?' she asked, smiling, trying to keep it light, and Angelo shrugged.

'It doesn't matter.'

After the race they went with the other VIPs into a glittering ballroom. Tuxedoed waiters passed around yet more champagne as well as chocolate-dipped strawberries, caviar, pâté. Food Lucia had never had before and didn't really like, although she helped herself to several strawberries. Angelo kept surveying the ballroom, his eyes narrowed as if he were looking for someone. He barely spoke to Lucia, and her unease turned to pure feminine annoyance.

'Angelo—'

'Come here.' He took her elbow, striding forward towards a man Lucia recognised from earlier, Gio Corretti—a son of Benito Corretti, a cousin of Angelo's.

The man inclined his head slightly in cool acknowledgement and Angelo smiled back, although there was no friendliness or warmth in that curving of lips. He looked hard, unyielding, ruthless. Underneath her hand his arm felt as if it had been hewn from granite, forged from steel.

'You lost quite a bit tonight,' Gio remarked as he shook Angelo's outstretched hand. Angelo's smile deepened, became even colder.

'Pocket change, Gio.'

'Ah.' Gio Corretti nodded slowly. 'I see.'

Lucia didn't see anything at all. The men stared at each other, Angelo cold, Gio chillingly remote. Lucia felt like screaming at them to behave—but of course, to all intents and purposes, they were behaving. No fisticuffs, no hurling of insults. Just this cold, hard, glittering anger. Like the diamonds Angelo had wanted to buy for her, costly and soulless.

'I'm not the one you're fighting, you know,' Gio said quietly, and Angelo's whole body stiffened as if he'd been jerked on a string.

'Who said I'm fighting?'

'Aren't you?'

'It's business.'

'Some business.' Gio shrugged, turned away, and Angelo stood there, his whole body quivering with tension, with anger. *With hurt.*

Lucia could feel it coming off him in waves, knew he felt like he'd been dismissed, rejected by a Corretti. What she saw in Gio Corretti was a grudging respect for a self-made man like Angelo, but Angelo hadn't seen it.

'Angelo…' she murmured, and he shook his head, shrugged off her arm.

'Let's go.'

As relieved as she was to get out of there, she didn't like the way he seemed about to stomp off, pulling her along with him. 'Don't you think—'

'I've done what I came to do,' Angelo said flatly,

and reaching for her hand, he led her swiftly out of the ballroom.

They didn't talk until they were in the Porsche, speeding back towards Palermo, the night inky-black all around them.

'What was that all about?' Lucia asked quietly.

'What do you mean?'

'Why did you bring me there, Angelo? Why did you go yourself?' She shook her head, bewildered, uncertain, starting to get angry. 'You certainly didn't go because you enjoyed the experience.'

'Did you?' Angelo tossed back, and she leaned her head back against the seat.

'No, not at all. But does that really surprise you? I've never—' She stopped suddenly, and Angelo glanced at her with narrowed, knowing eyes.

'You've never what?' he prompted softly.

'I've never wanted to be in that kind of crowd,' she finished, choosing her words with care. 'Have that kind of life.'

Angelo arched an incredulous eyebrow. 'You've never,' he stated disbelievingly, 'wanted more out of life than making other people's beds, cleaning their damn toilets—'

'It's a job, Angelo. It's respectable, it pays—'

'There's more to life than a *job*.'

'Oh, yes, there is. There's love and family and children and happiness.' Her throat clogged and her chest hurt. She didn't know how they'd got into this argument, but she had a gut instinct that the only way to get out was to wade through. She swallowed hard. 'But I don't think you meant those kinds of things.'

'No, I didn't.' Angelo stared straight ahead, flexed his fingers on the wheel. The night-shrouded landscape passed by in a blur of black. Lucia closed her eyes. She didn't like where this conversation was going. He didn't say anything else, and she thought they might spend the entire journey back to Palermo in this stony silence. A question burned in her gut, churned its way up her throat.

'How much money did you lose?'

'Does it matter?'

'I think it does.'

Angelo threw her a quick, irritated glance. 'Why? I have plenty. And you don't even like me to spend it on you, so—'

'It's not about the money.'

'What, then?'

She shook her head wearily. 'Perhaps you should tell me that.'

'Stop talking in riddles, Lucia—'

'Then you stop putting me off,' she retorted. 'You didn't bring me to the Corretti Cup as a date, did you, Angelo? You didn't even buy me that dress or want to buy me those ridiculous diamonds because you wanted to please me or make me happy.' It was all becoming horribly clear, like wiping the steam from a mirror. Slowly, surely, she could see the whole, awful reflection.

'Why do you think I did, then?' Angelo asked in a colourless voice.

'Because you wanted to show me off. Show yourself off.' Lucia spoke mechanically; she felt weirdly lifeless, almost as if she didn't care about it any more. 'You went to the Corretti Cup to thumb your nose at all the Correttis you still hate, even though it's been fifteen years since you left. Even though you probably have more money than they do now. That's why you bet on the losing horse, isn't it? Just to show you could lose however much money and it didn't matter.' More mist cleared; the reflection

sharpened. 'And that's why you bought the hotel.' The
realisation lay heavily within her. 'What are you trying
to do, Angelo? Ruin them?'

'Anything that happens to them, they deserve.'

'They *deserve*? Does anyone deserve to be ruined?
Why are you even angry at them, Angelo? It's your father you're really angry at and he's—'

'Don't,' he said in a low voice, 'talk about my father.'

'Why not?'

He let out a low breath and shook his head. 'I just
don't want to talk about him.'

Lucia sat back against her seat and closed her eyes.
She felt utterly drained, her mind numb and empty. She
should have thought about this, she realised dully. She
should have expected this. She remembered how angry
and bitter Angelo had been as a child; had she thought
he'd changed?

That was why she didn't like all this power and
wealth, she knew now. It really wasn't about the money.
It was about the reason, the motivation. The revenge. The
hard core of bitterness and anger Angelo would never re-
linquish. How could love flourish in such a heart? How
could it even survive?

They'd reached Caltarione, and Angelo pulled up in
front of her apartment. Tinny music and raucous laughter
spilled out from the bar beneath. Lucia opened her eyes
and saw Angelo staring straight ahead, his jaw bunched,
his body tense.

'I don't even see why any of it matters,' he said flatly.
'It has nothing to do with us.' Lucia just shook her head.
She didn't know how even to begin to explain. 'Why
does it bother you?' he demanded, his voice harsh now.
'It's not as if any of the Correttis have ever done you a
good turn, Lucia. Or as if you cared about them—did

you?' His voice hardened in suspicion, and Lucia turned to him slowly.

'What are you saying?' she asked in a low voice.

'Why are you so defensive of the Correttis?' Angelo challenged. 'Did one of my half-brothers offer some comfort while I was away—maybe you wanted to be with a *real* Corretti—'

Lucia didn't think. She just reacted, reaching out and slapping Angelo hard across the face. He blinked, and she watched an angry red handprint bloom across his cheek.

He reached up with one hand and touched his cheek, his expression one of cold disbelief. Lucia held her breath. She didn't regret slapping him, not one bit, but she regretted everything else. This whole evening. This argument. The man he'd become.

Angelo held his hand up to his cheek, his expression coldly remote, and Lucia stared back, her chest heaving. Then his face crumpled and he covered it with both his hands as he let out a shuddering breath.

'*Dio*, I'm sorry,' he said, the words coming out on a half-groan. 'How could I say such a thing to you? I didn't believe it for a moment.' He dropped his hands and looked at her with such aching bleakness that Lucia suddenly felt near tears herself. 'Forgive me, Lucia. Forgive me for everything. I'm such a bastard—a true bastard, and not just one by birth. I've treated you terribly. I always have.' He drew in a ragged breath. 'I can't do this.'

She reached out and cupped his cheek, the one still red from her slap. 'You *are* doing it, Angelo. Just saying that is more than you've ever done before.'

He grimaced. 'That's not saying very much.'

'Still.' She tried to smile. 'It's something.'

Angelo stared at her, his eyes glittering, his chest

heaving with ragged breaths. 'Let's get out of here,' he said suddenly. 'Out of Sicily. Being back here—it makes me someone I don't want to be. Let me take you somewhere, Lucia—somewhere you've never been, away from all of this. Just for a little while.'

'But my—' She stopped, because she could not mistake the desperation in Angelo's voice. She knew, in her own way, she'd been as stubborn as he was, refusing his gifts, refusing to change or even give an inch of her life over to this man. But maybe now they both needed compromise. Escape.

'Please, Lucia.'

She smiled again and slowly leaned forward to kiss his lips. 'Yes,' she answered. 'Let's escape.'

CHAPTER ELEVEN

ANGELO GAZED AT Lucia sitting across from him in his private jet and smiled. He'd made the right decision, leaving Sicily for a little while. Escaping, just as Lucia had said. He'd hated how he felt there, trapped as the boy he'd once been, determined to prove himself yet still dismissed.

He remembered how Gio Corretti had turned away from him, indifferent, dismissive, and his heart burned inside him. Perhaps Gio would think differently when he took over another chunk of Corretti Enterprises. Last night, after he'd left Lucia, he'd put several meetings into place with various shareholders in Corretti Enterprises's different interests. He might have to wait on Corretti Designs, but other companies under the Corretti umbrella were ripe for the taking. And he intended to take.

'You're frowning,' Lucia said quietly, and he returned his distant gaze to her, taking in the blueness of her eyes, shadowed grey by a moment's worry. She didn't understand, Angelo knew. Didn't share his need to equal the Correttis, to rise above them.

'Sorry, I was lost in thought.' He leaned forward to brush his lips against hers, all his plans for meetings and takeovers momentarily forgotten as her mouth met his. She tasted so unbearably sweet, and he longed to take her in his arms, to lose herself in her generous warmth.

They'd hadn't done more than kiss since that unforget-table, tempestuous night at his villa. He hoped that might change today. Tonight.

'So you haven't even told me where we're going,' Lucia said, and Angelo was gratified to see her eyes clear to sapphire. 'Not too far away, I hope.'

'No.' He glanced out the window and smiled. 'We're almost there.'

Twenty minutes later the jet touched down. As she stepped out onto the tarmac Lucia clutched her hands together, turned to Angelo with shining eyes. 'Paris.'

'You always said you wanted to go.'

'I did, didn't I?'

He drew her towards him, unable to resist kissing her again. 'I hope it lives up to your expectations.'

'I think it will,' Lucia murmured as she kissed him back.

Angelo felt his insides lift, lighten. Coming here had been such a good idea. Here, away from Sicily, their childhoods, the memories and prejudices, they could be themselves…and learn to love each other all over again.

Lucia felt as if she were floating. She was finally in Paris—and with Angelo. It was her birthday and Christ-mas all in one, everything she'd ever wanted. Almost.

They rode a limo into the city, and Lucia kept her nose nearly pressed to the glass as she watched the monu-ments flash by: le Place de Concorde, l'Arc de Triom-phe, the huge Louvre with its winking glass pyramids and of course the Eiffel Tower, a glorious steel pinnacle piercing the sky. She had a postcard of each one, but the reality, even from behind the tinted window of a limo, was far better.

'I want to see it *all*,' she breathed, and Angelo chuckled.

'And you will. But first let's check in and get something to eat.'

They checked into the Presidential Suite at the Georges Cinq Hotel, and after the bellhop had left Lucia walked around slowly, taking in the antiques, the huge marble bathtub, the private terrace. She'd cleaned such rooms, of course, working at the hotel, but she'd never stayed in one before.

She stared out at the City of Light dazzled by a noonday sun and shook her head in wonder.

'Do you like it?' Angelo asked, and to her own shame she heard an uncertain note of vulnerability in his voice.

'Do I like it?' she repeated, and turned around. 'It's the most amazing place I've ever been. It's even better than the penthouse suite at the Corretti!'

He chuckled softly. 'For now. I intend to make the Corretti the most luxurious hotel in all of Europe.'

'And you'll manage that easily, I'm sure.' Away from Sicily, from the memories and prejudices, she felt her resistance to Angelo's wealth melt away. He was a different man here, and she was a different woman. Finally they could be the people they wanted to be, the people they were meant to be, loving each other.

She walked towards him, reached for his hands. 'Thank you for bringing me here, Angelo.'

She felt his tension ease, saw his countenance lighten. 'Thank you for coming.' He drew her towards him and she came willingly. 'I'm glad we escaped.'

He slid his arms around her and she pressed her cheek against his chest, felt the reassuring thud of his heart. 'It felt like a close one,' she whispered, and his arms tightened around her.

'I know.'

She didn't say anything more, didn't want to drag

them both down into argument once again. They had time to work out their differences, time to change and heal. 'Let's go see the city,' she said instead, and he laughed ruefully, his arms still around her.

'I have some good ideas of what we could do right here, you know.'

Her heart seemed to turn right over, her insides tightening with longing. She had a good idea too, and if it actually came down to a choice between seeing the Eiffel Tower and making love with Angelo...well, the postcard really was a good likeness, wasn't it? Although the thought of actually making love with Angelo—not just a moment's grasped pleasure, a one-night stand—thrilled her and terrified her in equal parts. It would be so much *more*.

Still chuckling, Angelo released her. 'Come on. I couldn't live with myself if I didn't let you see the Eiffel Tower.'

It was better than the postcard, Lucia decided as they took the lift to the top viewing level. The city lay spread before them in a living map, the sky cloudless and blue above. Angelo slipped his hand in hers as they stared out at the endless view.

'Is it as you imagined?'

'Better.'

'It's nice when things live up to your expectations,' he said dryly.

Some strange impulse made her ask, 'Has this lived up to your expectations, Angelo?'

'This?' he repeated, his voice turning just a little guarded and Lucia gazed at him openly, wanting, even needing, this honesty between them.

She wasn't really sure what she was asking. 'Success,' she said after a pause. 'Wealth. Power. Revenge, even—all of it. Has it lived up to your expectations? Is it everything you hoped it would be?'

Angelo squinted as he gazed out at the city. 'Wealth and power have their advantages.'

'But do they fill that emptiness inside?'

She felt him tense, saw his eyes narrow and his pupils flare. 'What are you talking about?'

'Do you remember?' she asked softly. 'When your— when Carlo Corretti died, and you came and found me. Do you remember what you said?'

She could tell by the way his mouth tightened and he looked away that he did. *He'd dead, Lucia, and I don't feel anything. I just feel empty.*

'Why are we talking about this?' Angelo asked, his tone even and yet also edged with impatience, annoyance. 'I thought we came to Paris to forget about all that, at least for a little while.'

'Is it wrong of me to want to know? To want to know you?'

He let out a sigh. 'Not wrong. Just…difficult. We'll argue about it, Lucia. I know that. You don't see things the way I do.' A fair point, yet she knew the implication was that he was seeing things correctly and she wasn't.

Lucia decided to leave it. Why ruin a perfect afternoon by insisting on a discussion she wasn't sure either of them were ready to have?

'We don't have to talk about it now,' she said quietly, and with a grateful smile Angelo turned from the railing.

'There's plenty more to see in this city, you know.'

They spent the afternoon touring the sights, taking in the endless steps of Montmartre and the quaint, narrow streets of the Latin Quarter, the modern Centre Pompidou and the ancient Louvre.

They wandered down the Champs-élysées and Angelo

insisted on buying her a dress for dinner, a strappy black number that made Lucia feel both sophisticated and sexy.

'And we'd better not forget the shoes,' he murmured, his eyes glinting, and she laughed, realising he'd noticed her old shoes from before. 'How about these?' He'd stopped in front of an exclusive-looking boutique and pointed to a pair of diamante-encrusted stilettos. The heel was at least five inches high.

'They're ridiculous,' she protested.

'True,' Angelo agreed solemnly. 'But you do love them.'

Lucia had to admit that she did. She'd never possessed anything frivolous or extravagant before, and suddenly those silvery stilettos seemed the best shoes in the world.

Angelo led her by the hand into the boutique, and a few minutes later he was slipping one of the stilettos onto her foot.

'I feel like Cinderella,' she said with a laugh, and he glanced up at her with passion-darkened eyes.

'You're my Cinderella.'

'That's the only one I want to be.' She swallowed, her heart suddenly starting to pound, and then stood. She felt about ten feet tall in the heels, and she tottered around the shop, feeling outrageous and yet so very sexy.

'We'll take them,' Angelo told the sales assistant. He pulled Lucia close so only she could hear his whispered words. 'I have a fantasy of seeing you wearing those and nothing else.'

A blush fired Lucia's body and she glanced away. 'That sounds like a…an interesting fantasy,' she murmured.

By the time they'd arrived back at the hotel Lucia was exhausted but also happy. All afternoon Angelo had been relaxed, fun, even silly. He'd been the boy she had missed, the boy she'd fallen in love with. Underneath the hard gloss of wealth and power he was still there, and the realisation made her heart sing with joy.

As she walked into the suite, still amazed by the sheer luxuriousness of the place, she stopped suddenly for the doors to the private terrace were ajar, and she could see a table there, laid with linen and flickering with candlelight.

She turned back to Angelo. 'How—?'

'I'd like to say it took great planning and precision, but all it really took was a phone call.'

'Even so,' Lucia murmured, touched more than she could say by his thoughtfulness. She gave a slight grimace, gestured to her plain T-shirt and capris. 'I think I have half the dirt of Paris on me.'

'There's no reason why you can't make good use of that huge marble shower,' Angelo said with a glint in his eyes. 'We both could.'

Lucia's breath caught in her chest as she remembered how they'd made very good use of the shower in Angelo's villa. He laughed softly and shook his head.

'No, there will be time for that later. Bathe and we'll eat first.'

'All right.' She headed for the bathroom, peeled her clothes from her body and stepped under the hot, powerful spray. Why, she wondered as she washed her hair, did Angelo's words feel a bit like a temporary reprieve? She wanted to make love with him, had dreamt of it, and yet…

She was afraid. Afraid that now they were actually trying to have a real relationship, sex might ruin it. She might disappoint him. He might walk away afterwards.

'Stop it,' she said aloud, her words lost in the shower spray. 'Stop waiting for the worst to happen.' She'd lived her life like that for too long already. Now she wanted to hope. To believe.

Trust was a choice.

She wore the strappy black dress Angelo had bought for her earlier, and the silver stilettos. Gazing at her reflection in the mirror, she hardly recognised herself. Her hair tumbled loosely about her shoulders, and her eyes were smoky and dark with anticipation. With passion. As for the dress…it clung to every curve before flaring out about her thighs. The silver stilettos made her legs look endless.

Taking a deep breath, she headed out to the terrace. Angelo was already out there, having showered and changed into a pair of charcoal-grey trousers and a white button-down shirt, open at the throat. His hair curled against his neck and as he turned to her his eyes blazed almost emerald and for a moment Lucia forgot how to breathe.

In, out, lungs filling—she had to tell herself, remind her body of its basic functions because every sense, every cell and neuron, was short-circuited by awareness.

She loved him so much.

'Bellissima,' Angelo said softly as he came towards her. 'Mi cucciola.' She didn't mind the endearment then, knew it was part of their history, who they were.

He took her hands in his and drew her to the table. 'Good enough to eat,' he said, and Lucia laughed.

'And I'm starving.'

She didn't really remember what they talked about that evening, only how easy and relaxed it seemed. How happy she felt, and how happy she knew Angelo felt; the tautness was gone from his body, the shadows from his eyes.

The City of Light had settled into silence for the evening, the sun streaking its last orange rays across the horizon. As the sky deepened into indigo, Angelo reached for her hand and pointed to the Eiffel Tower.

'Watch.'

The last of the sun's light sank from the sky and the lights of the Eiffel Tower came on, transforming the tower into a diamond-like jewel in the centre of the city, sparkling with lights against a darkening sky.

'Oh,' Lucia breathed as she gazed at the lit tower with wonder. 'It's beautiful. I'm so glad I saw it.'

'I'm glad I saw it with you.'

She turned back to Angelo, and saw he was looking at her with heavy-lidded, languorous intent. She swallowed, then whispered, 'Make love to me, Angelo.'

He smiled and drew her up by the hand away from the table, and then from the terrace to the sumptuous bedroom with its huge four-poster bed.

He stood her in front of it, his hands cupping her face. 'You're trembling.'

'I'm…nervous.'

He frowned. 'Why?'

'Because…this is different, isn't it? It should be different. The other times—it was rushed….'

He slid his hands from her face to her shoulders, sliding his fingers through the heavy mass of her hair. 'I don't think it was too rushed in the shower,' he murmured, and she chuckled in acknowledgement, the sound wavering on the still air.

'Yes, I know, but…it still felt temporary. I still thought it was a one-night—'

'This is not for just one night,' Angelo said softly, silencing her words. 'This is the beginning, Lucia, of for ever.' And then he kissed her, softly, his lips brushing across hers, a whisper, a greeting, before her lips parted beneath his and he went deep as her mind went blurry, awash with pleasure.

Slowly, reverently, he slipped the straps of her dress from her shoulders and she stepped out of the garment, wearing only her underwear and the silver heels.

'Ah,' Angelo said as he gazed down at her, drinking her in. 'My fantasy. Almost.' Smiling, he reached forward and undid the clasp of her bra. He slid her panties down her legs and she kicked them off. She was naked, save for the shoes.

And amazingly, she didn't feel embarrassed or uncertain. She felt powerful. Sexy. And incredibly desired. Smiling, she reached for the buttons on his shirt. 'And now it's time for my fantasy.'

Angelo's eyes were dark as he gazed down at her, his voice a husky murmur. 'Which is?'

'You wearing nothing at all.' She slid the shirt from his shoulders and then, fumbling only a little, went for his belt. She drew it through the loops and heard Angelo's breath come out in a hiss as she undid the button of his trousers and then slid them down his legs. His boxers followed and now they were both naked.

Lucia kicked off her shoes. Angelo laughed softly. 'There goes my fantasy.'

'I think I can do better.'

'I'm sure you can. In fact, my fantasy is becoming less and less about shoes and much more about you—and me.' Tugging on her hand, he drew her to the bed, pulling aside the duvet, and then took her into his arms and she curled into him, sliding her legs along his, her softness against the hard, muscular planes of his chest and abdomen. In the comforting cradle of his arms she remembered how good he felt, how *right*. How much she missed this warmth, this connection, and how she never wanted to be without it again.

That connection strengthened with every touch, every kiss, every caress. Lucia arched against him, gasping aloud as he touched her in every intimate place, hands and mouth, fingers and lips. And she touched him back, tentatively at first and then with growing confidence and power, revelling in the way he responded, drawing his breath in a hiss through his teeth as she followed the path blazed by her hands with her mouth. She knew every part of him now, and yet she wanted to know more. Needed more, craved that full union, when her body would be joined with his wholly and utterly.

'Angelo…'

'I'm here, *mi cucciola*,' he whispered as he rolled her onto her back, his body poised over hers. '*Amore mio*. I'm here.' He slid a condom on and then joined his body with hers, filling her right up so she gasped again, her nails biting into his shoulders as she wrapped her legs around his waist and drew him even more fully into herself.

'I—' she gasped, unable to manage more as his body drove her closer and closer to shattering completely. 'I love you—'

'I love you,' Angelo said, his voice breaking on the words, and then he kissed her as her body convulsed around his and the world fell apart and came together again, a more beautiful and perfect whole than ever before.

His words still reverberated through her as she lay in his arms, sated and sleepy. *I love you*. He'd actually said it. But had he meant it? Or had it simply come from the intensity of the moment.

'You're wondering if I meant it, aren't you,' Angelo said softly. He brushed a strand of hair away from her face and Lucia turned to look at him, unable to dissemble.

'Did you?'

'Yes.' He sounded quiet, certain, and yet a little sad. 'Yes, although this is so new for me, Lucia. I've never loved anyone before. I've never let myself.'

'I know,' she said softly.

'But I love you. It doesn't make it easy or comfortable.' He let out a shaky laugh. 'But it feels right. And I can't live without it now. Without you.'

They made love again, even more slowly and languorously this time, and afterwards they showered, washing each other before they made love a third time until Lucia laughed, her face buried in Angelo's neck.

'I'll be exhausted tomorrow.'

'Good thing we can spend the whole day in bed, then.'

'Don't you need to be anywhere?' she asked once they were back in bed, snuggled against each other, this time to sleep. Angelo slid his fingers along hers in turn, not speaking for a moment.

'I can spare a day or two,' he finally said, and Lucia could not keep the disappointment from whispering through her.

'A day or two,' she repeated, and he rolled over to face her.

'This time. But there will be other times and places, Lucia. Other escapes.'

She stared at him, wanting to accept what he said, wanting to believe in it, and yet something held her back. 'What is it?' he asked, and drew her fingers to his lips. 'You're frowning.'

'I don't want a relationship of escapes,' she said after a moment. 'What are we escaping, Angelo?'

He sighed and rolled onto his back, his hand still loosely clasped with hers. 'I didn't mean it like that.'

'How did you mean it?'

'Just…' He shrugged. 'We'll have other holidays. Other cities, other hotels—I want to show you the world.'

'And I want to see it with you,' she said, wishing she could leave it at that, and be content with what they had. Yet she couldn't. That fear still lurked her inside her, whispered its taunts. She knew she wanted to silence that sly voice for ever, and the only way to do that was by speaking it aloud.

'But seeing cities—travelling the world—that's not real life, Angelo.'

'It could be.'

She shook her head. 'What about—what about my life back in Sicily? Your life? What will happen when we return?'

'We can decide what happens. You don't have to return to work as a maid—if you don't want to.'

She knew it cost him to say that, to not demand she quit. He'd never wanted her scrubbing floors, cleaning toilets. And frankly, it wasn't a job she really liked, so why had she clung to it? Out of pride, perhaps, as well as fear. Quitting her job to await Angelo's pleasure felt like the actions of a mistress or a whore, not an equal.

'I don't know what else I would do,' she said after a moment.

'I've been thinking about that. You enjoy helping women like Maria, don't you? With their reading and writing?'

'Yes…'

'Why not start a literacy charity for women like her? Women who had to quit school at sixteen or even younger to work. You could be involved on the ground level, help teach them yourself. I could provide the initial funding—'

She felt an incredulous bubble of hope rise up inside her and she squeezed his hand. 'You would do that for me?'

'Of course I would. And for them, as well. I would have liked to keep at school. I know what it's like to feel frustrated by your own lack of education.'

Softly she kissed his lips. 'You're a good man, Angelo.'

He slid his arms around her and they lay there in silence for a moment, thoughts tumbling through Lucia's mind. *Just leave it,* she told herself. *Leave it and be happy. This is so much more than you ever dreamt of, ever hoped for.* Still she spoke.

'And what about you? When we return to Sicily?'

'What about me?'

She took a breath, prayed for courage to see this through. 'What kind of man will you be, Angelo? Because it's still in your power to decide.'

She felt his emotional withdrawal like a physical thing, as if the very air around them had cooled. He rolled onto his back, slipped his hand from hers. 'I am who I am, Lucia.'

'I know you are, and I love you. But you said yourself how returning to Sicily made you someone you didn't want to be. I don't want you to return and still find you're acting like that person, not when I know who you really are. I know how much goodness you're capable of.'

He stared up at the ceiling, not answering, and Lucia held her breath. He had to see what she meant. He had to give up this awful idea of revenge—

'You're right,' he said at last. 'I don't want to be that boy with a bloody lip and broken dreams. The boy who's always been rejected or reviled. And when I come back to Sicily that's who I feel like, a beggar at the Correttis' feast.' He turned to face her, and determination blazed from his eyes. 'That's why I'm doing this, Lucia. You might see it as some kind of cold-blooded revenge, but it's different than that. I'm showing them—and myself— that I'm not that boy any more. That I'm someone to be reckoned with—' He stopped, his eyes narrowing. 'What?'

Lucia swallowed past the thickening of tears in her throat. 'But, Angelo,' she whispered. 'I fell in love with that boy.'

For a moment she thought he understood. His mouth twisted and she glimpsed that old bleakness in his eyes. Then his mouth firmed and his eyes shuttered. 'Then the question is, do you love the man that boy has become?'

She swallowed again, her throat aching. Everything aching, because she hadn't expected it to come to this so quickly, so terribly. Moments ago they'd been making love. 'I love you, Angelo, but this revenge you're desperate to pursue…it's tearing you—and us—apart. You can't see it, but it is. Why do you think you got that migraine—'

'I've always suffered from headaches.'

'And why do you think that is? Why do you think you still feel so restless and angry, even when you have all the power, all the wealth, you could possibly ever need or want? Why do still feel so empty?'

He stared at her hard, and she thought he might not answer. He might turn away, and then what would she do? How could she make him see how this was destroying him—and any chance their love had?

'Why do you think that is?' he finally asked evenly.

'Because revenge doesn't satisfy you, Angelo. Wealth,

power, any of it—no matter how many companies you buy up, or how many Correttis you grind into the dust, you'll still feel as empty as you did the night of your father's funeral, when you came to me—'

'Don't.'

He rolled away from her, into a sitting position, so she was facing his taut back. Lucia sat up, clutching the duvet to her, knowing they had to have this conversation. The only way was through. 'I must. Our love—any love—can't survive this kind of cold-blooded destruction, Angelo. You have to let it go.'

'It's a business deal, Lucia.'

'No, it's not. It's so much more than that. You might be able to tell Gio Corretti it's just business, but you can't lie to me. You're doing this because you're still the hurt little boy whose father wouldn't acknowledge him, and you hate that.'

'Of course I hate it,' he snapped. He rose from the bed, reached for his trousers. 'You think I want to feel like that again? You think I want to look into the Correttis' sneering faces and see how they've dismissed me?'

'And you think ruining them will achieve anything?'

'Yes—'

'No, Angelo,' Lucia said quietly. 'It won't. It might make them respect you, but that's not what you want.'

'Oh?' He turned to her, dressed only in his trousers, one eyebrow arched in cold incredulity. 'What do you think I want, then?'

'You want them to love you.' She might as well have hit him. He jerked back as if she'd slapped his face. 'And they won't,' she forced herself to continue. 'You can't make someone love you, Angelo. But I love you. I love you with all my heart, and it's love that fills the emptiness, that feeds the hunger. Let my love be enough.'

Angelo didn't respond. He stared at her, his face expressionless, every emotion veiled. Lucia held her breath and waited. What would she do if he said it wasn't?

She would, she realised hollowly, leave him. She would have to.

'Don't make me choose,' he finally said, and it was a warning.

'And if I do?'

'I said, don't make me.'

'Because you will choose revenge.'

'It doesn't have to be like that,' he said, impatient now. He reached for his shirt and shrugged into it. '*Dio*, Lucia, you're the one bent on destruction. Why are you trying to ruin what we have? It's been good so far, hasn't it?'

'It's been amazing,' she whispered. 'It's been the most wonderful experience of my life.'

'So why not just let it go? Why are you always asking for more of me?'

'Because that's what love does, Angelo.' She choked back a sudden sob. 'That's what love is. You don't love half a person. You love all of them, everything, and that's how I want to love you. But I can't—'

'You can't love me if I continue with this?' he finished. 'That sounds like conditional love to me, Lucia. That sounds like you trying to manipulate me as surely as I was trying to when I suggested you become my mistress. I wanted to put you in a compartment of my life, I see that now. In a nice, tidy little box. I wanted to manage you. Now you're doing the same to me.'

'It's not like that,' she insisted. Tears slipped down her face, cold and silent. 'I'm trying to free you from the box you've put yourself in—'

He flung up one hand. 'Enough. I've had enough of

this ridiculous arguing. *Dio*, nothing I ever do will be enough for you.'

'That's not fair. I've never asked for any of this, Angelo. Not the diamonds or the clothes or money or trips to Paris. I just want you. The real you.'

'This,' Angelo said flatly, 'is the real me.' And then he turned and walked out of the room.

CHAPTER TWELVE

ANGELO GAZED MOODILY out the window of his private jet at a grimly cloud-laden sky. The weather had turned grey and cool and after the argument with Lucia last night it suited his mood perfectly. Although if the weather truly suited his mood, a storm would surely be raging, just as anger surged inside him.

Who the hell did she think she was, telling him all that psychobabble? Insisting he wanted the Correttis' *love*? It was absurd, pathetic. Yes, maybe he'd dreamt of such things once upon a time, when he'd been a foolish boy—but now?

Now he wanted revenge. He wanted justice. Didn't she see that? Why couldn't she understand this integral part of himself? And how could she even pretend to love him, when she wouldn't accept this?

Restlessly Angelo settled into his seat. The obvious answer was she didn't love him, never had, just as he'd first thought. She'd convinced herself, perhaps, that she loved him, the him she'd plucked from her own head. He hadn't lived up to that sappy fairy-tale prince, so here he was, flying back to Sicily alone, about to take over more of the Corretti holdings. This morning, after Lucia had left, he'd arranged several private meetings with the shareholders he thought most likely to cave. He could have control of Corretti Designs by this evening. Lucia's leaving had just made him more determined to dominate Corretti Enterprises.

I'll show her.

He stilled in his thoughts, felt his insides curl in something like shame. He sounded like a little boy. He was acting like a little boy…like the little boy she'd claimed he still was, looking for love.

And she gave it to you. She'd asked him to let it be enough, and he'd told her it wasn't. She wasn't.

Resolutely Angelo set his jaw and stared out the window. Lucia had asked too much. He couldn't give up this. He couldn't imagine what life would look like if he did. She wanted to talk about emptiness? He'd be a damn *void* if he let go of this. Of revenge, of proving himself, of finally, *finally—*

Finally what?

Would acquiring one more Corretti company—or two, or a dozen—really make a difference? Would he feel satisfied then, complete? *Happy?*

He sat back in his seat, his jaw bunched so tight his teeth hurt. He knew he wouldn't. And yet even so he could not imagine giving up, letting go—because that thought was still more terrifying than the emptiness he lived with every day.

Lucia gazed around at the tiny bedroom in the hostel near the Gare du Nord where she'd gone after leaving Angelo that morning. It was a far cry from the palatial suite at the Georges Cinq, but it would have to do. It was within her budget, at least.

Angelo, she knew, had been shocked that she had insisted on leaving right then. He'd thought she was making some grand gesture, but it had been simpler, and more awful, than that. She was simply preserving her sanity. She couldn't spend another moment in his company, never mind return to Sicily in his private jet, and not break down. Beg for him to take her back, just as her mother had her father.

How many times had she curled up into a ball in her bed while she heard her mother's noisy sobs from downstairs, her father's gruff replies? And then the slamming of the door, and her father disappeared for a week, a month, however long his money lasted until he was back, to her mother's shaming joy, for more. And then he'd left for good…just as Angelo had.

Except you were the one to leave. You walked away before he could.

A ripple of unease shivered through her, and she tried to shrug it off. She'd made the right decision; she knew she had. As long as Angelo was bent on proving himself in this awful, twisted revenge there was no way a relationship would work. She knew that, had felt it.

And yet—

Did you have to push him so hard? So far? So quickly?

Restlessly Lucia rose from her narrow bed and opened the door. The hallway of the hostel reeked of sweat and boiled vegetables, and she felt as far from home as she ever had. Tears stung her eyes and she blinked them back quickly as she strode towards the front door. Too late for regrets.

She spent the next few hours wandering around Paris, lost in a haze of her own misery and doubt. She could not shake the feeling that she'd made a terrible, terrible mistake.

But what choice had she really had? To go back to Sicily and watch as Angelo ruined the entire Corretti family or died trying? Watch him become more bitter, more determined—and emptier all the while? The end would have happened, sooner or later. She'd just hurried it along.

That's why you pushed him. You were still protecting yourself.

Trust was a choice, and she hadn't trusted. She'd pushed Angelo towards an impossible ultimatum because she was still afraid he was going to walk away. So afraid—and so she'd made him.

She might have told him she was acting out of love, but she hadn't been, not really. She'd been acting out of fear. She'd always been acting out of fear.

Gazing blindly at the Eiffel Tower in the distance, Lucia let out a choked sob. She had made a terrible mistake—and she didn't know how or if she could fix it.

The last of the sun's rays were streaking the sky, and just as before, the moment they'd faded the lights switched on, and the Eiffel Tower shone jewel-bright. She remembered how only last night Angelo had shown her, his eyes warm and bright with love. *I'm so glad I saw it with you.*

Why hadn't she believed in that boy? Why hadn't she given him the time, space and support to make the decision she knew he was capable of? Instead she'd pushed. She'd pushed him away.

And now she needed to get him back.

'It's not that we don't *trust* Luca Corretti—'

'Of course not. This is simply a good business decision.' Angelo smiled coolly at the banker from Milan who would help to orchestrate his insider's coup. With him he could convince the other shareholders to depose Luca as CEO and put him in his place. Corretti Designs would be his. Yet all he could think as he looked at the man's paunchy face was *traitor.*

And all he could feel was emptiness.

He didn't care about Corretti Designs. He knew adding another company to his portfolio wouldn't appease any of the restless emotions inside him, the anger and the hurt and the need.

Only Lucia had done that. Only loving Lucia could do that now.

'Signor…Corretti?' The man stumbled slightly over his name. Angelo lifted his gaze, gave him another cool smile.

'I have the document right here. We need six signatures—half of the board—on it before I can act accordingly.'

'Of course.'

Resolutely Angelo pushed the paper over to the man. He watched him take out his fountain pen, scan the document that would give him control. He thought of Luca's steely authority, the grudging admiration he'd felt for his cousin.

It's not business. Not for you.

No, this had never been about business. Never about money or power or even revenge. It had been, he knew, just as Lucia had told him, about love. About wanting to be loved, accepted—and knowing that the Correttis never would.

But Lucia had. Lucia always had.

'Don't sign.'

The banker looked up in surprise. *'Scusi?'*

'Don't sign.' Angelo smiled grimly. 'I've changed my mind.'

The man's jaw slackened. 'But…the company—'

'Luca Corretti is perfectly capable of turning his company around if need be,' Angelo said. 'I don't need to do it.' He reached for the document and tore it neatly in half. 'I don't need to do any of this.'

With the man still staring at him in slack-jawed amazement Angelo rose from the table. 'And now I'm afraid I must take my leave of you. I have a plane to catch.'

It had taken her the better part of a night and day to get back to Sicily. She didn't have enough money for the airfare, and so she'd taken a train to Milan, another to Genoa and then a twenty-hour ferry to Palermo. By the time she arrived at the hotel she was exhausted, dirty and in desperate need of a bath and a hot meal. She pushed all of it aside in search of the one thing that truly mattered. Angelo.

The bellhops stepped back as she entered, eyes widening in surprise. Perhaps they didn't recognise her as one of the chambermaids, and she certainly didn't look like a guest.

The concierge came hurrying forward. *'Scusi, signorina.'* Her eyes were flinty, her smile perfunctory. 'May I help you?'

'I'm looking for Angelo Corretti.'

'I'm afraid he's not available—'

'I'll just go see for myself.' She strode past the woman who, she could see, was already calling security on a pager. Great. She'd get kicked out of the hotel and fired from her job. So be it. This was more important than any of those things.

She pressed the button for the lift, prayed it would come before security escorted her out. She saw two uniformed men heading towards her just as the doors pinged open—and Angelo stepped out.

The look of incredulous amazement on his face mirrored, she was sure, her own.

'Lucia—'

'*Scusi*, Signor Corretti.' One of the security guards grabbed her arm. 'She just came in—this way, please, *signorina*….'

'Unhand her now.' Angelo's voice was low and deadly and the guards immediately stepped back. 'This woman is not only an employee of this hotel, but my special guest.' He glanced back at her, and his gaze roved hungrily over her face. Lucia felt the first wonderful flare of hope. 'Lucia,' he said softly, urgently, and she swallowed hard.

'Can we…can we go somewhere to talk?'

He nodded, and Lucia started forward. Then he shook his head. 'No, what I need to say to you, I can say here, in front of everyone.'

That didn't sound good. 'But—'

'You were right, Lucia. You were right about everything.'

'Oh, Angelo, I wasn't—'

'I went in pursuit of what I told myself was my dream and I felt only emptier. Lonelier. You're the one who fills me, Lucia. The one who loves me, and I threw the most important thing in my life away with both hands and for what? Just more emptiness. More bitterness.' He shook his head slowly. 'I'm done with it. Done with revenge, done with buying up businesses as a way to change the past or myself or the way others think of me. I'm done with all of it, Lucia.'

'Oh, Angelo.' Tears slipped down her cheeks as she reached for his hands. 'I came here to tell you that I was wrong for pushing you so hard. Forcing you to choose when you weren't ready, when everything between us was still so new. I did it because I was afraid, because even then I was bracing myself for you to walk away from me. If I made you do it, it would be better some-how—but of course it wasn't. It was awful. It was the worst thing in the world.'

'I'm not walking away now,' he told her in a low voice. 'I'll never walk away from you, Lucia. I was a fool to have let you walk away from me. I love you, and I want to live the rest of my life with you, to grow old with you and have more children if you're willing.'

'Yes.' Her throat was so tight she could barely get the word out. 'Yes, I want all of that, more than anything.'

'So do I.' Angelo smiled, his own eyes bright. 'So do I.'

And there, in the middle of the marble lobby of the Corretti Hotel, he sank to one knee, his hand clasped with hers as he looked up at her with love-filled eyes. 'Lucia Anturri, I love you more than life itself. Will you marry me?'

Wordlessly Lucia nodded. Her throat ached too much and her heart was too full to speak. 'Get up,' she finally managed with a tearful laugh. She pulled him to his feet. 'Get up so I can kiss you.'

'I think I can manage that.' Smiling, Angelo drew her into his arms and kissed her soundly, as around them the staff and guests of the Corretti Hotel began to cheer.

* * * * *

A WHISPER OF DISGRACE

SHARON KENDRICK

To Tony "The Vet" Abbott...who is a fabulous person to see plays with and who has provided plenty of animated (geddit?) discussions and laughter over the years.

CHAPTER ONE

THE BOTTLE WAS cold, but not nearly as cold as the ice around her heart. Rosa lifted the champagne to her lips and drank another mouthful as she tried to dull the pain. She wanted to wake up and find that the past few days hadn't happened. She wanted to be the person she thought she'd always been. And she wanted that towering man on the other side of the nightclub to stop watching her with that dark and unsettling stare of his.

The flashing lights and loud music were making her feel giddy—or maybe that was just the champagne she'd been glugging from the moment she'd walked in. She wasn't really used to the sharp, bubbly flavour and she didn't really like it—mainly because she'd been brought up on the wines of Sicily which were rich and warm and red. Or at least, she'd been allowed the occasional half-glassful, topped up with water—watched over by the fiercely protective eyes of her two brothers.

Except that they were not really her brothers, were they? From now on, she had to start thinking of them as her half-brothers.

Rosa gripped the neck of the bottle, a shudder running down her spine as she forced herself to confront the unbelievable truth. That nothing was as it seemed, nor ever would be again. The discovery had been brutal and she'd found out in the worst possible way that she'd been living a lie all her life.

And she was nothing but a fake.

'*Mademoiselle?* You are ready?'

Wordlessly, Rosa nodded as the nightclub attendant gestured towards the podium on which various women had been attempting to pole dance all evening. It would be fair to say that most of them had been making an absolute hash of it, despite the fact that they were slim and blonde and incredibly fit. But then, all the women on this part of the French Riviera looked like that. Rosa was the one who stood out like a sore thumb with her mahogany hair, olive skin and the generous curves— which were currently spilling out of her brand-new crimson dress.

She placed one leg rather unsteadily on the podium, wondering if she would be able to dance in the kind of heels she wouldn't have dared wear back home in her native Sicily. But who cared if she stumbled? And who cared if her dress was the shortest thing she'd ever worn? Not her. Tonight she was going to shrug off the old Rosa, who had cared so much about appearances and doing the right thing. Tonight she was going to embrace a brand-new Rosa—one who had grown a tougher skin so that nobody could hurt her ever again. On this privileged strip of French coastline known as the Côte d'Azur, she would emerge from her protective shell into a glittering and unrecognisable creature—and her transformation would be complete.

She took another slug of champagne and put the bottle down, but as she stepped up onto the podium, she found her gaze locked with the man on the other side of the club—the one with the dark hair and the powerful body. He was still watching her—and something in the speculative amusement which glittered in the depths of his eyes made Rosa's stomach perform an odd kind of flip. Hadn't anyone ever taught him that it was rude to stare like that? And even more rude to ignore that poor woman who was practically draping herself over him.

The music began as Rosa gripped the pole, thrusting her pelvis towards it, the way she'd watched the others do. She'd never even seen a pole dance before tonight—nor would she ever have dared enter a competition for enthusiastic amateurs. But shock could make a person behave in a way which was completely out of character.

Snaking one leg around the slippery pole, she began to move. She could feel the smooth, cold metal sliding against her bare thigh. The alcohol was relaxing her and the hypnotic beat of the music began to suck her in. And suddenly it was easy. Easy to lose herself in the sensual sway of the music and forget about her own particular heartache. Her movements seemed instinctive—as if she had been born to dance this way. As if rubbing her body against a static piece of metal was the only way to go. Closing her eyes, she raised her leg even higher and tipped her head back, so that she could feel her long hair brushing against the floor. She began to grind her hips in slow and sensuous circles against the pole and, inexplicably, could feel the slow burning heat of excitement deep in her groin.

Through her dreamy reverie she could hear other sounds. A loud, whooping noise as she slid up and down in time to the music. The unrestrained clamour of male voices shouting enthusiastically as she clutched the pole and writhed against it. But Rosa didn't care who was shouting—she just kept her eyes tightly closed and gave the dance everything she'd got. It was the most cathartic thing she'd ever done and it wasn't until the music had stopped that she opened her eyes to find that a large crowd of men had gathered at the front of the stage to watch her.

For a moment she blinked at them, feeling like a prize exhibit being paraded in a foreign zoo. She found herself expecting to see the furious faces of her brothers.

Correction. Her half-brothers—but they were hundreds of miles away.

She straightened up and flicked her gaze over the assembled men, wondering how she was going to be able to make her way through them without pushing. Lots of them had their shirts open to the waist and their chests looked all sweaty. She didn't want to touch them. She shuddered. She didn't want anything to do with them. All she wanted was another drink, because the aching in her heart was starting to return and a drink seemed the only way to numb it. She bent to pick up the bottle, when she felt the whisper of fingertips on her arm and, straightening up, she found herself staring into the blackest pair of eyes she had ever seen.

It was the man from the opposite side of the club. The one who'd been staring at her. Who up until ten minutes ago had been the object of some beautiful woman's attention. She tried to focus her gaze to look at him properly, and as his image blurred and then sharpened again, she thought that she'd never seen a man like this before. Standing up close to his hard body and staring up into his hawk-nosed face, Rosa could suddenly understand why that woman had been draping herself all over him. He seemed larger than life—as if he was composed of some dark, elemental force which dominated the entire room. His black eyes glittered—as if a fire was smouldering behind those long lashes—and his lips were full and sensual.

But he frowned as he glanced at the clamouring throng of men. 'You look to me like someone in urgent need of rescuing,' he said, in an exotic accent she didn't recognise.

The old Rosa might have been intimidated by such a man—that's if she had ever been allowed to get within six feet of him by her overprotective family. But this new and tipsy Rosa was feeling no such thing as intimidation. Instead she looked into his eyes and felt an undeniable excitement—as if she had just found something she hadn't expected to find. Something she hadn't even realised she'd been looking for. 'And you're just the one to do it, I suppose?'

'I'm the perfect candidate for any kind of rescue mission, my beauty. Be assured of that.'

Trying to dampen down the excitement which was fizzing through her veins, she looked around her in mock surprise. 'But I can't see your white horse anywhere.'

'That's because I always ride a black stallion, although never in France. He's big and he's powerful and he's not particularly partial to nightclubs.' His eyes were gleaming as they gazed at her. 'Unlike a woman who doesn't seem to realise what havoc she was creating when she performed that incredibly sexy dance a few moments ago and nearly had the whole place in melt-down.'

Rosa's smile became a little glassy, aware that the level of flirtation was escalating by the second. And she was feeling more than a little daunted by it because this kind of thing was way outside her experience. Even during her university days in Palermo, the men she'd fancied had steered clear of her when they'd discovered who she was. Because what man in their right mind would get involved with a Corretti woman, a woman they wouldn't dare touch for fear that one of her brothers or cousins would come after them?

She'd never met anyone who hadn't been intimidated by the reputation of her powerful family and she wouldn't have been allowed anywhere near a man like this. A man who was sizzling out so much sex appeal that she wondered if her fingers might burn if she reached out and touched him.

She knew that the sensible thing to do would be to turn around and walk away. To go back to the hotel she'd booked into and sleep off the champagne. She would wake up in the morning—probably with a splitting headache—and decide what she was going to do with the rest of her life.

But Rosa wasn't feeling sensible. She was feeling… defiant. Because defiance was easier to deal with than heartbreak and loneliness, wasn't it? Defiance made you feel alive, instead of flat and empty and wondering just where your life was going. 'I don't want to be rescued,' she said, a touch petulantly as she took another swig of champagne. 'I want to dance.'

'Now that,' he said steadily as he removed the bottle from her hand and handed it to someone standing nearby, who accepted it without comment, 'can also be arranged.'

He took her hand and led her towards the dance floor and Rosa was aware of a sudden and heady sense of danger as he took her into his arms and the music began to throb out a sultry beat. He was so tall, she thought—taller than any other man she'd ever seen. And his body felt so strong. She licked her dry lips. A woman wouldn't stand a chance against a man like this. The thought thrilled her, rather than scared her as she knew it should have done. 'I don't even know your name,' she shouted.

'That's because I haven't told you.'

'And are you going to tell me?'

'I might—if you're very good.'

Recklessly, she said, 'And if I'm not?'

He didn't miss a beat. 'In that case, I will definitely tell you—because there is nothing I like better than a woman who isn't good. My name is Kulal.'

She tried saying it. Rounding her lips she sounded out the first syllable and then, letting her tongue touch the upper palate, she murmured the second. 'Ku-lal.'

'Mmm. I like the way you say it. It sounds very sexy on your lips.'

Rosa giggled. 'Stop it!'

With a sudden hard beat of lust, Kulal pulled her closer and felt her melt against him, as if she'd been waiting all night to have him do that. And wasn't it like that for him? Hadn't his senses been ignited from the moment he'd set eyes on her and seen those soft lips parting with a look of innocent wonder, which certainly didn't match the sinful splendour of her voluptuous body? He could feel the way her breasts were pushing against his chest and he sucked in a breath of longing as he dipped his mouth to her ear. 'Now let's see if you can dance as well on the floor as you did on the podium, shall we, my beauty?'

The slick words which flowed from his lips were warning Rosa to be careful. Because there was a reason for the expression 'paying' someone a compliment—her ruthless family had taught her that. You told a woman she was pretty and she would put out for you—wasn't that how it worked? Hadn't she grown up watching the male members of her family as they'd put their own heartless seduction campaigns into action? Men like this wanted only one thing from a woman like her and she'd been brought up to guard her honour and integrity. But that was before the world had changed. Before the values she'd held so dear had been held up as shallow and worthless.

So she pushed away her doubts and instead glanced up at him, batting him a coquettish look she hadn't even realised had been in her repertoire until now. 'You're going to mark me out of ten, are you?'

'If you want.' His hands tightened around her waist.

'But I warn you in advance that I can be a very harsh judge.'

The words came out almost before she realised she'd said them. 'I'll take the risk,' she said.

'Good.' His lips nuzzled against her neck. 'I like a woman who takes risks.'

Rosa could feel the whisper of his mouth on her bare neck and she closed her eyes with pleasure. This was… bliss. His arms had tightened around her and she realised that dancing with him was different to dancing with anyone else. He seemed to be making up the rules as he went along, completely ignoring the rhythm of the music and moving them around as if this was a slow waltz instead of a vaguely jumpy beat. And she was letting him. Why wouldn't she let him? Why, he could carry on doing that all night, he was so good at it.

'Do you like that?' he queried softly as the palms of his hands skated possessively over the curve of her bottom.

Her sudden, heady sense of freedom and the sensation of listening to her body's desires made Rosa bold and she didn't shrink away from the way he was pulling her even closer. 'Yes.'

'I thought so. I like it too. I like it very much.'

Kulal closed his eyes as he felt her fingertips move to his shoulders. He could feel the brush of her silken hair against his cheek and the wave of desire which swept over him was so strong that he was filled with an unbearable need to touch her more intimately.

But even though he'd always been known as a mould-breaking prince, Kulal respected his position enough not to throw his royal role into jeopardy. Dancing with a woman who was clearly an exhibitionist was one thing, but making love to her in a public place was quite another. So that even though they were shielded by the bobbing crowds around them and even though the flashing lights obscured most of their movements, he did not do what he wanted to do. Which was to play with the tips of her breasts through the thin satin of her mini-dress. Or to slide his hand up her thigh and touch the undoubtedly moist heat which would be searing its way through her panties.

That's if she was wearing any.

He swallowed, wondering if she could feel the sudden jerk of his erection.

He'd noticed her the moment she'd walked into the nightclub—but then, her shiny red dress had left little to the imagination. She had the type of body which was deeply unfashionable—especially here, in the South of France. She didn't look as if she spent hours at the gym and she didn't look as if she existed on a punishing diet either. The kind of diet which always left women with that furrowed and slightly anxious look—as if they were worried they might pass out from hunger. Instead she was ripe and luscious—like a juicy mulberry just before it fell from the tree.

He'd noticed the way her hair had tumbled like dark satin all the way down to her waist and her dress had skimmed the smooth expanse of her bare thighs. Their eyes had met across the dance floor—he had seen her eyes widen as if she had been surprised—and in that moment he had known. Just as he always knew when a woman wanted him. She was his for the taking and he wanted to take her as soon as possible—because one day very soon, this kind of sexual dalliance would be a thing of the past.

Kulal felt his mouth flatten in resignation, for the duty and the protocol of an arranged marriage loomed close on his horizon and his carefree playboy days were numbered. Even if he and his new bride were to agree to an 'open' marriage—or at least 'open' for him—he knew that in future he would have to conduct his affairs discreetly. He came from the kind of culture where wives turned a blind eye to their husbands' indiscretions, but marriage brought with it certain responsibilities. Gone would be the days of walking into a nightclub alone, and walking out with a beautiful woman on his arm.

He pressed his lips against the warm, fleshy shell of her ear as they moved in time to the music. 'What's your name?' he questioned.

'Rosa,' she replied, instinctively leaving off the 'Corretti' bit. He might have heard of her notorious family or he might not, but she wasn't going to take that risk. Tonight might be her night for behaving recklessly, but not stupidly.

'Rosa,' he repeated, running his palm down over the thick spill of her dark hair as if he was stroking the flank of his favourite mount. He smiled as he felt her wriggle in response. 'I like that too. Are you Italian?'

'Yes,' Rosa managed, even though it was difficult to speak when his earthy scent was overpowering her. Who cared that she was being a little economical with

the truth? She was Sicilian through and through, and
her family would have erupted with rage if they'd heard
her claiming to being Italian! But it was easier this way.
And she no longer owed her family anything, she reminded herself fiercely. Not a single thing. 'Yes, I am.'

'And do you make a habit of pole dancing in nightclubs, Rosa?'

She shook her head. 'Never done it before in my life.'

'Interesting. Why not?'

Rosa screwed up her face because this was a path
she didn't want to venture down. She shook her head.
'Tell me about you instead!'

But Kulal was coming to realise that he didn't want
to have to shout to make himself heard, and he didn't
dare stay on the dance floor with her much longer. Much
more of her rubbing her voluptuous body against him
and he would be unable to move. So why not cut to the
chase and continue this conversation somewhere more
private—like the seclusion of his villa complex, with
the convenience of a nearby bed?

'Why don't we go somewhere a little quieter?' he
suggested.

Rosa swayed. She wished he'd given her some kind of
warning before he'd loosened his grip on her like that,
because suddenly she felt like a ship which had broken
anchor. 'Like where?'

Kulal frowned as a flicker of irritation skittered over
him. Why did women always do this? Why did they pretend total innocence when they both knew exactly how
the night was going to end? Trying to suddenly play the
innocent was never going to work for someone as foxy

as her. He shrugged. 'I know a place with an amazing view, where we could sit and watch the stars.'

'Oh, I love the stars,' said Rosa dreamily.

'I love them too. So why don't we get out of here and find our own little piece of heaven?'

He made the words sound so poetic, Rosa thought as a feeling of wooziness shimmered over her again. She tried to remember the last time she'd eaten but it seemed like a long time ago. 'Okay,' she agreed carefully.

And Kulal smiled, for it was as easy as he had expected it to be. What Kulal wanted Kulal got. That's what they always said about him. He'd never had to fight for anything or anyone—except for the one person he'd really wanted, and it hadn't been possible to fight for her.

She was looking up at him now and the expression on her face was so soft and…trusting—and he didn't want her to look at him that way. He wanted her hard and hot and sexy. 'Let's go and find my car,' he said, his gaze skating over her bare arms and legs. 'Do you have a jacket, or something?'

Rosa blinked. Did she? She couldn't recall. She stared down at the satin minidress which was skimming her thighs. She remembered buying it in that ridiculously expensive boutique in Antibes just a few hours earlier, along with the towering shoes which complemented it. It matched the crimson bag which was hanging from her shoulder on a gilt chain, but she didn't remember it coming with a jacket.

'I don't think so,' she said vaguely.

The look that Kulal shot her was tinged with apprehension and, as he steered her through the packed dance floor, he suddenly began to regret his impetuous offer. She might look like every man's fantasy come to life, but now her gait was distinctly unsteady and he began to wonder just how drunk she was. He liked women who weren't good, that much was true, but he liked them to be sober.

His hand resting in the small of her back, he felt her stagger as they stepped outside the club and he caught her and steadied her. Thank God there were no paparazzi around, he thought grimly as he gently levered her into the back of the waiting limousine and she slumped back in the seat with her long legs splayed out in front of her, her eyelids fluttering to a close.

For the first time in his life, Kulal found himself tugging down the hem of a dress in a vain attempt to introduce a modicum of decency. Now was not the time to make the observation that she *was* wearing panties. Or that they were lace, by the look of them. 'Just how much have you had to drink?' he demanded.

That deeply accented voice penetrated her woolly thoughts and Rosa's eyes snapped open. The fresh air had made her feel very peculiar but suddenly she felt safe in this luxurious car. And he was still here, she thought. Her black-eyed rescuer from the nightclub who'd held her so closely on the dance floor. She felt very safe with him. So why wasn't he still holding her? Holding her so tightly that she could forget everything except the sensation of him touching her.

'Come over here and kiss me,' she mumbled as his jet-dark eyes swam in and out of focus, before the effort of keeping her eyelids open became too much and she closed them again. 'Please. Just kiss me.'

Kulal caught hold of her arms and gave her a little shake as he tried to wake her—but he didn't bother hiding his feeling of disdain, or his growing anger for having allowed himself to get into a situation like this. Did she really think that he wanted to kiss her when she was in that kind of state?

'Rosa,' he accused. 'You are drunk!'

'I know I am.' Her head lolled back against the soft leather seat as his unfamiliar words washed over her. 'And it feels fantastic.'

'If you could see yourself you would not think that,' he raged. 'For a drunken woman is never a pretty sight.'

'But a drunken man is okay, I suppose?' she mumbled. Because wasn't this what she'd grown up with? One rule for men and a different one for women. Oh, why was the world so unfair?

'I don't approve of anyone losing control of themselves in such a way as this, no,' he retorted. 'Which is why I'm taking you home.'

The word mocked her enough to make her lips curve into an empty smile. 'Home?' she questioned, and for the first time a trace of bitterness crept into her voice. 'You're going to have a bit of a problem with that one. Because I don't have a home. Not any more.'

Kulal leaned over her, only just managing to avoid the arms which were reaching up in an attempt to snake themselves around his neck. He wasn't interested in this particular alcohol-fuelled sob story. He just needed to get rid of her and he needed to do it quickly. 'Where are you staying?' he questioned urgently.

At this, her eyes snapped open and, blurrily, she looked up at him. She tried to sit up, but somehow the effort of moving was just too much. And he had brought her attention to a much bigger problem. Where *was* she staying?

'I've no idea,' she mumbled, tucking her legs underneath her. It was comfortable here and she didn't want to go anywhere else. She wanted to stay with this man with the dark face and glittering eyes because he made her feel safe and he made her feel excited. She gave a luxurious yawn as she snuggled down against the soft leather seat. 'So I guess I'd better stay with you.'

CHAPTER TWO

WARM SUNLIGHT FLOODED over Rosa's face and for a moment she wriggled, reluctant to leave the hypnotic dream which felt curiously realistic.

'I know you're awake.'

The hard, accented voice crashed into her dream and shattered it—even though it was the voice of the man who was responsible for the erotic images which had punctured her restless night.

Her throat feeling as dry as a summer beach, Rosa opened her eyes to find a pair of black eyes trained on her, but there was no lazy speculation or flirtation in them this morning. All she could read was anger and... She cringed. Yes, that was definitely contempt she could see flickering in their ebony depths.

Woozily, she looked around her in an attempt to get her bearings as she tried to piece together the jigsaw memories of last night. Her head was pounding and her mouth felt dry and claggy and she had the feeling that something was very wrong.

Something was. She stared down at herself in horror as she realised that she was in a very large bed—and she was completely naked!

Clutching the fine linen sheet to conceal the jiggle of her breasts, she sat up and stared at the man she knew only as Kulal, who was standing glaring at her from the end of the bed, looking like some kind of dark and avenging angel.

'What happened?' she demanded.

'You don't remember?'

'If I remembered, I wouldn't be asking—would I?'

The disdainful twist of his mouth deepened. 'You want to know if we had sex?'

Rosa felt her cheeks grow hot as she stared at him, appalled by his crude question. But beneath her horror beat the memory of how good it had been to have been held by him on the dance floor and she could feel an unwanted tingling in her breasts. She felt as if she'd left one nightmare and woken up in a different one—and she was going to have to be strong if she wanted to get out of this with any degree of dignity. And she could be strong. She'd proved that, hadn't she? She had survived her mother screaming vitriol at her as she'd made her vile confession. And she'd faced the unbelievable and heartbreaking truth, that her beloved father—the single rock in her life—was not her father at all.

She prayed for the right amount of bravado as she stared into Kulal's furious face. 'And did we?'

At this, he smiled, and it was the coldest smile that Rosa had ever seen.

'Believe me, *garbuua*—if you'd had sex with me, you'd remember it, no matter how drunk you were.'

Rosa met the mocking expression in his eyes, telling herself that she wasn't going to be intimidated. She just needed to extricate herself from this regrettable situation—but first of all she must face facts.

'So we didn't?' she questioned flatly.

'No.'

She held the sheet a little tighter. 'Then how come I'm not wearing any clothes?'

'Because I undressed you.'

'You…undressed me? Why?'

'Why do you think?' he snapped. 'Because I wanted to feast my eyes on your delectable body?' And yet Kulal felt the sudden fierce beat of his heart as he tried to subdue the memory of her firm flesh as he had stripped her bare. He'd taken her clothes off on autopilot, averting his eyes when he had slithered that wispy little pair of lace panties down over her knees. In her uninhibited state she had grabbed him and pulled him down towards her—and he'd had the tantalising experience of having his head buried in her magnificent breasts before he had forced himself to move his aching body away. 'If you must know, I removed your clothes because I didn't think you'd want to leave here this morning wearing last night's crumpled dress, or underwear.'

The gap in her memory was making Rosa feel frightened but she wasn't going to let him know that. 'Is that so?' she said.

Kulal heard the disbelief in her voice and felt a slow anger begin to simmer inside him. Didn't she realise how lucky she'd been that someone like him had been the man she'd targeted last night? That somebody completely lacking in moral scruples could have taken her home and… His mouth hardened. 'I'll tell you exactly what happened,' he bit out. 'You couldn't remember where you were staying, and just before you passed out on the back seat of my limousine, you announced that you wanted to stay with me.'

Rosa could do absolutely nothing about the blush which stained her cheeks. 'I said that?'

'You did,' he agreed grimly. 'Leaving me with little choice other than to bring you back here to my hotel. My plan was to get you inside as quietly and as unobtrusively as possible—but unfortunately, that was not on your agenda.'

She saw the furious accusation which had darkened his face. 'It wasn't?' she questioned as a trace of nerves began to creep into her voice.

'Indeed it wasn't. You decided that as many of the people in the immediate vicinity and beyond should know exactly what you wanted—and what you wanted was to go down to the beach and look at the sky....'

Oh, God. It was all coming back to her now. He'd promised to take her somewhere to look at the stars. He'd said that to her in the nightclub as he'd held her in his arms. And in that moment, she felt as if he'd been offering her a slice of paradise. 'What...what happened?' she whispered.

'I decided that an excess of alcohol, a senseless female and close proximity to the Mediterranean were a potentially lethal combination and so I carried you in here, undressed you—and put you to bed.'

'And that's it?'

'That's it.'

'So where did you sleep?' she questioned pointedly.

He gave a short laugh. 'When you rent a hotel villa overlooking the Mediterranean, there tends to be more than one bedroom. In fact, there are three—so I slept in the one next door.'

Rosa's mind was spinning as she listened to his explanation, but the one thought which was uppermost was that her virtue was still intact—and that surprised her. Because she did remember the heady rush of abandonment she'd felt as he'd held her on the dance floor. She wasn't experienced, but she didn't need to be to realise that she'd been putty in his hands last night. That if he hadn't been so moral, then he would have been lying beside her now. Because she had wanted him. Come to think of it, she still wanted him.

He had moved away from the bed and now that he was at a distance it gave her a better opportunity to study him. She wondered where he was from—his rich accent certainly didn't sound Mediterranean and his skin was much too dark.

'Who are you?' she questioned suddenly.

Kulal tensed, realising that he had been expecting this question a whole lot sooner and knowing that his answer would bring with it a whole new set of baggage. Should he lie? Adopt some fictitious identity, knowing that their paths would never cross again? But that might add fuel to a possibly combustive situation. She had already humiliated herself through her drunken behaviour—if she then discovered that he was lying to her, then mightn't she take out her shame on him? He knew women well enough to know that they were impossible when you rejected them. So why not keep her sweet? Why not make her appreciate just how much he had done for her?

'My name is Kulal,' he said.

'I already know that bit. Where are you from—you're not Mediterranean, are you?'

'No, I am not. I come from a country called Zahrastan.' He searched her face for signs of recognition. 'Any idea where that is?'

She shrugged. 'I'm afraid I've never heard of it. Should I have done?'

Kulal told himself that he shouldn't have been surprised. He wouldn't really expect a pole-dancing socialite to know much about the Arabian principality which produced a vast tranche of the world's oil supply, would he? She probably thought of little else other than which colour she was going to paint her pretty little toenails each day. 'I suggest you try acquainting yourself with a map of the world if you want to find out its exact position.' His voice was dismissive as he slanted her a cool look. 'Now, have I answered all your questions to your satisfaction?'

She wanted to say that no, he hadn't. She wanted to ask him if they couldn't just forget about the disastrous way the evening had ended. If only it was possible to rewind life and stop at the bit you liked best. When she'd been dancing with him it had all felt so…promising. But the repressive note in his voice and the unwelcoming look on his face made her realise that this was not a conversation he was keen on extending. She lifted her fingertips to her temples as if that might help reduce the pounding inside her skull, but it didn't.

'My head hurts,' she said, painfully aware that the first and last hangover of her life should have been conducted in front of such a critical audience.

Kulal nodded as he saw an acceptable exit sign looming ahead. 'So why don't you get showered and dressed?' he suggested smoothly. 'Your things are hanging up in the bathroom and I can order you something to eat. You'll feel much better once you've had some breakfast—'

'I don't want any breakfast,' she snapped, realising that he couldn't wait to get rid of her.

'You ought to. When did you last eat?'

She shook her head. 'I don't remember.'

Reluctantly, he found his gaze drawn to her eyes which had been illuminated by the bright sunshine, and for the first time he noticed that their darkness was broken by flecks of green and gold which made him think of the filtered sunlight you sometimes found in a quiet forest glade. But despite their natural beauty, there was no disguising the shadows which lay beneath them—shadows which were not caused simply by her smudged mascara. Her eyes looked empty, he realised—as if she had seen something which had haunted her. And she was pale. Very pale. Beneath that smooth olive skin of hers, she had the pinched look of a woman who had stopped caring—not about her appearance, but about life itself.

And that was not his business.

He was a royal prince and he was about to announce his engagement to a royal princess. The last thing he needed was to start worrying about the welfare of some spoiled little rich girl who had got herself plastered. Thank God he'd been strong enough to walk away from the promise of her amazing body—he should start being grateful for the lucky escape he'd had.

But something was nagging at his conscience and he found himself unable to ignore it.

'You're not leaving here until you've eaten something,' he said forcefully.

'And you'd be prepared to stop me, would you?'

He raised his eyebrows. 'I don't intend to pick you up for a second time if you pass out and I don't want the drama of a French ambulance screaming to a halt outside. So why don't you do something sensible for the first time in your life and eat something?' he said, turning on his heel and heading for the door.

Rosa stood watching as the door banged shut behind him and she could have burst into howls of frustration. How dare he judge her and find her wanting—when last night he hadn't been able to keep his hands off her?

He could do anything he liked, she realised, because she had put herself in a position to be judged. Angrily, she pushed aside the sheet and headed for the bathroom, recoiling as she caught sight of her reflection in the huge mirror. It was a shock on so many levels, because walking around naked wasn't something she ever did. In Sicily, she always wore a silk nightgown to preserve her modesty because that was how she'd been brought up.

'Imagine if there was a fire in the middle of the night,' her mother had once said, in that tart way she had of speaking to her only daughter. 'And the fireman found you naked and indecent. That is not the way a lady behaves, Rosa.'

As she stood beneath the torrential jets of the shower, Rosa's lips curved with derision. She had just accepted her mother's opinion, hadn't she? The way she always did. Never realising that the woman who had brought her up so strictly was nothing but a cheating hypocrite.

Quickly, she turned on the cold tap—hoping that the shock of the icy water might wash away the memories of the past few days, but it wasn't easy to forget her mother's dramatic confession. She stayed in the shower until she had scrubbed herself clean, and afterwards she found an unused toothbrush and paste and located her clothes and hairbrush. By the time she heard a knock on the bedroom door, she felt a million times better and she psyched herself up to face the judgemental face of Kulal.

'Come in,' she said crisply, her heart beginning to race as he walked in. 'I'm ready.'

'So I see,' Kulal said, reluctantly letting his gaze drift over her. Her feet were bare and the crimson minidress brushed the smooth skin of her thighs. For a moment he felt a powerful wave of temptation as he imagined taking her back to bed, before he swatted it away. She was trouble, he told himself. Last night, he might have been swayed by her beauty and her dancing, but in the cold light of day he knew she was best avoided.

'I've ordered breakfast to be served on the terrace,' he said. 'So why don't we go downstairs?'

Hunger made Rosa nod her head in grudging agreement and she followed him down a wide marble staircase and out onto a terrace, where a table had been laid with croissants, juices and jams, and what looked like a dish of iced mango. The terrace overlooked landscaped gardens and, in the distance, she caught a glimpse of the sapphire sea. It felt as if they were in a self-contained world of their own—a private little bubble which was miles away from the hustle and bustle of the French Riviera. 'Did you say this was a hotel?' she asked curiously.

'It is, but I always rent one of the two villas which are attached to it. They come with their own gardens and that affords me more privacy.'

Rosa sank into one of the wicker chairs and looked up into the flatness of his eyes. 'Which makes it easier to get rid of unwanted overnight guests in the morning, I suppose?'

He sat down opposite her—a movement which immediately heralded the appearance of a butler bearing a large silver pot of coffee. Let her know exactly where she stands, Kulal told himself. Tell her the truth, even if the truth hurts. 'That is always a consideration to take into account,' he agreed.

Rosa stared at the inky coffee which was being poured for her before Kulal waved the butler away. She wasn't going to cause a scene about what he'd just said, when all he'd done was be honest. It would have been much worse if he'd pretended otherwise—if he made out that he'd never taken a strange woman back to his hotel before. And wasn't she all done with lies and subterfuge? 'Wise man,' she said lightly.

Her casual tone made Kulal relax and he sat back in his chair. So she was going to behave herself, was she? He guessed she must have done this kind of thing plenty of times herself. The slightly stilted morning breakfast after a night of red-hot sex.

His mouth hardened as he forced himself to face the frustrating and rather laughable truth. Because you haven't actually had sex with her, have you?

He watched as she pulled a croissant from the bread basket and began to cover it in strawberry jam. With her dark hair drying in the sunshine and her body smelling of soap rather than perfume, he thought how different she looked this morning. Her face was completely bare of make-up so that she looked very young and almost innocent. Her pink lips were so delicious that it seemed a crime not to lean across the table and kiss them, and for a split second he imagined his tongue licking its way inside her mouth. Until he remembered the way she'd been writhing her hips around the pole last night and forced himself to dampen down his ardour. What chameleons women were, he thought. How they changed faster than the seasons! She was about as innocent as one of the houris who charged men by the hour for their services.

Even so, as he watched her lift a glass of *jus de pamplemousse* to her lips, he couldn't ignore the undeniable regret that he hadn't made love to her. Because she would be an amazing lover. The sexual connoisseur in him told him that—even if he hadn't witnessed the sensational way she'd been moving on the podium last night. As he'd put her to bed, her beauty had been revealed to him in all its shockingly sensual glory. He had felt deliciously firm skin as he'd peeled the little dress from her body. And it had taken more strength than he'd ever needed to walk away and spend a restless night in the bed next door.

He waited until she'd finished eating, until she had dabbed those delectable lips with a napkin, before putting down his own coffee cup and subjecting her to a steady stare. 'I'm assuming that by now you've remembered where you're staying?'

Rosa winced. What would he say if she told him that she'd never been drunk like that before? That she'd just discovered that her mother had cheated with her husband's own brother—and her whole world had been smashed apart?

How would he react? Well, he might believe her or he might not, but that would make no difference to the fact that he couldn't wait to get rid of her.

'I'm staying at the Hotel Jasmin,' she said, getting to her feet. 'So if you wouldn't mind calling me a cab, I'll get out of your way.'

Kulal rose from the wicker chair, knowing that he could easily send her home in his own car, but it was a pretty distinctive car and it would inevitably connect them. This part of the Riviera was always crawling with paparazzi, eager to capture the indiscretions of celebrities. They'd been lucky enough not to have been seen last night when he'd had to carry her inside—so maybe he should count his blessings and get rid of her as anonymously as possible.

'I'll get reception to organise it for you,' he said. 'And arrange for someone to show you through to the main part of the hotel.'

Rosa felt like a piece of garbage which was headed

for the recycling bin and wondered if it was possible to feel any worse than she did right then. She was never going to touch another drop of alcohol in her life! And she was never going to dance with dark and dangerous-looking strangers in nightclubs. She nodded as she looked up into his black eyes, unprepared for his sudden movement as he touched her hair before running his fingertips lightly down the side of her face in a gesture which felt almost gentle.

'Just do yourself a favour, will you?' he said roughly. 'And stay off the booze in future.'

His words affected her far more than they should have done and Rosa recognised how lucky she'd been in her choice of rescuer. He had plucked her from the sweaty scrum in the nightclub and danced with her, and then she had blown it. She had got drunk and passed out but he hadn't taken advantage of her sorry state, even though it would have been easy for him to do so. And if he was clearly appalled by her behaviour—well, who could blame him? She was pretty appalled by it herself and she'd never get another chance to show him that deep down she wasn't really like that. Worst of all was that she would never know what it was like to kiss him....

The old Rosa might have slunk off—but of course the old Rosa would never have found herself in such a compromising position. And the new Rosa wanted to have a taste of pleasure—just one—before she walked out of his life for good.

She stood up on tiptoe and framed her hands around his hard jaw before leaning forward to brush her lips over the sensual curve of his mouth. 'Thank you,' she whispered. 'For your hospitality and your chivalry.'

For a moment he didn't move and it was as if her soft words had turned him to stone. Rosa could see a little muscle working overtime at his temple before he drawled out a sardonic reply. 'I'd like to say that the pleasure was all mine, but that wouldn't be true.'

She looked at him uncertainly. 'No?'

'In fact, it was an evening which fell pretty short on the pleasure quota for both of us, and I'm wondering whether it might not be too late to remedy that....'

Rosa was unprepared for the decisive way that he pulled her against him and the equally decisive way that he drove his mouth down onto hers. His hands were cupping her head and her hair was spilling through his fingers and suddenly he was kissing her like she'd never been kissed before. She could feel the instant flowering of her breasts and a delicious warmth between her legs. Did he know that? Was that why he thrust one hard thigh between hers, as if sensing that might help alleviate the sudden aching she could feel at the most intimate part of her body?

'Oh,' she said against his lips, swallowing down her sense of wonder. 'Oh.'

With an effort, he tore his lips away and looked down into her upturned face. 'How commendably circumspect I have been with you, my beauty,' he said shakily. 'But that all ends as of now. You are no longer drunk and I am no longer angry. This may be one of the most ill-judged decisions of my life, but I want you—and, sweet heaven, I am going to have you. Right now.'

His emphatic statement should have daunted her, but it didn't. She suspected that he didn't particularly like or respect her, but suddenly Rosa didn't care. She didn't care about anything other than the way he was making her feel. Why shouldn't she taste the pleasures which seemed to drive everyone else in the human race, except for her—poor, protected Rosa, who had been shielded from the world for so long? Her lips were dry but somehow she managed to echo his words as she felt his thumb tease its way over one painfully erect nipple.

'I want you, too,' she whispered. 'And right now is fine with me.'

With a hard smile of satisfaction, he bent his head to kiss her again and Rosa never knew what would have happened next had she not heard the sound of an embarrassed cough behind them. With a start, they sprang apart—as if they'd been caught red-handed at the scene of a crime.

And maybe they had, she thought. Because there, standing at the edge of the private garden watching them, was a man as dark-skinned as Kulal himself, though his head was dipped with the faintest degree of subservience.

She watched as a look of anger darkened Kulal's face. 'What the hell is going on?' he demanded. 'Why the hell are you disturbing me, Mutasim—creeping up on me like a spy?'

Rosa thought she'd never seen a man look more embarrassed than Mutasim did as Kulal's words fired into him, and she noticed that the stranger hadn't met her eyes. Not once.

'I beg your indulgence at this untimely intrusion, Your Highness,' said Mutasim softly. 'But your brother, the king, craves your company at the earliest opportunity.'

Rosa's lips parted in shock as the words registered in her befuddled brain. She looked up at Kulal, her bewildered eyes asking him a silent question.

Highness? King?

Were they playing some sort of joke on her? Talking in some kind of code? But her confusion was quickly superseded by shame as Kulal took no notice of her silent plea. Completely ignoring her, he walked over to the dark-skinned man and began to speak in a low voice, in a language she couldn't begin to understand.

And Rosa felt completely invisible.

CHAPTER THREE

'So what did you think you were playing at, Kulal?'
The king was shaking his head in disbelief. 'When you
decided to take some drunken pole dancer back to your
hotel?'

For a moment Kulal didn't answer. Instead he sat
back in one of the ornate chairs in the throne room and
stared up at the old-fashioned fan which was whirring
in the vaulted, golden ceiling. He was back in the ancient palace in which he'd been raised, having flown
to Zahrastan as soon as he had received word that the
king wished to speak with him. He'd never received a
summons quite like this and it occurred to him that he'd
never seen his brother look quite so exasperated either.
Not even during that time when he had caught Kulal
leaving one of the chambermaid's rooms, smoothing
down his ruffled robes and smirking all over his face.

Or the time when Kulal had 'borrowed' one of the
palace cars for an unauthorised trip into the desert when
he was barely sixteen and nobody had known that he
could drive. On both those occasions—and, indeed, on
many more—righteous anger should surely have come
flooding the younger prince's way, but it had not. It was

almost as if it had been expected that he should behave wildly—and everyone knew why. Weren't motherless children always indulged?

As two royal princes of a fabulously rich desert kingdom, the two men should have been close but an accident of birth meant that they had grown up living two very different lives. Hazail was the older, the heir to the throne, and the defining factor of his life had always been that he would one day inherit the crown. It had been Hazail's destiny which had occupied most of their father's time as he had tutored his elder son in the art of ruling a powerful desert kingdom.

Kulal had simply been the 'spare'—the extra boy child born as an insurance policy to ensure the line of succession. He had been brought up by a series of amahs—female servants who had adored him but had lacked the strength to discipline the strong-minded little boy. Consequently, he had been given freedom—perhaps a little too much freedom for so strong and so wilful a character. But that had never compensated for the heavy weight which had hung over him since his mother had died—a shocking death which had sent the country spiralling into deep mourning. And Kulal had been marked out by that terrible loss, for she had died saving his life. Deep down he knew that was the reason why his father and his brother had always been so distant towards him. He knew that subconsciously they blamed him for the queen's untimely end, even if logic told them that it was nothing but the cruel intervention of fate. Of two people being in the wrong place at the wrong time.

Perhaps it had been to make up for their emotional distance that they had tended to overlook Kulal's misdemeanours. But it seemed that they were not being overlooked this time. Hazail was pacing the floor like an expectant father, before turning back to his younger brother, still with that exasperated expression on his face.

'She wasn't a pole dancer,' Kulal protested as he picked up a golden goblet and swirled the pomegranate juice it contained.

'No?' Hazail looked at him. 'It is fiction, then, that she was seen writhing around in a nightclub, showing much of her underwear in the process? That is simply a figment of my informant's imagination, is it?'

'Which informant?' Kulal demanded, trying to dampen down the vivid image of Rosa's curvaceous body as it had twisted itself around the pole. Or the fact that his brother's damned servant had interrupted him just as he had started to seduce her!

'That is surely beside the point,' answered Hazail coolly. 'Unless you're denying that you took this exhibitionist back to your hotel with you?'

Kulal shrugged. 'No, I am not denying it.'

'She seems a little outré even for your extravagant tastes, Kulal.'

'I know.' Kulal met the question in his brother's eyes with a faintly bemused shrug, because he couldn't have begun to describe the sensation which had washed over him when he'd watched Rosa walk into the nightclub that night. Lust didn't begin to cover the hunger he'd felt when he'd seen her. There had been something in her eyes—a look which had seemed so at odds with the provocative curves of her body and which had called out to something inside him. He had noticed the defiant way she'd lifted the champagne bottle to her mouth and the small rush of foam which had trickled erotically over her lips. And then she had begun to dance....

Kulal felt desire shiver over his skin as he remembered that dance. It had been an invitation to sex. The most blatant and beautiful invitation he had ever witnessed and he had simply been unable to resist it. He had walked towards her like a man on autopilot, with his heart thundering and his body on fire. 'But she is very beautiful,' he said simply.

'There are a lot of beautiful women in the world, as well you know,' came Hazail's dry rejoinder. 'Surely you could have found someone a little more suitable to have sex with?'

Kulal wanted to protest that they hadn't actually had sex, but his fiercely masculine pride would not allow him to make such a disclosure, especially not to his brother. 'I'm not really clear about why there has been a big drama about it, Hazail?' he drawled. 'Why the sudden interest in my sex life?'

'Because you are engaged to be married—in case it had slipped your mind. And therefore it is inadvisable for you to behave like a rutting stag!'

Kulal thought of his serious-faced fiancée—a blue-blooded princess who hailed from the neighbouring country of Buheiraat. He thought about the matter-of-fact way the two of them had sat down to work out an agreement for their forthcoming nuptials. He thought about her complete lack of passion and compared her to the fiery and responsive Rosa, and his heart sank.

He shot his brother a cool look. 'I made a single, minor transgression, Hazail,' he said. 'I hardly think that puts me in the category of "rutting stag." And besides, you know how these things work. Ayesha will not be expecting her prince to come to her on her wedding night as a cowering innocent. She will expect her husband to be experienced in matters of sexuality.'

'Well, Ayesha's expectations are now academic,' said Hazail. 'Since the wedding is now off.'

Kulal stilled. 'The wedding is off?'

'Yes. She has sent word to the palace through one of her envoys that she will no longer marry you.'

Kulal's eyes narrowed. 'Why not?'

'Why do you think?' exploded Hazail. 'Because word has got back to her about your exploits, that's why! You seem to forget that modern princesses are different to the way they used to be. They are no longer prepared to turn a blind eye to behaviour which they find intolerable. And you have hardly been the soul of discretion on this occasion, Kulal. A discreet liaison is one thing, but openly spending the night with a complete stranger is something else.'

Kulal's mouth hardened because it had been the loud and drunken Rosa who had made it into such a spectacle. If she hadn't been so damned predatory, this might never have happened. He glowered at his golden goblet and slammed it down on the table. 'I will write to Ayesha, wishing her all the very best for her future happiness,' he said. 'And we will forget that this unfortunate incident ever happened.'

But Hazail was shaking his head. 'That's the trouble—we can't just forget it. If only it were that simple.'

Kulal frowned. 'You're not making any sense.'

The king leaned back in his chair. 'You do realise the identity of the woman you spent the night with?'

'Of course I do.' Kulal felt a beat of frustration harden his groin, his erection conveniently concealed by the silk robes he always wore when in Zahrastan. And although it felt like an exquisite form of torture, he allowed a picture of her luscious curves and dark hair to form in his mind. 'Her name is Rosa.'

'Her name is Rosa Corretti!'

Kulal's expression remained unchanged, for he did not care to admit that the brunette's surname was news to him. 'Mmm. That's right. Corretti. She's Italian,' he said, as if imparting some important nugget of information.

'No, she is not Italian,' said Hazail. 'She's Sicilian. And not only is she Sicilian, but she comes from one of the most powerful families on the island.'

'So?'

'So her brothers are probably going to come after you. In fact, the whole damned family is probably going to come after you after you compromised her reputation by spending the night with her.'

Kulal shrugged. 'Then let them come,' he said carelessly. 'For I am afraid of no man!'

'Your courage has never been in question, but you don't seem to realise the gravity of the situation, Kulal.'

Hazail bit his lip with the closest thing to anxiety Kulal had ever seen. 'The influence of the Corretti family extends all over the world and they do not take the virtue of their womenfolk lightly. I'm not joking—this could be political and economic dynamite for our country if it were to erupt into some kind of international scandal.'

There was silence for a moment as Kulal mulled over his brother's words. Were this Corretti family such a big deal, then? He remembered everything he had heard and read about the Sicilian culture. That the men were proud and the women were pure. His lips twisted scornfully. Except that Rosa Corretti was the least pure woman he'd met in a long time!

'Do you think they might respond to bribery?' he mused. 'Shares in one of our oil refineries might buy their silence.'

Hazail shook his head. 'This is one situation where I suspect that bribery will not work—for there are very few ways to appease a Sicilian family when their honour is involved.'

For a moment, Kulal was silent as he considered the options which lay open to him and forced himself to acknowledge that there were remarkably few. He thought about Rosa Corretti and her soft pink lips. He thought about her magnificent breasts and waterfall of dark hair and he felt a corresponding pang of pure and frustrated lust. Surely there was something he could do to remedy a potentially explosive situation?

And then an idea began to form in his mind, an idea so simple that he was surprised it had taken him so long to come up with it.

'I suppose I will have to marry her,' he said.

Hazail stared at him. 'Marry her?'

Kulal shrugged. 'Why not? A short-term marriage would suit both parties very well. It would rescue her "honour," silence any overprotective brothers and it might work in our favour. Think about it, Hazail. We sell the story as some kind of love match and Princess Ayesha will be seen as magnanimous for agreeing to cancel her wedding to me. And just think how the press will seize on it!' He gave a mocking smile. 'The Arabian version of Romeo and Juliet!'

The king's mouth fell open. 'You're serious, aren't you?'

'Entirely serious.' Kulal smiled as he allowed his body to anticipate the pleasure of reuniting with his little Sicilian firecracker. 'I shall go to Rosa Corretti and ask for her hand in marriage.'

There was a pause as the king looked at him. 'This is remarkably good of you, Kulal,' he said quietly.

'Ah, but I am not doing it to be "good,"' Kulal corrected silkily. 'I am doing it because I can see no feasible alternative. Look on it as an act of supreme patriotism, if you will. Let's just say I'm doing it for the sake of my country.'

CHAPTER FOUR

ROSA HAD BEEN crossing the room towards the bathroom when the sudden rap on the door halted her in her tracks. She could feel a sudden clamminess on her forehead and her heart began to pound with something which felt very much like fear. Who on earth was that knocking at this time of night? She wasn't expecting any visitors and this wasn't the kind of hotel which offered room service. More importantly, nobody knew she was here.

Or at least, only one person did and she doubted she'd ever see him again.

But her heart began to race as a series of ghastly possibilities began to crowd into her mind. What if Kulal wasn't the only person who knew of her whereabouts? What if her brothers who she must now refer to as her half-brothers had discovered she was here? They might have been horrified to find out that she didn't share their father—and that their mother had brought shame and disgrace to the family with her behaviour. Their eyes may have deadened with anger on discovering that she was not their true blood sister, but surely twenty-three years of guarding her as fiercely as a lion might guard its cubs could not be forgotten overnight?

Mightn't they have decided to bring her back to Sicily themselves? Wasn't that the gist behind the text which she'd received? The one which had simply said, Come home, Rosa.

She had ignored the text, just as she had ignored the one which had followed shortly after. In fact, she'd hurled the phone at the wall so that it had fallen in shattered and useless pieces on the carpet. But she planned to get herself a new, cheap one tomorrow morning and then none of the Correttis would have her new number. Which meant that none of them would be able to contact her.

And in the meantime, why was someone still knocking on her door like that?

She stayed rooted to the spot, praying that it was a case of mistaken identity. A drunken reveller, perhaps— for there were enough of them in this part of the South of France. She felt her skin redden. Because hadn't she been one of those drunken revellers herself the other night, when she'd made such an awful fool of herself in front of that arrogant man, Kulal? It was ironic, really. She'd grown up surrounded by arrogant men and seen the heartbreak they could wreak on women, so why hadn't she chosen someone softer and easier as the man she had decided she wanted to take her virginity?

Briefly she shut her eyes because the most humiliating thing of all was that he hadn't wanted her. He'd put her to bed after too much champagne and the disdain on his face the following morning had been clear. It was only when she'd practically thrown herself at him that he had deigned to kiss her. She wondered if they would have gone all the way had the kiss not been interrupted by that other man, the one who'd started talking about a king.

She still couldn't quite believe the words he'd uttered. Something about the king 'craving his company.' Did people really talk like that any more? Perhaps they were some kind of double act who trawled holiday areas pretending to be people they weren't. Operating some kind of cheap scam.

'I know you're in there.'

The terse words carried through the closed door and put a swift halt to Rosa's swirling thoughts. Because that deep voice with the strange accent was horribly familiar and she was unprepared for the wave of desire which made her skin grow heated. A curling expectation began to unfold somewhere deep inside her and it wasn't a feeling she particularly welcomed. She thought of his cruel face and hard body and her heart began to pound. What was the matter with her? He was probably nothing but a weird imposter—some fake sheikh—and she didn't have to answer the door to him.

Oh, why hadn't she turned the lights off?

Because you weren't expecting a late-night visitor, that's why.

'You can try ignoring me if you want, Rosa, but I'm not going anywhere,' persisted the voice. 'And if you stretch my patience too far, then I may be forced to break down this door.'

What a caveman he was! Rosa racked her brain for some kind of response and decided to attempt an audacious piece of bravado. 'And what if I'm not alone?' she demanded. 'Don't you think you might be disturbing something—that I might want a little privacy?'

From the other side of the door, Kulal gritted his teeth as a slow rage began to build inside him. Bad enough that he was being forced to enter a union with this tramp of a woman, but that she should dare to keep him waiting was intolerable!

'Then I'd advise you to tell your paramour to get dressed and to get dressed quickly, since he might not enjoy facing me in my current mood.'

Rosa shivered at the forceful intent behind his words. She should have been shocked by his arrogance, but she was Sicilian and therefore she wasn't a bit shocked. She was used to outrageously chauvinist behaviour within the Corretti clan itself, but this man was making the male members of her own overbearing family seem like absolute pussycats.

Reluctantly, she unlocked the key and opened the door, her senses assailed by the overpowering scent of jasmine from the darkened gardens as she stared at the man who was standing on her doorstep.

He was exactly as she remembered him. No, that wasn't quite true. She'd spent the past two days trying to play him down in her imagination, telling herself that it had been her highly emotional state which had made her react to him in such an uncharacteristic way. Telling herself that he was nothing special, that he was just a man who was aware of his appeal to women and who played on it.

But she had been wrong. More than wrong. Because tonight, his undeniable sexiness was edged with something potent—something which suddenly made her feel innocent and fragile. He looked as if he meant business—and it wasn't just the way he was dressed, in a dark and sombre suit, which emphasised his powerful physique. He looked as if he hadn't shaved that day so that his dark jaw was faintly shadowed with stubble. It was a look which was essentially masculine and subtly modern, yet it didn't match the expression in his black eyes. Because that was the antithesis of modern—it was darkly glittering and almost primitive.

She swallowed. 'What do you want?'

'A little courtesy might be a good place to start. I'd like to come in.'

To Rosa's disbelief he didn't bother waiting for her assent, just walked straight past her. 'You can't just barge in here like that!' she protested.

'Too late. I just did. So let's not waste any more time with futile protestations. Shut the door like a good girl, will you? I want to talk to you.'

Fury came in many forms and the form which was visiting Rosa right then was making her speechless with a growing anger. Like a good girl, he had said—and hadn't she run away from Sicily to escape precisely that type of patronising attitude? It took a moment or two before she could compose herself enough to suck in a deep breath and manage to turn it into an outraged question.

'What are you doing here?' she demanded.

'Are you going to shut the door, or am I?'

She kicked it shut before she could ask herself why she wasn't calling hotel security—if such a thing existed in this place—to have him ejected. Maybe because there seemed something distinctly unfinished between them—something which still needed to be said. But she wasn't going to let him think that she was a pushover, even though her heart was now racing for a very different reason. She had behaved like a stupid fool the other night and she didn't intend to do so again. 'I didn't think we had anything left to say to each other, after that man Mutasim bundled me into a taxi the other day.'

He didn't appear to be listening to her for his eyes were trained on the closed door in the far corner of the room. 'So is there some thwarted lover in there?' he questioned softly. 'Cowering in fear as he puts his clothes back on?'

For a moment Rosa was tempted to say yes, wondering if he would have the bravado to actually go in and confront some fictitious man. But deep down she knew the answer. Of course he would. She could tell from the tension in his powerful body that he was afraid of nothing. Or no one.

But then, neither was she, she reminded herself. Not any more. She'd spent her whole life being bossed around by autocratic men and being reined in by old-fashioned rules, and the new Rosa Corretti had no intention of continuing with that repressive tradition. So this Kulal—whoever he was—had better understand that, before she kicked him out of here for good.

'No, I haven't got anyone cowering in the bedroom—not that it's any of your business if I had,' she snapped. 'I was about to go to bed myself when I was rudely interrupted by your unwanted appearance.'

Kulal felt his pulse quicken. So she was alone, was

she? Alone and probably as hungry for him as she'd been the other night. And wouldn't that be the easiest way to get her to agree to his proposition—by getting her horizontal? His lips curved with the hint of an expectant smile. Because a woman would agree to pretty much anything when a man was making love to her.

Now that he was safely in her hotel room, he allowed himself to study her closely—thinking that she looked very different to the sexy strumpet who had writhed around the pole in her tiny crimson dress the other night. Her dark hair was tied over one shoulder in a single plait and she wore a heavy, silken robe, which shimmered to the ground as she moved. A classy kind of garment, he thought approvingly. And even though it covered every inch of her body, the delicate fabric still clung to every delicious curve, reminding him all too vividly of what lay beneath.

'You are looking very beautiful tonight,' he murmured.

Rosa stiffened because the calculating look she'd seen hardening his eyes was completely at odds with the silken caress of his voice. And yet stupidly, her body couldn't seem to stop reacting to him. She wanted him to pull her into his hard body and she wanted him to kiss her again. But he was trouble. She knew that. He might exude an undeniable appeal which was clawing away at something deep inside her, but she sensed an undeniable danger about him.

'I asked what you were doing here,' she said quietly. 'And so far you haven't come up with a satisfactory answer.'

Kulal frowned. She was certainly behaving very differently this evening. She wasn't coming on to him at
all, or making any indication that she wanted to continue
the delicious kiss which had been abruptly terminated
by the appearance of his brother's aide.

'We need to have a conversation,' he said.

'At this time of night?'

He nodded. The concealing cloak of nighttime was
infinitely preferable to a meeting conducted in the harsh
light of the Mediterranean sunshine. And even though
this rather humble hotel was not the kind of place which
usually attracted the paparazzi, his striking looks always made him the subject of prying eyes. 'I'm afraid
so.'

'Then you'd better hurry up and get on with it, Mr...?'

He met the challenge in her voice, thinking how spectacular her eyes were, as they looked at him with imper-
tinent challenge. 'I think you were made perfectly aware
by the interruption which took place yesterday that I
am not a "Mr,"' he said shortly. 'In fact, I am a prince.'

'A prince?' she echoed, like someone waiting for the
punchline to a joke.

He nodded. 'Although I prefer to think of myself as
a sheikh first and a prince second. I am Sheikh Kulal
Al-Dimashqi, the second son of the royal house of Zahrastan.' He elevated his dark brows in careless question.
'But perhaps you have found out a little more about me
since we were parted so abruptly. Was your interest not
piqued by the stranger you almost had sex with?' He
gave a mocking smile. 'Especially when you discovered
that his brother was a king.'

Rosa glared at him, trying to ignore his crude taunt. 'If you must know—I thought that you might be involved in some kind of scam.'

'A scam?' he echoed.

'Yes. That man turning up and announcing that the "king" wanted to see you.' She gave him a scornful look. 'People pretend to be aristocrats all the time! It helps them get into expensive hotels without paying.'

He gave the room a deprecating glance. 'Then I don't imagine they'd be targeting a place like this, do you?'

Rosa didn't rise to the taunt. Why should she, when it was true? She'd chosen the hotel precisely because it hadn't been expensive. Because it was the last place on earth that you would ever expect to find a Corretti staying and therefore it was unlikely that any of her family would come looking for her here. But the Hotel Jasmin was exactly what she needed in her troubled state. She liked the peace of the place. The laid-back attitude and the old-fashioned gardens. There were mostly French people staying here and the service was simple and unobtrusive. There were no tourists, no dull international menu or any Wi-Fi connection which might have encouraged people to sit around, tapping away on their computers so that you felt as if you'd walked into a giant office.

'If you don't like it, then leave,' she said quietly. 'I'm not stopping you.'

Kulal hesitated—and for him, such hesitation was rare. But this conversation was not going according to plan. For a start, she had not fallen on him with lust in her eyes and a body impatient for the pleasure he could give her. He had thought that he would be in her bed by now and yet he was nowhere near it. She seemed completely different to the woman who had begged him to kiss her and he began to wonder why.

'I know who you are,' he said suddenly.

Rosa didn't react. It had been one of the first lessons she had been taught—never show a stranger what you are thinking. She had broken that rule the other night, under the influence of the unaccustomed champagne, but she would not be repeating such a fundamental mistake tonight.

'And who am I?' she questioned lightly, thinking that perhaps he could provide a better answer than any she could come up with. Because she didn't seem to know who she was herself any more.

He sucked in a deep breath. 'Your name is Rosa Corretti and you are a member of the prestigious Sicilian family of that name.'

Rosa nodded. At least he hadn't come out with the usual accusatory stereotype, as people usually did. They discovered that you came from a powerful family with a sometimes questionable past, and assumed that you were all gangsters. Hadn't that been one of the reasons why she'd been so protected during her upbringing—to keep her away from the judgement of the outside world, as well as to protect her innocence?

'Bravo, Sheikh Kulal Al-Dimashqi,' she said softly. 'And what else have you found out about me?'

He stared at her. 'Nothing,' he said, his words edged with frustration.

'Nothing?'

He shook his head. He had some of the best intelligence sources in the world, but when it came to finding out more about the daughter of Carlo Corretti, it seemed that they had come up against a brick wall. There was plenty about her two brothers and a whole bunch of colourful cousins, but Rosa might as well not have existed for all the information they'd been able to provide. 'Absolutely nothing. Oh, I know which schools you went to and that you studied linguistics at the University of Palermo, but other than that, not a thing. No lists of lovers and no recorded misdemeanours. No earlier experimentations with pole dancing. You come from a society which seems expert in keeping secrets,' he observed caustically.

Somehow Rosa suppressed a bitter laugh. He didn't know the half of it. Not just a society which was good at keeping secrets, but a family which was riddled with them. 'I think I would agree with that,' she said coolly.

Kulal was starting to feel confused and it was not a feeling he was used to. Because Rosa Corretti was perplexing him. The other night, her sexuality had shimmered off her half-clothed frame like the bright haloes of light which gleamed around the planet Saturn. But tonight, she seemed proud and untouchable. And why was the daughter of such a wealthy dynasty staying in a humble hotel room like this?

'So what brings you to the French Riviera?' he questioned.

Rosa wondered what he would say if she told him. How he would react if she explained that her identity crisis was very real and not the characteristic angst of some spoiled little rich girl. And for a second she was tempted to tell him. To unburden herself to someone who didn't know the Corretti family, and who didn't particularly care about them. Wouldn't it be liberating to share her terrible story with someone else and to free herself from the resulting poison which had flooded through her veins?

But old habits died hard and Rosa was too well-taught in the art of keeping secrets to dare divulge the darkest one of all to this man who was dominating the small room. She could tell him something, yes—she just could not tell him everything.

'I wanted to get away,' she said, giving a careless shrug of her shoulders as if to add credence to her statement. 'To escape from home and see a little of the world. Lots of women my age do that. It's perfectly normal.'

But a trip to see the world did not tend to make a person look so haunted, Kulal thought. His eyes narrowed. 'So it's a temporary trip?'

'I guess.'

'And when are you planning to go back?'

His question was unexpected and it made her confront what she had been doing her best not to confront. Rosa shuddered. Back to what? To a home she no longer recognised and a family who had changed beyond recognition as the result of a few spilled and deadly words?

'I'm not,' she said forcefully. 'I'm never going back to Sicily!'

CHAPTER FIVE

KULAL WATCHED ROSA closely as she bit out her heart-felt words—more closely than he usually bothered to watch any woman, but by now she was beginning to perplex him. He had seen the play of emotions which had crossed her beautiful face when he'd asked her about her native Sicily. He had seen wariness and fear. Disgust too. Yes, he had definitely seen disgust when she had declared that she was never going back home. Someone more curious might have wondered what had caused such an extreme reaction, but he had never been a man to delve too deeply. He was more interested in the facts than in what lay behind them.

'So you will find employment here?' he mused. 'Or perhaps you are wealthy enough to live comfortably without any need to go out to work?'

If he hadn't hit on such a raw nerve, then Rosa might have told him to keep his intrusive questions to himself. Because there always had been money whenever she'd wanted it and plenty of it too. A trust fund had been put in place for her from the moment she'd been born and she'd been able to access it any time she liked. Sometimes she'd wondered what life might have been like if she'd had to save up in order to buy the latest expensive pair of shoes she'd coveted, but that was something she'd never experienced. At least, not until now. Because quickly following the text summoning her home had come another, informing her that all access to her funds had been frozen. That there was no more money to be had.

She knew exactly what her family were trying to do.

They were trying to force her to go back to Sicily by starving her out!

She'd known that they could be ruthless. She'd seen them dispose of enemies and workers—even husbands and wives—she just hadn't realised that the same ruthlessness could be directed at her.

She stared at Kulal as his question lodged in her mind, suddenly realising that even if she did try to go out to work that her options open to her were very limited. She had a respectable degree in languages, but she wasn't actually trained in anything, was she?

'Actually, I'm not wealthy,' she said. 'Not any more.'

'So what are you going to do?' he persisted.

Frustration made her turn on him again. Was he getting some kind of kick by watching her squirm? 'What I do or I don't do is none of your business.'

'But I could make it my business.'

His tone had softened and instinctively Rosa stiffened, for she suspected that this was a man who didn't really do soft. She looked at him suspiciously. 'Why would you do that?'

'Because I think we could offer each other mutual help in a time of mutual need.'

She looked at him suspiciously. 'I'm not sure I understand.'

He took a step forward, closing some of the space between them, and he saw from the sudden tension in her body that she was acutely aware of that fact. As was he... 'I think you're running from something, Rosa,' he said as he stared down into her big, dark eyes. 'Something or someone. I also think that you're hiding—that you don't want anyone to know you're here. And that you're broke. Or at least, if not broke, then rapidly running out of funds.'

Rosa swallowed because his proximity was making her feel as unsettled as his perception. And how spooky was that, when pretty much everything he'd guessed had been true? Soon after she'd found out that her funds had been frozen, she had sold a bracelet to a second-hand jeweller in nearby Nice, but had received much less for it than she'd been expecting. And wasn't it funny how money didn't seem to go anywhere, especially when you weren't used to living frugally? Especially when she'd blown most of her budget on a tiny crimson dress which had got her into all this trouble.

'Why are you so interested in me?' she whispered.

Kulal's mouth flattened into an uncompromising line. Time to destroy any emerging fantasies which might destabilise what he was about to say. 'I'm not interested in you, *habeebi*,' he said softly. 'But more in what we can offer each other.'

Beneath the slippery fabric of her gown, Rosa felt the prickling of her skin and she wasn't sure if it was excitement or fear. Was he going to suggest that they continue where they'd left off the other day, when they were so rudely interrupted in the garden of his hotel villa? And if he did say that…if he pulled her in his arms and kissed her with the same kind of hungry passion she'd tasted the other day, would she honestly be able to push him away?

The words seemed to be having difficulty leaving her mouth, but she knew she had to say them. 'What kind of offer?'

Kulal's lips curved into a smile of satisfaction as he read the unmistakable signs of sexual desire on her face, and knew he was home and dry.

'My offer of marriage,' he said.

His words echoed around the room and a feeling of unreality began to wash over Rosa as she stared into his black eyes. She tried to wonder what it would be like if he'd made his suggestion with some degree of affection, rather than with that cruel and calculating expression. But she was a Corretti, wasn't she? And therefore ideally equipped to deal with his proposal in the same businesslike way as he'd made it.

'Marry you?' she said drily. 'Don't you have someone more suitable you could ask? Perhaps somebody you've known longer than five minutes, in a relationship which is founded on more than lust and insults?'

Briefly, Kulal thought of Ayesha and wondered whether now was the time to reveal his broken engagement. In terms of getting the Corretti girl to agree to his plan, surely it would be better to keep it secret? But he remembered the bitterness on her face as she'd spoken disparagingly about 'secrets' and figured that she was bound to find out some time. Far better it came from him than from some mischievous news source.

'Actually, I had a fiancée,' he said. 'Until very recently.'

Rosa's eyes narrowed. 'How recently?'

There was a pause. 'Until yesterday.'

The brutal time scale meant that no mental calculations were necessary and she stared at him in disbelief. 'You mean you…you made love to me when you were engaged to another woman?'

He gave a short laugh. 'I don't classify kissing someone who has just hurled themselves into my arms as "making love."'

'You bastard,' she said quietly. 'You complete and utter bastard. You know damned well that if I hadn't been drunk then, you would have ended up in my bed that night.'

Kulal only just managed to repress a shudder. It was outrageous that he was going to have to marry a woman like this. A woman who showed no shame about spreading her favours so widely. Yes, he liked his lovers to be liberated—of course he did—but a wife was something completely different. That a royal prince should take such a tramp as his bride was unthinkable! Until he reminded himself that this was intended to be nothing but a temporary marriage and that her virtue was irrelevant. He remembered the way she'd kissed him. The way she'd pressed her delicious body into his so her magnificent breasts had flattened against his chest. At least she would come to the bridal chamber with a satisfying degree of sexual knowledge.

'I was behaving no differently to how men have always behaved,' he drawled.

'You mean you expected your fiancée to ignore your outrageous behaviour?'

'I expected my fiancée to know nothing about what I was doing,' he said. 'But it seems I was wrong. And it also seems she didn't understand that a man owes it to his future bride to gain as much experience as possible before he takes her innocence on their wedding night.'

Rosa almost laughed at his insolence. 'Is that supposed to be a joke?'

'What's funny about it?'

'You're making it sound as if you were doing her a favour by sleeping with as many women as possible.'

'That is one way of looking at it,' he agreed seriously. 'And it is certainly a valid point. Generations of men from all cultures have taken a comprehensive amount of lovers before tying themselves down to marriage. For no woman wants a man who is a novice in the art of lovemaking.'

'And no woman wants a man who is so arrogant that he doesn't realise what a jerk he's being!'

'A jerk?' he ground out. 'You dare to call the sheikh of Zahrastan a jerk?'

'I do when it happens to be true.'

His eyes narrowed, but he could not deny the rush of blood to his groin, because her unprecedented insolence was inexplicably turning him on. 'And tell me this, Rosa Corretti—are you always so outspoken?'

In truth, no—she wasn't. The old Rosa was often button-lipped and uptight. She never voiced the scandalous thoughts which sometimes plagued her because that was the way she'd been brought up. To be serene and calm and ladylike. To hide her feelings behind a polished exterior. But what had been the point of playing her obedient role to perfection when everyone else had been deceiving her?

This man Kulal had deceived her too. He hadn't bothered telling her he was engaged to be married when he had practically glued himself to her on the dance floor, so why on earth would she tread carefully to spare his feelings? She doubted whether he had any!

'My outspokenness is irrelevant,' she snapped. 'And you haven't explained why you've made this astonishing proposal of marriage.'

'To protect my reputation,' he said.

She gave a short laugh. So he was self-serving as well as arrogant. 'Surprise, surprise.'

'And to protect yours.'

'I don't know what you're talking about.'

There was a pause while he chose his words, though he was finding it difficult to keep the irritation from his voice. 'My brother has found out that we spent the night together, so the information is out there. From what I understand, your own family is pretty good at information gathering.' He glanced at her from beneath the half-shuttered lids of his eyes as he watched her body tense. 'How do you think they might react if they discover you've been sleeping with an Arabian prince?'

She shuddered to think how they'd react if she'd been sleeping with anyone. 'But we didn't sleep together!' she hissed. 'You know we didn't.'

'And you think anyone is likely to believe that?'

Distractedly, Rosa rubbed the palm of her hand back and forth over her lips as his words hit home. With a shudder, she tried to imagine Alessandro and Santo's reaction to the news that their baby sister had been be-having like a *puttana*. The family would still be reeling from her mother's shocking disclosure—which would probably make their reaction even harsher than normal. She was still a Corretti, wasn't she? And a female Cor-retti, to boot. Bottom line was that her innocence would be seen as having been compromised, and all hell would be let loose. She could imagine them sending out a gang of heavies to bring her back again. Even worse—they might come and get her themselves.

'*Mannaggia,*' she whispered unthinkingly. 'What a fool I have been.'

It occurred to Kulal that not once during the entire conversation had she made any attempt to flirt with him, nor to show any kind of gratitude that he was of-fering a solution to her predicament. Why, she barely seemed aware of the bed in one corner of the room—a fact which was now beginning to dominate his thoughts. If it had been anyone else, he would have taken her into his arms and started to kiss her, but her face was so full of a simmering rage that he thought it unwise to try. He was beginning to realise that the situation was balanced on a knife edge, and that now he wanted her to agree to a plan which had initially repulsed him.

Because Kulal was an expert at finding the good in a bad situation. It was what had sustained him during his lonely childhood. He had refused to dwell on the fact that his mother's love had been brutally torn from him, and to focus instead on the unparalleled freedom which he had enjoyed within the palace walls. He had learnt to be utterly self-sufficient and hit out at anyone who should ever dare to pity him.

Now he looked at Rosa Corretti and thought about the benefits of having her as his wife. He thought about what enjoyment her curvaceous beauty would afford him. A body which he had touched only briefly would become his to play with as he pleased! And once his passion for her had worn off, he could send her on her way.

'A short marriage which can be dissolved once the dust has settled,' he elaborated. 'A marriage which could be beneficial to us both.'

She had lifted her head and was staring at him as if she was seeing him for the first time and didn't very much like what she saw.

'Beneficial?' she snorted. 'I think not. I think that marriage to you would be something of a nightmare.'

'Are you so sure?' he mocked.

'Absolutely positive!' she asserted, until she forced herself to confront an alternative which was even worse. She couldn't go home and yet she couldn't stay here with rapidly dwindling resources. Even if she ran to somewhere else and found herself a humble job, her family would surely come after her and find her. She forced herself to smile. 'But I can see that it would have some advantages.'

'You mean you're now agreeing to my proposition?'

'Only on certain conditions.'

'I'm afraid that won't be possible,' he stated softly. 'You don't get to bargain with a sheikh.'

'Oh, but I do!' she said firmly. 'Because you need this marriage more than I do!'

'You think so?'

'I know so.' She shot him a look of pure challenge. 'You're afraid of what my brothers might do when they find out about our liaison, aren't you?'

'Are you out of your mind?' His lips curled with derision. 'Kulal Al-Dimashqi is afraid of no one, Rosa. Not now and not ever. But I love my country and the fallout from our ill-advised night together could bring shame on our royal house.' There was a pause. 'You have no need to worry about tying yourself to me for a lifetime if that is what gives you cause for hesitation, for I will happily give you a divorce once a suitable time has elapsed.'

Rosa mulled over his words, aware that he was offering her a way out. It might not have been the way she would have chosen, but she wasn't exactly being dazzled by choice, was she? 'How long?' she questioned. 'Will we have to be married?'

He glimmered her a cool smile. 'How does a year sound?'

'Like eleven months too long?'

'I can assure you that it will fly by,' he said smoothly. 'Because time always does. Before you know it, the year will be up and I will send you on your way with a fortune big enough to guarantee your independence and a lifetime's memories of sexual bliss.'

Rosa met the gleam of his ebony eyes. His sexual boast was shocking and his arrogance was second to none, and yet... It seemed such a stupid thing to feel, but in the midst of all her confused emotions, she was aware only of a feeling of safety when she looked at him. Because whatever faults he possessed, she felt sure he would protect her. Nobody would dare come near her if Sheikh Kulal Al-Dimashqi was fighting in her corner.

Even if she could wave a magic wand—which is what she'd originally wanted—she knew now that her old life was over. She couldn't go back. She'd fled to France and booked into a cheap hotel and sold an old family bracelet and nearly got herself laid. For the first time in her life, she'd felt as if she was really living—the way her brothers were allowed to live—instead of existing in the pampered little bubble they'd created for her.

She'd tasted freedom and found it a heady brew and she could never return to the life she'd known before. All those eyes watching her. All those unspoken codes she'd grown up with, and the expectation which came with them. That Rosa was a good girl and that one day she'd marry some suitable Sicilian who had been picked for her.

If she was going to have to endure the ignominy of an arranged marriage, then why shouldn't she arrange it herself? Especially as this particular marriage had a get-out clause. She wanted independence and Kulal had offered it to her. He had offered her a generous pay-out too. For the first time in her life she would be independent! Imagine being able to do as she wanted, without having to run to someone else for permission. Her traditional family could not object once she'd got that all-important band of gold on her finger.

'It's a very tempting offer,' she said.

'I find it's always wise to make your offers tempting. It usually gets people to agree to them.' A smile slid across his lips as he slanted her a quizzical look. 'And your "conditions" are?'

Rosa hesitated. She had been about to tell him that it would have to be a celibate marriage. That she would not have sex with a man who thought so little of women—a man who had been prepared to cheat on his ex-fiancée without a flicker of conscience. But she could see now that such a demand would be impossible to enforce. Could she really imagine saying no to the sexual advances of a man like Kulal Al-Dimashqi? Could she really picture herself trying to resist him? She felt the sudden lurch of her heart.

Not in a million years.

She looked at the black eyes which glittered in his hawk-like face and in that moment she suspected he knew exactly what she was thinking. She could feel her skin tightening as their gazes clashed in recognition—as if her body was silently acknowledging the sizzling connection which blazed between them. She might not like what he stood for and she might disapprove of his views on women, but she wasn't stupid enough to deny that she wanted him.

The fact that he could treat his ex-fiancée so badly told her he wasn't a man to be trusted, but what man was? Even her own uncle had cold-bloodedly bedded her mother! She wasn't looking for trust, or softness—or any of the things which most women wanted when they took a husband. And with her family background, she certainly wasn't looking for love. Her mouth flattened. Definitely not love. She wanted someone to show her how to become a woman in the fullest sense of the word—and Kulal would be the ideal candidate. She would take from him everything he was prepared to give and then she would walk away.

'I've decided to waive my conditions,' she said, her airy tone matching the careless shrug of her shoulders.

Kulal saw the way her colour had heightened and again he smiled. 'I rather thought you might,' he murmured, his gaze drifting down to where her luscious breasts were jutting against the satin of her robe. He could see the nipples hardening as he watched them and he felt the responding jerk of desire. 'And that pleases me.'

'But I don't want my brothers finding out,' she continued. 'Because they'll try and put a stop to this wedding, if they do.'

For a moment he contemplated the idea of challenging her brothers—or laughing aloud at the very idea that their supremacy could challenge his. But why fight a battle which was ultimately pointless? They would get their precious Rosa back when the year was up. 'There are things we need to decide, but we can easily put them on hold.' His voice was husky as his gaze drifted once more to her nipples. 'And start occupying ourselves a little more pleasurably.'

She looked at him. 'Meaning?'

'You know very well what I mean, Rosa. Your body certainly gives every indication of doing so. And there's a bed right over there, just waiting.'

Rosa flinched as she crossed her arms over the betraying tightening of her breasts. 'Don't treat me like a whore, Kulal,' she said quietly. 'Or I'll walk away from this proposed union right now.'

He saw the way she had lifted her chin. Saw the glint of steel which had entered her dark eyes—and in that moment she looked very proud and very Sicilian. A formidable woman, he recognised as he inclined his head in a gesture of grudging acknowledgement. 'Very well,' he said softly. 'If such games amuse you, then we will obey convention and wait a little longer—and the anticipation will add spice to my growing hunger. I shall send a car for you in the morning. And in the meantime, you might want to give some thought to some appropriate attire.'

Her fingers touched the slippery silk lapel of her robe. 'What do you mean—appropriate?'

He wanted to say that stark naked would be his first choice and the skimpy crimson dress which had done such dangerous things to his blood pressure would be a close second. But not in public. In public she was going to have to play the part expected of her. They both were.

'Something which a future princess might wear on the way to meet her prince.'

She thought about the few clothes she had flung into her suitcase just before her impetuous flight from Sicily. 'I'll try.'

'And make sure you bring all your belongings with you.'

She looked at him warily. 'Why, where am I going?'

'To Paris.' He gave the ghost of a smile. 'To begin your new life.'

CHAPTER SIX

A NEW LIFE.

Kulal's words played repeatedly in Rosa's mind the following morning as she crammed down the lid of her suitcase. Was it possible to just shrug off your old life and emerge without any traces of it clinging to your skin? She snapped the suitcase closed. All she knew was that she was going to try—she was going to lose her troubled past and step out into a new and unknown future as the sheikh's bride.

Remembering Kulal's directive about appropriate attire, she chose a silk chiffon dress the colour of raspberry sorbet and black shoes which made her feel very tall—but she wore no jewellery, not even the ring her father had given her for her sixteenth birthday. Platinum bright and studded with emeralds, her hand felt strangely bare without it for she was never without it glittering on her little finger. But now it seemed to mock her and the relationship she'd enjoyed with her father. It made her question whether that, too, had been false, like everything else around her.

Had he known? she wondered. Had he realised before his own violent death that the daughter he'd so adored had been the child of the brother he detested? Had he been broken-hearted and careless as a result—dropping a match in that cavernous old warehouse which he and his brother had owned so that they had burned to death, their tortured cries carrying out on the hot, Sicilian breeze?

She was grateful for the loud knock which broke into her troubled thoughts and she opened the door to find Kulal's driver standing there. Wordlessly, he took her suitcase from her, leaving Rosa to follow him. But her questions about Kulal's whereabouts were met with a polite shrug. As if he didn't understand what she was saying—even when she spoke to him in French—and Rosa got the feeling that he understood her very well.

Her feeling of isolation grew as the car headed out towards the airport and she peered out of the window at the upmarket holidaymakers. Against the azure backdrop of the sea, there were women in tiny shorts, big sun hats and even bigger pairs of sunglasses as they hung around the harbour areas, as if waiting for an owner of one of the luxury yachts to pluck them up and sail them away to paradise. She thought how carefree they all looked as they fished around in their giant leather bags. As if they had nothing more taxing on their minds than when their next coat of lipstick needed to be applied. She wondered if they even noticed her—the woman in the expensive limousine being taken to marry a man who was little more than a stranger.

The powerful car slid to a halt at the Nice airport and she was escorted straight out onto one of the airstrips, where a large plane stood waiting on the tarmac.

Its gleaming jade-and-rose bodywork reminded her of some oversize exotic bird and a steward wearing matching livery ushered her on board. The light in the cabin was dim and it took a moment or two for her eyes to adjust to the sight of Kulal reclining on one of the seats, reading through what looked like a pile of official paperwork. He looked utterly relaxed, with his long legs stretched out in front of him and one arm pillowing his ebony head. Reluctantly, she ran her eyes over him in unwilling appraisal, unable to deny the sheer physical perfection of the man.

Did he hear her quiet intake of breath? Was that the reason for his enigmatic smile as his gaze flicked upwards?

'Don't look so frightened, Rosa,' he said softly, his eyes making their own leisurely journey down over the entire length of her body.

'I'm not frightened,' she answered, trying to convince herself it was true, even though that lazy scrutiny was making her skin tingle in a very distracting way. She told herself that she'd met enough powerful men in her twenty-three years to make her impervious to them. But she'd never met anyone who had looked at her quite like that before. He had removed his jacket and was wearing dark trousers and a white shirt with the sleeves rolled up. She could see the crisp sprinkling of hairs on his powerful forearms and, despite his relaxed pose, she was very aware of all the latent strength in his muscular body.

'Come over here and sit down,' he said, patting the elongated seat beside him.

She approached with the caution of someone walking towards an unexploded bomb, knowing it would sound naive if she complained that the angle of the seat made it look more like a bed. Yet a couple of days ago she'd wanted more than anything to find herself in bed with him. She wondered what had happened to that new and confident Rosa Corretti, who had looked at this man and decided that she wanted him.

Was it because this morning he was exuding a sex appeal which seemed intimidating and for the first time she realised that he was planning to deliver? That things had moved beyond the hypothetical and sex had become a reality. She was aware that his initial relaxed pose had gone and been replaced by a sudden tension—as if he, too, had suddenly acknowledged the close confinement of the aircraft cabin as the outer doors slammed shut.

She slid into the seat beside him, aware that he was still watching her, his dark eyes seeming to drink in every move she made. She told herself that she mustn't be intimidated. That she needed to be more like the woman who had pole danced her way into his line of vision, rather than the one whose heart was now beating out a thready tattoo. 'I hope that what I'm wearing is "appropriate,"' she said.

'Utterly.' He watched as she smoothed the delicate material of her dress over her bare knees. 'You will need an entirely new wardrobe to cope with the demands of life as a princess, of course—though I don't imagine you'll have much of a problem with that. I've yet to meet a woman who doesn't salivate at the thought of buying new clothes, especially when someone else is picking up the bill.'

Levelly, she met his gaze. 'Are you going to spend all your time denigrating women?'

'Not all my time, no.' His smile was edged with pure danger. 'I'm sure we'll be able to come up with something more exciting to fill our time.'

'Because…' She didn't want to let this go. She didn't want him to keep making comparisons—because wouldn't that just tap into her crippling certainty that she was going to disappoint him? That he had signed up for something and was going to get something completely different. 'I'm sure your knowledge of women is comprehensive—it's just a little off-putting if you're going to keep reminding me of the fact.'

'I'm sure your knowledge of men is equally comprehensive, Rosa.'

'You'd be surprised.'

'I doubt it. I've yet to meet a woman who surprises me.'

Rosa gave a little shake of her head. What a cynic he was. Shouldn't she have tried to hook up with someone softer—and kinder? Someone who wouldn't have whirled into her life like a very sexy tornado. The plane engines began to flare into life and suddenly she started to laugh—the unexpected sound taking her by surprise because it seemed a long time since she'd laughed at anything.

He raised his eyebrows. 'What's so funny?'

'Everything.' She looked at him. 'Within the space of a few short hours I've become the kind of person who steps onto a private jet with a man I don't really know—a man I'm going to marry. I'm going to be a princess and I'm going to live in Paris and I don't have a clue what my life will be like. It just doesn't…' Her voice trailed off as she met his eyes and shrugged. 'It just doesn't feel real, that's all.'

Once again, Kulal saw that fleeting look of vulnerability—the one which didn't match the sensual lips and hedonist's body. The one which was making his gut twist with an inexplicable unease. 'If it's any consolation, it feels pretty bizarre to me too,' he said flatly as the irony of the situation hit him—not for the first time.

He should have been contemplating matrimony with a high-born royal from a neighbouring country but instead he found himself with Rosa Corretti, the daughter of a nefarious Sicilian family with a terrifying reputation. One who flaunted her body like a hooker, but who had since denied him all but the briefest kiss.

His mouth twisted into a hard smile. He could feel the exquisite hardening of an erection beneath the fine cloth of his Italian trousers and he shifted his body a little. Why should he have to wait a second longer to enjoy all the sensual possibilities which her beautiful body offered?

From the galley, the steward appeared with a tray and Kulal said something terse in his own language, so that the man set the drinks down on the table and then quickly disappeared.

Rosa saw the way that Kulal's knuckles had suddenly clenched against the hard outline of his thighs. 'Is something wrong?' she asked.

'Something is very wrong.' Turning to her, he lifted his hand to touch her face, his finger slowly tracing the outline of her lips. 'You are driving me crazy, Rosa. I am aching to possess you and I cannot wait much longer.'

Rosa swallowed as he moved his hand downwards so that it was now lying directly over her breast and she wondered if he could feel the wild beat of her heart. His words were so…brazen. He made sex sound so straight-forward—as if doing it and wanting it was perfectly natural—but she had no idea how to answer him, because she had been brought up to think that it was wrong and forbidden.

'You are silent,' he observed, his fingers now drifting down over her belly before coming at last to rest on her knee. 'That is good. So often a woman destroys the mood of love with her inane chatter.'

Part of her wanted to scream at him for his arrogance, but no scream came—and how could it, when his hand had now drifted beneath the hem of her dress and she was holding her breath to see what he would do next?

His fingers began to slide upwards and Rosa's eyes closed as desire began to flicker over her skin—a desire which was powerful enough to obliterate any lingering feelings of guilt. He was drawing little circles just above her knee and, while it was exciting her, it was also frustrating the hell out of her. She began to wish that he would touch her somewhere else—touch her where she was beginning to ache like crazy. And maybe her restless little wriggle told him that, because his fingers had now crept up to reach the bare skin of her thigh. The warmth coiling somewhere deep inside her began to spread over her whole body and she could hear the loud thunder of her heart. Her thighs seemed to be parting without any conscious action on her part, and she expelled a breath of disbelieving pleasure as his fingers brushed intimately against the searing heat of her sex.

'Mmm,' was all he said.

'Kulal,' she breathed.

Waves of shock and excitement washed over her as he pushed aside the moist panel of her panties and began to move his finger against her aroused flesh and Rosa thought that nothing had ever felt this good. Nothing. She could hear strange, gasping little sounds echoing around the cabin, which she realised must be hers. She could feel the tension as her body strained towards something tantalising which seemed just out of reach. Something which surely promised more than it could ever deliver. And then it happened—almost without warning—like a shower of fireworks exploding unexpectedly in the sky. She found her body contracting with the most exquisite sensations, the force of them taking her by surprise. It felt like flying—and then afterwards it felt like floating down into some dreamy place, all boneless with the pleasure which was still washing over her. She gasped aloud as her head fell back. Her tongue snaked out to touch her mouth and even that made her sensitive lips tremble and for countless minutes she just lay there, drifting in and out of the most incredible daydreams.

'Unzip me,' he whispered.

His words broke into her dreamy thoughts and Rosa's lashes flew open to meet the opaque smoulder in his eyes. But there was no softness in them—nothing but hard-edged desire. Her gaze flickered to his groin and her nerve failed her.

'I can't,' she whispered.

'Why not?' He frowned. 'What's wrong?'

Rosa bit her lip and felt the sharp indentation of her teeth. A million things were wrong and, stupidly, the one which seemed to bother her most was the fact that he hadn't even kissed her. She realised that she had just had her first orgasm but Kulal had made it happen with all the cold-bloodedness of a scientist performing an experiment in a laboratory. She might want to learn all about sex but she hadn't intended her first real lesson to take place on an aircraft, and she certainly didn't want to be treated like some sort of faceless puppet.

She felt like someone who'd never skated before being put on an ice rink and told to dance. The other night when she'd been drinking, she'd been filled with an unfamiliar bravado as she had flung herself at him. Even the next morning, she'd still been disorientated enough to make an uninhibited pass at him. But now that the moment of truth had arrived, she was scared.

So why not tell him? Why not be upfront with him? Surely even someone as hard-hearted as Kulal might be gentle if he realised the true depth of her inexperience.

She drew in a deep breath and let the words out slowly. 'I'm a virgin.'

'Sure. And I'm Peter Pan,' he murmured, guiding her hand towards his groin.

'No,' she said weakly as she snatched her fingers away. 'I'm serious.'

He drew back from her and she couldn't quite make out the expression on his face. Surely that wasn't boredom she could read there?

'So am I, *habeebi*, so am I. So why don't we leave the role play until our appetites have grown a little more jaded? I know the fantasies which turn women on and we can do the "innocent virgin being ravished by the big, bad sheikh" to your heart's content, but for this first time, shall we just stick to what nature intended and adjourn to the bedroom?'

Rosa stared at him as his harsh words registered themselves in her befuddled brain. He didn't believe her! He didn't believe she'd never had sex with a man!

A wave of shame washed over her. Why should he believe her, after the way she'd behaved? He had signed up for a woman who shimmied around in a revealing dress, not an overprotected Sicilian girl who'd never felt the intimate caress of a man's hands on her body until now. And mightn't he be disappointed if he knew how naive she was?

Her mind began to race. This was supposed to be a marriage of convenience, for her convenience as much as his, but it wouldn't be very convenient for him if his new wife was a hopeless novice, would it? Maybe it would be better if he discovered the truth on their wedding night—when it was too late to turn around and tell her he'd changed his mind about marriage?

She tugged her dress back down.

'What do you think you're doing?' he demanded.

She met his incredulous look, trying to imagine what

a more experienced woman might say in such a situation. 'You're planning to have sex with me?'

'What do you think—that I want to discuss the state of the world's economy?' He glared at her. 'Of course I'm planning on having sex with you. Isn't that what you've been practically begging me to do since we first met?'

Rosa pursed her lips together, although she conceded that he did have a point. 'You want this to be our first time together?' she questioned. 'When any number of your crew could walk in and discover us?'

'I don't think so,' he snapped. 'My crew have strict instructions not to disturb me whenever I have a woman on board. No one will dare to come in.'

Rosa felt sick. Was he setting out to humiliate her, as she had seen men humiliate women so often before? 'You make a habit of having sex on this plane, do you?'

'No, Rosa, you're the first,' he drawled sarcastically. 'What do you think?'

'I think that as your fiancée, I should be shown a little respect.'

'Having sex with you doesn't show a lack of respect.'

She shook her head, because how could you shake off a lifetime's indoctrination in a couple of minutes? 'And what if I told you that it would make me feel cheap?'

He leaned back and surveyed her, one finger slowly tapping his lip. 'But acting cheap didn't particularly bother you when I made you come just a few minutes ago, did it?' He saw her blush with what looked like intense embarrassment but he did not heed it, his own intense frustration making him want to drive his argument home. 'Nor did you seem to feel cheap the other night, when you shamelessly flaunted your body at the club for all to see.'

She swallowed. 'I was drunk.'

'And do you make a habit of getting drunk? Is this something I should know?'

She met the accusation in his eyes and shook her head. 'No, I don't make a habit of it,' she said quietly. 'In fact, I've never been drunk before that night.'

His gaze grew thoughtful. 'So something led you to drink from the champagne bottle, like a workman slaking his thirst in the heat of the midday sun? Something which disturbed you enough to behave in a way which you say was uncharacteristic?'

His perception was appealing and Rosa wondered how much to tell him. She'd never been close enough to a man to even think about admitting what was on her mind before, though come to think of it, she hadn't known real intimacy with anyone. Her relationship with her mother had always been strained—and her two brothers would have run a mile if she'd started talking to them about feelings. They were Corretti men and they did that Corretti thing of buttoning up all their emotions—that was, if they even had any emotions.

Rosa had never known what it was like to speak from the heart, and as she looked into Kulal's cool black eyes she wondered if she could trust him enough to dare.

Yet what did she have to lose?

'I had just discovered something about my family,' she said.

Kulal forced himself to look interested in what she

was about to say, even if the last thing he was interested in was talking about her family. But he had learnt much about women during an extensive career spent seducing them, and had discovered that a little patience shown at the beginning paid dividends in the long run. He injected just the right amount of curiosity into his voice. 'And what might that have been?'

Rosa hesitated, knowing that she risked making her mother sound like some sort of slut if she told him the truth—and that women were inevitably compared to their mothers. But she had to remember that she wasn't trying to impress him. It didn't matter what he thought of her, not when her place in his life was so temporary.

Even so, she felt the painful twist of her heart as she said the words out loud and the bitter memories came flooding back. 'I discovered that my father was not really my father.'

Kulal shrugged. 'I imagine that must have been disturbing.'

'Yes, Kulal, it was disturbing,' she said drily.

'But you must realise that such a situation as yours is not terribly unusual. Don't they say that one in twenty-five children in the west are brought up by a man who is not their biological father?'

She blinked, because the last thing she had expected from him was a careless kind of acceptance. 'How strange that you should know something like that.'

'Not strange at all.' He shrugged. 'I happen to be something of an expert on these matters, since I've been the subject of several paternity claims.'

Her eyes opened wide and she felt the sudden anxious beat of her heart. 'You mean, you've got...children?'

He gave a short laugh, because she might as well have asked him if he had ever taken a trip to the moon. 'No, Rosa, I do not have any children—though one of the downsides to being a sheikh is that women have tried in the past to get themselves impregnated, in order to secure themselves a place in my life.'

Rosa stared at him in horrified fascination. He came out with the most outrageously chauvinistic statements—worse than her own brothers' at times—and yet somehow he managed to get away with it. Was that because his sophisticated exterior didn't necessarily reflect the true man underneath?

Because on the surface he might look like a modern playboy, with his sleek designer suit and his private jet, but beneath all the trappings he was nothing short of primitive. He was powerful and wealthy, yet he certainly wasn't predictable. His matter-of-fact response to her admission about her paternity had surprised her, and had removed some of the emotional sting from its tail—something she hadn't thought possible. And wasn't part of her grateful to him for that? Just as she was grateful for the almost effortless way he had just given her an orgasm.

Her cheeks grew pink as she remembered the way she'd let him touch her and the way that had made her feel. She couldn't carry on feeling daunted by his sexuality, could she? Despite what she suspected was a very selfish nature, he had just proved to be the most generous of lovers. And surely she should be generous back.

How difficult could it be to give a man pleasure? Why not get it over with, so that it was out of the way and that she wouldn't have to dread it any more?

She lifted her hand to his face, letting her fingers slide over his sensual mouth, and even that brief touch felt electric. As she let her hand drift to the unopened neck of his silk shirt, she could see the suspicion which narrowed his eyes and her words of explanation came out in a breathy rush. 'Maybe I've changed my mind,' she whispered. 'Maybe we could make love after all—if you say that your staff would be sure to leave us alone.'

There was a split-second pause. A moment when she saw anger and frustration darken his face, before he swiftly removed her hand from his neck.

'You think you can play with me, as a cat would a mouse?' he demanded. 'That I am a man who can be picked up and put down? Are you nothing more than a tease, Rosa?'

'No!' she protested. 'I never meant to tease you. I was nervous, that's all—but I think I'm over that now.'

'Well, that's too bad,' he responded acidly, shifting his aching body away from her. Maybe it was time he showed her who she was dealing with—that he was not the kind of man to tolerate a spoiled little girl's sexual games. His smile was cold. 'It's not going to happen. At least, not right now. The flight to Paris only takes fifty minutes and I'm afraid we've wasted most of them talking.'

Rosa felt her heart clench. Wasted them? When she'd opened up to him like she'd never done to anyone else? When she'd let him touch her body as nobody had ever touched it before. When she'd decided that maybe she could trust him enough to tell him the truth about her parentage, only now it seemed that he was throwing it all back in her face. When would she ever learn that the only person she could really trust was herself?

'How silly of me,' she said lightly.

'Very silly,' he agreed, though the tremble of her lips made him briefly wonder whether it was worth telling the pilot to circle the plane so that he could indeed seduce her. Wouldn't ridding himself of this terrible ache make such an indulgent breach worthwhile?

And yet, hadn't he been partially responsible for this very unsatisfactory turn of events? He had been leaning forward, about to kiss her, when he had been arrested by the look on her face as he had touched her so intimately. He had never seen a reaction so instant nor so rapturous and hadn't he just watched her with a kind of dazed voyeurism, instead of undressing her and starting to make love to her?

He shifted his body as he decided against a delayed landing. Maybe it was better this way. The fantasies he had been building about his feisty little Sicilian should be enjoyed in slow time—not in some rushed explosion of need in the rather limited confines of an aircraft.

He snapped shut his seat belt and subjected her to a cool stare. 'In life, I find that timing is everything. Maybe that's something you should bear in mind for the future, Rosa.'

CHAPTER SEVEN

KULAL'S BREATH CAUGHT in his throat as Rosa entered the Damask reception room of the Zahrastanian Embassy, looking like a vision in her bridal finery. He stared at her, finding it hard to reconcile the pole-dancing tempt-ress with the woman walking slowly towards him. By necessity, the white gown she wore was modest, cov-ering her entire body so that only her hands and her neck were left bare. Her dark hair was coiled on top of her head and the lace-trimmed veil was held in place by a priceless diamond-and-ruby tiara from the Al-Dimashqi collection.

Inexplicably, he felt the sudden twist of his heart, for she looked… His gaze drifted over her and he gave a small shake of his head. She looked beautiful. More beautiful than any woman he'd ever seen and he won-dered if his senses were inevitably heightened by the significance of the ceremony which was about to take place.

They had been apart ever since his car had dropped her off at the Plaza Athénée Hotel yesterday, after a tense and silent journey from the airport. He had spent the night alone at his own apartment, simmering with a sexual frustration which was completely new to him. Naked, he had tossed and turned in his vast bed while the events of that bizarre flight to Paris had taunted him. Rosa had refused to have sex with him, and had then inexplicably changed her mind, just before coming in to land. He had never met such a capricious woman before!

The wedding had been scheduled—without fanfare—to take place within hours of their arriving in the French capital because he didn't want the world's press to get wind of it. Inevitably, word would get out sooner or later and then the palace's slick PR machine could whirr into action. But someone must have talked—the way they always did—which had meant that he'd been forced to clear a path through the waiting photographers who'd been standing outside the embassy when he had arrived earlier.

But now his bride was here and any lingering misgivings he might have been harbouring were dissolved by that tentative look she was slanting at him from behind the misty cover of her veil. How well she played the part, he thought approvingly. That faux shyness was remarkably convincing and he knew that the embassy officials would approve of her demure appearance.

'Rosa,' he said as he stepped forward and raised her hand to his lips.

Rosa could feel his warm breath on her fingertips and the tantalising promise of his touch only added to her general feeling of disorientation. Even discounting the fact that she was standing in an exquisite bridal gown in the middle of the Zahrastanian Embassy, the man she had agreed to marry now looked like a stranger.

Today, his playboy reputation and urbane appearance were nothing but distant memories. The immaculately cut suit had been replaced by a flowing garment of white silk and his hair was covered with a headdress of the same colour, held in place by an intricately knotted band of golden thread. He looked dark and indomitable, and the starkness of his robes seemed to emphasise the chiselled contours of his face.

Rosa swallowed down a feeling of nerves. 'The place is swarming with press,' she said.

Kulal shrugged. 'Weddings are news, I'm afraid.'

'Particularly a wedding involving a sheikh who was recently engaged to someone else and particularly if he's marrying a woman from a notorious family,' she answered drily. Rosa stared down at the sparkle of her brand-new ruby-and-diamond ring, which had been hastily despatched to her hotel by motorcycle courier late last night. She supposed there might have been less romantic ways for a man to give a woman an engagement ring, but right now she couldn't think of one. She looked up into his face and once again she couldn't help herself from being stirred by his proud, dark beauty. 'I can't imagine how my family are going to react when they find out what I've done.'

'They're going to have to accept it because they'll have no choice. And you'll no longer have to fear their influence, Rosa, since from now on you will come under my protection.'

Protection. It was a word which meant different things to different people, but it had particular resonance for someone from Sicily and Rosa gave him an ironic smile. 'One cage exchanged for another, you mean?' she questioned lightly, glancing up at the high, moulded ceilings of the exquisite embassy room. 'Even if this cage is considerably more gilded than the one I knew at home.'

'You seem to forget that this marriage is nothing but a temporary arrangement,' he said softly. 'One which has been manufactured to satisfy our critics. It's not as if it's going to be a lifetime commitment.'

Kulal's words nagged at her conscience throughout the short service which followed and Rosa thought about the woman he'd previously been engaged to. Had she heard about this wedding and was she lying and sobbing her heart out on some faraway pillow, thinking about the man who got away?

And then, rather more selfishly, Rosa thought about herself, knowing that she was here on false pretences, in more ways than one. She held out her hand so that Kulal could slip on the glittering diamond wedding band, knowing that he'd be expecting great things from her in the bedroom and she wondered how he was going to react when he discovered the truth. What was he going to say when he discovered that the only thing she knew about sex was that amazing orgasm she'd had on the plane?

'You may now kiss the bride,' said the celebrant.

Rosa stared up into the gleam of Kulal's eyes and held her breath as she waited, but the swift, almost per-functory graze of his mouth over hers left her feeling oddly rejected.

Her disappointment was so great that she summoned

up the courage to rise up on tiptoe to put her lips close to his ear. 'That wasn't much of a kiss.'

'I agree that it was briefer than any kiss I have ever given any woman, but I fear that once I start kissing you, I may not be able to stop.' He linked his fingers in hers and gave them a squeeze, putting his lips to her ear so that nobody else could hear. 'And perhaps it would be inappropriate for me to ruck up that pretty dress and take you unceremoniously against the wall, which is what I feel like doing.'

'Kulal!' The word trembled from her lips. 'That's the kind of thing a savage would say!'

'But perhaps my "savage" words turn you on, my beauty.' His black eyes gleamed with challenge as he observed the sudden flush of colour in her cheeks. 'Am I right?'

And although she shook her head to halt his erotic line of questioning, the truth was that he was turning her on. Turning her on in a way she wouldn't have thought possible, especially when all he was doing was holding her hand. Rosa could feel her breasts pushing against the bodice of her gown, as if they were anxious to be freed from their lacy confinement. Her mouth was drying and her skin was tightening with anticipation, so that she felt almost dizzy. But even though she felt a little daunted by this rush of unfamiliar sensations, she met his eyes with a sudden fearlessness, recognising that this was her opportunity, her time to grow. She had married Kulal to be free and independent, not to cower in the corner just because he was making her body respond to him in a way which was perfectly natural.

'Yes,' she said softly. 'Your words turn me on. They turn me on very much, if you must know.'

She saw the sudden tension which passed over his face before he nodded. 'Then let's get this next bit over with,' he said, sliding his arm around her waist. 'Let's go outside and give the press exactly what they want.'

But despite his warning, Rosa was unprepared for the wall of blinding light as the embassy doors were opened onto the street, where the small number of photographers had grown into a jostling crowd.

'Rosa!' someone yelled as the flashlights flared. 'What do your family think about you marrying a sheikh?'

'Rosa, how do you think Kulal's ex-fiancée is feeling today?'

Rosa could feel herself stiffen, but Kulal pressed his fingers into the flesh at her waist.

'Smile,' he instructed softly. 'Look like you're having fun.'

But she felt almost paralysed by the flashbulbs and the damning nature of the questions and maybe Kulal realised that, for suddenly he turned her towards him, his lips parting so that she could see the gleam of his teeth.

'Seems like I'm going to have to kiss you properly after all,' he said.

'And is that such a hardship?' she whispered.

'Everything about me is hard at the moment,' he commented drily as he lowered his mouth onto hers.

For a moment, the only thing Rosa was aware of was the press going crazy, but then the outside world blurred and faded and she was aware of nothing, other than the sensation of his lips exploring hers. Desire raced through her, as if he'd turned on some powerful current. As if she was on fire. She pressed the palms of her hands against his chest, revelling in the feel of his powerful torso, until she realised that he was pulling away from her and that the kiss had come to an abrupt end.

His eyes were impossible to read as he stared down into her upturned face, as if he was seeing something there which he had not expected to see. 'That's the first time I've ever kissed a woman in public and I don't think it's an experiment which needs repeating. I think I'd better get you back to my apartment as quickly as possible,' he said, his mouth barely moving for fear that some clever lip-reader in the press corps could pick up on what he was saying. 'Before we're hauled up on a charge of public indecency.'

Rosa could feel herself blushing as his bodyguards began to clear a way through the press, but she was surprised when Kulal waved a dismissive hand at the driver, who was opening the door of his official car. 'No. We'll walk,' he said. 'It isn't far.'

'But, Highness—'

'I said we'll walk.' And with that, he took her hand in his and began to lead her along the street, his mood unexpectedly buoyant as they began to walk along the wide boulevard. He stared down at their interlocked fingers, suddenly aware of the fact that he'd never held hands with a woman in public before. Her skin was the delicious honeyed shade which denoted her Sicilian upbringing, but his own was very much darker and there seemed to be a certain erotic association about the contrast between the differing hues. 'And smile,' he added softly.

It was the most bizarre experience of Rosa's life, walking in her lace wedding dress through the exclusive streets of the sixteenth *arrondissement*, her new husband beside her in his flowing white robes. Bodyguards speaking furiously into earpieces shadowed them all the way and people stopped what they were doing to turn and stare. She saw cars slowing down and drivers leaning out of their windows to capture their image on cellphones, and there were yet more press waiting outside his upmarket apartment block. She wondered if there would have been quite so much fuss if Kulal hadn't been wearing his traditional robes—and that only added to her sense of unreality. As if he was some kind of fantasy figure, rather than an ordinary man. But he isn't an ordinary man, she reminded herself, and this whole marriage was the stuff of fantasy.

He gripped her hand tightly as yet more flashbulbs exploded in her face, but this time she felt much less intimidated. She waved away the question of what her family would think or how her brothers would respond. Sustained exposure to something meant that you could get used to it and Rosa found she was even able to smile at one of the more persistent lens men. She felt breathless with nerves and a growing excitement as they walked into the foyer and took the elevator up to the penthouse suite, with Kulal watching her in speculative silence all the while, as if he didn't quite trust himself to speak. She kept telling herself that she wasn't going to be scared by what was about to happen. She had wanted adventure, hadn't she? Well, she had certainly found it!

Still silent, he opened the door to his apartment and Rosa stepped into a huge entrance hall. She had been prepared for luxury and she wasn't disappointed. Impressionist paintings adorned the walls and she'd never seen so much antique furniture outside of a museum. On dark, wooden floors lay faded silk rugs which looked centuries old and she wondered how many different pairs of feet had walked over them. She thought that a place like this could never really feel like home—or more specifically her home, until she remembered that it was never intended to be.

She found herself trained in the spotlight of his dark eyes as he watched her, like a hunter silently following the progress of its quarry.

'Drink?' he questioned.

'Just…some water would be fine.'

He led her into an incongruously modern kitchen of steel and granite and poured her a glass of ice water which she drank standing up, still in her wedding dress. She noticed that he didn't drink anything himself, and when she'd put her empty glass down, it was to find him still watching her.

'I want you in my bed,' he said simply.

She held her breath for a long moment before she expelled it. 'Then take me there.'

She could sense the growing tension in his body as he led her through a maze of corridors straight into the biggest bedroom she had ever seen, where vases of crimson roses stood on every available surface, their powerful perfume scenting the air. Tall windows overlooked a perfect vista of Paris, where the Seine was glittering in the afternoon sunlight, and beyond that she could see the arching fretwork of the Eiffel Tower.

'As you see,' he said. 'I have made every preparation for our honeymoon. I have even arranged for the sun to shine.'

Rosa glanced around the room, thinking that it looked gorgeous, but slightly unreal—as if a magazine shoot was about to take place. A vast four-poster bed played host to banks of pillows and shiny cushions and a bottle of champagne stood in an ice bucket on a small table nearby. And now there was nothing to stop them. No curious air crew or officials or intrusive cameras hovering nearby. Now she could give herself up to what she had been aching to experience for so long. She was going to start living the way other people lived, and for the first time in her life she was going to have sex.

She saw that he was staring at her and the pounding in her heart increased.

'Do you know, I have never seen a woman look more beautiful,' he said, swallowing down an inexplicable lump in his throat and finding himself surprised by his reaction. Was that because she had resisted him? Because she had not let him have her on the plane? He had never waited so long to have sex with a woman and the postponement of pleasure was making him ache. With a commanding finger, he beckoned to her. 'Come here.'

The look in his eyes was so irresistible and the yearning inside her so strong that Rosa went straight into his arms.

'I think it's time that I undressed you,' he said unsteadily. 'Don't you?'

'Yes,' she answered, with shy assent.

First he removed the ruby-and-diamond tiara and put it down on a nearby table and then he unclipped her veil with dextrous fingers and let it slither to the ground.

She closed her eyes as he lowered his head to kiss her and she honestly thought she might pass out with the sheer pleasure of that kiss. She was aware of the powerful scent of the roses and the way his hands were moving over her body, caressing her curves as if he was determined to explore every inch of her. She scarcely noticed him sliding down the long zip of her dress until it had pooled in a circle of lace around her ankles and she was left standing in nothing but her underwear. The cool air rushed onto her skin as he dragged his mouth away to study her and she should have felt nervous, but the expression in his gaze was making her feel anything but nervous. This felt right, she thought exultantly. Like what she had been created for.

'You look...' But Kulal's voice trailed off because, once again, the sight of her had taken his breath away. Her breasts were spilling out of a low-cut white bra and the matching high-cut panties were digging slightly into the soft curve of her hips. He'd never seen a woman who looked so fleshy before and it took a moment before he could compose himself enough to speak again. 'Exquisite,' he finished raggedly. 'The most beautiful thing I have ever seen.'

Rosa reached her hand up to touch his face, his words filling her with confidence as she reminded herself of the woman he had been attracted to—the one who had danced so provocatively on that podium. She had not been shy. So she began to tug at the white silken head-dress as if undressing a man was something she did every day of the week. 'Why are you wearing this?' she asked as she removed the whole contraption, including the woven golden headband. 'I've only ever seen you in a suit before.'

He took the headdress from her and threw it on top of the tiara. 'Because usually I prefer to blend in. I find that people are much more accommodating when they think you're just like them.'

'But you're not?'

He laughed. 'Of course I'm not. I am like few other men—for how can I be? I was born in a palace and reared as a son of the desert. People always see me as a playboy and I can act that role to perfection. But in my heart I am a sheikh.' There was a pause as he looked at her. 'And for once I wanted to look like one.'

'Why?'

There was a pause as Kulal considered her question but the truth was he didn't know what had motivated him to reach for his thawb this morning, instead of a sleek designer suit. He frowned as he forced himself to remember that this was all for show. That the symbolism of the ceremony meant nothing. 'For the press, of course.' He traced his finger over the centre of her cushioned lips. 'It will make a great picture in tomorrow's papers.'

Rosa nodded but she could feel a sinking sensation of disappointment. So he had been playing up for the cameras all along. Was that the reason for the kiss on the steps of the embassy, the one which had felt so electric—because it provided a great photo opportunity, rather than because he'd been longing to kiss her as she had him?

But this was what she had signed up for, wasn't it? An expedient marriage which they could both walk away from.

'It will make a fantastic picture,' she agreed, stepping out of the discarded dress and staring up at him, her heart now beating very fast. She was just going to have to forget about her feelings and be the woman he thought she was. That woman would have listened to nothing but the desire which was rising up inside her, making her want to rip off his silken robe and feel his skin beneath her fingertips. And maybe he'd read her mind, for he kicked off his shoes before suddenly peeling the garment from his body in one swift movement, and Rosa gasped when she realised that he was completely naked underneath.

Kulal smiled, for her gasp pleased him—though it was certainly not the first time he had been greeted with such a reaction when a woman saw his body for the first time. He reached down to touch the hard ridge of his erection as he met her startled eyes and gave a lazy smile. 'Worth waiting for?'

Rosa swallowed down a mixture of excitement and fear because she'd never actually seen a naked man before, but she mustn't beat herself up about it. She reminded herself that generations of women had started their wedding night in a similar state of ignorance. It might be old-fashioned, but it certainly wasn't a crime.

'Definitely,' she said truthfully, and it was obviously the right thing to say, for he gave a satisfied nod before picking her up in his arms and carrying her over to the bed.

She felt the soft mattress dip beneath their combined weight, and as he lowered his head to kiss her, she was aware of his practised fingers removing her underclothes until she was as naked as he was. He kissed her with a passion which left her breathless—as if he was making up for lost time, and under the sweet and relentless torment of his tongue, Rosa moaned with pleasure.

His hand was on her breast, his fingers tiptoeing their way down over her belly, and suddenly her own hands were exploring him and it felt like the most natural thing in the world. She revelled in the hard planes and muscular lines of his body, which were so different to the fleshy contours of her own. She thought about what had happened on the plane and she wasn't sure how fast these things were supposed to move, but they seemed to be happening very fast indeed. For a moment Kulal pulled away from her to tear open a little foil packet which was lying on top of a cabinet next to the bed—and maybe he saw her confusion because in the midst of stroking it on, he gave a satisfied smile.

'I told you that I had everything prepared for our honeymoon.'

He moved over her and she could feel the wetness between her thighs and the slight resistance as he started to push inside her. For a moment he stilled and she prayed that he wasn't going to stop, so she sank her lips against his shoulder and grazed at his skin with her teeth. And the simple gesture seemed to flick a switch somewhere deep inside him as, with a low growl, he began to move.

It wasn't anything like how she'd thought it would be. She hadn't realised that it would feel so…intimate. That the joining of their flesh would make her feel so incredibly close to him. She was pliant in his arms, content to let him lead and to learn from him, so that when he lifted up her thighs she wrapped them around his back. And when his hands slid beneath her buttocks to pull her even closer, she gasped aloud at the sensation of his deeper penetration.

She knew what an orgasm felt like, but the one she experienced now was magnified by the sensation of Kulal deep inside her body and his mouth exploring hers in the most sensual of kisses, his fingers tangling luxuriously in her hair. Sensation ripped through her like a forest fire as every pore of her body seemed alive with a blissful kind of awareness. She felt her back arching helplessly beneath him and dug her nails into his back as the incredible spasms ripped through her. It took a while before she opened her eyes to find him watching her, black eyes narrowed with every sweet thrust he made. And then those eyes became wild and hectic, his movements increasing before he made a guttural cry and slowly came to a shuddering rest on top of her.

For a while she felt dizzy and overcome by the most delicious wave of torpor. Her fingers crept up to his shoulders and began lazily to knead at the flesh there. She wished that she could capture that moment and bottle it, knowing that if she could it would sustain her for the rest of her life.

'You were a virgin,' he said at last, breaking the silence.

'Yes.' A pause. She prayed that would be enough because she didn't want to break this delectable mood, but his dark eyes were hard and questioning and, reluctantly, she shrugged. 'I told you that on the plane.'

Kulal rolled away from the cushioned curves of her body and shook his head. He remembered the first time he'd ever had sex, at the age of sixteen—and afterwards the palace maid had given him a hand-rolled cigarette. He remembered the way the rough tobacco had scorched its way down into his lungs and he had never smoked since, but now he found himself wishing that he could inhale some of that sickly sweet smoke and make himself dizzy.

'I didn't believe you,' he said slowly. 'You certainly didn't act like an innocent.'

'Blame the drink.'

'And what else do I blame, Rosa? Or should that be "who"?' He lifted her chin with his finger and the green and gold flecks in the depths of her eyes looked bright and vivid. He saw the uncertainty which flickered across her face, that strange vulnerability which appeared when you least expected it, and he shook his head in disbelief. 'You're twenty-three years old and you've never had sex with a man before today?'

'I thought we'd just established that.'

'I'm asking why.'

'And do you always subject your lovers to questioning, straight after...' She thought about how best to phrase it. She knew that people called it 'making love,' but there'd been no love involved in what had just happened, had there? 'Straight after having sex with them?' she finished baldly.

'Up until now, no. But then up until today I've never had a virgin—or a wife, come to that.'

'Bit of a double whammy?' she questioned flippantly.

'You can wisecrack until the sun comes up, but I'm not going to be satisfied until you've answered a few of my questions.'

Rosa wriggled uncomfortably, because she didn't want to think about it. She didn't want to think about anything. All she wanted was to hang on to this delicious warmth which was still pulsing through her body. She wanted to cling on to the amazing memory of what had just happened until it happened again, but she could see from the hard glint in his eyes that he had no intention of letting her avoid his questions. Why was he so damned persistent? she thought.

'I lived a very restrictive life in Sicily,' she explained. 'It's not unusual there, even these days, for a female to be wrapped in cotton wool until she is married. I was the only girl and I had two fiercely overprotective brothers, except that they...'

Rosa's words trailed off and Kulal heard the sudden bitterness which had crept into her voice. 'They what?'

Rosa pursed her lips together, her first instinct to come up with some fabrication about her past, but what was the point of telling lies? If she shocked him with the ultimate truth, then maybe the marriage would be even shorter than either of them had intended. Except that suddenly she realised she didn't want it to be. She felt as if they'd only just started on their own particular journey and she wanted more of it. Even if it wasn't real, she wanted more of that stuff which felt like intimacy.

'They're not my brothers. I've just discovered that they're actually my...half-brothers.'

He frowned. 'I don't understand.'

How could he possibly understand when she was still having difficulty grasping the facts herself? So that now she would be forced to say out loud the words which still made her want to retch. 'That's why I ran away from Sicily,' she said, and drew in a ragged breath. 'Because I found out something which rocked my whole world.'

'Go on,' he said.

She stared at him, wishing more than anything else that what she was about to tell him wasn't true. But it was. True and horrible and irreversible. She swallowed. 'There was a huge family gathering—a wedding which never happened—and my mother got drunk. Very drunk. I could hear her shouting, even above the sound of the music, but I couldn't quite make out what was being said. And when I did, well—' She swallowed down the bitterness which had taken up residence in her throat. 'I couldn't believe it.'

She remembered her mother's face looking flushed and contorted. She remembered the sudden lull in the music as Carmela's slurred words had echoed around the room. Awful, shocking words which had chilled her to the bone. They still did. Rosa tried to stop her lips from trembling as she stared into Kulal's face, but it

seemed that this was something else which was beyond
her control. She took another deep breath. 'I discovered
that my father was not my father,' she said.

'You already told me that on the plane.'

'I discovered that my father was in fact my uncle,'
she finished painfully, just so that there could be no
misunderstanding. 'My mother slept with my uncle.'

She was unprepared for the violence of his reaction.
She saw his face darken as if some kind of violent storm
was brewing there. She sensed that he was about to
move away from her even before he actually did. He
unpeeled himself from her warm body and got off the
bed, walking to the other side of the vast room where he
stood there surveying her, as if she was an alien species
who had just dropped into his life from another world.

CHAPTER EIGHT

SHIVERING FROM HIS sudden departure from the bed and from the new coldness in his eyes, Rosa met Kulal's accusing gaze.

'Your mother slept with your uncle?' he demanded in a voice which was icy with disbelief.

'Yes.' She tried not to flinch, thinking that it sounded even worse when it came from someone else's lips. And Kulal clearly thought so too, because his face had frozen into a sombre mask. 'But this is terrible!' he flared. 'I have rarely heard anything more shocking.'

'You think I don't know that?' she questioned. 'You think I wouldn't give everything I owned for it not to be so?'

'Is this not incest?' he questioned, almost as if he was speaking to himself.

'No! No!' And to Rosa's horror, she burst into tears. All the tears she'd been bottling up ever since her mother had blurted out the horrible truth now came spilling out. She hadn't dared to give in to the danger of crying before, terrified that once she started she might never stop. She had needed all her energy and her strength to get away from Sicily and the dark web of deceit which had been woven into her life for all these years. But now that the tears had begun, they seemed unstoppable. They slid down her cheeks and onto her breasts, dripping from the prominent curves to fall in a growing damp mark on the pristine linen sheet. 'I d-don't know what it is, but it's not that,' she declared raggedly. 'My mother and my uncle were not related by blood.'

'But they were related by honour!'

'Yes, they were!' She glared at him, wiping away the falling tears with a clenched fist. 'Don't you think this has been difficult enough, without you, a complete stranger, getting on your high horse and taking the moral high ground?'

'But I am not a "complete stranger," Rosa. I am your husband!'

His words seemed to bring her to her senses and she shook her head. 'But only as a symbol,' she whispered. 'As an expedient measure which suits us both. You're not a real husband, Kulal—and a marriage of convenience doesn't give you the right to stand in judgement of me, especially when this was something which was completely out of my control.'

For a moment there was a silence. Kulal stared at the fierce set of her lips, as if she was determined not to cry again. And he saw something in her which he recognised with a painful twist of his heart. Something he had buried so deep that he had almost forgotten its existence but which was now reflected in Rosa's tearstained eyes. It was powerlessness, yes, but it was anger too—that in a single moment, your life could change for ever. For him, it had happened when his mother had scrambled up a rock to go to the aid of her trapped child. For Rosa it had happened when her mother had looked at her husband's brother with lust in her eyes.

Damn the past, he thought viciously. And damn the never-ending repercussions of that past.

He walked across the room towards her and sat down on the edge of the bed, watching her gaze slide briefly to the roughness of his naked thighs before she turned her head to stare into his face instead. He could see the wariness which had frozen her features and he took one of her cold hands in his. 'You should have told me all this before,' he said.

'And would you have still married me?'

There was a pause as he imagined the reaction of the press, if ever this were to get out. He could read the desperate question in her eyes and he knew it would be the easiest thing in the world to tell her what she wanted to hear. But wasn't it about time that people stopped lying to Rosa Corretti?

'I don't know,' he said heavily.

It was not the answer she wanted, but strangely enough it comforted her. Much better to hear the harsh truth than honeyed words which meant nothing. And this was an honest relationship, wasn't it? That's what it had been from the very beginning. They hadn't pretended to feel things they didn't feel and they didn't need to say things they didn't mean. 'You think it's an easy thing to tell someone something like that?' she questioned. 'That I'm not burning up with shame having to admit it to you now?'

He heard the guilt which had distorted her voice and

once again he felt the simmer of anger. 'Of course it's not easy. But this is not your shame. You are nothing but a victim in all this, Rosa.'

'And I don't want to be a victim! I'm fed up with being a damned victim!' she declared, shaking her head so that her dark hair flew wildly about her bare shoulders. 'But what would someone like you know about that?'

He heard the resentment in her voice and usually he would have brushed away her question, with all its inquisitive undertones. He didn't tell women things about his feelings or his past because there was no need to. He kept his secrets hidden from everyone, even from himself. But her admission had made him feel uncomfortable—more than that, it had ignited painful memories which had lain dormant inside his own heart for so long. What could you say to a woman like Rosa Corretti, who had been forced to face such an intolerable situation? Wouldn't it only be human kindness to open the door on his own suffering?

'I know more than you would ever guess,' he said slowly. 'And at least you can rest assured that the dark secret in your life and the consequences of that secret were outside your control. At least you are not responsible for what happened to you.'

She could hear the terrible pain which laced his words and saw the way that his face had frozen into a forbidding mask. The hard gleam in his eyes was piercing through her—as if daring her to ask him more—and she suspected that a look like that might put most people off. But Rosa did dare, because what did she have left to lose? 'What happened?'

Kulal shook his head, but that did nothing to keep the memories at bay. He remembered a story that his English tutor used to tell him. The story of a man called Orpheus, who had been told never to look back. But Orpheus had looked back and had been left broken-hearted as a result. Kulal had never forgotten the moral of that story—that looking back could destroy you, and going forward was the only way that you could survive. 'It doesn't matter,' he said bitterly.

'Oh, but I think it does,' said Rosa softly. 'And I think you want to tell me.'

He turned on her then, his face dark with the deepest sorrow Rosa had ever seen, and she held her breath as she waited.

'I caused the death of my mother,' he said bitterly.

For a moment she didn't speak. She wanted to brush away the bald statement like unwanted dust, but the suffering she saw on his face warned her not to make light of it. 'How?'

Kulal glowered. He had been expecting her to respond with a placatory 'Of course you didn't!' because that was what everyone always said, even if their accusatory eyes carried an entirely different message. 'You want to hear how?' he demanded. 'Then I'll tell you.'

Rosa leaned back against the pillows and shiny cushions and nodded. 'Go on, then.'

There was something so unexpectedly calm about her that Kulal did something he'd never done before. He completely disregarded the fact that she was naked and that her cushioned breasts were just crying out to have him lay his head on them. Instead he opened his mouth and let out the words which had been smouldering away inside him for so long that they seemed to taint the air with their darkness. 'I was six years old,' he said. 'And a very naughty child, apparently.'

She nodded. 'Most six-year-old boys are naughty.'

'I don't need you to try and reassure me, Rosa!'

'I was merely pointing out a fact.'

'Well, don't!'

She shrugged. The fury in his voice would have been off-putting to a lot of people, but she had grown up with furious men whose word was law and she knew how to deal with it. She lay very still and watched him.

Kulal picked his next words carefully; he felt like someone plunging his hand into a basket of fruit, knowing that angry wasps were buzzing inside. 'It had been a hot summer, piteously hot—with the worst drought our country had ever known. Sandstorms had been raging in the desert for weeks and we had all been confined to the palace. We were going stir-crazy. I remember feeling that so vividly. I remember the constant drip of sweat, despite the fans that whirred overhead. My older brother was away in Europe, and I missed his company. But my mother said we would go on a picnic as soon as the weather improved and one morning the storm just died down, as if it had never happened. There was a strange calm to the air—and even though my mother complained of a slight headache, I was eager to leave.'

He was silent for a moment. How eccentric the memory could be, he thought. How was it that something which you'd blocked for over thirty years could suddenly reappear in your mind, as crystal clear as if it had happened the day before? Were these things he remembered himself, or things he had been told? Or maybe they were just a combination of things he had pieced together after the event.

'We were driven out to Saxrasahl—a very famous dried-out plain which was once an oasis and is surrounded by intricate rock formations.'

Rosa nodded. She wanted to say that it sounded beautiful, but this was something she could never say, for his voice was leaden with the sound of approaching doom and she knew he would never associate such a place with beauty.

'We ate our food, but I was eager to play and there was nobody to play with. My mother's headache had grown worse and the driver and the bodyguards were too hot to join in with me. My mother told me to stay within eyeshot, but I remember being engrossed in my game. I remember climbing to the top of a rock, but the dryness of the terrain meant that it started to crumble. I…screamed.' He closed his eyes and his heart began to pound. 'And I heard my mother's voice calling my name—and soon after that, I saw her face appear, for she had climbed the rock to find me.'

He stared down at his hands, as if he might find some comfort in those tight, clenched fists. The silence seemed to go on and on until Rosa reached out and touched one shoulder which was so hard and unyielding that he might as well have been carved from stone.

'And then?'

He lifted his head and it was as much as she could do not to recoil from the heartbreak written in his eyes. 'Her foot slipped. The bodyguard yelled—for he was only feet away from her—but it was too late. She fell.'

She forced herself to ask the painful question, because what else could she have said in the circumstances? 'And she died?'

He shook his head. 'Not straightaway. She was airlifted to hospital but she never came out of the coma. She slipped away two nights later, with my father holding her hand.' A father who had never really forgiven him and a brother who had returned from Europe to accuse him of putting their beloved mother in danger. Later, both men had done their best to try to make up for the words which they'd uttered in the depths of their own grief, but it had been too late. And no blame or accusation had ever been more condemnatory than that which Kulal had directed at himself.

As his voice died away, Rosa stared at him, wondering what on earth she could say to a tortured man who had just bared his soul. What words could possibly bring him comfort? She thought about everything he had missed—all the cuddles and the warmth and knowing that somebody who loved you more than anyone else in the world would always be there for you. And then she felt a sharp and bitter pang of understanding, because she'd never had a mother like that, had she? She moved closer, her arms slipping around his neck as she offered him all the comfort in her heart.

'I'm sorry,' she whispered. 'So very sorry.'

He tried not to flinch but the warmth of her body

was irresistible. He had told her more than he'd ever told anyone. His playboy mask had slipped and she had glimpsed the real and ravaged face behind. He felt raw and he felt vulnerable. He felt all the things he had vowed never to feel again.

'It doesn't matter,' he said unevenly.

'Of course it matters.' She saw the bleakness etched onto his features as she dared to bring up the one glaring omission from his story. 'When your mother died, did you never think that perhaps her headaches might have been contributory? Was a post-mortem ever done?'

'No!' Her questions only added an extra layer of pain to his bitter memories and, pulling away from her, he steeled himself against her look of concern. Did she think that he was regularly going to bare his heart to her and subject himself to this kind of pain? And if that was the case, then surely it was his duty to enlighten her.

'That's it, Rosa,' he said flatly. 'We've had this conversation because maybe it was necessary, but we won't be having it again. We've looked inside our individual wardrobes and seen all the skeletons hanging there, but now we're closing the door on them. Do you understand?'

She heard the finality in his voice. 'If that's what you want.'

His eyes narrowed. 'Yes, it's what I want, but maybe it's not what you want. Because this wasn't what you signed up for, is it?'

'I don't think either of us really knew what we were signing up for.'

'Which is why I'm giving you the opportunity to walk away.'

'Walk away?' Rosa blinked at him. 'What are you talking about?'

'Leave. Go on. Leave now. Why not? It makes perfect sense. You'll still get your pay-off—only you'll get it sooner than you ever anticipated. Because I think I've done rather better out of this marriage deal than you.' He forced himself to say the words—wanting her to hate him, because if she hated him, then she would go. She would go and he wouldn't have to look into her eyes and realise that she knew his secret and that she had seen his pain. 'Just think, Rosa—all that money I'm prepared to pay for having taken your virginity. You can walk away now—free and independent, just like you wanted.'

But Rosa didn't move because she knew exactly what he was doing. He was regretting having confided in her and now he was trying to drive her away. He was offering her money and trying to make her sound like some kind of whore in the process—something she'd emphatically told him she would not tolerate. Hoping that she'd leave here in some kind of rage.

A few hours ago and she might have been tempted, but that had been before he'd taken her to his bed. Before he'd shown her what she was capable of feeling. There was a reason it was called sexual awakening, she realised. Something had happened to her, and it was all down to him. It felt as if she'd been existing in a shadowy place before Kulal had brought her senses to life. And she didn't want to lose this feeling.

'Going is the last thing I want,' she said, and knew she hadn't imagined the long breath which escaped from his lips.

'Then what do you want?'

She took the edge of the linen sheet and began to pleat it between her fingers, because that was easier than looking into those piercing black eyes. She recognised that she wasn't ready to go it alone—at least, not yet. Not when the world outside Sicily still seemed such a big and frightening place. Wasn't the whole point of this bizarre marriage that Kulal could give her something which nobody else could? Not just the money which was going to buy her independence, but a sexual education which had only just begun. And why should anything be allowed to spoil the best thing that had ever happened to her?

Looking up, she pushed the heavy fall of hair back from her face and the movement caused her heavy breasts to sway. She saw him shift a little and her attention was caught by the growing erection between his thighs and in that moment she felt shy and powerful, all at the same time. 'I want you to teach me everything you know.'

He stared at her, knowing that he should distance himself from her and yet how could he when she looked so damned gorgeous? How could he force her to leave when he wanted her so much that he felt he could explode with need? He could smell the lingering scent of sex on the air and could feel the erratic beat of his heart as he leaned forward and bent his lips to her neck. 'Anything specific you have in mind?' he questioned unevenly. 'The history of Zahrastan, maybe? Or the new energy proposals I'm setting out next week?'

She tipped her head back. 'About pleasure,' she whispered through dry lips. 'Teach me everything you know about pleasure. I'll be your wife and one day I will walk out of your life. But in the meantime…'

'What?'

She wriggled again, more impatiently this time. 'Please?'

He drew back to see the sudden rush of colour to her cheeks and something made him want to show her who was in charge. To show her that, ultimately, he was the one who called all the shots. And perhaps the first lesson she needed to learn was how to articulate her own desires, instead of expecting him to second-guess them. Because only that way would she ever be truly independent. 'Please, what?' he prompted softly.

Rosa met the dark gleam of his eyes, and swallowed. 'Please will you do it to me again?'

CHAPTER NINE

KULAL STROKED HIS fingertips over the silken curtain of dark hair which lay spread all over the pillow and felt the inevitable hardening of his body.

'I know you're awake, Rosa,' he said softly. 'So why don't you open your eyes and kiss me?'

Rosa stirred as the sheikh's voice penetrated her dreamy thoughts and, obediently, she let her eyelashes flutter open. He was lying next to her, propped up on one elbow—deliciously naked and gloriously virile, studying her body as if it was the most beautiful body he'd ever seen, which was what he had told her in the early hours of this morning as he had pulled her hungrily into his arms. Each morning she woke up to a similarly appreciative reaction, but it still took some getting used to.

She pushed the blanket of mussed hair away from her face and yawned. 'But I might have been asleep,' she objected.

He glanced at his wristwatch. 'It's nearly midday.'

'And it's Saturday. Or are you saying that it's impossible for someone to be asleep if it's nearly lunchtime?'

'I knew you weren't asleep because you've been

wriggling that delicious bottom—' he smiled as his arm
snaked around her waist and he turned her around, so
that his erection was pressing hard against her belly
'—against me for the past half-hour. So it was a toss
between going for a cold shower, or seeing if I might
be able to get you to do something more interesting
than sleeping.'

She leaned forward, brushing her mouth against his
and feeling the instant shimmer of lust which flamed
over her skin. 'You can always get me to do that,' she
said, her voice sounding almost shy as he cupped her
buttocks to pull her closer. But wasn't it insane to feel
shy, when in the few short weeks since their marriage
Kulal had stripped her bare in just about every way
there was?

He had taught her so much. He had shown her that
sex was something to be enjoyed and savoured, not
something furtive and shameful. In short, he had liberated her from a lot of her own hang-ups and all she
was trying to do now was avoid getting too dependent
on a man who was never intended to be anything other
than a temporary fixture. 'In fact, you can get me to
do just about anything,' she finished softly, and saw
his eyes darken.

'I know,' he said. 'And I'd be happy with pretty much
anything you'd care to do to me right now.'

'Oh, Kulal.'

'Oh, Rosa,' he murmured back, and lowered his head
to kiss her. He thought that her lips felt cool and tasted
of the peppermint tea she'd brought back to bed when
they'd first woken. Her arms tightened around him and

the desire he felt grew stronger—his heart beating out a crazy rhythm as he pushed one hard thigh against the fleshy softness of hers. He thought how perfect she was in his arms, how their lovemaking just got better and better and pretty much took his breath away every time. And he thought how their honeymoon had surprised him in all kinds of ways.

At first, they had barely left the apartment—with only the occasional trip to a theatre or a restaurant punctuating their lazy days and long nights of sexual exploration. For the first time in his life he had cleared his diary and turned off his phone—because he never took a holiday. Never. He told himself that it would be a useful experiment to see if his charitable foundation could function well without him, but deep down he knew that wasn't the real reason. The truth was that he didn't want to leave Rosa's side. He couldn't get enough of her; he couldn't seem to keep his hands off her. And when they had ventured out, he had felt like a tourist in his adopted city. She'd made him do things he would normally never have dreamt of doing, like climbing as far as it was possible up the Eiffel Tower—with his bodyguards trailing behind them. And when he had remonstrated that he did not wish to join in with other sightseers, she had halted his objections simply by kissing him.

'You're never too cool to see the whole of Paris from the top of the Eiffel Tower,' she'd giggled against his lips. And later that week they had taken a riverboat down the Seine and she had looked up the name of all the bridges in her guidebook and recited them to him. They'd sat and drunk coffee incognito at the famous

Café de Flore and made two similarly unrecorded trips to the theatre. In fact, they'd managed to avoid a single press photographer capturing any honeymoon images and to Kulal this had felt like a small triumph—especially when he'd realised that she actually hadn't been interested in being photographed with him.

He'd even taken her shopping—something he'd never done before, although he'd picked up plenty of inflated bills in his time. But with Rosa it was different. She didn't seem bothered about the cost of things and he enjoyed dressing his new wife with clothes which befitted a princess. Just as he enjoyed buying—and removing—the outrageous scraps of silken underwear which could barely contain her luscious curves.

He still couldn't get his head around it. What was the appeal of lying next to her and just watching her—as if the sight of the slow inhalation and exhalation of her breath was the single most fascinating spectacle in the world? Usually he absented himself pretty early, because he didn't like women hanging around him in the morning. He liked his space and his privacy. He liked the feeling of being alone—the way he'd always been.

But not with Rosa—and he was still trying to work out why.

Was it because she gave herself to him so completely? Because she was all his and only his—like a newly minted coin which had been held by no other person? With her, he felt primeval. Something possessive and powerful gripped him whenever he held her, something which battered at his senses like a raging storm. Perhaps that was the ancient power of the marriage vows—that no matter how carelessly the words had been spoken, they still managed to convey a profound significance to the couple involved.

He moved his head down between her thighs, hearing her breathless little gasp of anticipation as he began to lick her. He revelled in the taste of her sweet-sharp stickiness and the way that his fingers sank into her soft hips—just as he revelled in her orgasm as she bucked helplessly beneath his tongue. He stayed there for a while, his lips pressed hard against her until at last she grew still and then he moved over her, and into her. He closed his eyes as he lost himself in her slick heat. Allowed the urgent rhythm to spiral them both up to a place so high that the slow and incredible fall back to earth left him breathless, and spent.

He must have fallen asleep, because when he opened his eyes it was to the smell of strong coffee and the sight of Rosa sitting on the window seat in a silken robe the colour of claret, with the glory of Paris framing her like an Impressionist painting.

'I've made you some coffee,' she said.

'I can smell it.' He sat up as she placed it on the table beside the bed. 'You make the best coffee in the world.'

'This is true,' she said seriously. 'Because I'm Sicilian and we do the best of everything.' But as Rosa lifted the pot to pour her own coffee, she was aware of how hollow her words sounded. She used to revel in her Sicilian roots and identity, with the fierce pride which had been drummed into her ever since she could remember. Being born and raised on the beautiful Mediterranean island had always given her a feeling of belonging. She'd felt part of her family and also part of the bigger island community, which had always existed there. But not any more. Her mother's betrayal seemed to have had even wider-reaching repercussions than she'd originally anticipated. Not only had her relationships within the family been dramatically altered, but a wall of silence seemed to have descended since Rosa's dramatic flight from her homeland.

'Have you heard anything from your family?' he questioned softly.

Had he read her thoughts, or had her wistfulness shown on her face? She didn't want to show him she was hurt because she was trying very hard not to be. But it did hurt that neither of her brothers had been in touch, even though she'd emailed them her new phone number and told them she was now married and living in Paris.

'I've heard from Lia,' she said slowly. 'She's the half-sister I never knew I had. The one I insulted after my mother had dropped her bombshell. I wrote and apologised for the way I lashed out at her and she was so sweet. She said she understood. She also said she'd always wanted a sister—she just hadn't been expecting to find one quite so dramatically! But I guess we'll never get to know each other now.'

Kulal frowned. 'There's nothing stopping you going back to Sicily, you know—if you wanted to speak to them face to face,' he said. 'I could take you there, if it would help.'

Rosa shook her head. And have everyone cluster round and want to find out about her glamorous new husband? She wasn't that good an actress and somehow she couldn't bear the pity she'd have to endure when her family discovered the truth of why they'd married. 'I told you—I can't imagine me ever wanting to go back. There's no place for me there now. The person I used to be doesn't exist any more.'

Because the new Rosa was now a princess, even if it was only a very temporary role. She didn't get to wear a crown but she got to share the bed of a man who was a real-life prince. A desert sheikh—a man who couldn't seem to get enough of her…and much as she revelled in his attention, she knew it was getting dangerous. She'd been feeling that for days now. It happened every time she opened her eyes and saw him lying next to her and it continued throughout the day. She hugged the memory of their lovemaking to her like a delicious present. She'd never felt so contented—nor ecstatic—in her whole life and she knew that it would be madness to allow her feelings for Kulal to grow.

But how did you stop yourself feeling something when your heart was determined to do the opposite? She picked up her cup and sipped her coffee. She could not afford to get too attached to her husband, because one day they were going to split. She knew that. She'd signed that damned pre-nup, hadn't she? The one which offered her a massively generous amount of money, in exchange for a 'clean break' settlement? She just needed to train herself to get used to that bald fact and to maintain some kind of emotional distance.

She tried telling herself she was okay with it, when Kulal announced that their honeymoon was over and that he was planning to return to work at his foundation the following Monday. But the reality was that she'd wanted to cling to him and beg him not to go and that feeling had scared her more than her very real dilemma—about how to usefully spend her days while he was working.

'I'm not sure what I'm going to do all day in Paris, with you back at the office full-time,' she said.

He glittered her a smile. 'Do more of what you did in Sicily. You were a lady of leisure there, weren't you?'

Rosa didn't let her smile slip, even though it wasn't the most flattering way to describe her former life. It was true she hadn't had a career, though she'd been awarded a respectable languages degree from the University of Palermo. But it had been difficult to find a job which hadn't been vetoed by her controlling family. She'd done bits of interpreting work whenever she could, but opportunities were scarce. So she'd ended up with a part-time administrative job at the university where she'd studied—and it had felt a bit like stepping back in time. As if she hadn't progressed much beyond the student she'd once been.

'I wasn't exactly a lady of leisure,' she defended. 'I did have a part-time job—'

'Well, there's no need for you to have a part-time job now,' he said, a touch impatiently. 'Just enjoy your days and let me pick up the bill.'

Rosa tried not to feel offended by his dismissive words just as she tried to throw herself into her new life as a stay-at-home Parisian wife. She explored more of Paris and the many attractions it had to offer. She walked everywhere—always tailed by the ubiquitous bodyguard—and began to gain the confidence which came from learning the geography of a once-strange city. In the mornings she took in a gallery or an exhibition, and in the afternoons she went to see a film and her once-fluent French began to improve as a consequence.

But she got a distinct sense that she was simply filling in time, that she was becoming like many of the other rich expatriates who counted away their hours with culture. She began to look forward to Kulal's homecoming with more enthusiasm than she told herself was wise. He didn't want an eager woman throwing herself at him like an underexercised puppy whenever he came home from work, did he? He wanted a woman who'd had an interesting day, because surely that way she'd be more interesting herself.

One evening, he came back late from the office and went straight into the shower, and when he walked into the bedroom, Rosa was sitting in front of the dressing table in her bra and pants, blow drying her hair.

'You haven't forgotten we're out to dinner tonight?' he questioned, momentarily distracted by the sight of the lace-covered globes of her breasts.

'No, of course I haven't.' She put the hairdryer down and watched his reflection as he began to rub a towel over his damp body. 'We're seeing someone from a TV company, am I right?'

'You are. Actually, the executive producer of one of France's most successful independent companies, who wants to make a documentary about Zahrastan.'

She met his eyes in the mirror. 'Maybe that's a good thing—to place it in the minds of the public.' She leaned forward and slicked some lipstick over her mouth. 'I'd never heard of Zahrastan until I met you.'

'Precisely.' Roughly, he rubbed at his hair. 'We need to let the world see that we're not some big, bad oppressive dictatorship. The biggest problem was persuading my brother to allow a foreign crew to enter the country in order to film.'

'And he was agreeable?'

Kulal laughed. 'Oddly enough, he was very agreeable—since he's notoriously prickly about foreign opinion. But I think he's decided that Zahrastan has to be seen as embracing the modern world.'

'And do you...' She hesitated, because since that first night, when he'd poured out the blame and guilt he'd felt about his mother's death, he'd barely mentioned his brother. In fact, the frankness of that night had not been repeated, even though she had tentatively tried to get him to open up on more than one occasion. But he had blocked her moves with the skill of a seasoned chess player. She got the feeling that he had allowed her to see a rare chink in his armour and had no intention of repeating it and it frustrated the hell out of her. Because wasn't it natural to want to chip away at that armour and see more of the real man beneath? Didn't that kind of intimacy feel just as profound—maybe even more profound—as anything which they shared during sex? She sucked in a breath as she watched him pull on a white shirt. 'Do you talk to your brother much?'

He raised his eyebrows, as if she had somehow overstepped the mark. 'Obviously we've spoken about the film crew. How else would I know his feelings on the subject?'

The faint sarcasm which edged his words was new but Rosa wasn't going to give up, because this was the first opportunity she'd had in ages. 'I don't mean about that. I mean, about…about what happened to your mother.'

She saw him stiffen before his eyes suddenly became cool and watchful. Like a snake's eyes, she found herself thinking as a little flutter of trepidation whispered over her skin.

'Sorry?'

'I just thought—'

'Well, don't,' he snapped. 'Because there's nothing left to say on the subject, Rosa. I thought we'd already decided that.'

His words were steely—they sounded like a metal door being slammed—but Rosa wasn't going to give up. She knew the danger of locking away painful things. You locked them away and they festered and then one day they all came bubbling out in a horrible mess. Wasn't that what her own mother had done? 'I just get the feeling that there's so much between you which isn't resolved. That maybe—'

'Maybe nothing,' he clipped out, and now his words were coated with ice. 'I told you those things because…' Kulal felt a brief flicker of anger, but it was directed at himself as much as at her. What the hell had possessed him to tell her all those things? To open up his heart in a way which was unheard of? 'Because you'd given me a brief glimpse into your own sorry family saga and I decided it was only fair to try to redress the balance. But I didn't tell you so that you could suddenly decide to "fix me."' He stared at her. 'You have enough things to worry you, Rosa—and if you feel the need for some sort of redemptive programme in your life, then I suggest you might try working on your own stuff first.'

His attack had come out of nowhere and it startled her. Rosa stared into his hawk-like face and thought that his expression looked cruel and almost…unrecognisable. Except that wasn't strictly true, was it? He had looked at her that way when she'd woken up in his villa. When she'd found herself alone in his bed and discovered him staring at her as if he didn't like her very much.…

She fished around for something to say. Something which wouldn't involve bursting into tears and demanding to know why he'd felt the need to spoil everything with his cruel words. But instead, she fixed him with a questioning look which was very polite and utterly shallow. 'What kind of documentary?'

He nodded, as if approving her sudden change of subject. 'A groundbreaking one, with not a camel in sight.'

She gave the smile she knew was expected of her before walking into her dressing room to choose something to wear. Her hands were shaking as she pulled open the closet door, but she tried to tell herself that she couldn't heap all the blame on Kulal.

Because in a way he was right, wasn't he? She hadn't worked out any of her own stuff. She still felt bitter and hurt by what she had learnt about her parentage. She had run away from her family, but it seemed that her family had been happy to let her go—and she was surprised by the sharp pain she felt as a result. Had she thought she was still their precious Rosa who could do no wrong? That they'd come seeking some kind of reconciliation or to comfort her, when the reality was that they would have been furious and humiliated by her desertion?

She began to riffle her way through her clothes, picking out an ankle-length dress, which Kulal had chosen for her himself. It was a simple red dress, but the beauty was in the fabric which clung like molten syrup to her curves. Skyscraper heels in ebony leather and loose hair completed the look, though impulsively she clipped a scarlet silk flower behind her ear at the last minute.

Kulal's reaction to her appearance was gratifying, although she had to reapply her lipstick after he'd kissed it all away, and still glowing from the sweetness of that kiss, she decided that she was going to forget the bitter words he'd spoken. What was the point of ruining the evening ahead, especially when he looked so…gorgeous. His dark, sculpted features were highlighted by the fact that he was newly shaved and his ebony hair gleamed in the early-evening sunshine as they stepped into the official car.

Was it normal to feel this way? she wondered. To want to touch him at every given moment and run her fingers over each inch of his body? But she didn't give in to her desire—just sat serenely beside him on the back seat of the large car, asking him intelligent questions about the proposed documentary, so that by the time they arrived in the trendy Marais area of the city she felt composed. As if she had been born to walk into swish restaurants by the side of a man who had caught the attention of every person in the room.

The TV executive was called Arnaud Bertrand, and if she'd been with anyone other than Kulal, Rosa might have found him attractive. His chiselled jaw and sensual mouth hinted at his earlier career as an underwear model, before he'd realised that it was far better to rely on his brains, rather than his beauty. Or so he told Rosa, during a lull in the conversation, when Kulal was busy talking to the location manager about the practicalities of taking a film crew to Zahrastan.

'Whilst you,' he mused, his eyes moving to the bright flower she wore in her hair, 'could rely on both, I think. Brains and beauty.'

'I'm not beautiful,' she said quickly.

'You don't think so?' Arnaud narrowed his eyes. 'With that lustrous hair and perfect skin, you remind me of Monica Bellucci. And you are the wife of one of the world's most powerful men, a man who could have any woman he chooses. That in itself speaks volumes about you.'

Rosa bit back a wry smile. If only he knew why Kulal had ended up with this too-curvy Sicilian with a complicated past! 'And I'm certainly no academic,' she said, swiftly changing the subject and wondering if he paid such lavish compliments to every woman who entered his radar.

'But you're a linguist, right? You speak French and English—and Italian, of course.'

Rosa shrugged. 'Plenty of people do.'

'But plenty of people do not look like you, Rosa.

You have a freshness about you—and a vibrancy too.' Arnaud lifted his wine glass to his lips, and over his shoulder Rosa thought she could see a faint frown appearing on Kulal's brow. 'Tell me, would you be interested in taking a screen test?'

Rosa blinked. 'You mean for television?'

'Of course for television—that's my medium.'

'I don't act,' said Rosa bluntly. 'And don't they say that the camera adds ten pounds? I'm completely the wrong shape for the small screen—I'd fill it!'

'Ah, but I believe in smashing stereotypes,' said Arnaud softly. 'I'm trained to recognise that certain *je ne sais quoi* which the camera loves and I think you have it. I'm not expecting you to act, just do a brief test. Would you be interested?'

Telling herself that it would be rude to refuse his offer—or maybe that it would simply be easier to go along with it—Rosa took his card and slipped it into her handbag.

'Ring me,' he said, and then turned back to talk to Kulal.

The dinner was delicious and the wines kept on coming and Rosa felt wonderfully replete as their car arrived to take them home. But even though she made a few predictable comments about how well the evening had gone, Kulal merely answered her in clipped monosyllables. His powerful body seemed tense and forbidding, but she was feeling expansive—and more than a little bit randy—so she trickled her fingertips over his forearm. But he didn't react and, feeling foolish, she quickly removed her hand as if it had been contaminated. He didn't say another word until they were back at the apartment and the lights which bounced nightly off the Eiffel Tower were flickering over the huge sitting room, making it seem as if they were standing in the centre of a silent fireworks display.

'You seemed to hit it off very well with Arnaud,' he said slowly.

'That was the whole point, surely?' She clicked on one of the lamps, telling herself she was imagining the scowl of accusation on his face. 'I was there as your wife, to support you—and the best way I could do that was to be friendly.'

His black eyes bored into her. 'Did being friendly involve thrusting your breasts in the face of the executive producer?'

Rosa tensed as she heard an ugly and unmistakable note in his voice. It was a note she knew too well from having grown up in a family of powerful men. Men who had an overabundance of male testosterone and an overinflated sense of their own importance. It was possession—pure and simple—and it made her skin turn to ice.

She tried to keep the tremble of outrage from her voice. 'That's a completely unreasonable thing to say.'

'You think so? Then why did he give you his card? You think I didn't notice that?'

The card was buried at the bottom of her handbag and Rosa honestly didn't think she would have given it another thought if Kulal hadn't challenged her, but his attitude was riling her. More than riling her—it was making rebellion stir up inside her. Because hadn't she fled Sicily precisely to avoid this kind of domineering attitude? To stop people treating her as if she was some puppet whose strings they could pull at will.

'He asked me if I was interested in taking a screen test.'

'You?'

'Yes, me, Kulal—is that such a bizarre thing for him to have said?' she demanded, pushing aside the nagging voice which reminded her that he was only echoing her own initial reaction.

'And you told him no?'

She heard the certainty in his voice and drew in a breath as her emotions began to wage a sudden and dramatic war. She knew what he wanted and she knew she could please him by telling him exactly what he wanted to hear—but then what? You caved into a bully once and that was giving him carte blanche to bully you all over again. She had planned to do nothing about Arnaud's offer of a screen test, but now she was beginning to have second thoughts. She stared at her husband, not liking the Kulal she was seeing tonight, knowing that he had no right to dictate what she should or shouldn't do. Because surely he hadn't forgotten that this marriage wasn't real?

'I haven't told him anything,' she said. 'At least, not yet.'

There was a pause as Kulal stared at her. 'But you're going to tell him that you're not interested,' he said.

Rosa's mouth dried as she felt the sudden tension in the room. Because that had been a statement, not a question. Or rather, it had bordered on being an order.

Rebellion flared up inside her once more. 'I'm going to hear what he has to say,' she answered stubbornly.

Kulal could feel a tight knot of anger but he could feel something else too. A flicker of something which burned beneath the anger and which was growing like a weed inside him. Something painful and intolerable. Something unfamiliar and yet horribly recognisable. He rammed his hands deep into the pockets of his trousers—something he couldn't remember doing since he'd been a schoolboy and had been sent to that terrible prep school in England. But he didn't want her to see the bunched tension of his knotted fists. Because wouldn't that reveal the fact that he was in pain—and he didn't want to be in pain!

He gave a tight shrug of his shoulders. 'Suit yourself,' he said coolly. 'I'm going to bed.'

Rosa watched him go. He'd sounded so dismissive, as if he didn't want her to share his bed that night. She licked her lips. So was she going to let herself be intimidated? Crawl off to sleep in one of the empty bedrooms as if she'd done something wrong, when all she'd done was to consider a perfectly reasonable offer which had been made to her.

Like hell she was!

She went to the bathroom and stripped off her dress, then brushed her hair and washed her face—and when she had removed every trace of the evening, she heard something behind her and glanced into the mirror.

Not something.

Someone.

Kulal stood behind her—completely naked and com-

pletely aroused by the look of him. On his face burned
an expression she'd never seen there before. Was it anger
or desire, she wondered, or a potent mixture of both?
She saw the heat in his black eyes and instinct was telling her that maybe sleeping in one of the spare rooms
was a better idea than slipping into the marital bed when
he was in this kind of mood. Anything would be better
than having to face that undiluted rage on Kulal's face.

But that was before he put his arms around her. Before he dropped his lips to her shoulder and traced a
line there—the words he uttered made indistinct by his
kiss. But they were not tender words. They were words
of want, not words of need. They were graphic words
about what he wanted to do to her, and although the
baldness of his erotic wish list made her feel that she
should beg for sleep and ask him to wait until morning,
Rosa did no such thing.

His hands were far too clever to let her escape. His
fingers made her weak with longing and so did his lips,
so that by the time he entered her from behind, she was
as turned on as he was. Turned on enough to watch their
dual reflections in the mirror when he urged her to do
so. Turned on by the sight of her own orgasm—and just
as turned on by the sight of his.

But even though the kiss he gave her afterwards was
lazy and sticky, he disentangled himself sooner than she
wanted him to. She wanted him to stroke her and comfort her; to tell her to forget about the hurtful things he'd
said. But he didn't. The only thing he told her was that
he needed to do some work before he slept.

And he didn't follow her to bed.

CHAPTER TEN

ROSA AWOKE TO an empty space beside her and when she blinked open her heavy eyelids it was to see Kulal pulling on a jacket. He was dressed for the office in dark trousers and a pristine white shirt and she shifted a little to get a better look at him, but she noticed that he made no acknowledgement as she stirred.

She sat up in bed, a chill creeping over her skin as she remembered the angry words of the previous evening which had culminated in that cold, almost anatomical sex in the bathroom. She shivered. At the time it had turned her on like mad to see the wild passion flaring in their eyes, as they'd watched their reflected images bucking their way to fulfilment with all the guilty pleasure of voyeurs. But now it all seemed curiously empty. Vividly, she recalled those big, dark hands cupping her breasts and the look of fierce intensity which had shadowed his face as he'd thrust into her. It was like watching a rerun of a porn show and felt like the emotional equivalent of a hangover and her cheeks began to burn with shame. How could she have let herself do that, when in the previous few moments he had been damning her with his snide accusations about flaunting her body? Accusations which hadn't even been true.

Which left the question of how she was going to handle the situation this morning. Did she bring up the whole painful subject and risk one of those dreadful circular arguments which went nowhere? Or should she just be grown up about what had happened? Forget what had been said the night before and start the new day on a new and positive note.

She sat up in bed. 'Morning!' she said cheerfully.

He turned round then and Rosa could see the shuttering of his dark eyes.

'I didn't want to wake you,' he said.

Suddenly, she felt self-conscious. He was dressed in that immaculate suit, while beneath the sheet she felt naked and vulnerable. She wondered if he, too, was remembering last night's erotic scene in the bathroom, and some unknown instinct made her pull the sheet a little higher. 'I didn't realise you were going to work so early.'

He shrugged. 'There are things I need to do.'

The smile she attempted was more difficult than she'd thought—especially when he was talking to her in that polite, cool tone, as if she was someone he'd just met at a party. No, maybe not at a party—because then he would be smiling back at her. He wouldn't be looking at her with that flat expression in his eyes. 'Surely as the boss, you can be excluded a crack-of-dawn start!' she said, her voice just a little too bright.

'It's not a question of being excused, Rosa—more that I have plenty of ongoing projects which need my attention.' Kulal buttoned his jacket, acknowledging how false her words sounded. And suddenly he realised that the honeymoon was over; it had ended last night when those dark feelings had taken him to a place he hadn't wanted to go. When he'd looked at her and experienced a blinding jealousy at the way she'd flirted with the Frenchman throughout dinner. He remembered the painful pounding of his heart as he'd stared into an abyss which had seemed uncomfortably familiar—and it had taken all his energy to regain his usual clarity of mind.

He wondered if she was feeling more reasonable today. If she'd woken up and realised that Arnaud Bertrand had simply been using her as a means to try to get closer to him. He surveyed her curvaceous body which was outlined by the white sheet. 'So what are you planning to do today?'

For a moment she hesitated, because she knew the most acceptable way to answer his question. She could fake a light excitement about visiting some art gallery or exhibition, or recount the synopsis of a film she was intending to see.

But Kulal's behaviour last night had scared her. It had shown her the ruthlessness he was capable of. It had painted a dark picture of what he could be like if things didn't go his way, and it had served as a timely warning that she needed to protect herself. She needed to guard against her own stupid emotions—the ones which had started tricking her into thinking that Kulal had started to care for her. Because he hadn't. She didn't have a special place in his heart just because the sexual chemistry between them was so hot.

It was important to remember something else too—

something she hadn't dared admit until now. That if she let herself start to care for him, then she would get hurt. Badly hurt. She'd go back to being a victim—the kind of woman who things happened to, instead of making them happen for herself. And he wasn't exactly falling over himself this morning to tell her that he had spoken impulsively and out of turn, was he? He wasn't apologising for all those insults he'd thrown at her last night.

She remembered the way she'd capitulated to her controlling family for all those years and she twisted a strand of hair around her finger. 'I thought I'd give Arnaud a ring.'

'Arnaud Bertrand?'

'He's the only Arnaud I know.'

He could feel the rapid flare of rage, but somehow he kept his expression neutral. 'I thought you'd decided that wasn't a good idea?'

'I don't remember saying that.'

'Maybe not in so many words.' His eyes narrowed as he tried not to dwell on the area of her breasts which was not concealed by the sheet. 'But in the cold light of morning, perhaps you've considered the general unsuitability of a sheikh's wife flaunting herself on television.'

'I wasn't planning to do anything to bring your name into disrepute, Kulal.'

'No pole dancing, then?'

'That's unfair.'

'You think so? You wish to deny the past, perhaps?'

She met the accusation in his eyes and she wanted to tell him to stop doing this. To stop it right now before he did irreparable harm to what they had. She wanted to rewind the clock back to yesterday morning, when his words had been tender, not harsh. 'You know why I pole danced,' she said quietly. 'I was drunk and I was running away from an impossible situation. You know that.'

His black eyes continued to bore into her. 'So what are you running away from this time, Rosa?'

She could feel the hammering of her heart as she clutched at the sheet. 'I'm not running from anything,' she said. 'I'm just trying to find out what talents I have. I want to grab every opportunity which comes my way, because I'm aware that the clock on this marriage is ticking away. And that when we part, I want to know who the real Rosa Corretti is and what she's capable of.' She stared at him in appeal, wanting him to understand. Praying that he would understand.

He picked up a file of papers. 'Then I must wish you well,' he said.

His words were dismissive and Rosa could feel her fingernails digging into the palms of her hands as he headed out of the room without even bothering to kiss her goodbye. Damn him and his prissy attitude, she raged silently as she heard the front door slam behind him.

Defiantly, she showered and dressed—and although she always felt at her thinnest in black, she remembered reading somewhere that you should never wear black in front of the camera. So she put on a green silk dress which brought out the emerald flecks in her eyes, and after a couple of cups of strong coffee she rang Arnaud Bertrand.

'Madame de la Désert,' he said slowly. 'This is a surprise.'

Rosa sucked in a deep breath, wondering if his offer had just been something meaningless which he'd tossed out during a lull in the dinner party conversation. 'Did you mean it when you suggested the screen test?'

There was a pause. 'But of course I meant it,' he said smoothly. 'I never say anything I don't mean. Can you come in for a test this afternoon?'

She thought afterwards that if he'd scheduled the test for the following week, then she might never have taken it. Maybe that was why he did it so quickly. All Rosa knew was that later that day she had the car drop her off at the TV studio, which was situated on the Avenue de la Grande Armée. The building overlooked the Arc de Triomphe and Arnaud told her that the iconic backdrop was often hired out to visiting foreign broadcasters.

'You don't seem too nervous,' he observed as he ran his eyes over her silky green dress.

Rosa gave an automatic smile. My husband doesn't want me to be here, she found herself wanting to say. I keep thinking about him, instead of the reason I'm here—and that's the reason why I'm not nervous. But she forced herself to push the memory of Kulal's face from her mind and to flash a bright smile at the TV executive instead. 'Surely nerves in front of the camera are a bad thing?'

'They certainly are.' Arnaud smiled back as he led her into the studio, where the lights were belting out a heat as fierce as a tropical sun. 'How good are you at ad-libbing?'

Rosa shrugged. 'I have no idea.'

They stood her in front of a giant green screen and explained that the weather report was one of the few things on television which didn't require an autocue. They told her that Paris was going to have sunny spells throughout the day, but that there would be scattered showers overnight. And then they asked her to talk about it on camera for thirty seconds, without a script.

She was a natural. Or at least, that's what they said afterwards, when she'd finished her slot. Just as the last few seconds were ticking away, she had turned to the camera and said, 'Sometimes I wish I was back in Sicily, where the sun always shines.' She'd heard shouts of laughter in her earpiece, and when Arnaud came to collect her from the studio floor, he'd been grinning—as if he'd just done something very clever.

He took her for coffee afterwards and told her that he'd been entirely correct and she did have that certain *je ne sais quoi* which made the camera love her. That it was a rare commodity but television gold. They couldn't offer her much at the moment, but they thought she'd be perfect for a daily 'novelty slot,' just after the lunchtime news.

She received the news with the enthusiasm she knew was expected of her, but when she left the café to slide into the back of the waiting limousine, all she could think of was how she was going to break it to Kulal. And wasn't that crazy? Because this was the chance of a lifetime—and wasn't this marriage supposed to be about freedom?

She had to start taking control. She was legally contracted to be Kulal's wife for another ten months and she certainly couldn't spend it moping around the place, wishing he felt stuff for her which he clearly didn't. If she didn't like something, then she needed to change it. And if she couldn't change him, then she needed to change herself. Couldn't she show her sheikh husband that it was possible to live in harmony, if they both made the effort? That they could compromise if they wanted to, just like any other modern couple.

She felt filled with a new sense of purpose as she took the elevator up to the apartment, and when Kulal arrived home she was waiting for him out on the terrace. She had mixed a drink of his favourite rosewater and pomegranate juice and his eyebrows rose speculatively as she held up the frosted pink jug. 'Drink?'

'A drink would be perfect,' he said, pulling off his jacket as he went out onto the terrace and joined her. He had thought that he would arrive home to an atmosphere, that she might be sulking in response to his obvious disapproval of her intention to ring Bertrand. But it seemed he had been wrong, for he'd never seen her looking quite so relaxed.

Sinking into one of the chairs, he watched as she bent to drop ice into the glass, his gaze resting on the curve of her bottom, and his heart began to accelerate as she handed him the drink. She was wearing her hair loose, just the way he liked it, and her flame-coloured dress accentuated her exotic colouring. Not only did she look good, but she was behaving in a way which pleased him since her attitude towards him was undeniably accommodating. Did this mean that she had reconsidered her rash statements of this morning? His gaze was approving as he took a sip of his drink and let out a rare sigh of contentment. 'I must applaud you, Rosa,' he said. 'For this is exactly how a man likes to be greeted after a hard day at the office.'

She waited until he'd put his drink down before she walked over and sat on his lap, looping her arms around his neck. 'And have you had a good day?'

'When you wriggle on my lap like that, it makes me forget—other than to say that it's getting better by the minute.'

She dipped her head forward and brushed her mouth over his. 'Is it?' she whispered.

He didn't answer, just put his hand up to anchor her head so that he could kiss her, and Rosa felt the shimmering of desire as if whispered over her skin. Her hands reached out to frame his face, her fingertips tracing the hard outline of his jaw and feeling the faint rasp of new growth there. Her fingers crept upwards, so that they could feel the hard slant of his cheekbones beneath the silken skin. And all during her tactile survey of his face, he continued to subject her to that sweetly drugging kiss so she was startled when, abruptly, he terminated it, pushing her away by a fraction so that he could look directly into her eyes.

'What's the matter?' she managed through dry lips. 'D-don't you want to make love?'

'You mean here?'

She wondered how best to respond. Up until now, Kulal had been the dominant one—not surprising given his vast experience and her complete lack of it. But she'd had a pretty intensive introduction to sex, hadn't she? Surely she'd had enough tuition for her to take the lead for once. Maybe that was what he wanted her to do.

'Of course here,' she whispered as she drifted her hand down to his groin, where he felt as hard as steel, and began to stroke him through the straining material of his trousers. 'I want you now. I can lift up my skirt and you can just slip inside me. No one need know a thing.'

The explicitness of her words excited yet shocked him and Kulal recognised a subtle shift in power between them as his body responded instantly to her touch. For a moment he allowed himself the fantasy of following through. Of allowing her floaty dress to conceal what was going on underneath. Of unzipping himself and pushing deep inside her honeyed heat. Gripping her wrist to arrest the movement of her captivating fingers, he put his face very close to hers. 'You don't think we can be seen?'

Rosa swallowed. 'This terrace is completely private.'

'Nowhere is completely private. There are long-range lenses and buildings all around which offer perfect vantage points.' His black eyes shot out black fire which blazed over her. 'Unless you are turned on by the thought that someone might be watching? Perhaps deep down you are longing for the kind of notoriety which would come from being the first woman to be photographed having sex with the sheikh?'

She stared at him, her heart beginning to pound painfully in her chest as she heard his unjust and harsh accusation. 'Is that what you think?' she whispered. 'Is that what you really think?'

'I don't know what to think. You are a constant series of surprises to me, Rosa—surprises which are becoming more apparent by the day. I had no idea, for example, that you were a frustrated television star.'

Shaking her head with indignation, she jumped off his lap and ran back inside the apartment but she quickly realised that he was following her. She could see his huge shadow dwarfing her and could hear him pressing a button so that the blinds floated silently down, leeching the room of all brightness and colour. She turned, seeing the look on his face.

'Don't,' she said, her heart quickening.

'Don't what?' he questioned. 'Don't continue what you started outside, only without the possibility of some paparazzi salivating over his camera? I thought that was what you were angling for, Rosa.'

The prospect of sex when he was looking as aroused as that made Rosa's body tremble for his touch, but pride made her shake her head with a sudden fury. 'Don't keep treating me like some mindless puppet who can't think for herself,' she said fiercely.

Her unexpected words made him halt in his tracks and he deliberately made his voice grow silky. 'But I'm just acting in your best interests. Surely you can see that it was unwise for us to be intimate outside, with the possibility that we could be seen by the paparazzi?'

'Yes, I can see that,' she said impatiently. 'But there are more diplomatic ways to tell me than by making me sound like some little tart who is seeking a crude kind of notoriety.'

There was a pause for a moment as he considered her words, his eyes travelling over her hurt and angry face before, slowly, he nodded. 'I'm sorry,' he said.

For a moment she thought she'd imagined it. She stared at him in disbelief. Had Kulal actually said *sorry*? 'You are?' she questioned cautiously.

'Of course I am.' He gave a heavy sigh. 'You've just given me what is probably the best homecoming I've ever had and all I've done is throw it back in your face.'

For a moment Rosa was too overcome to respond. Because Kulal had used an emotive word which could mean so much, especially to someone like him. Homecoming. Coming from a man whose own home life had been shattered by the death of his mother—wasn't that the greatest compliment he had ever paid her?

'It's okay,' she managed, but she was shaking with emotion all the same.

'I can be an ungrateful bastard at times,' he admitted as he stepped forward and took her in his arms. 'I guess part of me was still worried that you'd gone ahead and allowed yourself to take Bertrand's ridiculous suggestion seriously.'

Rosa stilled as the truth dawned on her. He thought she'd changed her mind. That she'd opted for the docile role of compliant wife—the role he obviously expected of her. That she was doing what he wanted her to do. She bit her lip. So what did she tell him? She could play safe by phoning Arnaud in the morning and telling him she'd changed her mind, thus guaranteeing harmony in her marriage. But at what cost? Was she going to have to subjugate everything about herself which didn't please this demanding sheikh? And for what? For him to turn around and leave her when the year was up, no matter what she did.

'You think it was a ridiculous suggestion?' she said carefully.

His lips gave the flicker of a smile. 'I'm afraid it was. I know what these people are like, Rosa. He wants to make sure that I give him permission to film in Zahrastan, which is why he chose to flatter you. People often try to target powerful men through their wives. Though if he was a little more discerning, he might have realised that his behaviour has angered me and that I dislike men fawning over you in such a way.'

For a moment Rosa was so outraged that she couldn't speak, even though his attitude was one she was used to. One she'd grown up with... He was making her sound like a racehorse, or a fancy car which another man was attempting to joyride. How dare he speak of her in such dismissive tones? She stared up at him, trying to stop her voice from trembling as she spoke. 'You think that's the only reason he showed interest in me—to get close to you?'

'Not the only reason, no. Any man with a pulse would want to get close to you in an altogether different way.'

Rosa nodded. 'So you wouldn't approve of me taking a screen test to appear on French TV?'

He gave a cynical smile. 'What do you think?'

'I think you'd better get your head around the fact that I've done exactly that.'

His eyes narrowed as she wrenched herself out of his arms. 'What are you talking about?'

'It's quite simple, Kulal. I went into the studios this afternoon and they gave me a try-out. They said I was very telegenic and so they've given me a slot.'

'They've given you a slot?' he repeated dangerously. 'On national television?'

'The very same. Only a tiny slot—it's true. But at least that means it won't be too disruptive to our lives.' She stared into the steely gleam of his black eyes. 'And next week I start presenting the weather report on the lunchtime news.'

CHAPTER ELEVEN

THE INTENSE LIGHT felt hot on her cheeks, but Rosa didn't mind. The brightness of the studio made some of the other presenters grow overheated, but not her. She was used to the glaring blaze of the Sicilian sun, so a few television lights weren't going to make her sweat! She flashed a wide smile as she finished her segment, reminding viewers to remember to pack an umbrella 'if you don't want your nice Parisian clothes to get wet!'

As always, her final comment made the crew smile, just as it would make the nation smile. In the instantly accessible world of television, Rosa had become a bit of a star, which was something she'd never envisaged.

Her rise to prominence in the national consciousness had all happened so quickly—and her popularity had been picked up by the press, during a quiet summer when there wasn't very much news. Newspaper analysts had been quick to question 'Why Rosa?' because she wasn't an obvious choice to be a pin-up. France had a recognised template for beauty, and Rosa didn't fit it. She was curvy and she didn't wear black. Her clothes were the colours of an exotic bird's plumage and she wore flowers in her hair. She should have been invisible in a place where thinness reigned supreme and women worshiped at the altar of high fashion. But people liked her. Men liked her because she was the stuff of forbidden fantasy, and their wives liked her because they didn't perceive her as a threat. French department stores had reported an increased demand for colour-blocked clothes. A glossy magazine had even urged its readers to throw away their diet books and 'channel your inner Rosa.'

Then had come the discovery that before her marriage to one of the world's most powerful men, Rosa had been a Corretti—and all hell had broken loose. Suddenly, she had become even more sought-after. The studio bosses asked her to do an extra weather slot on the highly prestigious breakfast show, but she'd said no, because who in their right mind would want to get up at three in the morning? Even farmers slept for longer than that! Requests for interviews began to pour in but she told Arnaud to refuse them all. She knew her family would go ballistic if journalists started to pry into its chequered history. And she knew that any more exposure would make Kulal even angrier than he already was....

'Just why are you doing this, Rosa?' he had demanded one morning, just before he'd stormed off to his office. 'Pursuing a useless career as a weather announcer? Telling people what they can already read on their cellphones!'

Those had been his actual words—words which had been intended to wound and which had hit their target full-on. Rosa had swallowed down the hurt she'd felt.

If only he had given her a few crumbs of praise, then she might have refused the offer of the Friday teatime slot in addition to her regular lunchtime one. If he'd told her that her French accent was flawless—which was what everyone else said—or that she'd managed to make women who felt bad about their bodies feel better about themselves, then she might have cut back or even deferred her fledgling career until after the marriage had ended.

But Kulal wasn't in the business of praising. He was in the business of making her feel like she had overstepped the mark. As if she had no right to do anything with her life if it dared to interfere with his.

She arrived home late one Friday after a meeting with Arnaud, and when she rushed into the apartment Kulal was standing waiting for her. His gaze ran over her, his black eyes lingering on the rose in her hair, and she saw the almost imperceptible twist of his lips. The fresh flower had become her 'trademark' and was provided by the studio before every show, but she'd forgotten she was wearing it and it was now probably wilting.

'You're late,' he observed caustically. 'And your face is covered in make-up.'

She touched her fingertips to her cheek and they came away the deep bronze colour of the heavy studio foundation. 'I wanted to get away as quickly as possible.' She drew in a deep breath and smiled. 'To get home to you.'

'That's very considerate of you, but have you forgotten that we were supposed to have been going out tonight?'

'Out?' She looked at him blankly, and then clapped her hand over her mouth in horror. 'Cocktails at the French Embassy!' she breathed. 'Oh, Kulal—it slipped my mind completely. But it's not too late, is it? We can still go.'

'It is too late, and the sheikh is never late,' he snapped. 'It would be an unspeakable diplomatic breach!'

'I'm sorry.'

With a growing feeling of frustration, Kulal stared at her, wanting to kiss her and yet wanting to rail against her all at the same time. Did she think that this situation she had manufactured was in any way acceptable to him? That he would ever tolerate being consigned to second place in her life? 'Obviously you're having difficulty fitting me into your busy schedule, Rosa.'

'That's not fair. My work hardly impacts on your life at all. Why didn't you remind me this morning?'

'Because it is not my place to remind you!' he bit out as he found himself longing for the days when she'd always been there, waiting. When he'd needed to do nothing but open the front door before she would be nestling in his arms—a package of curvaceous warmth and eager kisses. He remembered the way they used to sit on the terrace and watch the sun going down, before the lights of the city brought it to vivid life once more. 'You think I have nothing better to do than to act as your social secretary?'

'No, Kulal,' she said tiredly. 'I don't think that.'

She went into the bathroom to shower away the heavy make-up, and when she returned she thought that his mood was better. But maybe that was because she was wearing a light summer dress which came to just above the knee. She could see the instinctive gleam of his black eyes as he pulled her into his arms and kissed her. One kiss led to another, and then another—and sex always made Kulal feel better. Actually, it usually did the same for her, but today she was left feeling strangely empty as she lay in his arms afterwards.

The weather that weekend was amazing—the sky a clear and vaulted blue and the sunshine bright and golden as it shone down on one of the world's most beautiful cities. They spent Saturday morning in one of the flea markets, followed by a stroll around the Tuileries after lunch. Most of Sunday took place in bed.

'Doesn't this feel fantastic?' murmured Kulal as he traced lazy circles all over her stomach. 'And don't you feel fantastic—all soft and sensual?'

Sensation shivered over her. Yes, it felt fantastic. It always did. Rosa felt her heart clench, knowing that she was going to miss this when the year was up. Could she ever imagine being physically intimate with another man like this? She shuddered. Never in a million years! Could she imagine a life without Kulal full stop? A sudden darkness crept into her heart as she nestled closer to his naked body. 'Do you ever think about what's going to happen when we dissolve the marriage?' she questioned.

'There's no point,' Kulal said, but her question had destroyed the mood and he rolled away from her. He had learnt never to project—even though sometimes he saw the dark wings of the future flapping ominously on the periphery of his vision. 'We made a decision and we're sticking to it. What's to think about?'

Rosa watched as he got out of bed and headed for the door, returning a few minutes later with two glasses of white wine. She took hers and began to sip at it, but her thoughts were troubled and she couldn't seem to shake them off. She'd told herself right from the beginning that she didn't believe in love. That she wasn't looking for love—but wasn't it peculiar how sometimes love seemed to come looking for you? How it could creep up on you and wrap its velvet fingers around your heart without you realising—even when the man in question could be stubborn, demanding and autocratic? Reason seemed to have no effect on her volatile emotions and she knew why.

She had fallen in love with her sheikh husband even though that was the last thing which either of them wanted.

No further mention was made of the future which meant that by Monday morning the atmosphere between them was serene. The missed party at the embassy was long forgotten and the goodbye kiss they shared as Kulal left for the office was lingering.

'I wish you didn't have to go,' she said.

'I wish that too.'

She wriggled her body against him. 'And I promise I won't ever be late again.'

Kulal gave an odd kind of smile before brushing his lips over hers one final time. 'Let's hope not.'

Rosa went to the studios, but as the crew began to mike her up for her segment, she thought that they didn't seem as chatty as usual. And afterwards, when she went to the dressing room to wipe off her make-up, there was a knock at the door.

It was Arnaud Bertrand and she raised her eyebrows in surprise, because he didn't usually come to her dressing room.

'Have you got a minute?' he said awkwardly. 'I need to talk to you.'

'Talk away.' She smiled at him in the mirror. 'Do you mean here, or would you rather go next door and we can get some coffee?'

'No, here is fine.' He looked slightly uncomfortable, his hands digging deep into the pockets of his trousers. 'Rosa, there's no easy way to say this, but I'm afraid we're pulling your slot.'

She turned round. 'What do you mean?'

'The bosses have decided that it's no longer working.'

She gazed at him blankly. 'But…I don't understand. You told me that everyone loved the feature. You said that you hadn't had so much fan mail since Johnny Depp gave that interview.'

He didn't quite meet her eyes. 'I'm afraid it's out of my hands.'

Rosa frowned as her heart began to pound loudly in her chest. 'Something's happened, hasn't it?'

Arnaud looked even more uncomfortable. 'Nothing has happened.'

'You're not a very good liar, Arnaud.' Her eyes narrowed. 'Has this got something to do with my husband?'

'I can't—'

'Oh, I think you can. Tell me!' she said, and then softened her voice. 'Please.'

There was a moment of silence before he gave a sigh of resignation. 'Okay, I'll tell you—but you didn't hear it from me. It does have something to do with your husband. In fact, it has everything to do with him. He's threatened to pull out of the documentary if we don't stop…' He shrugged his shoulders. '"Monopolising my wife" was how I think he phrased it.'

Rosa flinched to think that any man could be old-fashioned and chauvinistic enough to march up to a bunch of TV executives and tell them something like that. 'And you're willing to just cave in?' she questioned heatedly. 'To let this go just because you want to make some damned documentary about his country?'

Arnaud shook his head. 'It's not just the documentary!' he said. 'It's everything else. Your husband is a powerful man, Rosa—not just in Paris, but pretty much everywhere else. And you don't make enemies of men like that.'

The realisation of what Kulal had done suddenly hit her and Rosa felt sick. Her heart was pounding and her chest felt so tight that Arnaud reached out towards her in alarm.

'Mon dieu!' he exclaimed. 'But your face is like chalk! Sit down, and I will fetch you some water.'

But she shook her head. 'I don't want anything,' she said fiercely. But that wasn't quite true, was it? She wanted to regain her honour and her pride and there was only one way she was going to do that.

She flipped through her address book before going

outside, ignoring Kulal's official limousine which was waiting for her just as it always was. Quickly, she darted down one of the side streets and felt a flash of triumph as she gave her bodyguard the slip, before clicking onto the map section of her phone. Her footsteps were rapid as she walked to the sixteenth *arrondissement* until she had reached the ornate nineteenth-century building which housed Kulal's foundation.

She realised that it was the first time she'd ever been inside the building and she saw the receptionist's look of shock as she walked in.

'I'm Rosa,' she said automatically, knowing how hot and dishevelled she must look after her dash across the city.

'You are the sheikh's wife,' breathed the receptionist, her look of shock deepening. 'And I have seen you on the television.'

'Where is he?' Rosa asked quietly. 'Where is the sheikh?'

'I'm afraid he is in a meeting, and I'll have to—'

'Where is he?' Rosa repeated, and then spotted the staircase on the opposite side of the lobby. He would be at the top of the building—of course he would—because powerful people always chose their vantage points up high, so that they could look down on the rest of the world. She ran up the stairs, two at a time, until there was nowhere left to go and she passed another receptionist who had clearly been warned that trouble was on the way. The woman shot a horrified glance in the direction of a set of double doors and that look told Rosa everything she needed to know.

She burst in through the doors to see a huge table with lots of men in suits sitting around it and they all looked up as she appeared. But only one man dominated the room with his powerful presence. A man with black eyes and dark skin and the demeanour of a desert warrior, despite the sleek outlines of his Italian suit. He was getting to his feet and all the men were looking up at him in alarm, before staring at her again.

'Rosa,' he said in a voice she'd never heard him use before. 'What an unexpected pleasure.'

'I want to talk to you.'

'Can't this wait until later?' he questioned. 'Because as you can see, I'm in the middle of a meeting which has taken some time and trouble to organise.'

'No, it can't wait!' she flared, hearing the onlookers draw in a collective shocked breath and she recognised then that people spent their lives appeasing Kulal and giving him exactly what he wanted. And how could that be good for him? 'So either you get rid of them now, or we're going to have an audience while I put to you a few very pertinent questions!'

'Gentlemen, looks like we're done here,' said Kulal, but Rosa couldn't miss the unmistakable glint of anger in his eyes.

They stood in silence while all the men filed out, and when the door had been closed, Kulal looked at her and she saw that the glint had become a quietly smouldering blaze.

'So, are you going to give me some sort of explanation for this unwarranted intrusion?'

'Are you?' she retorted.

'I'm not in the mood for riddles, Rosa!'

'Aren't you? Well then, let me spell this one out for you! Did you…' She gripped on to the back of a chair to steady herself, aware that her voice sounded all croaky. Kulal gestured towards the water jug on the table but she shook her head furiously, as if he was offering her a beaker of poison. 'Did you put a stop to my weather slot?'

There was a moment of silence.

'I want the truth, Kulal! Did you?'

He shrugged. 'I'm no television executive,' he said. 'It's not within my power to do something like that.'

'But it's certainly within your power to threaten to withdraw permission for filming to begin in Zahrastan, isn't it? And it's certainly within your power to lean heavily on investors, if that's what it takes. Is that what you did, Kulal?'

He looked at her for a long moment and then he gave a curt nod, as if he had just come to a decision. 'Yes, I did it—and you want to know why? Because I don't think it's such a heinous crime for a husband to want to see more of his wife. A wife who is only mine for a year! Why should I wish to share her with millions of viewers and the people who read those dreadful magazines?'

Rosa's throat was so tight that it felt as if it had an invisible cord clenched around it and it took a moment or two before she could respond with any degree of clarity. 'So you just stormed in and took control? You decided that because you didn't like it, that you would change it. Because even if it is only for a year, you don't really want a wife, do you, Kulal? What you want is a doll— a doll you can play with whenever you want. Someone that you can dress and undress and put to bed. Something you can walk away from in the morning, knowing exactly where your little doll has been all day, because one of your damned bodyguards has been tracking her.'

At this moment, an urgent-sounding buzzer on his desk began to go off and Kulal leaned over to press his finger on it. 'Yes…?'

Rosa recognised the frantic tones of the bodyguard who had been assigned to her that day. 'Boss, I've lost the princess.'

'Don't worry, I've found her.'

'You see!' She glared at him as he clicked off the connection. 'You even make me sound like a doll—or a package which has inadvertently gone missing.'

'As my wife you require a security issue!' he flared. 'You cannot deny that, Rosa!'

'I'm not here to talk about my security!' she flared back. 'I'm here to talk about the fact that you heavy-handedly put an end to my burgeoning TV career and you didn't even have the courtesy to tell me!'

His mouth tightened. 'And is this television slot really so important to you?'

She shook her head as hot, infuriating tears began to spring to her eyes. 'You're missing the point,' she said. 'I left one life because people expected me to behave a certain way. I was trapped and controlled and told what to do every minute of the day. And you're doing exactly the same thing! You promised me freedom and independence and you've given me the opposite.'

'You'll get your freedom and independence when

the marriage is over,' he said, his hands clenching into tight fists.

'And it'll be too late by then,' she said, and now her voice was trembling. 'Kulal, you're making this very difficult for me. You don't want a wife with a career, but neither do you want a wife who you'll let close enough to love you. Can't you see that I'm between a rock and a hard place here?'

His eyes flicked over her and he steeled himself against the tears which were sparking so brightly in her eyes. He remembered the night of their honeymoon when she'd sobbed against his bare chest as she'd told him about her mother's betrayal and a shiver of something dark and empathetic had whispered over his skin. But the intensity of those feelings had made him feel raw and vulnerable—and hadn't he vowed that he would never allow himself to feel that way again? He drew a deep breath as he stared at the flyaway mess of her dark hair and the flushed sheen of her face. 'Can we discuss this later?' he said. 'When you've calmed down a little, and maybe had a chance to brush your hair?'

Rosa almost choked with frustration, until she realised that maybe this was exactly what she needed—to hear him utter the truth in all its stark brutality. Get out of his life, she told herself. Get out now while you still can—before he sees just how much he has hurt you. She sucked in a deep breath. 'I'd like that drink now, if you don't mind.'

He poured her a glass of water. 'I can ring for some ice, if you like.'

'No, thanks.' Her smile was wan as she gulped down

the tepid liquid. 'Tell me, Kulal, do you always get exactly what it is you want?'

Her words took him back. He thought about what they used to say about him in Zahrastan. *What Kulal wants, Kulal gets.* But not always. Not the one time when it really mattered, when his heart had been shattered into a thousand little pieces—and he was damned if he was going to risk that happening again. 'You're talking in riddles again,' he said.

'Am I? Yet you're a highly intelligent man. I'm sure you can understand exactly what I'm talking about, if only you'd let yourself. But there's no need to look so worried. The discussion's over and I'm going now.'

'And we'll talk about it some more tonight.'

'Of course we will.' The lie came easily to her lips, just as it had come to his. Because Kulal had no intention of talking about this any more. She knew that. The decision had been made—his decision—and he would just expect her to get used to it. To go along with it, like a good little girl. She could imagine the scene which would enfold tonight. The hungry kiss, heightened by all the tension, and then a session of lovemaking powerful enough to push any nagging doubts from her mind. Well, not any more. Because Rosa Corretti was through with being manipulated. She was going to start taking control of her life, as of now.

She looked up at him, but it felt as if her face might split in two with the effort it took to smile. 'I'll see you later.'

CHAPTER TWELVE

KULAL SHOULD HAVE felt better after Rosa had gone, leaving him alone in his vast office. He told himself that she needed to understand that they'd made a deal and that he wasn't prepared for her to start reneging on it. He hadn't signed up for someone who wouldn't be there when he needed her. Until he reminded himself fiercely that he didn't actually need anybody—because need was dangerous. It made you dependent and it made you weak.

He pulled a pile of papers towards him and started to read them, but the afternoon passed by much too slowly. He knew that he could have left the office any time he pleased, since he didn't have any more meetings planned, and even if he did, he could always cancel them. But he didn't go home. Why should he go home early to a woman who didn't appreciate him?

What Kulal wanted, Kulal got.

The words stayed irritatingly in his head, like an advertising jingle which wouldn't go away, and his temple was throbbing by the time he took the elevator up to the apartment. As the doors slid open he wondered what was the best way to handle what had happened earlier. He could quietly take Rosa aside and tell her that he wouldn't tolerate a repeat of such a hysterical scene but mightn't that make her stubborn? Mightn't the argument then continue into the evening, when he had plenty of other things he'd rather be doing with her than arguing?

And he had made his point, hadn't he? He had won. There would be no more missed cocktail parties, nor would they be disturbed by any phone calls from the infernal Bertrand. There would be no more business colleagues telling him that their wives had seen a picture of his wife in a magazine.

The apartment was strangely silent—there wasn't even any music playing—and Kulal walked through to the drawing room to see if Rosa was out on the terrace. But the French windows were closed and there was no sign of her with a forgiving smile on her beautiful lips as she sashayed towards him in one of her vibrant dresses.

'Rosa?' The word echoed around the vast rooms like something shouted into a tunnel. 'Rosa!' he called once more, but there was no reply.

He told himself that she must have just gone out for a while. But she didn't do that, did she—because where would she go? The galleries were shut for the day and there was no need for her to perform the multiple tasks which fell to other, less exalted women. She didn't need to shop or to cook or to clean. She was a princess and that was why she needed to behave like a princess!

A faint frown creased his brow as he remembered the frustration on her face when she'd confronted him today. The anger spitting green and golden sparks from her dark eyes. He remembered the messy spill of her hair and her shiny face—a look which was worlds apart from the usual sleek grooming of his former lovers. He thought about the wilted rose tucked behind her ear, and a wave of lust so strong washed over him that for a moment he just stood very still and closed his eyes.

He was just about to phone her, when he walked past the dining room and saw the cream-coloured envelope which was lying on the oak table and his heart missed a beat. He stared at it for a moment, and when he walked over and picked it up, he noticed almost impartially that his fingers weren't quite steady.

It was the first thing she'd ever written to him and, judging by the tone, she intended it to be her last.

'Kulal,' it read. Not 'dear' Kulal or 'darling' Kulal— or any of the other sweet things she had sometimes whispered to him when he was deep inside her body— but just his name, stark and emotionless, just like the words which followed.

I imagine you'll be pleased to discover that I've gone, especially after that rather unfortunate scene at your office today. I'm sorry if I embarrassed you in front of your colleagues, but please be assured that it won't ever happen again, because I'm leaving and I think you'll agree that's best.

Since I won't be honouring our marriage contract, you can tear up the pre-nup. All I'm taking are my wedding and engagement rings, which you told me were mine to keep. I'll probably sell them and set myself up with somewhere to rent, before I look for a job. And one day—who knows?—I may be able to pay you back for them, in full.

Thank you for all that you have taught me, which turns out to have been a lot more than just about sex.

I hope you can find it in yourself to be happy and I wish you nothing but good things.
Yours ever,
Rosa.

'No!' He felt a dry and tearing pain as he crumpled the piece of paper tightly in his hand and it fell in a ball and bounced soundlessly on the table while Kulal dug his phone from his pocket.

He punched out her number, unsurprised when it went straight to voicemail and a curiously flat-sounding Rosa said that she would return the call as quickly as possible. Which was clearly not going to happen. He left two messages before letting out another howl of rage, tempted to hurl the damned phone against the wall. And he remembered Rosa telling him she'd done just that when she'd run from Sicily, when she'd wanted to cut off all communication with her family. And now she was running from him. He had gone from his privileged position as her husband and her lover to being cast out in the cold. And he had no one to blame but himself. He had convinced himself that he was fearless and strong and yet he had been so scared of dealing with his emotions that he had built a wall around them. He had allowed a tragedy in his past to blight any possibility of a future and he had pushed away the woman he loved.

A wave of pain hit him. A pain so intense that it felt

like an iron fist clenching its way around his heart. Where was she?

He dialled his chief bodyguard. 'I want you to find someone for me,' he clipped out.

'Anyone you like, boss. Who is it?'

There was a pause as, for one brief moment, Kulal confronted his own fierce pride and knew that he was going to have to let it go. Who cared if his bodyguards discovered that his wife had left him? Who cared about anything other than getting Rosa back again?

'My wife.'

'The princess has gone?' questioned the bodyguard in surprise.

'Yes, the princess has gone!' snapped Kulal. 'Because your people weren't doing their job properly. They let her leave the studios unguarded and now she's managed to give everyone the slip. And if you value your future you'll find out where she is by sunset tomorrow.'

They did better than that—they had located Rosa by the following afternoon and Kulal was astonished to discover that she'd flown back to Sicily.

Sicily?

She'd told him she'd never go back there! She'd told him that no way was she going to get involved with her dysfunctional family ever again.

'Is she staying with her family?'

'No, boss. She's all alone in a beach house on the eastern side of the island.'

Kulal nodded. 'Prepare the plane,' he said grimly.

It occurred to him when his jet touched down several hours later that her powerful family might have attempted to try to stop him from entering the country, but he was wrong. It also occurred to him that maybe he should have waited until the next morning to see her, for the sun was already beginning to sink in the sky as his waiting car drove away from the airfield. But for the first time in his life he couldn't bear the thought of waiting—no matter how much bigger a psychological advantage that would be.

Eventually, the car bumped to a halt and the driver pointed to a solitary beach house in the distance, barely visible through all the trees and shrubbery. It was in part of a nature reserve and the area was impassable to all cars. Kulal found himself thinking that the gleaming limousine wouldn't have stood a chance of negotiating that narrow path. He told his driver to go and he told the car containing the accompanying bodyguards to follow, waving aside their protests with a flat and implacable movement of his hand.

'I don't want anyone else here,' he said fiercely. 'Now go.'

'But, boss—'

'Go!'

He stood and watched the powerful vehicles roar away to make sure they obeyed him. Large clouds of dust puffed around their gleaming paintwork as the two cars became little black dots in the distance. And suddenly, he felt an unexpected wave of liberation. It was, he realised, a long time since he'd gone anywhere without being shadowed by one of the guards who had been part of his life for as long as he could remember.

For the first time, he allowed himself to look prop-

erly at his surroundings, taking in a deep breath of the
scented air. It smelt of lemon and pine and he could hear
the massed choir of the cicadas echoing over the hills.
The baked vegetation was surprisingly green—with
flowers dotted here and there—and in the distance he
could see the deep cobalt of the sea. He stared down at
his feet and some instinct made him slip off his loafers
and carry them.

The warm sand was gritty between his toes and as
he walked along the narrow path he felt that sense of
freedom again. Was that because for the first time in his
life he was following his heart? Because in this moment
he was no longer a royal prince and sheikh, but simply
a man who had come to make amends with his woman.

The beach house which lay ahead of him was modest,
just a one-storey building with a wide, wooden veranda
looking out to sea. The beauty lay in its position—the
matchless view and the solitude—and suddenly Kulal
wondered what he was going to do if Rosa wasn't there.
How would she react if she came back later to find him
waiting for her? Would she turn the might of the Corretti
family against an estranged husband she could rightly
accuse of stalking her?

He didn't care. Let the Correttis come. Let them all
come. He wasn't going anywhere until he'd looked into
Rosa's eyes and told her what she needed to hear.

He moved silently, for at heart he was a child of the
desert, taught how to blend into whichever landscape
he inhabited. He thought fleetingly that Sicily was as
beautiful as everything he'd ever heard about it, and
that he'd like the chance to explore it further. And then

he saw her and his footsteps halted, so that he stood perfectly still.

Sitting at the far end of the veranda, her legs dangling over the side, she was shaded by an umbrella pine tree but was wearing a sun hat as an extra precaution. The hat looked new and was made of straw—its crown festooned with a bright mass of orange and pink silk flowers, which matched her sundress. He could feel a lump forming in his throat as he watched her staring intently out at the sea. He wanted to stand there all day watching her but he thought that she might turn around and be startled. More than startled.

'Rosa,' he said softly.

For a moment Rosa didn't move, telling herself it was like one of those fantasies which schoolgirls sometimes concocted. The ones where the object of their affections would suddenly be spirited in front of them, no matter how unlikely that scenario would be.

'Rosa,' said the voice again.

Her fingernails dug into her thighs. Bad enough that she should be without him—but did she also have to suffer auditory hallucinations which were designed to torment her?

Slowly, she turned her head and her breath froze in her throat. She could hear the loud thunder of her heart as he held up the palms of his hands, like someone in an old cowboy film, admitting surrender.

'I didn't mean to startle you,' he said.

'Well, you did.' She tried not to feast her eyes on him, but it was impossible. How could you not look at him and keep on looking, when he seemed like a dark and sculpted god who had just been planted in the Sicilian landscape? He was wearing pale linen trousers and a pale silk shirt—the sleeves rolled up to reveal his dark, hair-roughened arms. From this distance she couldn't really see his expression, but as he grew nearer she noticed that his feet were bare. Kulal walking in public in bare feet? She looked over his shoulder to the landscape behind. And where were his bodyguards?

It didn't matter. None of those questions were relevant because he was no longer part of her life. She'd escaped from him and his controlling ways. Nothing had changed. Only the externals. She had left him and his home in Paris and she was starting a new life for herself. It wasn't going to be easy because she still wanted him, but she was going to do it. She needed to do it.

He was closer now. He was stepping down onto the veranda so that she could see the dark gleam of his eyes and she knew she ought to tell him to just go away and leave her alone, but in that moment she discovered that her sense of curiosity was stronger than her sense of self-preservation.

'What are you doing here?' she questioned, trying to inject just the right note of careless sarcasm into her voice. 'No, don't tell me—you've come to try to bring your little doll back to Paris. Is it time to brush her hair and put her back into her shiny box?'

Kulal stood looking down at her, reading the hurt and anger on her upturned face as he thought of all the inducements he could use to get her to return to Paris with him. He thought of all the things he could say to try to persuade her. Things she probably wouldn't believe—

and who could blame her? And he didn't know where to begin, because this was all new to him. He clenched his fists as all his buttoned-up feelings demanded to be set free, but habit made him want to resist. Damn it, why shouldn't he resist? There was a reason why he had put all his emotions into cold storage and it was a good reason. If you didn't allow yourself to feel things, then you couldn't get hurt.

But suddenly, it was no longer working. Whatever had protected him in the past was failing to protect him now for the pain in his heart was very real and very raw. He moved across the terrace and sat down beside her and he saw her body tense. For a moment there was silence.

'I miss you,' he said.

She shook her head. 'No, you don't. You just think you do. It's because I was the one who walked away and your pride is hurt. You'll get over it.'

'No, I won't get over it,' he said. 'I don't think I could, even if I wanted to. And I don't. I just want you back in my life because I love you, Rosa.' The words left his mouth in a breathless rush, but his voice was shaking with emotion as he finished his quiet declaration. 'I love you in a way I never thought I could love anyone, and that's the truth.'

Rosa could feel a horrible lump forming in her throat and the betraying flavour of salt in her mouth but she wasn't going to cry. Damn him—she wasn't going to cry. And she wasn't going to listen to his empty words either. He might have all the real power—the social and the economic power which came with his royal title—

but she had power too. She had the power to live her life as she wanted to. Without pain and without heartbreak. She shook her head. 'It's too late, Kulal.'

'No!' In the growing darkness his word was fervent as it rang out on the still, Sicilian air. 'Don't tell me that we don't all deserve a second chance when we screw up so spectacularly. And I recognise that I've behaved like a fool. You said in my office that you wanted to love me but that I wouldn't let you close enough. But I'm letting you close now. Are you telling me that your feelings for me have changed, Rosa? That twenty-four hours have altered the situation so radically?'

She tried not to be affected by the look of raw pain on his face as he spoke, but it was the hardest thing she'd ever had to do. Because of course she hadn't stopped loving him. Love wasn't something you could just turn on and off, like a tap. She wanted to take him into her arms and cradle him. She wanted to lose her heartache in the sweetness of his kiss—but what good would that do? This is short-term pain for long-term gain, she told herself fiercely. He just needs to win at everything and that's why he wants you back.

'I'm not the kind of woman you need, Kulal,' she said quietly. 'You need someone you can dominate. Someone who will do exactly what you want her to do. Some women might call that being masterful but I call it being a control freak and I'm afraid that I can't live like that. Not any more.'

His body tensed. 'You can have your TV slot back!'

'No!' Frustratedly, she shook her hands in the air.

'You don't understand! This is nothing to do with my TV slot.'

'But isn't that what drove you away?'

She stared at him. 'That was the final straw, yes. But what really drove me away was the fundamental inequality of our relationship. I don't want to live with someone who won't let me do something—so that only when I push and push will he change his mind and give me his permission. I'm a grown-up, Kulal. I don't need anyone's permission to live my life. Not yours, nor my family's. I've had that for too many years and I don't want it any more.'

He saw the sudden fierceness on her face. 'Why did you come back to Sicily?' he questioned suddenly. 'When you told me you would never return.'

There was silence for a moment as Rosa mulled over his question. 'Because I thought about something you said and realised that you were right. That I had no right to try to fix you, when my own life was so unresolved,' she said. 'I knew I needed to speak to my brothers and to my mother. Especially my mother. I needed to hear her side of the story. I needed to hear what made her betray my dad with his own brother, but then I had to let it go. Because it's her life, not mine.'

'And what did she say?'

'I'm meeting her for coffee tomorrow morning.' She nearly said, 'I'll let you know,' until she realised that she wouldn't, because tomorrow he would be gone from here. She wanted him gone from here. She needed him gone from here.

He saw the new strain on her face and his heart

twisted. 'I'm sorry for what you've been through with your family, Rosa—'

'Yes, I know that,' she put in, hating the betraying little crack which seemed to have crept into her voice. 'And that was one of the things I first loved about you— that you defied all my expectations. That once you'd got over the shock of my parentage, you supported me. And I was so grateful to you for that, Kulal. I thought you would judge me negatively, but you didn't. And then, when you opened up to me on the night of our wedding, I felt something like hope about the future. It felt as if two people who had been damaged could find comfort and solace in each other. But then you clammed up— and even though there were moments when I felt as if a real passion and friendship was there, it was as if you wanted to keep it locked away from me.'

'And I did,' he said slowly, her words unlocking a conundrum he'd never really understood until now. He stared at her. 'I guess I was terrified of getting too close to anyone. It felt like too much of a risk. Can you understand that, Rosa?'

She nodded as she heard the flicker of uncertainty in his voice and suddenly her man of steel seemed soft and vulnerable and she couldn't seem to stop her heart from reaching out to him. 'Of course I can understand,' she said. 'Your mother was torn away from you in a way which left you heartbroken. Worse still was that you blamed yourself. You still do.'

'You know why I blame myself,' he said quietly. 'You know what happened that day.'

'But you're not even sure about the facts, are you?'

she whispered. 'You've refused to look at the post-mortem report or speak to the doctors.' She saw him flinch but she knew she had to carry on. Because even though Kulal was no longer a small boy locked in a nightmare of guilt and loss, he was a man still suffering as a consequence of that day, and he would continue to suffer unless he confronted it. 'I think you should go back to Zahrastan and find out the truth. You told me that your mother was suffering from headaches prior to the picnic. Well, maybe the fall was a result of that. Maybe she would have died anyway—or maybe she wouldn't. You have to know, Kulal. You can't keep living your life burdened by guilt and neither can you keep avoiding risk, just because it's safer that way. You have to learn to take a chance—on me, yes, but more importantly, on yourself.'

He swallowed, struggling to cope with the new and very powerful feelings which were beginning to emerge. And he wondered if it really was too late. 'I'll go,' he said. 'And I'll face whatever truth awaits me there—but before I do, there's something you need to know. Something I never told you before, but which I should have done.' There was a pause as he looked down at the soft parting of her lips. 'That the first time I saw you, you spoke to something in my heart. I looked across that crowded nightclub, little realising that I was about to meet a woman who would change just about everything.'

'Kulal—'

'And that is why I am asking you—with all the earnestness at my command—can we please try again?

Because I love you, Rosa, and I want to be a real husband to you—in every sense of the word.'

She was swallowing frantically but it was no good, because the tears which had begun welling up in her eyes had begun to trickle down her cheeks. And she saw from the sudden darkening of his features that he was in danger of misinterpreting those tears and that's when she stopped fighting her own feelings. She gave in to what she'd been wanting to do all along and flung her arms around his neck, her face wet as she pressed her lips to his.

'Yes,' she said, whispering the words directly into his mouth. 'Yes in every language that I speak—and in yours too, which I have yet to learn. Yes, because I love you too—even though I tried to tell myself that I was crazy to love you. But I couldn't stop myself, no matter how hard I tried. And I want to spend the rest of my life loving you back, but only if you promise never to lock me out of your heart again.'

'I promise,' he said fiercely. 'Now will you please just kiss me properly before I go out of my mind?'

Her lips were pressing hard against his almost before he'd finished the sentence but the kiss felt different. It felt like a statement—and a seal. It felt almost life-changing. And maybe it was. She smiled as if she'd suddenly understood the world's best-kept secret as Kulal stood up and lifted her into his arms, before carrying her into the small, wooden house.

Because didn't everyone always say that true love had the power to transform?

EPILOGUE

THE AL-DIMASHQI PALACE shone in the late-afternoon light, rising up from the stark landscape like a beautiful fairy-tale castle in the distance and Rosa peered out of the car window with a fast-growing feeling of excitement. She had been longing to visit the desert kingdom of Zahrastan and now the moment was here at last. She could see turrets and domes and the tantalising glimmer of water in among the rose gardens and she gave a little sigh of anticipation.

Kulal squeezed her hand. 'Nervous?' he questioned.

'A bit.' She turned to look at him. 'I'm terrified your brother won't like me.'

'What's not to like?' His eyes were soft as he studied her. 'You are the woman who has tamed the tearaway sheikh. The proud Sicilian beauty my people are longing to meet.' He lifted her hand to his lips and kissed it. 'And the woman who has captured my heart so completely.'

'Well, when you put it like that.' She brushed her fingertips over his mouth, but her next words were hesitant. 'And how do you feel about coming back, Kulal? I mean, really.'

Kulal was quiet for a moment while he considered

her question. This was his second trip to Zahrastan in as many months. The first time he had come alone and it had been a trip of necessity, not of pleasure. He had gone to the hospital in the capital, where his mother had been taken following her fall. Assiduously, he had forced himself to read through all the records and then had spoken to the medical director, who'd been a very junior doctor at the time.

Vividly, Kulal remembered flying back to Paris. He remembered the hopeful expression on Rosa's face and the way it had become wary when he told her that the tests had proved inconclusive. That he still didn't know whether his mother's death had been caused by the fall or by some pre-existing condition. But that it was okay. He'd told her that too. It was all okay. The past had happened and there was nothing he could do to change it. All he had was the present—the glorious present, with his loving wife, who had taught him so much, by his side.

'I feel joy,' he said simply. 'And gratitude. That in finding you, I could find myself and learn to live in a way I never thought possible. And I'm looking forward to the celebrations.'

'Me too,' she said. 'Though I've had my reservations about the guest list.'

'Well, don't. I utterly forbid it. And I don't know why you're giggling like that, Rosa—because I do!'

He tightened his hand around hers. They were here in Zahrastan because the king wanted to throw a big party for his brother and his Sicilian bride. Kulal's former fiancée, Ayesha, would be there, with the Tuscan nobleman she had surprised everyone by marrying after Kulal had 'freed' her from their engagement. His lips curved. How life could constantly surprise! Rosa's family had also been invited and most of them were coming. There would doubtless be friction, though hopefully the august surroundings of the Al-Dimashqi palace might inject a little calm into the sometimes overexuberant nature of the Corretti clan.

And if it didn't? If there were noisy scenes and tears, and make-ups and break-ups? So what. What would be, would be. Kulal had learnt that there was much in life he couldn't control. He'd learnt that taking a risk was sometimes as necessary to life as breathing itself. He touched his hand to the gleaming crown of his wife's dark hair and smiled as he bent to kiss her.

And he'd learnt that love was the most necessary thing of all.

* * * * *

LET'S TALK

Romance

**For exclusive extracts, competitions
and special offers, find us online:**

Or get in touch on 0844 844 1351*

For all the latest titles coming soon, visit
millsandboon.co.uk/nextmonth

Want even more
ROMANCE?

Join our bookclub today!